Everybody would die. That wouldn't happen unless the enemy was suicidal, or totally insane. Neither possibility was completely out of the question.

"Have there been demands from anybody?" Brognola inquired bluntly. "Hamas, Al Qaeda, Iraq, China?"

Frowning deeply, the President said, "Thankfully not yet, and we can't make any inquiries. That would only demonstrate that we have no idea who is behind all of this. And as long as the enemy is not sure of exactly what we know, they'll be cautious. Afraid of our direct military retaliation. Even without nuclear weapons, America has a tremendous military. But if the enemy discovers the truth…"

The President didn't finish the sentence. He didn't have to. The big Fed understood. Then the enemy would be free to do whatever it wanted. The only thing holding the terrorist states in check had always been the threat of nuclear strikes from the U.S. If the news of the covert disarmament was released, an incalculable wave of terrorist strikes would sweep the free world like a plague.

DON PENDLETON'S

STONY

AMERICA'S ULTRA-COVERT INTELLIGENCE AGENCY

MAN ®

ACT OF WAR

A GOLD EAGLE BOOK FROM

W RLDWIDE ®

TORONTO • NEW YORK • LONDON
AMSTERDAM • PARIS • SYDNEY • HAMBURG
STOCKHOLM • ATHENS • TOKYO • MILAN
MADRID • WARSAW • BUDAPEST • AUCKLAND

First edition April 2008

ISBN-13: 978-0-373-61978-8
ISBN-10:   0-373-61978-2

ACT OF WAR

Special thanks and acknowledgment to
Nick Pollotta for his contribution to this work.

Printed in U.S.A.

ACT OF WAR

PROLOGUE

White Sands, New Mexico

In a muted rumble, a massive 757 jumbo jetliner streaked across the night sky, the aircraft rendered invisible by the sheer distance. Only a few scattered clouds marred the peaceful heavens, along with a dusting of twinkling stars, a few of them crawling steadily along, the motion betraying the fact they were actually telecommunications satellites.

On the ground, a warm desert breeze moaned among the tall cactus and scraggly Joshua trees, the gentle wind kicking up tiny dust devils that twirled about madly. Scattered among the low rock formations, crickets softly chirped looking for a mate.

Sipping at a cup of hot coffee, a bare-chested man wearing khaki shorts and hiking boots listened to the music of the desert night. The reddish light of the dying campfire cast his craggy features into harsh relief, making him appear older and more heavily scarred than usual. Military tattoos were clearly visible on both arms. Numerous shiny patches on his chest were circular scars, mementos from shrapnel and assorted bullets caught in a dozen firefights around the world. A holstered U.S. Army Colt .45 automatic pistol rested on his left hip, and a fully loaded M-16/M-203 combination assault rifle leaned against a nearby boulder. A fat 40 mm antipersonnel shell was tucked into the stubby grenade launcher.

Just a few yards away from the U.S. Army sergeant a small canvas tent was perched on the crest of the small hillock, the flap tightly zippered closed to keep out the scorpions and desert spiders. The sergeant knew that for some unknown reason the creatures loved to hide inside boots, and if a man wasn't careful pulling on his gear in the morning that would be a damn rude surprise.

Draining the cup, Sergeant Bruce Helford debated pouring another and decided it could do no harm. He was up for the night anyway. So far this tour of duty had been a cakewalk, and he had encountered nothing more dangerous than a couple of lost tourists looking for a gas station and some drunk college kids trying to sneak onto the military base for a thrill. Idiots.

Pretending to be a National Park ranger, Helford had forced a smile onto his face and helped the civilians on their way, then filed a report for taller fences. Whether anybody at the Pentagon ever read his reports about the incidents was unknown, but that was part of Army life. Besides, the sergeant knew that he was stationed here in the middle of nowhere purely as a precaution in the ancient military litany of being prepared for what an enemy could do, not for what they might do. There were a lot of heavy armament at the underground military base only a few dozen klicks away, and—

With a shock Helford realized that he could clearly see the cup of coffee in his hand. Then cold shock hit his guts as a bright light blossomed on the distant horizon.

Suddenly a low rumble steadily grew in volume and power until the ground began to shake. The campfire broke apart, startled birds took flight from the quivering Joshua trees and loose rocks tumbled free from the side of a low mesa.

Casting the steel cup aside, Helford reached for the Geiger counter sitting on the trembling ground, when a hot wind blew across the campsite carrying a strange metallic taste. Then the Geiger counter started to click wildly, the needle swinging up into the red zone and staying there.

Knowing he was already dead, the sergeant stood slowly, then broke into a sprint and charged to the tent. Diving inside, he snatched the military transponder hanging from the aluminum support pole, twisted the encoder to the proper setting and thumbed the transmit button.

"Watchdog Four to base," he said, his words becoming a shout as the rumbling noise mounted with increasing fury until it seemed to fill the world. "Watchdog Four to base! Code nine! Repeat, we have a code nine!"

But if there was a reply, it could not be heard over the now deafening hurricane wind howling madly across the landscape. Sand and small stones peppered the flapping sides of the canvas tent, the hot wind stealing all sound from the air and increasing the bitter taste in the man's mouth. Still shouting into the microphone, Helford flipped a safety cover and thumbed a red button to activate the emergency signal when the tent tore loose from the soil and flew away. Feeling stark naked, the sergeant raised a hand to protect his eyes from the terrible light searing the landscape. This was impossible! The hillock was much too far away from the armory. The distance had been checked, and rechecked, a dozen times by some of the best minds in America! There was no way that he should be able to actually see the glow, unless…

In stentorian majesty, a dozen fireballs grew on the horizon, the lambent columns rising upward to form the classic mushroom shape, each overlapping the other into a vista of hell.

Incredibly, the buffeting wind stopped, and the only sounds were the man's ragged breathing and the nonstop clicking of the Geiger. He knew what that meant. The calm before the maelstrom. Just then, a ghastly prickly sensation began to stab needles into his body. The hard radiation had arrived.

"Code nine!" the sergeant grimly shouted into the transponder, even though the radio was probably dead from the electromagnetic pulse of the multiple nuclear explosions. "Code nine! Nine!"

Swelling rapidly, a tidal wave of debris rose from the burning ground, a roiling wall of destruction that swept across the tortured desert, shattering trees and tossing aside boulders.

Doggedly determined to die performing his duty, Helford continued shouting a warning into the transponder until the airborne shock wave arrived. He was instantly crushed into bloody paste and blew apart in a red mist. A microsecond later the hillock broke into pieces. Then the heat wave arrived, the brutal thermal onslaught searing the ruined landscape into a hellish vista.

Still expanding, the nuclear detonations continued growing in power and fury until the nightmarish conflagrations seemed like the end of the world....

CHAPTER ONE

"Take a seat, Hal," the President of the United States said, gesturing. "We have a lot to cover and little time." In the middle of the room, there was a battered old wooden desk, office furniture from some forgotten time, along with a few metal chairs. Set close by was an array of telephones and a cafeteria-style wheeled service cart carrying a steaming urn of what smelled like fresh coffee and a heaping pile of sandwiches and small pastries. None of the food had been touched. For security purposes, Hal Brognola, Justice Department liaison and director of the Sensitive Operations Group, based at Stony Man Farm, had agreed to meet the President in a remote, secure location.

"Yes, sir." Sitting, the big Fed noticed that an Air Force colonel stood to one side of the President, holding a small leather briefcase. It was handcuffed to his wrist. Brognola promptly dismissed the man. That was the Football, the remote-control device containing the launch code for America's arsenal of nuclear missiles.

As the President and Brognola got comfortable, the Secret Service agents who had accompanied the President remained standing, their hard eyes boring holes into the Justice Department man.

"All right, here it is. At 0214 hrs this morning the entire nuclear stockpile of tactical nuclear bombs exploded at White Sands, New Mexico," the President said, passing over a manila file colored a deep crimson.

"Obviously not an accident," Brognola stated, accepting the folder. On the front were stamped the words, *Top Secret,* but the color alone was enough identify the high-level security status of the file.

"No, it was not an accident, nor a traitor or an enemy spy that infiltrated the laboratory."

"Are you sure, sir?"

"Yes."

"Interesting." Carefully pressing his thumb to the sensor pad of the small explosive device locking the folder, Brognola impatiently waited until he heard a beep, then he slid off the explosive charge and opened the folder. There were a lot of documents carrying the Top Secret notice, along with a bevy of high-altitude surveillance photographs carrying the NSA emblem. There was a lot of technical jargon that the big Fed skimmed, along with a summary from the Pentagon noting the nuke signatures. Brognola knew that every type of nuclear explosive in the world had a unique chemical signature to its blast, sort of like fingerprints, the composite metal carried trace elements of their origins. An expert looking at the spectrograph of a nuclear explosion could tell with absolute certainty which country had made the bomb. Once again, this was old technology, tried and true, proved a hundred times over.

Scanning the summary, the big Fed slowly began to frown. He had expected to find one foreign nuke signature among the roll call of American bombs. But it wasn't there. The White

Sands base had not been hit with a nuke that set off a chain reaction among the arsenal of weapons in storage. The first blast had occurred deep underground. The side caverns built to absorb nuclear detonations had done their job and kept the explosions from reaching the surface. Unfortunately, there had been half a dozen tactical nukes being loaded onto some trucks to be shipped the Sixth carrier fleet in the Persian Gulf. Those blasts had to have been visible for miles. There was a small note on the side that a perimeter guard pretending to be a park ranger had called in the blast before going off the air. No remains had been found to date, but the search would continue. To everybody else in New Mexico the incident was being hushed up as an earthquake.

Poor bastard probably saw the actually blasts, Brognola thought. If so, there's not going to be enough of him remaining to fill an eyedropper. But the military took care of their own, and whatever could be located would be given a proper funeral. How the living treat their fallen soldiers was the hallmark of any civilization.

"Every bomb in the place," the big Fed said out loud, placing aside the folder. "How is that possible?"

"We have absolutely no idea," the President said honestly, crossing his leg at the knee. "According to the security records recovered from the off-site bunker a hundred miles away, the status of the base was normal. There were no known intruders, no unusual incidents, nobody was acting oddly, no… nothing." He shrugged. "The entire arsenal of nuclear weapons simply detonated at exactly the same moment."

"All of them? Exactly?"

"All of the live bombs, yes. Thankfully the hydrogen bombs are kept disassembled for safety concerns, and only the cores exploded, but there were no thermonuclear reactions." The President recalled how surprised he had been to learn that a tactical nuke was basically the same type of weapon America had dropped on Japan at the end of World War II. In government slang, those were called atomic bombs by the old guard. But wrap a jack of heavy water around the core, add some tritium injectors and the atomic explosion became a thermonuclear reaction a thousand times more powerful. It was sort of like using a firecracker to set off a stick of TNT. The analogy didn't quite hold, but was close enough to the truth to serve as a nontechnical explanation to most folks. Sure as hell worked for him.

"Son of a bitch," Brognola muttered, loosening his necktie. "Sir, we're in deep shit."

"I concur, my old friend. The deepest shit imaginable." Accepting a cup of coffee from an aide, the President took a sip and made a face. Reaching out, he added more milk and sugar. It wasn't his first cup today, and far from the last.

"So there's more," Brognola said, reading the expression on the man's face. "Okay, let me have it, sir."

"At precisely the same time as our incident, the exact same time, I might add, the Russian Kornevko Nuclear Repository in northern Siberia, and an Israeli Tomcat jet fighter carrying a Class 2 tactical nuclear missile also exploded without known reason or cause."

Sitting back in his chair, Brognola exhaled deeply. The military had a saying about such things. Once can be an accident, twice may be a coincidence, but three times is always enemy action.

"It seems that some group has found a way to remote detonate nuclear weapons," the big Fed said, his stomach tightening into a knot from the words.

"Unfortunately, that is also our opinion on the matter."

"Anything from the TDT?" Brognola asked pointedly, laying aside the report.

"Sadly, no. And the Joint Chiefs checked with the Theatrical Danger Team immediately. Normally the TDT has got a plan for damn well everything, but this time…"

"Nothing?"

"Exactly."

"And the vice president must have checked with the AEC, CIA…" Brognola pursed his lips, mentally running through the entire catalog of alphabet agencies. Then he shifted mental gears. The facts were plain. Nobody in America must have any idea how the weapons were triggered, or else the President would not have summoned me, the Justice man thought. Fair enough.

"I'll assume that we are quickly disassembling our stockpiles?" Brognola asked, reaching for a cup of coffee.

"Across the board. Oak Ridge, Paris Island, San Diego, Fort Bragg, Arctic Base One, aircraft carriers, submarines…" The President made a circular gesture to indicate the all-inclusive process.

"I'm surprised the bastards didn't hit Oak Ridge first," Brognola admitted. "Maybe the enemy is not as good as we fear."

"Oh, they might have," the President admitted honestly. "But where the Oak Ridge Nuclear Weapons and Storage facility is located on the map—and where it is actually located—are two entirely different things. The atomic lab is well hidden, as protection from the old Soviet Union from blowing it out of existence."

Really? That was news to him.

"Certainly served us well enough today. If their stockpile of hydrogen bombs had detonated, half of the nation would be dying right about now from the radioactive fallout." Then Brognola frowned. "Any reactions from the nuclear power stations?"

"Thankfully, there was not, especially since all of those are near major cities," the President said, obviously pleased how fast the man thought.

"So this trigger effect only works on weapons, eh?" the big Fed mused, rubbing his chin. "That's something, at least."

"Unless the effect that set off the bombs does not work on power plants."

"Because they don't have a critical mass in the reactors?"

"That is the logical conclusion, but we may be wrong." Draining the cup, the President placed it on the table. He stared at it for a minute, his thoughts private.

"Hal, we're completely in the dark on this. An unknown enemy, with an unknown weapon and unknown goal. Did they try to destroy the Unites States and fail? Is this the opening round in a major conflict, or something else entirely?"

"What's been done already, sir?"

"Every tactical nuke is being taken apart while it is being moved far away from civilian population centers," the President declared. "Plus, until further notice, the nation will remain at DefCon Five, full war status. All military leaves have been cancelled, troops are arming, the Umbrella of fighter planes is out to maximum range and our entire stockpile of nonnuclear weapons is being prepared."

"How long until every nuke is disarmed?" Brognola asked, leaning forward in his chair.

The President gave the man a hard look. "Using every available technician...sixteen days."

"Sixteen!"

"Best we can do. On top of everything else, we're also

moving the bombs to secret locations, so the enemy can't find them."

"Unless they can sweep the entire continent with this triggering device."

"Agreed. In that case, we've already lost, and the death toll will be in the millions, the hundreds of millions if they get even the slightest bit lucky and set off a couple of plutonium bombs."

Brognola grunted at that. Too true. A radioactive death cloud would sweep across the globe, killing everybody. That wouldn't happen unless the enemy was suicidal or totally insane. Neither possibility was completely out of the question.

"Have there been demands from anybody? Hamas, al Qaeda, Iraq, China?"

Frowning deeply, the President said, "Thankfully not yet, and we can't make any inquires. That would only demonstrate that we have no idea who is behind all of this. And as long as the enemy is not sure of exactly what we know, they'll be cautious. Afraid of our direct military retaliation. Even without nuclear weapons, America has a tremendous military. But if the enemy discovers the truth…"

The President didn't finish the sentence. He didn't have to. Brognola understood. Then the enemy would be free to do whatever it wanted. The only thing holding the terrorist states in check had always been the threat of nuclear strikes from the U.S. If the news of the covert disarmament was released, an incalculable wave of terrorist strikes would sweep the free world like a plague.

"Even worse," the President continued. "If somebody, anybody, does make a demand, then we would have no choice but to comply. This isn't a matter of making policy, or standing tall, but outright survival. We're virtually helpless for sixteen days."

"Even less if the enemy demands access to our Keyhole and Watchdog satellites," Brognola added grimly, "then they could monitor our nukes, and stop them being moved or disarmed."

"Sadly, yes."

"Plus, any demands we receive may not even be the people behind the attacks," the big Fed noted pragmatically. "It could simply be some opportunist group claiming the credit and trying to sneak one past us. Nuke Israel, or a million Americans die. Release every terrorist held in American prisons, hell's bells, release everybody in all of our prisons. Or else."

"Or else," the President agreed solemnly.

"What do you want us to do, sir?" Brognola asked, standing.

"Find them," the President said bluntly. "Find them and kill them and smash their damn machine, whatever it is."

"You don't want it recovered?"

"Hell no, it's too damn dangerous. Smash it to pieces and burn any records, blueprints, schematics, whatever you find."

"Done," the Justice man stated, extending a hand. When the politician first took office, he had used euphemisms like "terminate with extreme prejudice," or "permanently eradicate." But that stopped. Troops had no confidence in a leader who couldn't give a direct order. There were no euphemisms used in the middle of a firefight. A soldier killed the enemy. Period. End of discussion.

"Alert," the communications officer announced, looking up from a laptop. "Message from PACOM for you, sir. Admiral Fallon at Camp Smith reports the nuclear destruction of the USS *Persing* missile frigate in the north Pacific Ocean. No survivors. The cause seems to be a tactical nuclear explosion. Navy Special Intelligence and the NSA are analyzing the Watchdog photographs for known radiation signatures."

"Understood," the President said. "Keep me informed of any further developments."

"Yes, sir."

"Better move fast, old friend," the President said. "The numbers are falling and time is against us."

Nodding in agreement, Brognola turned and headed for the door. America had the most powerful army in the world, along with a host of covert agencies, but to use any of them could reveal a fatal weakness and cause untold deaths.

Which left the deadly matter entirely in the hands of Stony Man Farm.

CHAPTER TWO

Yig-Ta Valley, China

Reaching the middle of the lake, the old man in the wooden boat back-rowed a little until the forward momentum was canceled and the boat was relatively still, rocking slightly in the gentle chop.

Whistling happily to himself, he opened a plastic box and carefully pulled out a large fishing net. It was discolored in several areas from numerous repairs done over the years with whatever was available, but the net was still strong and highly serviceable in his capable hands.

Shaking the net a few times to straighten out the folds and to warm up the muscles in his skinny arms, the fisherman then twisted sharply at the hip and the net flew out to land in the water with barely a splash to announce its arrival.

The small lead weights woven along the edge of the net dragged it down swiftly, and the man promptly began to haul the net up again, his fingers expertly testing for any additional weight that meant a catch.

But the net was empty, so he cast again. Fishing was more

of an art than anything else, and a man needed patience almost as much as a net. This time, the net held a dozen yellow fin trout. Happily, he emptied the net into the empty plastic box and cast once more. It was a long time ago, but he vaguely remembered when the lake had been a peaceful fishing village. However, a few years ago the Communists had sent in armed troops to throw everybody out of their ancestral shacks, and then had an army of workers build the massive dam. Now he came here to fish and recall better times. Somehow, the trout he caught always brought back memories of his idyllic youth. Silly, but true.

From the woods surrounding the lake there came a snap of a breaking tree branch, and the old man froze motionless, nervously glancing around, his heart pounding. Thankfully there was nobody in sight. Fishing on the government lake was strictly forbidden for some reason. It had taken a thousand men five years to build the huge concrete dam that blocked off the Wei River, creating the huge artificial lake. Now Beijing controlled the water for the crops, and the electricity for the lights and distant factories. Good for the government, but only more taxes for the struggling farmers and workers. Nobody was allowed to be on the lake, not even to sail paper boats on festive days or to send out a floating candle for a dead loved one. Scandalous!

Unexpectedly the entire lake shook, and the old man almost dropped the net from surprise. A ripple expanded to the shores and came racing back, the water seeming to rise quickly as huge bubbles came up from below like a pot about to boil.

Suddenly the middle of the watery expanse started to bulge, the surface rising higher and higher until it burst apart and exploded into a vertical column of fiery steam that blasted high into the air.

Screaming in terror, the fisherman threw away the net and

grabbed onto the gunwale of the boat as it was shoved aside by the strident explosion of steam. An instant later a deafening concussion vomited from the roiling depths, spreading the lake wide-open. A monstrous wave cast the old man and boat aside, sending them flying over the top of the concrete dam toward the distant mountains.

Horribly scalded, the terrified fisherman could only desperately hold on to the boat as it sailed through the air. Glancing down at the bubbling lake, he saw a wealth of writhing flames expand from the murky depths, then the boat hit the trees and blackness filled his universe.

Mounting in fury and volume, the nuclear fireball of the underwater Red Army weapons depot continued to expand, fully exposing the radioactive ruins of the illegal base hidden for years from the prying eyes of the annoying UN spy satellites. A split second later the physical shock wave crossed the churning expanse of the lake like an express train and the dam violently shattered, massive chunks of steel-reinforced concrete blowing out across the river valley below like the discharge of a shotgun. Ten thousand trees were mashed flat for half a mile, the destructive force of the fifteen DF-31 underwater missiles armed with tactical nuclear warheads was multiplied a hundredfold from being trapped under the lake. Tumbling wreckage from the destroyed dam plowed into the nearby hills like meteors throwing out geysers of earth and the boiling lake rushed through the yawning gap to thunderously churn along the river valley, destroying everything in its path. At a little vacation jetty, colorful boats were blown into splinters and rental cottages exploded, the startled families inside parboiled in a microsecond from the radioactive steam cloud, their death screams lost in the Dantian cacophony.

Disguised as an old barn, a military pillbox from the Glorious War for Freedom shuddered from the arrival of the searing torrent, the thick ferroconcrete walls withstanding the titanic pressure for almost a heartbeat before crumbling. Instantly dead, the soldiers tumbled away with all of the other debris propelled by the rampaging cascade.

TEN MILES DOWN THE Wei River valley in the small village of Tzang-Su, a teenage boy in a lookout tower dropped a pair of binoculars from his shaking hands. He was supposed to be looking for forest fires instead of trying to see into the bedroom of the girl that he was attracted to. But a flash from the north had caught his attention and his stomach lurched at the sight of the Wei River dam exploding like a house of cards.

A soft rumble could be heard, slowly increasing in volume, and the teen shook off the shock to spin around and rush for an old WWII radio sitting on a small table. A hurried glance informed him that the battery was fully charged, so he slapped the big red button on the side. He knew that would instantly send a signal to Beijing for emergency assistance. But could the soldiers in their helicopters arrive in time? The tidal wave from the dam could be seen moving above the treeline…no, it was moving *through* the forest, crushing aside the thick trees like blades of grass!

Suddenly from the nearby village the air-raid siren began to loudly wail, the noise rapidly increasing in volume until the windows on the homes and cars shook from the raw force of the clarion warning.

Everybody stopped whatever they were doing at the noise. The dam had broken? Surely this was only another government test. There hadn't been a hard rain for many months….

Then the townspeople caught the muted vibration and saw

the nearby river start to dramatically rise, climbing over the wooden docks and spreading across the streets, small vegetable gardens and freshly mowed lawns.

Shrieking hysterically, the people of Tzang-Su dropped whatever they had been doing and blindly raced for the public library. There was a large bomb shelter located in the basement, a holdover from the WWII. Long ago, the stout bunker had protected their grandparents from the aerial bombardments of the hated Japanese, and then had saved their parents from the brutal "political cleansing" of the Red Army. Now it would save them all from this onrushing disaster!

But upon reaching the library, it was painfully apparent that the bunker was too small to hold everybody in town. Instantly the people began to frantically struggle to be the first inside the imagined safety of the small bunker. But as more, and even more people attempted to jam into the zigzagging antiradiation corridor leading to the lead-lined door, fighting broke out among the mad press of bodies. Women began to shriek, men cursed, children wept. Knives flashed, guns fired. Soon, fresh blood flowed on the dirty concrete floor, and it became impossible to tell the living from the dead in the raw chaos.

The savage battle was still raging when the boiling wave of radioactive water thundered around a curve of the river valley, the churning wash a hideous slurry of steaming mud, broken trees and lifeless human bodies.

Looming high above the fishing village, the nuclear tsunami seemed to pause before slamming onto the village like the wrath of an angry god, flattening the wooden homes and smashing apart the few brick buildings. The sound of shattering glass overwhelmed the warning siren, and then it went silent, vanished in the maelstrom. A split second later the wave exploded through the side of the library, sending out a halo of stained glass to slice apart the people struggling to get into the ridiculously undersize bunker. Unexpectedly a flood of cars and tree trunks tore away the roof and punched more holes in the stone block walls. Still fighting among themselves, the cursing townsfolk screamed in terror as the water hit, the deadly waters rushing through every opening and crevice with trip-hammer force.

Less than a moment later, the flood swept past the ruined village, leaving behind a grotesque vista of smashed wreckage and a thousand steaming corpses....

Stony Man Farm, Virginia

DESCENDING FROM THE darkening sky in a rush of warm air, the Black Hawk helicopter landed gently on the field of neatly trimmed grass. However the people inside did nothing for a moment, as the turboprops continued to spin overhead. Then a red light flashed green on the elaborate control console and the pilot turned around to give a thumbs-up to the passenger.

"All clear, sir!" he shouted over the rush of the engines. The Stony Man weapons array had been deactivated.

Hal Brognola slapped the release on his safety harness, exited the helicopter and hurried to the waiting SUV that would take him to the farmhouse.

A short ride took the big Fed to the main buildings. No one was there to greet him, so Brognola went through the security protocol, entered the farmhouse and walked briskly to the elevator, nodding to the staffers that he passed on the way. Stepping inside the car, he pressed the button for the basement.

The elevator started downward and soon stopped with a gentle jounce. As the doors slid open, the big Fed gave a half smile at the sight of Barbara Price, Stony Man's mission controller, hurrying his way.

A stunningly beautiful woman with honey-blond hair, Price carried herself with the total assurance of a trained professional. As a former field agent for the NSA, Brognola expected no less.

"Hello, Hal," she said.

"Wish I could drop by without bad news sometime, Barbara," Brognola said. "Have you read the preliminary report?" They continued on toward the tunnel that would take them to the Annex.

"Yes, I already have Aaron and his team busy digging up intel on the matter."

"Excellent."

"Anything new to add?" she asked bluntly.

Without comment, Brognola removed a sheet of paper from his briefcase and passed it over. As she read the update, Price noted that the red striping along the edge of the document was still brightly colored. If the paper had been run through a scanner or copier, the red stripes would have faded to pink. This was an original document, direct from the Oval Office.

"So the Chinese did have a secret missile silo at the bottom of that lake," she stated, handing it back. Where her fingers had touched the paper, brown spots began to appear from the warmth of her skin.

"More likely it was only a weapons cache to hide the nukes from our Watchdog and Keyhole satellites, but yes," Brognola agreed, tucking the sheet away and closing the briefcase with a hard snap. "A lot of innocent civilians died in the flood, and more will perish from the poisoned drinking water. That whole section of the Wei mountain farmland is not going to be habitable until the rains come in the spring."

Which would wash the contaminated soil down the river, and out into the sea, Price realized privately. Where it would be carried on the currents across the world. A nuclear explosion in Beijing would end up on the dinner table of America two years later. The world seemed huge, but in reality was a very small place, and with the advent of modern technology it was getting smaller every day.

Without speaking, the man and woman entered the tunnel, each lost in their own thoughts. They continued to walk, deciding not to take the electric rail car that would take them to the Annex.

Reaching the end of the tunnel, Brognola stayed back as Price placed a hand on a square of white plastic embedded into the smooth concrete wall. Sensors inside the pad checked her fingerprints, along with her palm print.

When the scanner was satisfied, there came a soft beep and the plate went dark, closely followed by the sound of working hydraulics. Ponderously, the security door began to swing away from the jamb.

Moving quickly, Brognola and Price stepped past the door and made their way to the Computer Room. The air was cool and clean, although tainted by the smell of burned coffee. Several people sat at a series of computer consoles. A small video display set alongside the main monitor showed a vector graphic map of the world, blinking lights indicating the state of military alert for every nation. Another side screen swirled with high-resolution photographs of the weather above the North American continent, the images broadcast live from a NASA satellite. The only sounds came from a softly burbling coffeepot at in a coffee station and the tapping of fingers on keyboards.

This was the Computer Room, the heart and quite literally

the mind of Stony Man operations. Located on the next level down, just below the terrazzo flooring, was a unbelievably huge Cray IV Supercomputer, the titanic machine cooled by a steady stream of liquid nitrogen to keep the circuits working at their absolute optimum level.

This was the base of operations for the background soldiers of Stony Man Farm, the vaunted "electron-riders" of the covert organization. A cadre of unstoppable computer hackers, part data thieves and part cybernetic assassins, who patrolled the info net of the world and sometimes did more with the press of a single button than an army of soldiers could with missiles and tanks.

"Well, good morning!" John "Cowboy" Kissinger called, looking up from the monitor he studied.

A former DEA agent, Kissinger was a master gunsmith and in charge of all the firearms used at the Farm. He made sure that anything the field teams needed was instantly available, from conventional weaponry to experimental prototype. His workshop was stockpiled with everything from the P-11 underwater pistol used by the Navy SEALS, to the brand-new 25 mm Barrett rifle. He even created some of the specialty weapons used in the field by Able Team and Phoenix Force.

"What are you doing here?" Brognola asked brusquely. The man usually stayed in his workshop.

"Helping us," Kurtzman said, grabbing the wheels of his chair in both hands and nimbly turning toward the new arrivals.

Resembling a grizzly bear in a badly rumpled suit, Aaron "The Bear" Kurtzman was the head of the cybernetics team. A master code breaker and expert in cipher technology, Kurtzman had quit his lucrative job on the Rand Corporation's world famous think tank to use his skills where they were most needed, bringing a measure of justice to the world, instead of just making more millions for fat businessmen already rolling in cash.

"Cowboy read the report on what happened in New Mexico, and had some suggestions to offer on where to look for more data," Kurtzman added.

"Suggestions?" Price asked curiously, crossing her arms.

"Gunsmiths like to talk about weapons. It's more than our job, you know, it's a calling," Kissinger said. "So I often lurk online, listening to the gossip about this and that, cut out articles from the trade journals and such, always keeping a watch for anything odd going on, anything that just doesn't sound right."

"He knew about the new 7.8 mm QBZ Chinese assault rifles before the Chinese army did," Kurtzman stated. "Cowboy has sent us in the right direction numerous times."

"Always considered that antinuke thing just a load of bull," the armorer said. "But now…" He shrugged.

"Are you trying to tell me that somebody knows what triggered the nukes?" Brognola demanded, placing his briefcase on the polished floor.

"Of course not. But I do remember hearing something about an odd rumor from the cold war. The story was that some scientist in the Netherlands, Swedish maybe, or possibly Dutch, had invented some sort of device to stop a nuke from detonating, or something along those lines…different people told different versions, you know?"

"But the essence of the story," Kurtzman added, "is that the KGB heard about the device, found it, killed the scientists involved and stole the blueprints."

"Or so some of the rumors go," Kissinger finished, resting

a hand on the back of the wheelchair. "Other folks say the CIA stole it, but you know how that goes."

Yes, Brognola did. Anything odd that happened in the world, some people immediately blamed the CIA.

"So, how old is this rumor?" Price asked, trying to see over the shoulders of the three people clustered around a console.

"About a decade or so."

She started to scowl, then stopped. Just because something was old, didn't mean it was harmless. There briefly flash in her mind the memory of how the French invention of the table fork had been introduced to England back in the Middle Ages. The French had been using forks for many years, but overnight the English discovered that the simple eating utensil fit perfectly through the eyeslots on a suit of armor. A fork that cost only pennies could easily kill a nobleman supposedly invulnerable inside a suit of highly expensive armor. The world of peasants versus knights was almost overturned until the helmets were quickly redesigned. Simple things could become very deadly in the right—or wrong—hands.

"Any truth behind the tale?" Brognola queried.

"Nothing yet, still checking," Akira Tokaido said, rock music seeping from his earbuds.

"Let us know when you have anything," Price added.

"No problem." Unwrapping a fresh stick of chewing gum and popping it into his mouth, the handsome Japanese American was the youngest member of the cyberteam. It was joked that Akira had chips in his blood. The natural-born hacker could instinctively do things with computers that others took years to learn. Kissinger had taught the young genius how to shoot a gun on the Farm's firing range, but in his official government profile, Tokaido's weapon of choice was listed as a Cray Mark IV Supercomputer.

"Could this be another jump start?" Carmen Delahunt asked from behind a VR helmet. A wealth of glorious red hair cascaded from underneath the utilitarian device strapped around her head, and both hands were encased in VR gloves as she stroked open files and seized data from foreign computer banks.

"A jump start?" the big Fed prompted.

"Oh. During a past mission we cracked open a couple of NATO nukes to use the radioactive cores to kill the terrorists trying to steal them. Could something similar be happening now?"

"Possible, but unlikely," Kurtzman said grimly, cracking his knuckles. "Besides, we had the access codes, these new folks do not."

"True."

"Perhaps only tactical nukes have been set off so far because of their compact electronics," Brognola suggested, taking a chair and sitting. "Thermonuclear weapons have ten times the protective circuitry, right?"

"Absolutely true," Professor Huntington Wethers stated, removing the cold pipe from his mouth only to place it back again. Since smoking was strictly forbidden on the premises, he was forced to merely chew the stem of his beloved briar while on duty. "However, all of the superpowers have different types of electromechanical protection for their nukes. Nobody knows how to set off every type of nuclear device. This must be a matter of preexciting a subcritical mass of U-235 to achieve threshold."

Tall and lean with light touches of gray at his temples, the distinguished black man had formerly been a full professor at the University of California, Berkley, teaching advanced and theoretical cybernetics until the call came to help fight the criminals of the world.

"Threshold," Kissinger stated, giving a sideways grin. "Why not just say explosion. It's a perfectly good word."

"But wildly inaccurate," Wethers replied, then smiled. "Out of curiosity, does your automatic pistol use gunpowder, John?"

"Gunpowder?" The armorer arched an eyebrow. "What is this, 1920? Firearms haven't used gunpowder since the invention of cordite! Well, we still call it gunpowder, but the technical name is propellant, that's a form of stabilized fulminating guncotton…" He stopped, then grinned. "Point taken."

"Would a neutrino bombardment work?" Delahunt asked.

"Not unless these people have a working neutron cannon," Price declared. "And our Watchdog satellites are now keyed to detect the sort of induced magnetics needed to operate that weapon."

"Plus, according to the videotapes I've seen, nobody near the nukes died before the explosions," Brognola noted. "So this could not be caused by a beam of focused neutrinos."

Going to the coffee station, Price poured herself a cup of coffee, adding a lot of cream and sugar. She took a sip and made a face. Good God Almighty, Kurtzman liked his brew strong enough to melt teeth. He seemed to have come pretty close with this batch, too.

"Maybe we're looking in the wrong direction," Price suggested. "Perhaps somebody has simply found a way to ignite the C-4 used inside a nuclear weapon. That would slam the uranium together and cause a nuclear blast." Then she scowled. "No, we've seen videos of the guards near the attack sites. Several of them were carrying M-203 grenade launchers, and those 40 mm shells are armed with C-4. Damn!"

"Okay, do all nukes have anything in common, aside from C-4 and uranium?" Brognola asked, furrowing his brow.

"Tell you in a minute." Kurtzman turned back to his console. Rolling the wheelchair into place, the big man locked the wheels and started quickly typing on the keyboard. Within moments the screen was scrolling with mathematical equations and complex molecular diagrams.

"And the answer is… Well, I'll be damned. Thulium," Kurtzman growled, poking a stiff finger at the rotating graphic of a molecule on the screen. "It seems that every nation uses some sort of thulium shield to protect—" the man grinned as he looked up at Price "—to protect the C-4 plastic explosives inside their nukes."

"Do they now," Price muttered, narrowing her gaze in concentration. Okay, the cyberteam had gotten hold of a very slender thread. The enemy was somehow exciting the thulium, which in turn triggered the C-4, causing an early explosion. They now knew what was happening, but not how, why or the much more important who.

"Akira, see if anybody has ever done theoretical work on the possible long-range stimulation of thulium," Brognola ordered, leaning forward in his chair.

"No," Kurtzman countered. "Pull up all of the files on thulium. Everything there is available, mining operations, common and military uses, research projects…everything!"

"Already have," Tokaido said calmly, tapping a button.

Pulsating into life, the main wall monitor divided into four sections, each slowly scrolling with text and mathematics.

Biting a lip, the big Fed struggled to read all of the screens at the same time, when Price gave a hard grunt. "Wait a second!" she barked. "There on screen three! Go back a bit."

Stroking a fingerpad, Tokaido did as requested, and everybody perused the text. It was a Pentagon document on foreign-weapons research. The file was ten years old and marked as abandoned.

Reaching for his ceramic mug, Kurtzman took a sip of the black coffee. "Code name Icarus," he muttered. "That's it, just the project name? No details?"

"Very little," Tokaido admitted, accessing the file. "Less than a page. The Pentagon wasn't interested in obtaining more since the project was a failure. Why, does the name mean something to you?"

Removing his pipe, Wethers answered. "In Greek mythology, Icarus was given wings of feathers and wax. He flew too close to the sun, the wax melted and he plummeted into the sea."

Tokaido shrugged. It was as good as any place to start.

More data came onto the screen. "Okay, Project Icarus was a top-secret research project by the Finnish government conducted around 1989," Kurtzman announced. "Believed to be some sort of electromagnetic shield designed to stop a nuclear blast. The project was abandoned a year after it started."

"During the cold war," Kissinger said in a low voice. "And Finland is sure as hell part of the Netherlands."

The people in the room became galvanized at the simple pronouncement.

"So the rumors were correct. Sort of. But a nuclear shield?" Delahunt said. "That's ridiculous! Scientifically impossible."

"That could have simply been the cover story," Brognola explained. "Lord knows I've had to spin some whoppers in my career to cover the work that goes on here."

A dimple appeared on her cheeks. "Fair enough."

"No way the Finns are behind this," Price declared resolutely. "They are some of the staunchest supporters of world peace."

"The Chinese invented gunpowder, but they still got shot by the Japanese in both of the Sino-Japanese wars," Kurtzman retorted. "Somebody may have just have run across this research and finished the project, or simply stolen it outright. Are any of the Finnish scientists or politicians involved in the project still alive today? Anybody we can question for details?"

"Checking," Tokaido said, typing on his keyboard.

"Negative," Wethers announced, hitting a button to slave his monitor to the wall screen. Old photographs of men and women in laboratory coats appeared on the screen, short profiles scrolling alongside each face. "They have all passed away from natural causes."

"But they only look to be about forty years old," Price said carefully, as if weighing each word. "If this picture was taken in 1989, that would only put them in their sixties now."

"All of them are dead?" Brognola demanded suspiciously. "All?"

"I have the death certificates," Wethers said, checking the screen. Then he frowned. "What in the world… These are fake. Look at those dates! It is statistically impossible for fifty people working on a project to all die on the exact same day." He tapped the scroll button to flip pages. "Car crashes, heart attacks, fell off a bridge, drowned…this is a wipe-out!"

"Has to be," Kurtzman growled. "Somebody must have hit the lab and killed everybody there, and the Finnish government disguised the deaths as accidents."

"The natural choice is the Soviet Union, which means the KGB," Brognola said. "But the KGB was disbanded when Russia became a democracy."

"The KGB also sold off a lot of their stockpiles of tanks, planes, submarines and even some nukes," Delahunt noted. "They might have sold the Icarus blueprints to anybody."

"Excuse me, this man is not dead," Tokaido said casually.

"Eh? I have the files right here," Wethers stated, shifting his pipe to the other side of his mouth. "Fifty people, fifty death certificates."

"True, but I cross-checked with their families to see who got the estates of the deceased scientists, settled their bills and so on." He moved a mouse and a single picture appeared on the wall monitor. The man was pudgy with thick wavy hair, horn-rimmed glasses and a small mustache. "Only the family of Dr. Elias Gallen did not apply to his insurance company, and he carried term life."

"He's not dead," Price said with a hard smile. "The son of a bitch survived the attack, and the Finns pretended that he was to try to save his life from further assaults."

"Got a location?" Brognola demanded urgently. "If he can tell us exactly what we're dealing with here…"

"Checking…" Tokaido said, frowning slightly. A minute passed, then two. Five minutes.

"Need any help?" Kurtzman growled impatiently, fingers poised over his keyboard.

"Not really," the young man answered slowly, both hands working furiously. "These records are still on magnetic tape in some Finnish archive, and they load slower than a Bolivian firewall… Yes, got it!" He swung away from the console. "All right, there is no record of them changing their mailing address, driver's license or anything similar."

"Be the mistake of a rank amateur if they did," Kurtzman interjected rudely.

"However," Tokaido continued unabated, "when the Treasury Bureau of Finland closed the personal accounts of Dr. and Mrs. Gallen, that exact same amount was sent to a numbered Swiss bank account in Geneva." The man smiled.

"Then shifted to a Chase Bank in Mousehole, Wales, United Kingdom."

"Always follow the money," Price said with a nod. "Good job, Akira."

"Got an address?" Brognola asked. In spite of all the years working with these people, he was still amazed at how fast they could unearth information and track down people.

"It's 14-14 Danvers Road," Kurtzman answered, studying a small window display. "That's a house, not an apartment complex, so there should be a name on the land file. Good thing David McCarter got us those MI-5 access codes… The land belongs to a Mr. and Mrs. Daniel Cartwright. I'll cross-reference that with the Royal Motor Division—she does not have a driver's license, but he does—give me a sec, download-ing the JPEG now." On the wall monitor was a the slightly blurry photograph of a pudgy man with thick wavy hair, the temples winged with silver streaks, horn-rimmed glasses, a large mustache and an old scar along the right cheek. It was clearly an old bullet scar. Everybody in the room had seen enough of them to know those on sight.

"Any fingerprints?" Brognola asked hopefully.

"No need, that's him," Tokaido stated confidently. "Same blood type listed on his organ-donor card, and still on the same medication."

"What for?"

"Some sort of cancer. Checking…"

"Working with high-voltage electronics for many years often causes leukemia, cancer of the blood," Wethers said un-expectedly.

Dutifully, Tokaido bent into the screen. "Confirmed, he has leukemia," he announced after a few moments. "The medical records also show his wife was admitted to St. Frances Hospital in Wales last year, also with leukemia…she died six months ago and was laid to rest in Heather Grove cemetery in Sussex."

"Exhume the body," Brognola ordered. "I want to make sure it is her and not him."

Pausing in his blowing of a bubble, Tokaido looked pained at the request, but nodded. "We'll know for sure by noon tomorrow," he said, and went to work contacting Scotland Yard, routing the request through Brognola's Justice department e-mail account. The British police regularly did the Farm small favors, assuming the requests came from Justice.

"All right, I hacked the bank and got his credit card," Delahunt announced smoothly. "The account for his wife was closed last year, and the dates match her supposed demise."

"What about him?" Price asked.

"He spent a lot of time drinking at the local bars, months actually, then went to Amsterdam for a—" Delahunt coughed delicately. "Shall we say he had a lonely man's weekend adventure?"

"Everybody grieves in their own way. All I want to know is, where the frag is he now?" Kurtzman asked. "Exploring the forbidden delights of Hong Kong? Going down under in Australia?"

"Australia?"

"Prostitution is legal there."

"Is it? Well, the card shows he took British Airlines Flight 255 to Nashville, Tennessee, and he is staying at the Tuncisa Casino and Hotel in Memphis. Room 957, the Heartbreak Hotel suite."

In spite of the situation, Brognola almost smiled at that. "He's an Elvis fan?"

"And who isn't?" Kissinger said languidly.

"Has Jack gotten in touch with Able Team yet?" Price

asked, standing from her chair. Jack Grimaldi was the chief pilot for Stony Man and often carried the field teams to and from battlegrounds. There wasn't a machine with wings or rotors that Grimaldi couldn't fly, including space shuttles.

"Just a few minutes ago," Kurtzman replied. "They were getting some R and R visiting Toni in Los Angeles, and not answering their cell phones, so I sent some blacksuits after them as you suggested. Thankfully, Ironman heard about New Mexico on the radio and the team is already on the way."

"Excellent. When they arrive, send the team to Memphis and bring in Professor Gallen," she ordered. "We need him alive."

"Consider it done."

"What about Phoenix Force?" Brognola asked.

"They're going to Finland, to check the former location of the lab," Price answered curtly. "Or rather, they will be soon. Unfortunately right now they're incommunicado on that search-and-rescue mission to Sardinia. No way out of that."

Although irritated, the man accepted the information. Soldiers couldn't very well answer a cell phone in the middle of a firefight. One small distraction could cost a hundred lives. There was nothing to do until McCarter called the Farm, either announcing a successful mission or asking for an immediate air strike.

The big Fed took a deep breath, then let it out slowly. "How soon until they call in?"

Price checked the clock on the wall above the room's entrance.

"Just about any time now…" she answered as the hands moved forward with a mechanical click.

CHAPTER THREE

The Isle of Sardinia

It was a moonless night and the stars were bright in the heavens. Sitting on a rock, the man in loose clothing was cleaning his fingernails with a pocketknife when he went stiff, his eyes going wide in shock. His hands twitched from the effort to grab the AK-47 assault rifle laying across his lap, but they refused to obey even the most simple command.

There was pain, searing pain, at the back of his head, and the guard realized that he had been stabbed in Death's Doorway, the tiny fissure located near the right ear. Slide in a thin blade right there and your victim was paralyzed, twist the blade and they died instantly, like turning off a light switch. Click, dead. The guard had done it many times over the years to policemen, judges, even a few women who had refused to cooperate, but he never knew how much it hurt. The pain filled his body like electric fire. It was beyond agony! But he couldn't make a sound. Not a sound.

Then there was pressure from the blade, a flash of light and eternal blackness.

With a soft exhalation, the dead man slid off the rock onto the white sandy beach, the assault rifle splashing into the blue sea.

"One down, fifty to go," T. J. Hawkins whispered, wiping the blade clean before sheathing it. A decorated member of the elite Delta Force before joining Stony Man, Thomas Jackson Hawkins, T.J. to his family and friends, was a big man, lightning-fast in his movements and a stone-cold killer on the battlefield.

"Firebird One, this is Texas. The clubhouse is open," Hawkins said, touching his throat mike.

As silent as ghosts, more men rose from the scraggly juniper bushes of the low hillock and approached the rocky rill, moving from shadow to shadow. Past the hillock rose huge sand dunes that extended for miles. This section of Sardinia was often called the Sarah of Italy. Others called it purgatory, the gateway to hell.

Carefully studying the coastline, David McCarter kept the Barnett crossbow steady in his grip, the blackened tip of the arrow as reflectionless as the sky above. A quiver of arrows for the crossbow was strapped across his back and a MP-5 machine gun was slung at his side, the barrel tipped with a sound suppressor.

There was a tunnel straight ahead of the Stony Man team, a dark recess going straight into the bowels of the earth. Sardinia was famous for its gold mines, the island honey-combed with a warren of passages. But McCarter knew this abandoned mine was a dead end. The slavers were a lot smarter than that. They had been plying their trade for decades, and nobody had ever gotten closer than the length of a knife blade before.

Until this night, McCarter thought grimly. A former mem-

ber of the SAS, David McCarter was the leader of Phoenix Force, a former SAS commando and an Olympic-class pistol shot. Every man on the team owed his life to McCarter a dozen times over, and had repaid the debt in equal numbers. Their bonds of friendship had been forged in fields of blood.

On the surface, the island of Sardinia was a tourist's paradise, the fjords filled with more yachts and pleasure craft than all of the fishing boats of the entire chain of twenty-three islands combined. The beaches were made of the purest white sand, as pristine as newly fallen snow, and the sea was almost supernaturally clear. During the daylight, it was possible to look all the way to the bottom of the shoals and see the wrecked stone columns from the time of the Roman Empire.

However, the criminal elements of Sardinia began to kidnap young women from Italy, Albania, Greece, Turkey, Spain and Sicily, hauling them away to a secret location. There they were brutalized until their spirits finally broke and they learned to accept their new position as sex slaves. Branded like cattle, the girls, mostly teenagers, were sold on the world sex market to high-priced whorehouses in Bangkok, harems in Arabia and South America or to millionaire sadists seeking fresh victims for their private torture rooms. If the girls refused to obey, or tried to escape, they were brutally killed.

Italy lost an estimated thousand teenage girls a year to the monstrous slavers. Numerous ships had been caught at sea, and occasionally some girls were rescued alive. But the slavers disliked witnesses, and often tossed them overboard still locked in their heavy steel chains.

If the flesh merchants were arrested by NATO forces, they went to stand trail in the world court. If taken by the Italian military, the slavers were executed at sea with a bullet to the back of the head. Nobody had ever accused the Italians of

being soft on crime. But the lure of huge profits was too strong an incentive, and in spite of everything the UN, Interpol, Italy, Greece and Turkey could do, the foul practice continued.

There were few villages along Costa Verde that afforded privacy to anybody who did not wish to be observed. Far out to sea, Arlentu Mountain was a basalt fortress rising on the horizon from the last volcanic eruption hundreds of years ago. It was a landmark for passing ships to find the safe deep-water harbors. The mountain was also an excellent way for the slavers to navigate without using radar or radio beacons, which might give away their position.

Pulling a palm-size computer from a pocket of his combat suit, McCarter checked the position on the blinking red dot. The slavers were smart, he'd give the bastards that, but not smart enough. A raiding party had captured a water-skiing party that morning, and one of the guests was the daughter of a American senator, with a low-jack chip embedded into her earlobe. It was a precaution that some politicians and the members of their families, took against kidnapping. The chip had been steadily emitting a pulse, giving her exact location. Unfortunately, her father had been in conference until noon and only learned of her disappearance then. The senator immediately called the President, who then called Stony Man. Hours later Phoenix Force was moving through the night, tracking a tiny blip that hopefully still was attached to a living woman.

"There are no proximity sensors in the area," Rafael Encizo said, checking the EM scanner in his hand. "We're clear to proceed."

Encizo was a short stocky man, with catlike reflexes. Slung across his chest was an MP-5 machine gun, and stun grenades

festooned his web harness. A compact .38 Walther PPK rode in a high belly holster, a Tanto combat knife was sheathed upside down near his shoulder for fast access and plastic garrotes dangled from a breakaway catch on his belt.

"Are we heading for that?" Calvin James asked suspiciously, his accent pure southside Chicago. "Jails make a good cover for covert ops. Nobody wants to go near them, and any trouble can be attributed to an attempted escape."

Rising far to the south, the black outline of a Sardinia penitentiary stood against the starry sky, a stoic reminder that not everybody on the island was involved in the black market of selling human beings. Like everywhere else, most of the people were just trying to make a living and protect their families. But not all.

"Trail goes this way," McCarter said, checking the locator.

"Just hope we're tracking a girl and not merely an ear," Gary Manning stated, working the slide on a KGB Special pistol.

Satchel charges hung from both sides of his combat suit, while a standard-issue MP-5 submachine gun was slung across his chest. Usually, he carried a .50-caliber sniper Barrett rifle, whose titanic cigar-size bullets could shoot through a brick wall. But that was for open terrain, and the work tonight was going to be close quarters, probably hand to hand. Which is why he was also carrying disposable plastic garrotes, stun grenades and the KG-B Special.

Actually, the automatic pistol was simply a Beretta 9 mm with an oversize ejector port to prevent jamming. But the bullets were truly unique. Invented long ago by the KGB, the shells carried half-charges that propelled a miniature piston forward inside the casing to slap the soft-lead bullet forward. However, the 9 mm piston then jammed into the narrow 7 mm

mouth of the casing virtually welding into place from the heat and friction. That stopped all of the propellant gases from escaping, along with any noise. The KGB Special wasn't a silenced gun, but carried silenced bullets. The only sounds made were the click of the falling hammer and the click of the piston. The subsonic rounds had a pitiful range and poor penetration. But for this kind of a soft probe, where silence was vital, it was pure death, especially in the talented hands of Gary Manning.

Suddenly soft bells began to tinkle, and the Stony Man commandos dropped into combat posture, snicking off the safeties of their weapons. A moment later a deer strolled into view from around a boulder, its leather collar studded with tiny bells.

"A pet?" Encizo asked, easing his finger off the trigger of his submachine gun.

"No, the island is full of them," James replied, checking behind them in case this was a diversion. "They roam free by the thousands, like reindeer in Iceland."

As the deer began to walk along the sandy beach, Hawkins gave a hard grin. "Which is why there are no remote sensors. They'd be going off every five minutes with these things wandering around."

"All the better for us," McCarter said, comparing the vector graphic on the device to the terrain around them. "Okay, this way. I'm on point, T.J. and Gary cover the flanks. One meter spread, silenced weapons only." First and foremost, this was a rescue mission. Get the girls out alive. Afterward, there could be a reckoning with the slavers, but not before. The image of the criminals throwing their "goods" overboard flashed into his mind, and a rage filled the former British soldier. He checked the arming bolt on his MP-5 submachine gun.

Easing through the jumbled array of boulders dotting the landscape, Phoenix Force slipped through the moonless night, watching for sentries and trip wires. There were sure to be additional safeguards aside from the one sleepy guard.

The salty smell of the sea became sweetened by the perfume of the maccia shrubs and myrtle. The team jerked their weapons upward at an odd noise, then relaxed when it was only a vulture winging by overhead. They only hoped it wasn't an omen.

Following a dried riverbed of smooth stones, the Stony Man team soon reached a big granite tower set alongside a low hill, partially hiding it from the beach. All around them rose granite cliffs, impossible to climb. It was a box canyon, with the stony riverbed the only entrance.

"Mine," Hawkins whispered into his throat mike.

Everybody froze.

Dropping to one knee, Hawkins moved aside the loose stones to reveal a squat land mine. Only the burnished pressure plate had been exposed, a small coin set among the loose stones. Pulling a garrote from his belt, Hawkins cinched it tight through the locking safety and heard the mine disarm. The weight trigger had been set to maximum, probably so that one of the wandering deer wouldn't set the charge, but an escaping girl would have her legs blown off. Nasty.

A few yards away McCarter whistled softly, and bent to neutralize another. Then Encizo did a third, followed by James. Proceeding with extreme care, the team cleared a wide path down the middle of the riverbed until finally reaching an ancient Roman pavilion. Marble stairs rose from the riverbed and led directly to a large stone tower, which dominated the box canyon.

Spreading out, the Stony Man commandos checked for traps, but reached the crumbling fortress without incident.

Apparently, the granite tower had once been a tourist attraction, as there was a sign announcing the prices for a guided tour. But now the entrance was blocked. A weathered sign printed in Italian, Sardinian, French and Japanese listed the structure as dangerously unstable, about to collapse at any moment. The message was clear: keep out or die.

"Bullshit," James muttered, holstering his pistol and running a scan of the door. He found no electronic sensors and went to work on the lock. A moment later they heard a subdued click and the door swung aside, revealing only darkness.

Donning their night-vision goggles, the team switched from starlite to UV and slipped into the ruin. The night vanished, replaced with a black-and-white view of the world in sharp detail.

The inside of the granite tower had been reinforced with concrete plastered on the walls. Rubber mats lined the ancient stones, and winding stairs led to the tower and down to the basement. Checking their weapons, Phoenix Force descended into the bowels of history.

The center of the stone steps was worn from two thousand years of bare feet, sandals, boots and sneakers. Small recessed niches dotted the wall. Most of them were empty, but a few contained modern Coleman lanterns. Reaching a landing, McCarter saw a short, plump statue of a naked woman sitting in a niche, the smiling figure holding a spear and a sheath of wheat. That was the mother goddess, protector of women and children. The Briton felt repulsed at the thought of the crying prisoners dragged past the ancient idol as some sort of horrible joke. Or was it more than that?

Going to the statue, McCarter switched from UV to in-

frared. Sure enough, the navel of the plump little goddess glowed faintly. Still warm from the touch of a human hand. Gently, the Stony Man commando inserted a finger into the navel and felt the stone give slightly.

Across the landing, there was a click and a section of the smooth concrete wall separated. Also switching to infrared, Hawkins inspected the door and pressed a palm to the only glowing area. There was a second click and the door swung aside, revealing a long narrow tunnel cut through the rock of the hill.

His weapon at the ready, Hawkins took the point position again and moved swiftly into the passageway, holding his pistol in a two-handed grip.

The last to enter, James pulled out a small block of C-4 from the satchel charge, shoved in a radio detonator and hid the explosive wad alongside the secret door. Just in case.

Exiting the tunnel, Hawkins found a huge room carved into the rock. Wooden pallets were placed in orderly lines along opposite walls and large cisterns stood in the corners.

"This was the barracks for the soldiers," McCarter stated, glancing around. The place was enormous, suitable for a small army. He spotted small brass placards on the walls showing where racks for spears and swords used to be located. Now there were only rough outlines left by the smoke of primitive candles.

"Some sort of a museum exhibit," Manning observed warily. There was no concrete down here. The walls were raw stone, covered with a ripple pattern of chisel marks from the artisans who had hammered the room into existence two thousand years ago.

"I don't like this," Encizo muttered, looking around quickly. There didn't seem to be any other way out of the bar-

racks. "Which means that either we missed something or else…"

A ghostly whimper interrupted the thought, closely followed by a man's cruel laugh.

This was it! McCarter realized, the knowledge sending adrenaline pumping through his veins. The slavers were right on the other side of the stone walls. But where was the bleeding entrance?

Switching his goggles from UV to IR, Hawkins saw nothing unusual. He knew the team was missing something obvious, but what? They could start tossing grenades, but the moment they started, the jig was up for the girls.

Removing his goggles, McCarter pulled out a flashlight and clicked on the bright halogen light. Sweeping the beam around the barracks, he saw the hidden door immediately. Every one of the brass plaques on the wall was above a sleeping pallet, except one located on a black wall, the brass tarnished and dirty.

Clicking off the light, McCarter pressed the plaque and the nearby pallet slid aside silently on greased tracks. Worn stone steps led down again. The sound of laughter was louder.

"Just like Afghanistan," Hawkins whispered, readying a stun grenade. When the Soviet Union had invaded the ancient country, their battle tanks had been meet by booby traps designed centuries ago for Roman war chariots. Hinged sections of road opened wide and a tank dropped fifty feet onto solid granite. What killed horses two thousand years ago, only stunned the crew of the tank. But before they could recover, the Afghans poured gasoline through the air vents of the armored transport and burned the Soviets alive. Grisly, but effective.

Moving swiftly along the flight of stairs, the commandos found themselves descending into a huge natural cave. The

floor below was lined with rows upon rows of steel cages, young woman lying inside on piles of dirty straw.

Like animals in a zoo, James noted, feeling a furious coldness swell deep inside.

Several of the prisoners were weeping, the sound echoing slightly off the hard walls of the cave. Reaching the floor, McCarter switched to IR again, searching for any hot spots. Immediately he saw the rectangle of a door set into the far wall, the outline glowing with warmth. Jackpot.

The Stony Man team headed that way, moving past the rows of cages in the dark. The smell from the dirty straw was foul. There were no bathroom facilities for the prisoners. Obviously another part of the process designed to break their spirit. The soldiers hardened their hearts and concentrated on the mission. If the team started freeing the girls, some would began to shout, alerting the slavers. The only way to release them all was to take out the Sardinians first.

A soldier's burden, Hawkins thought grimly, trying to ignore the sobbing teenagers.

A guard armed with a cattle prod was sleeping in a chair beside the door. Manning and James grabbed his arms as McCarter clapped a hand across the man's mouth and slit his throat with a fast slash of a Gerber combat knife. The guard awoke drowning in his own blood and thrashed wildly for a few moments before going still.

With the sound of the dead man's life dripping onto the floor, Encizo went to the door and ran a check with the EM scanner. It was clean, no traps this time.

Hawkins took point again and tried the latch. It moved easily and the door swung aside on loud creaking hinges. Damn! The big Southerner brought up his MP-5 fast, but the next room was empty.

As their goggles adjusted to the bright electric lights, the Stony Many commandos saw rubber mats on the rock floor making paths through the torture chamber. There was no other word for the place. Gleaming steel tolls hung from hooks on the walls, and heavy wooden stocks, looking like something from the Middle Ages, were situated over rusty drains. Ripped clothing was piled to the side, mostly T-shirts and swimming suits. A stainless steel surgical table was filled with personal items, rings, eyeglasses, hair clips and such. Video cameras were mounted on tripods to record the humiliating strip, and the air was redolent with the smell of pine disinfectant. A hose lay coiled in a corner, the nozzle trickling water down a drain.

This must be where the girls were first taken to be stripped of everything from the outside world. A wooden butcher's block was surrounded by the remains of cell phones that had been smashed into useless rubbish, and the hopper of a nearby shredder was filled with the remains of wallets and credit cards. The last hope of escape was destroyed right before the helpless captives.

Across the room was a door made of burnished steel.

Moving in that direction, the team tightened their grips on the weapons as the metal door opened and out walked a whistling man with a coiled whip in his hand. The slaver paused, registering shock at the unexpected sight of a group of armed soldiers inside the underground base, then McCarter shot him in the face with the crossbow.

The barbed quarrel came out the back of his head, and the dying man wheezed in pain as he eased to the rubber mats on the floor. Already at the door, Hawkins kept it from closing completely with a knife blade, while Encizo and James pulled the rings from grenades.

A guttural voice laughed harshly and several men responded in Sardinian. The words almost made sense, the language was so close to Italian, but there were just enough differences to render it incomprehensible.

"Please," a young woman cried out in English. "My father is a senator! He'll pay anything you want for me! Anything!"

"We make more, you go Sudan," the first voice said in halting English. "Big show, daughter American senator."

There came the sound of ripping cloth, and the young woman screamed.

Instantly, Hawkins pulled open the door, Encizo and James tossed in their grenades, and the rest of Phoenix Force moved in with their weapons firing. A group of men was clustered around a young woman dressed only in bra and panties. They turned at the noise, cursed and shoved her aside to claw for the handguns in their belts.

Aiming carefully, McCarter put an arrow through the throat of a bald man holding a fistful of blouse, then dropped the weapon and pulled around his MP-5. Hawkins shot a Sardinian in the forehead, then rocked back as an incoming round hit him in the belly.

On the count of eight, the stun grenades detonated while still rolling along the floor, the bright flashes filling the room. Blinded by the light, the Sardinians began to shoot wildly, one of them blowing the face off the slaver standing right alongside. The glowing streaks of tracer rounds filled the air.

Over near a video-mixing board, two men worked the bolts on their Kalashnikov assault rifles, chambering rounds. Encizo took out one, Hawkins the other. The Sardinians died with their life blown out the backs of their chests.

Shooting as carefully as if he was at a gun range, Manning

placed four rapid head shots in a row, taking out the men clustered around the console.

Diving forward, James tackled the terrified girl to the floor to get her out of the line of fire, trying to keep her covered with his body. He grunted as a bullet hit his back, the NATO body armor under his fatigues deflecting the slug with a sharp whine. Screaming hysterically, the girl began pummeling the Stony Man operative with her soft fists.

"Delta Force, ma'am," James grunted as he took another bullet in the back. "You want to shut the fuck up and let us rescue you?"

Instantly she stopped struggling and looked into his face, tears of hope welling in her eyes. He could see that she had been badly beaten, her nose broken, and there were teeth missing, fresh blood smeared on her cheek and shoulder.

"Kill them," she begged with a sob in her voice. "Please kill them all."

"That's the plan," James replied, pulling out his Beretta and firing directly into the groin of a man coming their way loading a shotgun. Dropping the weapon, the slaver shrieked and tried to get away. James shot the man in the back, then again in the spine as the bleeding gunner started to slide limply down the wall.

A few moments later it was over and Phoenix Force quickly reloaded their weapons before going into the next room. Rising stiffly, James hauled the girl back to the entrance, hustling her away to safety. The first part of the mission was done. Now came the hard part—burning out this nest of vipers.

Kicking open the door, McCarter found a short corridor lined with curtained alcoves. It reminded him of a brothel he had raided once in Hong Kong. The implications were hor-

ribly clear, and he shoved the stubby barrel of the machine gun into the first sex room, seeking a target. A naked girl was strapped to small bed, a naked man trying to get a handgun free from the tangle of his clothing draped over a chair. McCarter stitched the slaver from groin to face, then departed while reloading. They'd come back later for the prisoners. This wasn't over yet by a long shot. The element of surprise was gone, and the Sardinians would start fighting back for real at any second. Every tick of the clock was a mark against the Stony Man commandos. This had to be a blitz.

Standing in a doorway, Hawkins was holding back a curtain and firing his MP-5 in short bursts, the spent brass arching away to bounce off the wooden jamb. Men screamed from within the alcove, followed by silence.

Going to the next curtain, Encizo paused and the fabric started to jump from the outgoing lead. He waited until the firing stopped, then swept in low, catching the bare-chested slaver as he dropped a spent clip from his Skorpion machine pistol. The little Cuban stroked the trigger and sent a wreath of 180-grain, steel-jacketed vengeance into the slaver.

Cringing behind a chair, a middle-aged woman stared at the act with a growing expression of delight. As the Sardinian fell, she leaped forward to pull a knife from his belt and attacked the riddled corpse in mindless fury.

Finishing another alcove, McCarter paused at the sight of his reflection moving in a wall mirror. Acting on a hunch, he fired into the glass, and a man fell out holding an AP grenade. As it rolled into sight, McCarter saw the ring was still attached. That had been too close! The NATO body armor they wore was good, but it didn't make a man invulnerable to head shots or concussion damage. Warily, the Briton checked inside the closet for any more hardmen and found a flight of stairs

leading deeper into the earth. Patting his chest, the Stony Man commando found that he was out of stun grenades. Returning to the room, he grabbed the AP grenade from the floor and tossed it down the stairs. As the lethal sphere bounced men shouted in fear and there came the sound of running boots.

Jumping down the short flight, McCarter landed in a crouch and saw a rough-hewn tunnel filled with men holding guns. Dodging to the left, the Phoenix Force leader opened fire with the MP-5, mowing them down. A few of the slavers fired back, the rounds ricocheting off the rock walls. When the clip was empty, McCarter pulled his 9 mm Browning Hi-Power and waded into the dying bodies, finishing off anybody who wasn't obviously dead.

Clearing out the last alcove, Manning reloaded his MP-5 just as a fat man rushed around a corner blasting away with an M-16. Coolly, Manning took out the fellow with a burst in the chest, then moved past the falling body to sneak a peek around the corner.

About a dozen men were opening plastic crates. A couple Sardinians were donning NBC suits, and the rest buckling on harnesses for XM-214 electric miniguns. Just one of those weapons could chew the Stony Man team into hamburger, and if the hardmen released VX gas into the prehistoric warren, everybody would die, including the girls still trapped in the cages.

"They've got VX and miniguns," Manning subvocalized into his throat mike, arming his last stun grenade. He couldn't risk rupturing the nerve-gas canisters.

Staying low, Encizo joined Manning just as a roaring hell-storm of lead blasted out of the room as the miniguns chewed a deep gap into the corner and wall, throwing off an explosion

of splinters. In unison, the two Stony Man commandos tossed their stun grenades around the corner, then quickly retreated.

As the grenades flashed into a triple flare, the slavers walked through the blinding light, firing their weapons everywhere, the spinning barrels of the miniguns vomiting high-velocity lead.

Crossing the streams, the Sardinian criminals chewed twin paths of destruction along the hallway and into the alcoves. Most of the curtains had been torn down, and they could see inside with no trouble. Still hacking at the corpse, the middle-aged woman was torn to bits.

Marching over the bodies of their fallen comrades, the two gunners proceeded into the studio, searching for the enemy, assuming it to be the Italian army again. But they could hardly believe the fools ever found their base, much less got this far inside. But the studio was also empty. Easing his grip on the firing handle, one of the Sardinians asked a muttered question. But the other man merely shrugged, uncertain of what to do next.

In the destroyed hallway, two of the bodies lying under the torn curtains raised into kneeling positions, and the Stony Man commandos cut loose with their MP-5 machine guns at point-blank range. The Sardinians flew backward from the concentrated barrage, their miniguns briefly firing to hammer at the stone ceiling before going as silent as the dead slavers.

Walking forward, Hawkins administrated a shot directly into the face of each Sardinian, just to make sure. Then Encizo pulled the power cords from the miniguns, rendering them inoperable.

"Okay, let's finish this," Manning said, slinging his machine gun. Pulling a Desert Eagle from a holster on his hip, the man clicked off the safety. His KGB Special didn't have anywhere near enough stopping power for this next part.

Slinging their machine guns, Hawkins and Encizo prepared their own handguns as they walked down the hallway, past the alcoves. There was a fast flurry of gunfire, then three slow deliberate shots.

Appearing in the smashed mirror, David McCarter carefully studied the war zone outside the alcove before emerging with his MP-5 in one hand and a thick book tucked under the other arm.

As he moved followed, the members of his team came around the corner.

"All clear?" McCarter asked.

The soldiers nodded.

"Well, I found the sales ledger," McCarter announced, tapping the fat volume with the hot barrel of the machine gun.

"Great," Hawkins muttered, working out a jam from his MP-5. "Then let's get out of this shithole." Saving the girls had been the mission priority, but this was the prize. The names and address in the book would send dozens of men and women to the gas chamber. Or whatever method of execution their assorted countries used to execute criminals in these so-called enlightened days. Hawkins had seen enough death in his career to understand that making somebody wait ten years on death row was a cruel and unusual punishment. A bullet to the back of the head was swift and painless, carrying much more mercy and compassion than the cannibals of society ever showed to their victims.

"I'll call in the rescue planes. Find some blankets, spare clothing, anything like that, and go help Calvin open the cages," McCarter directed. "And be gentle. The girls have been through double hell. If anybody doesn't want to leave her cage, then just unlock the door and let her be. To them, we're just another bunch of ugly guys with guns."

"Ugly?" Manning almost smiled at that, then he turned to Hawkins. "Must be talking about you."

Finally clearing the jam, Hawkins gave a snort. "Ugly in Texas is beautiful everywhere else in the world."

"I've been to Dallas, brother, and that dog won't hunt."

"Yeah, right."

"How about we bring along a peace offering?" Encizo suggested, reaching down to grab a dead Sardinian by the collar. He lifted the bloody corpse off the floor. "To show our goodwill."

"Now you're talking sense," Hawkins said, slinging the machine gun.

As the Stony Man operatives walked away, dragging the dead slavers along behind, McCarter worked the transceiver on his belt. The civilian cell phones would never have worked this deep underground, but the team had left a repeater unit hidden in the bushes on the surface. "Rock House, this is Firebird One," he said, touching his throat mike. "The clubhouse is clear, and the goods have been recovered."

"Excellent. Any breakage?" Barbara Price said, her voice wavering slightly from the interference of the surrounding rock.

Resting the hot barrel of the MP-5 machine gun on his shoulder, McCarter looked sideways at the woman in the alcove. "Yes," he said in a flat voice. "Send body bags along with the medics."

"Confirm. Sorry to hear that." Price sighed. "I'll contact the NATO frigate waiting offshore and have the prisoners picked up ASAP. As soon as the rescue helicopters arrive, proceed to your former staging area and wait for further instructions."

"Something local?" McCarter asked, pulling a cigarette from the packet of Player's in his shirt and lighting up. He

pulled in the dark smoke with little satisfaction. Maybe they hadn't gotten all of the slavers, and another nest of the vipers had been found. That's fine by me. Let's end this filthy practice, once and forever, he thought.

"Nothing local. We've got hot soup with breakage," Price said tersely. "Coffeemaker will relay details over a more secure line."

Coffeemaker had to be Kurtzman. "What kind of breakage?" McCarter asked, getting a bad feeling.

"Not over an open transmission."

That made McCarter raise an eyebrow. Open? These radios were protected by 254-byte encoding! The situation had to be really bad.

"Confirm," he stated, exhaling a long stream of smoke. "You sending Sky King?"

There was a crackle of background static. "Negative. Look for a man in dark clothing."

A blacksuit from the Farm would be bring them a plane, the leader of Phoenix Force translated. "Understood. We'll be ready. Over."

"Over and out," Price repeated, and the radio went silent.

Dropping the cigarette to the floor, McCarter crushed it under a boot, then went to inform the rest of the team. Their long night was over, but it sounded like an even longer day was just beginning.

CHAPTER FOUR

North Atlantic Ocean

The waves were low and sluggish, the thick waters of the Atlantic shimmering with the glassine effect of the nearly frozen brine. Peeking out from behind a few scattered clouds, the sun was high in the sky, but the light gave little warmth to the chilly world.

Standing on the bow of the HMS *Harlow,* the young boson swept the horizon with a large digital camera, his finger pressed lightly on the start button as if it were the trigger of an assault rifle. Standing closeby were the captain and the first officer, looking through computer-augmented binoculars.

"Anything?" the captain asked, an unlit cigarette jutting from a corner of his mouth.

"Nothing yet, sir," the first officer replied. "Boson?"

"Same here, Skipper," the man replied, swaying slightly to the motion of the deck as the missile frigate cut through the cold waters.

"Well, stay sharp!" the captain shouted above the wind. "It'll be any second now, and we won't get a second chance!"

"Aye, aye, sir!"

The salty wind was brisk, the sailors' uniforms slowly becoming damp as the material snapped against their arms and legs. High above them on the bridge were the gray half domes of the radar pods, and behind the bulletproof Lexan plastic windows could be seen more officers and crewmen with field glasses, monoculars, digital cameras and old-fashioned 16 mm chemical cameras, the boxy Nikons equipped with telephoto lens. This was going to be a historic day for Her Majesty's navy, hopefully, and every detail needed to be recorded.

"Look there, sir!" the first officer called excitedly, pointing starboard. "North by northwest!"

The captain replied with a grunt, but swung around to face the new direction, his hands tight on the binoculars.

Obediently, the boson followed their example. Through the electronic viewfinder, the sailor looked closely for any signs of submarine activity. The British navy was holding a live-fire test today of their new weapon, some thing called the Fire-lance. Unofficially, the rocket-powered torpedo had already been nicknamed by the sailors of the *Harlow* as the Thunder-fish.

Which was pretty accurate considering what the bloody thing could do, the boson thought, leaning harder against the safety railing to stop from swaying.

Removed from its regular duties, the *Harlow* was now on patrol outside the coastal wars of the Isle of Man, thought by some to be the most lonely spot in the North Atlantic that the UK still deemed to recognize as a royal possession. Just a lot of bare rock islands, hardly bigger than cricket field, and a million seagulls.

However, the royal missile frigate was not here to partici-

pate in the test, but assigned merely to be an observer. This was to be a battle of the titans, so to speak, and a vital stage in developing an adequate defense for the crown against this Russian aquatic killer. The British-made Firelance was going up against a Russian Squall purchased illegally on the black market by MI-5. Good lads all, the boson thought. Hopefully, the new British weapon could take out the Russian monster. Back during the cold war, the Soviet Union had invented the Squall, and the Iranians had their own version of the Russian superweapon. Sadly, the British navy was lagging behind in third place with the Yanks breathing hot on their necks. The boson smirked in pleasure. At least the French didn't have them yet, thank Jesus. That was some comfort, anyway.

The Firelance was incredible, with a maximum speed of 350 kilometers per hour. The captain had been forced to play the instructional video several times for the startled crew before they got over the shock of seeing anything move that fast under water. The torpedoes had a powerful rocket engine instead of propellers at the end, and a flat, armored crown, which seemed to be the secret to its success. The torpedo looked about as streamlined as a truck, and needed to be hard-fired into the water, not merely released like a regular torpedo. But when the Firelance hit the ocean, the impact caused a momentary shock wave effect that created yawning cavitation on the armored crown. In effect the concussion pushed aside the seawater for a split second, leaving behind a small empty space that was almost a vacuum. The Firelance flew through the shock wave, in a vacuum of its own creation. A Squall could blow any surface ship out of the water before the crew even knew it was under attack.

An abrupt disturbance in the pattern of the waves caught the attention of everybody. Excited voices rose from the

bridge. This was it! Then a humpback whale broke the surface for a moment to grab a breath and dived out of sight again.

Lowering the camera to clean the lens of spray, the boson hoped the big creature got the hell out of the engagement zone. Somewhere out there were two Royal Navy Vanguard submarines, and when the war games commenced, this was not going to be a safe place for innocent bystanders. Any minute now, the whale was going to find itself in more danger than a tourist in Liverpool.

There was subtle movement below the surface, the waves canting in different directions for only a heartbeat. Just long enough for the boson to catch sight of a periscope descending below the waves. Gotcha!

"Sub at four o'clock, sir!" the boson called out, tightening his grip on the video camera. Softly, the machine began to hum. "Range, one thousand meters!"

As the officers spun around, something flashed past the *Harlow* just below the surface. The blur was visible for a split second, then was gone.

"Mother of God," whispered the first officer, lowering his glasses. "Was…that our fish, or the Russian?"

"Who can tell?" the captain retorted, sounding excited and angry at the same time. "Look, there's the second fish!"

Another submerged object streaked past the bow of the frigate on a divergent course as the two aquatic hunters tried to find each other. Now it was machine vs. machine.

"Bridge, I want a sonar reading," the first officer said into a hand radio lashed by a cord to his belt.

"Negative, sir," came the prompt reply. "We've got a lot of hissing, but we can't track where it's coming from. They're just too damn fast, sir!"

"Both of them?"

"Aye, sir!"

"Excellent," the captain said, looking like a kid on Christmas morning.

Moving incredibly fast, the Firelance and the Squall zigzagged around the Atlantic, one of them trying to hit the submerged submarine, the other trying to prevent that very action. Then they were both gone and there was only the choppy waves.

Suddenly there was a tremendous flash of light from deep below, and the cold waters churned as the bubbling explosion rose to the surface. Every sailor on the *Harlow* cheered in victory at the sight. An explosion meant the Firelance had taken out the Squall! The Russian superkiller had just been defeated!

Maintaining a tight zoom on the churning patch of ocean, the boson frowned as he heard an odd ticking sound from behind, or rather, a sort of clicking. Suspiciously the sailor attempted to keep the video camera still as he glanced over a shoulder at the closed hatches of the missile launcher set into the main deck. The ferruled steel lids on the honeycomb were all tightly closed, but there was the oddest smell and then incredibly he saw fat sparks crackle on the outside of the WE-177 nuclear depth charges sitting in their launch rack. Stunned beyond words, the boson dropped the camera. Impossible! Those weren't even armed!

A split second later the *Harlow* was vaporized, the concussion traveling through the water to crush both of the British submarines in the area, the airborne blast also taking out the RAF Harrier jumpjet carrying the Minister of Defence who had wanted to see the live-fire test, but from a supposedly safe distance. Only seconds later, the British spy satellite relayed wire-sharp photos of the destruction to the headquarters for

the Ministry of Defence, and the prime minister was immediately alerted. The United Kingdom had just joined the list of nations attacked by the unknown terrorists.

Memphis Airport, Tennessee

WITH THE WHINE OF controlled hydraulics, the aft ramp of the colossal C-130 Hercules transport slowly lowered to the tarmac with a muffled crash, and a civilian van drove out of the huge airplane, jouncing hard as it make the transition from the sloped ramp to the smooth asphalt.

"Good luck," the voice of Jack Grimaldi said in the earphones of the men of Able Team.

"Same to you," Carl "Ironman" Lyons replied, shifting gears and moving away from the secluded landing strip.

As the man drove the van toward an access road running alongside the landing strip, the loading ramp of the Hercules rose upward and closed with a clang.

When the members of Able Team had arrived at Reagan National Airport outside Washington, D.C., they had found Grimaldi waiting for them in the Hercules, with their equipment van already loaded and strapped down for an immediate take-off. En route, the men changed their clothing and reviewed the information of the nuclear detonations while checking over their stores of weaponry. They had to move fast. If the enemy discovered that Professor Gallen was still alive, they would send an army of mercenaries to kill the man. Or worse, some other group would learn about the scientist and kidnap him, bringing a third party into the matter. It was possible that the Stony Man operatives would simply drive into Memphis, find the man, hustle him back to the Hercules and fly off without any trouble. But every second that passed put the odds against them.

"Hit the hotel first?" Hermann "Gadgets" Schwarz asked, draping a camera around his neck. Then he adjusted the silenced 9 mm Beretta pistol clipped to a breakaway holster on his belt. Taking on the role of a tourists for this assignment, the Stony Man team was casually dressed in loose slacks and loud Hawaiian shirts that perfectly covered the NATO body-armor underneath.

"Nobody stays in their hotel room on a vacation unless they're sick," Rosario "The Politician" Blancanales replied from the passenger seat, tucking a .380 Colt pistol snug in a similar holster at the small of his back. "We should hit Grace-land. That's the Mecca for all Elvis fans."

"Mecca?" Schwarz asked with a wry smile, checking the batteries in a stun gun.

"Metaphorically speaking."

"We'll hit the hotel first," Lyons stated, slowing the van as it headed for a tall wire fence that closed off that end of the Memphis airport. "Best to make sure he's actually here, before we hit Graceland. If we find the room in disarray with blood on the carpeting, then there's no sense looking for a corpse already floating in the Mississippi River."

"Plus, we can leave a bug behind, and lowjack his suitcase," Schwarz added, tapping the pocket of his shirt. "Just in case we miss him and he tries to run." Several ordinary-looking pens were clipped there, each of the intricate electronic devices worth more than most cars on the road.

"Readiness is all," Blancanales agreed, reaching up to slide aside a fake panel in the ceiling to take down a M-16/M-203 combination assault rifle. With expert hands, the former Black Beret made sure the 40 mm grenade launcher was loaded with a gel-pack stun bag. Just in case the professor didn't want to come along peacefully.

The so-called stun bags were nylon bags filled with soft gelatin pellets. The cartridges held only half-charges, but the nonlethal rounds still hit with enough force to break bones.

"Having a few guns doesn't hurt, either," Schwarz agreed, doing the same for his own assault rifle and then preparing the Atchisson autoshotgun for Lyons. The first couple of 12-gauge cartridges in the ammunition drum for the Atchisson were stun bags, the other twenty-four were stainless steel fléchettes. Perfect for blowing down locked doors or cutting a man in two.

When done, Schwarz tucked away the excess ammunition and closed all of the hatches until there was no sign of the arsenal within the ceiling and walls of the Ford Econoline 450. The van was a rolling arsenal of military weapons, and the rear was a compact electronic lab for Schwarz. Hidden compartments were filled with munitions, weapons, cash, clothing, medical supplies and anything else needed for the team out in the field. There were also three large blocks of thermite hidden inside the chassis in case it was necessary for them to destroy the vehicle. Burning at 2,000 Kelvin, the thermite would reduce the armored vehicle to a puddle of molten steel in a matter of seconds. It would be impossible for any police forensic expert to track who, and where, the van had originally come from.

Easing on the brakes, Lyons stopped the vehicle just past the wire fence and Blancanales climbed out to lock the gate behind them. Then the team proceeded toward Interstate 240. The traffic was light, the sky overcast, but not raining yet, and soon the sprawling city of Memphis loomed on the horizon.

Soaring skyscrapers marked the downtown area, bright steel and sparkling glass reflecting the streetlights. Neat rows of apartment blocks lined the bank of the mighty Mississippi, with small parks scattered around in artful disarray.

The water in the mile-wide river was dark and slow, with only a few pleasure craft darting across the murky surface. A fishing trawler moved slowly against the sluggish current, and a brightly lit paddle-wheel casino lolled majestically along, looking like something from another century.

"Behold, the Paris of the South," Schwarz quipped.

Dominating the entire southside of the bustling city was a colossal pyramid, the sloping sides tinted purple from neon lights. Lyons knew that was the Memphis Sports Arena, named not for the place of its birth, but for the ancient city the modern day metropolis was itself named after, Memphis, Egypt, on the Nile River. The gigantic arena was twenty-three stories high, taller than the Statue of Liberty, and easily held a crowd of twenty thousand people. Illuminated by search-lights at night, the Pyramid Arena could be seen for miles, and airline pilots had it listed on their visual reference chart as a landmark in case of any trouble with their GPS units.

"Huge place. We'll be shit out of luck if we have to hunt for Gallen in the Pyramid," Blancanales noted pragmatically, tucking a Homeland Security commission booklet into a pocket.

Few police actually knew what the ID looked like for HSA agents, and virtually no civilians did. So the booklets would open a lot of closed doors for the Stony Man commandos, and even if somebody called Washington, the official HSA records properly listed the three men as duly authorized operatives, thanks to a little creative hacking from Kurtzman and his team. As soon as this mission was over, the HSA files would be deleted, only to be recreated when needed. But there was much less of a chance of somebody in Homeland Security spotting any irregularities in the government files if the records didn't exist between missions.

"Caruthers," Lyons corrected. "The name is Caruthers now."

"But calling him Gallen let's the professor know that we are aware of who he really is."

"Fair enough."

"Sure hope he hasn't donned a disguise," Schwarz agreed somberly, pulling up a pdf on his U.S. Army laptop to check the picture of the scientist. "We can't exactly call out something in Finnish. That might give him a heart attack."

"Agreed. We may have to split up to hit more places," Lyons said, swerving to get out from behind a Mack truck hauling live hogs. On their way to the slaughterhouse, the fat animals peeked out from the dark interior, squealing unhappily as if somehow sensing their imposing doom. Lyons felt a brief impulse of sympathy for the animals, and only hoped it wasn't prophetic for the team. "If there's any trouble, we rendezvous at the Hercules."

"Check," Blancanales answered.

"No problem," Schwarz added, slinging the laptop over a shoulder. The portable computer had a thousand and one uses in the field, from opening electronic locks to deactivating lowjacks on civilian cars. It was also sheathed in galvanized titanium and was bulletproof to any caliber up to a .357 round at point-blank range. There were several small dents in the tough casing, testifying to the truth of the manufacturer's claim.

As they neared the downtown area, the traffic grew thicker, and Lyons tried to look confused as they drove past a Memphis Police Department patrol car, the officers casually watching the assorted cars and trucks flow past. To add some credence to the air of confusion, Blancanales pulled out a crumpled map, and started scowling unhappily until the police were left behind and out of sight, blocked by a Main Street trolley.

"And there she blows," Schwarz said, pointing a finger to the right. A few blocks ahead of them was the hotel-casino. It was definitely from the old school, the sort of thing that would have been seen in Las Vegas twenty years earlier, before the corporations took over and cleaned up the infamous Sin City.

But here, the Tunica Hotel was festooned with neon lights that blazed brightly even in the direct sunlight, announcing the hottest slots in town and a famous comic for an two additional weeks. The night's performance was marked as sold out.

Sparkles, garish paint, mirrors and plastic tinsel adorned everything else, and set among some neatly rimmed bushes were two colossal searchlights patiently waiting for the arrival of night. Cheery music played from speakers hidden in the bushes, a nearby water fountain spiriting up columns to match the beat of the country-western tune, even though it was performed only by violins and pianos. Rolling into the parking lot, the members of Able Team exchanged dour glances, but said nothing. Compared to the rest of the stately Southern metropolis, the hotel looked like a stripper in a nunnery.

The first couple of lots were full of cars, excited people pouring into the casino and weary ones stumbling into the hotel. Smiling politely, large men, probably guards, flanked the glass front doors, receivers in their ears to keep them in constant communications with Security. Video cameras were nowhere in sight, but Schwarz swept the front of the garish building with an EM scanner and found them all over the place.

"Smile, we're on *Candid Camera*." He tucked the scanner away. "Better try the back, Carl."

"That was the plan," Lyons replied, maneuvering past a

group of drunks stumbling past a bedraggled fellow staring forlornly at a single dollar clenched in his fist. Obviously he was not a big winner today.

Bypassing the front parking lot, Lyons drove around the hotel and parked behind an enclosed area, the pungent smell in the air telling them this was where the restaurant dumped its garbage.

The men waited for a few minutes to see if anybody would respond to their presence, then gathered their equipment into black nylon gym bags and left the van, locking it. Some low hedges masked the emergency fire exit, and while Lyons and Blancanales stood guard, Schwarz used a locksmith's keywire gun to shoot the dead bolt full of stiff wire. A sharp turn of the wrist and the lock disengaged without the alarm sounding.

"Easy as pie," Schwarz said, sliding the tool into the cushioned bag holding his laptop as the others slipped inside.

"Thus speaks a man who has never made a pie," Blancanales responded, his sharp eyes checking for trouble in the corridor. But there was nobody in sight, just rows of doors leading to rooms on either side. The sounds of laughter came from several rooms, and a couple was having a screaming match about something undetectable.

Closing the fire exit behind them, Schwarz reactivated the alarm, and they proceeded at a casual pace into the hotel. At an intersection filled with plants and overstuffed easy chairs, the team boarded the elevator and rode to the fifteenth floor. A family with two happy children and an unhappy teenager got on the elevator after them.

Chatting casually about the comic concert that night, Able Team strolled along the hallway, passing several more tourists and one drunk grimly determined to feed a fifty-dollar bill into a soda machine that was clearly marked Exact Change Only.

Going through a set of double doors, the team reached

room 1544. They listened for a moment for any odd sounds, then Lyons lightly rapped his knuckles on the door. There was no response. After a minute, he tried again to the same result.

Nodding at Schwarz, the Able Team leader went to a corner, while Blancanales stood guard, trying to stand in a way that would block any casual sight of his friend. Kneeling at the door, Schwarz looked it over carefully and smiled. He had been afraid that the lock on a luxury suite might be different from the standard hotel rooms, but the mechanisms were all the same. It was a standard electronic swipe, with a red and green light to tell the guest if they had inserted the keycard correctly.

Snorting in contempt, Schwarz got out the laptop, attached a small probe to the electronic lock and hit a few buttons. There was a short pause, then the door unlocked.

Pulling a stun gun into view, Lyons slipped into the room, the other two men close behind.

"Okay, this place is empty. Is there anything hot?" the Able Team leader asked, tucking away the stun gun and lowering the gym bag to the carpeting. There were no obvious signs of violence. Everything was neat and tidy, with some clothing hanging in the closet and the towels neatly folded over the chrome rods in the bathroom.

"Clean. No bugs or digital recorders," Blancanales announced, tucking away the device. He tried to keep disdain out of his voice, and failed miserably. The suite was hideously decorated with Elvis memorabilia; old posters from his movies, facsimiles of his gold records, newspaper clippings, a plaster bust of the King, a mirror with his silhouette etched into the glass and lots of photographs.

"Yeah, I think this is where kitch goes to die," Schwarz muttered, clicking on a UV flashlight and playing the eerie

blue light around, checking the curtains, carpeting, blankets and bathroom for any organic residue. Blood, sweat, urine, semen, any bodily fluid would give off a ghostly glow under the ultraviolet beam no matter how well the area was cleaned. Unless they use steam. But the room registered clean, merely in questionable taste. In Schwarz's opinion, while Elvis may have worn outrageous costumes on stage, in his private life, Mr. Presley would probably have run screaming out of a room like this.

"How clean?" Lyons demanded, his blue eyes narrowing suspiciously. "Has it been steamed?"

"No, there's soap scum on the bathroom towel and finger-prints on the TV set," Schwarz stated, turning off the flash-light. "Nobody has been killed here, and the room washed down to hide the fact."

"You sure?" the Able Team leader asked, lifting up the covers to check under the bed.

"Positive."

"Good," Blancanales said, inspecting the telephone.

Under his UV flashlight there were clear fingerprints on the buttons and a palm print on the handset, so Gallen had made a call to somebody. He could have just been asking housekeeping for more mints on his pillow, but maybe not. There was a pad and pencil near the telephone. Blancanales gently rubbed the pencil across the top sheet, but no words appeared, and there were no crumpled papers in the wastebasket. Damn, the man was tidy. It had to be his scientific training where a single mis-placed item could ruin months of hard work. Too bad. Slovenly people were always easy to track, the Puerto Rican thought.

Going to the dresser, Lyons opened the bottom drawer and began riffling through the contents for maps or brochures. If the professor wasn't here, then he was somewhere in the city,

and nobody wandered around a strange town with no idea where they were going. With luck, he'd left a clue to his whereabouts. If not, they'd have to hit the streets of Memphis and trust on luck. None of the Stony Man team put much faith in blind luck.

"Better do the mirror," Lyons directed, inspecting a drawer full of socks and underwear. "That'll give us some warning if he comes back."

"Done, and done." Taking the Elvis silhouette mirror off the wall, Schwarz laid it on the bed facedown. Pulling out a combat knife, he eased off the pressboard backing and used the tip of the blade to slice off a small amount of the silver backing. Next, he carefully positioned a metallic disk to the clear area and reattached the back before hanging the mirror on the wall once more. Pulling out his laptop, Schwarz touched a few keys and the plasma screen lit up with a sideways view of the hotel room. Adjusting the controls, the view rotated until it was right-side up.

"We're in business," he announced, closing the lid. "Any maps?"

"Not a damn thing," Lyons stated gruffly, closing the top drawer of the dresser. "Guess we're going to—" There was a knock on the door and everybody froze.

"Mr. Caruthers?" a man called from the hallway. "Hotel management, sir. There's a leak in the tub above your room. May I come in to inspect the bathroom, please?"

Instantly the team was alert. That had been a mistake. If there was a leak, the management would simply use a pass key to get maintenance into the room as fast as possible. Asking for permission meant the person on the other side of the door wasn't on the hotel staff.

Pulling out his .357 Colt Python revolver, Lyons mumbled

something into his palm to disguise the words as the other men took position on either side of the door. Shuffling over, Lyons paused, then threw open the door. Blancanales hit the startled man outside with his stun gun. The man grimaced, his arms and legs going stiff as the electric charge shot though his body. As Blancanales released the button, the stranger toppled over, breathing heavily. Catching the limp man under the arms, Schwarz dragged him into the suite and deposited him on the bed.

The newcomer was freshly shaved and dressed in a hotel uniform. His shoes looked hotel issue, and his fingernails were short and clean. All well and good. However, there was no wallet or car keys in his pants, or any other items—aside from a photograph of Professor Gallen tucked in his jacket pocket, along with a hypodermic syringe full of a dark blue liquid and a pair of steel handcuffs.

CHAPTER FIVE

Ochong Island, North Korea

A glorious sunset filled the horizon, the colors permeating the dense forest of oak trees and willows. Birds chattered constantly from the ruins of an ancient Buddhist temple, the lovingly carved stone blocks tumbling back into the earth they had been taken from a thousand years ago.

There were no roads in sight, no cities, no radio towers, nothing that would in any way hint at the presence of a large military force. Thick white mist moved like a disembodied spirit through the lush jungle. As the soldiers in the old Land Rover jounced along the gravel road, the way was becoming treacherous. Skirting a sharp cliff, the driver tried not to look down into the ravine, knowing that death was waiting for them on the jagged rocks a hundred feet straight down.

"Are you sure this is the correct way, sir?" the North Korean soldier asked, tightening his grip on the steering wheel as if it were a protective charm.

"Shut up and drive," the major said from behind his mirrored sunglasses, a smoking cigarette dangling from his thin lips.

Dutifully checking the GPS device bolted onto the dashboard, the driver tried to cross the ravine again, and this time successfully found the land bridge, a natural stone arch that connected the two parts of the island like a granite umbilical cord.

"Here we are, sir." The driver sighed in relief, stopping the Land Rover with a squeal of brakes.

The major scowled at the fog all around them with open dislike, then eased his tense shoulders. Women and the weather, a man could do little about either. Accept or ignore. That's all the choice there was available.

"Tea, sir?" a young corporal asked.

"Please." The major smiled, eagerly accepting a cup of the black brew from a Thermos. There was plenty of powdered milk aboard the Land Rover, but it was officially policy for soldiers to drink it with only sugar added.

Suddenly a white light appeared on the northern horizon.

"What is that, sir?" the driver asked, lowering his cup of tea.

Before the major could respond, the fog was blown away by a hot wind that left an odd metallic taste in their mouths.

Muttering curses, the major turned in the passenger seat and fumbled among the equipment boxes in the back to unearth a Geiger counter. The safety instrument added at the last minute in case of any trouble. The hidden cache of tactical nukes purchased on the black market needed to be checked every few days to make sure that none of the troops had decided to get rich quick and sell the bombs on the black market again. At least that one fool who tried put it on eBay first, the major noted, switching on the radiation counter. His death in one of the dreaded learning centers had been particularly gruesome.

Spitting away the cigarette, the major waited for the Geiger to warm up, then exhaled in heartfelt relief as the meter stayed

in the green zone, a long way from danger. Good. The nukes were the key to the huge North Korean army crossing the sixteen miles of the DMZ, the dark soil of the demilitarized zone so packed with land mines that sometimes even tiny birds landing on the ground set off a string of fiery explosions.

"Do not worry, Private," the North Korean officer said with confidence. "There is no danger." But the light kept getting brighter, the wind stronger, and there was a weird prickly sensation on his skin as if he was being stabbed by a million tiny needles.

"If you say so, sir," the driver said, hunching his shoulder and trying to look directly at the terrible white light. There was a low rumble building rapidly, the ground shaking enough to jiggle the speedometer in the dashboard.

Observing that reaction, the major openly cursed and thumped the Geiger counter with a fist. The needle in the meter promptly fell off, leaving behind a smear of dried glue.

Glancing up in horror, the major looked at the mushroom clouds forming exactly where the weapons cache was supposed to be located. Then everything went black. Reaching up to touch his face, the major cringed at the realization that he was blind.

"Sir, are you okay?" the driver asked, a raised arm blocking his face from the deadly illumination.

"Just fine, Private," the officer said in a deceptively calm voice as he reached into his shirt pocket and extracted a pack of cigarettes. "At ease. Care for a smoke?"

Startled by the uncharacteristic generosity, the driver started to reach for a cigarette, then suddenly realized the truth of the matter. Screaming hysterically, he jumped from the Land Rover and raced insanely through the bushes until reaching the land bridge. Maybe…if he dropped down far enough…away from the blast…

Running straight off the side of the granite bridge, the private was still falling toward the rocks below when the ground seemed to heave upward to meet him halfway as the underground nukes thunderously detonated.

High above the earth, the entire Korean island vanished in a series of nuclear explosions, the expanding shock waves forming a crude bull's-eye pattern to the watchful long-range video cameras of the orbiting UN, NATO and American spy satellites.

Memphis, Tennessee

BITING BACK A CURSE, Blancanales went to stand guard near the door, a 9 mm Colt pistol in one hand, the other adjusting the radio transponder clipped to the belt under his Hawaiian shirt. He quickly found the frequencies reserved for the federal government and carefully listened for any traffic in the area. If this man wasn't FBI or Homeland Security, that meant he was probably a mercenary sent from their enemy to kill the professor. Not sure which of those dark scenarios he preferred, the former Black Beret cycled up and down the bandwidths, even going into the forbidden military frequencies in his search.

With a grim expression, Lyons went over every inch of the unconscious man's clothing. Whipping out his laptop, Schwarz pressed the man's hand to a section of plasma screen, then tapped a few buttons. After a series of low clicks, the screen came alive with a small photograph, serial number and federal dossier.

"Mafia?" Lyons asked, looking up from his work at the telltale beep.

"Worse. He's FBI," Schwarz replied, closing the computer with a snap. "The damn federal hackers at Quantico must have

found out about the Icarus project and are looking for the professor."

"If they know, then others do, too," Lyons muttered angrily. He'd thought the Memphis police were staring rather hard at any car with out-of-state plates. "Rosario, any chatter?"

"Bet your ass. There's a lot of heavily encoded traffic on two of the federal frequencies, and on a military bandwidth," Blancanales said, wiggling his earpiece. "Company is coming, hard and fast."

"Gadgets, have Bear check with the staties and local P.D.," Lyons directed. "Let's see how badly they want the professor."

"All ready doing that." Schwarz adjusted the code and frequency of the transponder clipped to his belt. "Bear says there's nothing on the wire about the professor." He gave a humorless smile. "Seems like the FBI wants the matter kept on the QT just as much as they want the professor alive and kicking."

"Okay, let's go," Lyons said, grabbing the gym bag and hoisting it over a shoulder. Time was against them, and every second counted. Now it was a race to find the wandering professor, before the FBI hauled him in for questioning. Or an assassination team gunned down the man on sight.

Leaving the hotel room, Blancanales squirted glue into the dead bolt hole to seal it into place, and Schwarz peeled the backing off a small box-shaped object and pressed it to the ceiling, the sticky pad adhering tightly. Anybody trying to batter through the door would set off the motion detector in the bomb, releasing a nonlethal cloud of military BZ gas, knocking out everybody in the hallway. That would slow down the FBI a little bit, but not by much. The boys from the Bureau were smart and tough, even if their politically appointed leaders often were not.

Going to the elevator, Lyons reached inside and hit the button for the roof, then pulled out and started for the fire exit.

That was often a blind spot for folks as they firmly believed the doors could not be opened without setting off the alarms.

As the Stony Man operatives headed down the fire stairs, a group of large men in dark blue suits ran up the main stairwell, sleek 4.6 mm HK machine pistols held openly in their hands. FBI commission booklets were tucked into the breast pockets of their suits, the federal identification clearly on display.

"Spread out," a bald man directed, a flesh-colored wire going from the radio receiver in his ear and down into his shirt. "Weaver, Harrison, secure this corridor! McNalty, have hotel security turn off that elevator!" The men moved fast.

"Think they're really on board?" a hulking agent asked, sweeping the door to the room with an EM probe attached to a bulky scanner in his hand.

"Not unless they're stupid," the bald man said, scowling at the little box attached to the ceiling panel. "Now what the fuck is that?"

Reaching up with the EM probe, the huge black man took a step closer and with a soft poof, the BZ charges ignited and the thick clouds of swirling purple gas swirled about the hallway.

But the men merely clamped their mouths shut and started breathing through their noses. The biological filters stuffed inside each nostril making them wheeze slightly.

Scowling darkly, the bald man pointed wordlessly at the door, and the other agent pulled out a hotel security keycard. Inserting it into the lock, he saw the light flash green, but the door refused to open. The bald man asked a silent question, the other agent shrugged and, stepping back, the two men holstered their machine pistols to draw .357 Glock Magnum pistols. They fired in unison, the double report booming in the confines of the hallway. The door slammed open to crash into

the closet. Moving through the swirling cloud of BZ gas, the two men swept low into the room, their guns searching for targets.

REACHING THE FIRE EXIT, Schwarz slid a video probe under the door. On the screen of his laptop, there was nobody visible in the parking lot.

"Clear," he said, withdrawing the probe and deactivating the alarm.

A split second later there came a muffled sound of gunshots from above and then some sort of crash.

"Oh, no, it isn't," Lyons said, the former police detective feeling oddly pleased at how swiftly the FBI was handling the matter.

With a soft click, the fire door swung open and the Stony Man team left the building. Strolling casually to their van, the men checked the seals to make sure nobody had breeched the vehicle, then climbed inside and slowly drove away.

Easing into traffic, Lyons headed toward Memphis again, while Blancanales removed his sunglasses and passed out baseball caps. The men of Able Team would have to change their appearance, just in case somebody had gotten a glimpse of them at the hotel. A complete change of clothing was usually not necessary; simply altering one or two items was good enough in most cases.

"They found the video pickup," Schwarz said, lowering the lid of his laptop and sliding it into a recharging port built into the vehicle's wall.

"Already?" Blancanales asked, arching an eyebrow. "That was fast."

"They had an EM scanner of a type I've never seen before," Schwarz replied, worrying his mustache.

"Never?"

"Nope."

That was disturbing news. There wasn't much in the world of electronics that Schwarz didn't know inside and out. Blancanales took down the M-16 assault rifle and removed the 40 mm stun bag from the grenade launcher to replace it with an armor-piercing shell of high explosives.

"If they're that good, then these won't work," Lyons said, tossing the cap into the rear of the van and unclipping a microphone from the dashboard. The device resembled a cheap CB radio, nothing a would-be thief could possibly be interested in trying to boost. In reality it was a military transponder of astonishing power.

"Jungle Cat to Rock House." He spoke into the mike. "Uncle Hoover has joined the party, and wants to borrow a Finn. Any chance you can get them to visit Antarctica?"

"Negative, Jungle Cat," Kurtzman replied crisply. "I was just about to call you with the news. The earlier ID was a fake, planted by wax wing. These are not the real McCoy. These are not, repeat not, Uncle Hoover. Do you copy?"

Merging with the traffic, Lyons grunted at that. Wax wing, Icarus. Damn. Fake FBI agents. To pull off a stunt like that would require some serious hacking. And one mother of a powerful computer. No matter how good a computer expert was, not even Kurtzman could break into the DOD database without at least a Cray Supercomputer at his command. Only in the movies did somebody hack the White House with a regular PC.

"Confirm, Rock House, we will bank the Finn and remove any troublemakers from the game. Copy?"

"Roger," Bear replied, and the radio went silent.

"Fakes!" Schwarz said furiously, reaching for his laptop then pulling his hand back. If the enemy had fooled Kurtzman

for a whole ten minutes, there was nothing he could do to hack their location of a portable. It would be like hunting elephants with a derringer. Absolutely useless.

"Okay, our best bet is to find Gallen before these assholes do, and get him safely out of the state," Lyons said. "Pol, if our boy hasn't gone to Graceland, what else is there in this town for an Elvis fan to do? A wax museum, film retrospective, anything like that?"

"I'll check the Zagat," Blancanales said, pulling out a PDA and opening the electronic version of the international travel guide.

"And I'll have Jack warm up the Herc for an immediate takeoff," Schwarz said, pulling out a cell phone. "He already has the documents on board for an emergency departure ferrying a living heart to be transplanted to Seattle."

"Works for me." Twisting the wheel to maneuver around a bright red sport cars that looked like an oversize toy, Lyons turned onto Broad Street, then cursed as construction made him take a detour.

"Oh, hell, there's a hundred places!" Blancanales complained, using a thumb to scroll the tiny screen. "The Elvis Musical Museum, Elvis Miniature Golf Course, Elvis Dry Cleaner's, the Elvis Karaoke Bar…"

Under his breath, Schwarz muttered something about itching like a man on a fuzzy tree, and his partner shot him a stern look.

"No, wait, Gadgets has a good idea there," Lyons said, looking over the crowds of people streaming by on the busy sidewalks. "Which bar has the best Elvis impersonator? The absolute cream of the crop?" It would be a million to one chance of running across Gallen this way, but experience had taught the man that such things did happen, and only a fool would not take advantage of every opportunity coming his way.

"The very best Elvis impersonator would be—give me a moment—okay, that would be William 'Wild Bill' Fawcett. He's appearing at the Grotto tonight. That is on Third street. After that, the list of possibilities is endless."

"If this guy is so good," Schwarz asked pointedly, "then why isn't he playing the big room at one of the local casinos or riverboats?"

"He owns the Grotto."

"Good for him. Nice to hear of somebody supporting the arts."

"Got a location for this Grotto?" Lyons asked.

Reaching out, Blancanales touched the plasma screen in the dashboard and a map appeared. "Just a couple of blocks away."

"That close?" Lyons asked suspiciously, slowing at a traffic light.

"Memphis isn't that big a city. Everything is relatively close together."

"Fair enough."

Following the map, the Able Team leader easily found the nightclub and parked in back near the fire-exit door. In case they had to leave in a hurry. Inside, the bar was dimly lit, smoky and noisy, the clatter of dishes and drunken laughter mixing together.

There was a good crowd in the Grotto, a score of small tables filled with people drinking and talking. A chalkboard near the coat room announced that the Wild Bill show would start in a few hours. Trying not to scowl at the delay, the Stony Man operatives took off in different directions and did a fast recon of the premises in case Professor Gallen was there early. A few minutes later they regrouped at the bar.

"Not a sign of him in the bathroom," Schwarz said, taking a handful of peanuts from a bowl on the wooden counter.

"Ditto for the restaurant," Blancanales added, waving over the bartender.

"Thought I saw him for a moment near the stage," Lyons added, also taking some peanuts. "But it was just an old woman."

"Woman?" Schwarz asked, tilting his head.

"Let's just say that time had not been kind, and leave it at that."

"Afternoon, boys, what can I get you?" the bartender asked in a rich Southern drawl. The inflection sounded false. Probably something she did just for the tourists.

"Three beers," Blancanales said, laying a twenty on the counter. "Whatever you have on draft." The team was going to be here for a while. If the professor didn't show up for the concert, then they'd have to try Graceland, and after that the Forrest Hill Cemetery where Elvis Aaron Presley was originally buried before the Presley Corporation moved his body to Graceland. It was a long shot, indeed.

"Got a bar menu?" Schwarz asked, taking more peanuts.

"Sure. Best chicken wings in the state," the bartender said, drawing three draft beers, expertly keeping the foam to a minimum.

Lyons and Blancanales paid the woman no attention, but for some reason Schwarz could not take his eyes off her. Which was odd, since she was definitely not his normal type. She was pretty in a rough sort of way, but her blond hair obviously come from a bottle, her ample breasts were almost perfectly symmetrical indicating implants, both eyes were an unbelievable shade of blue, her skin color an impossibly smooth bronze. Bemused, Schwarz briefly wondered if anything about her was natural. Probably not.

Delivering the beer, the busty woman smiled coyly at the

man and he found himself impulsively smiling back. The name on her tag said Derrinda.

"Y'all want anything else?" she purred, setting down the frosty glasses. Derrinda rested an elbow on the counter and leaned artfully closer, exposing a megaton of bronze cleavage. "By the way, my friends call me Didi."

This close, Schwarz could smell her perfume, a heady mix of mimosa and honeysuckle. It reminded him of Shenandoah Park in the spring when all of the wildflowers came into bloom. The man started to speak when he caught a familiar face in the mirror behind the bar and all thoughts of romance vanished. It was Gallen!

"No, thanks, Dottie," Schwarz said, smiling broadly, looking past her shoulder to the reflection in the mirror.

"Didi," she corrected, her broad smile losing some of its warmth.

"Yeah, whatever. Keep the change, honey."

Scowling, the disappointed woman walked away. Sipping the beer, Schwarz double-checked the reflection against his mental file on the man. Yep, we have a winner.

"Hey, guys, did you say the show starts at four o'clock," he said softly, stressing the last couple of words.

Drinking their beers, Lyons and Blancanales casually turned to glance in the direction indicated. A small line of slot machines stood along the back wall, partially hidden from the rest of the tavern by an open trellis adorned with plastic flowers. Most of the seats were empty, the big casino down the street gathering in all of the early gambling. But standing over at a change machine was the elderly Finnish professor feeding dollar bills into a slot and scooping up piles of quarters.

Leaving their beers, Lyons and Blancanales pushed away from the bar and headed directly for the man, then separated

slightly so that they could approach from different sides. In two minutes he would be safe in the van.

Staying at the bar, Schwarz continued to eat peanuts, watching their every move in the mirror. Surreptitiously, he checked the stun gun in his pants pocket, and the 9 mm Beretta pistol holstered under his Hawaiian shirt.

"You do know that I was making a pass, right?" Didi said haughtily.

"Married," Schwarz snapped, ending the matter.

"You're not wearing a ring."

"It's not that kind of a marriage. I'm gay."

"Are you? Sorry," she muttered, turning away in a huff to serve other men sitting at the bar.

Meandering through the sea of tables, Lyons and Blancanales kept a close watch on the other patrons, making damn sure that nobody else was paying the professor any undue attention. But the coast was clear.

"Excuse me, did you drop this?" Lyons asked, proffering a twenty. "I found it over by the change maker."

Looking up from the slot machine, Professor Gallen stared at the bill, then at the big man holding the money. There was something about the stranger that inspired both fear and trust. The scientist had the feeling of being in the presence of his father. How very odd.

"Sorry, no, not mine," Gallen said with a forced smile. "Must be your lucky day."

"Yes, and no, Professor," Blancanales said, sliding into the next chair.

The old man went deathly pale. "What was that you called me?" he asked, hunching his shoulders as if braced for a blow. "I don't know anybody named Gallen. You must have the wrong person."

"Bad slip, Professor. We never used a name," Lyons said. "Somebody has built an Icarus and we need your help to try to stop it."

"How in the…" Gallen frowned. "Did you say some nation built more of the goddamn things?"

"What do you mean, more?" Blancanales demanded, grabbing the man by the arm. "How many did the Finnish government build?"

Before the professor could answer, there was a fast series of coughs from the bar.

Moving to block any view of the professor, Lyons and Blancanales saw four large men standing near the coat room. Two of them were redheads, one was bald, and the last was a heavily muscled man with dark skin. They were dressed in dark suits and sunglasses, looking exactly like FBI agents. But their jackets hung loose and unbuttoned and a glint of long blue steel was visible underneath.

These had to be the hardmen from the hotel, Lyons reasoned. How could they get here so fast, unless… Casting a glance backward, the man bit back a curse at the sight of Gallen holding his credit card. The idiot had to have been using the ATM to get twenties to feed into the change machine! He wanted to be furious, but in all honesty, why shouldn't the old scientist use the card? Gallen had no idea what was happening in the world at that moment, or that he was the target for an international manhunt. This was their mistake for not asking Kurtzman to run a block on his traveler's checks and credit cards.

"Look, sir! There he is!" the big man cried, pointing across the tavern with a finger the size of a sausage.

"Take him!" the bald man snarled, drawing a 9 mm Steyr machine pistol. Instantly the other men also reached into their

jackets and pulled out similar machine pistols equipped with acoustical sound suppressors. As their fingers touched the triggers, laser beams shot out of the tiny boxes attached below the barrel of each weapon. The red dots zigzagged across the nightclub, bobbing over people and tables, heading straight for the stunned professor.

Blancanales tackled Gallen, driving him to the floor while Lyons drew his .357 Colt Python and fired at the new arrivals. The thundering boom of the handgun shook the room, and everybody began to scream.

Ignoring the cries, the strangers opened fire with their weapons, tracer rounds from the little machine pistols stitching through the air to tear apart the wooden trellis, plastic flowers and splinters flying everywhere.

Moving behind a slot machine for protection, Lyons answered back with the booming revolver, the big-bore Magnum vomiting stilettos of flame from the pitted muzzle. The bald man grunted as he doubled over, holding his stomach, but then the man straightened and kept firing.

Son of a bitch was wearing body armor, Lyons realized, trying for a head shot. But in the smoky darkness of the club, with civilians yelling and running around, it was difficult to get a clear shot.

Darting forward, Blancanales went under a table, then stood, the glasses sliding off as he held the furniture as a makeshift shield. Walking backward, he covered the professor, who was trembling on the floor.

Unexpectedly, one of the redheaded men cried out, blood exploding from his arm, but it was just a flesh wound.

Standing behind the bar, Schwarz tracked the man with his Beretta, hitting him several times more, before the other guy took cover behind the salad bar and let loose a withering hail

of the sizzling tracers. Everywhere the rounds hit, a greenish splash glowed, the phosphorescent compound setting countless small fires along the wood paneling that covered the dark walls.

Popping into view, Didi cut loose with a sawed-off shotgun, the double report deafening inside the club. The assorted foodstuffs in the salad bar violently exploded, and the redhead spun with most of his face removed.

"Brother!" screamed the other redhead, and he drew a second machine pistol from under his jacket to blast both of the weapons at the bartender.

The first spray of rounds tore the cash register apart, electronic circuits and loose cash flying into the air. Dropping a clip and reloading, Schwarz stepped in front of the woman and answered back with copper-jacketed 9 mm parabellum rounds. The redhead shrieked as blood erupted from between his legs, inches below the body armor covering his torso. Twisting, the man waved his machine pistols madly, hitting the ceiling, civilians and the bald man, before collapsing to the floor.

At the sound of shattering glass, Schwarz looked to see Didi stagger into the mirror, both hands holding her throat, red blood gushing out between her slim fingers. The man felt sick at the sight, but there was nothing he could do, there was nothing anybody could do for that sort of wound. Her frightened eyes met his for a long second, a million emotions playing between the two people, then she folded to the floor, trembled and went still.

Suddenly the water sprinklers gushed into action from the ceiling, filling the nightclub with a fine spray of cold water. An alarm started to clang, and the civilians rushed out of hiding and headed straight for the fire doors.

Kneeling, Schwarz reached out to touch Didi's long hair, then spied a box of spare 12-gauge cartridges for the sawed-off. Holstering the Beretta, he snatched the box, found the scattergun and swiftly reloaded. There was blood on both.

Dripping wet, Schwarz stood and fired both barrels at a table blocking his view, the furniture blowing aside to reveal the black man pulling the pin on a grenade and releasing the arming lever.

"Incoming!" Schwarz bellowed, dropping behind the counter to reload again.

Something hit the wall above the smashed ATM, then hit the floor to roll in the watery darkness. Unable to see the grenade, Lyons shoved over a slot machine, which landed with a ringing crash. A split second later a roar filled the nightclub and the machine slammed into Lyons, shoving him aside to crash through the partially broken trellis. Stumbling in the downpour, the Able Team leader tripped on the edge of the stage and went sprawling. Incoming rounds peppered the musical instruments around him, creating a cacophony of noise. He fired back instinctively and was rewarded by a cry of pain.

Rolling off the stage, he hit the floor, landing on top of a wheezing man who was holding his stomach in both hands. There was a camera around his neck, a neat hole going clean through the device. Grabbing a wet napkin off the floor, Lyons moved to help but the man convulsed and shuddered for several seconds before stopping forever.

A blind rage filled the Stony Man operative, and he rose to charge for the killers, the Colt booming hot lead at every step. There was no return gunfire, and when he reached the salad bar, he could find only debris and spent brass shells. The fake FBI agents were gone.

A movement to his left made Lyons turn at the waist, and he stopped firing the Colt by the thickness of a prayer at the sight of Schwarz walking through the gushing downpour holding the sawed-off shotgun and his Beretta.

"They left," he said, looking over at his friend. There was blood all over the big blond man, but it was washing off, clearly none of it his own.

"Help Pol get the professor out of here," Lyons said, turning to sprint for the open fire exit.

Thankfully, the doorway was clear of frightened people, the civilians long gone, some of them still visible pelting down alleyways. Going to the van, the Able Team leader threw open the side door and slapped a disguised panel in the chassis to come up with a stubby rifle topped with a telescopic sight. Working the arming bolt, Lyons swung up the weapon just in time to see a red-and-black SUV pull away from the tavern, the tires squealing and smoking. That had to be the fake agents. Holding his breath, he tracked the speeding car for a precious minute as it raced through traffic, then stroked the trigger. But instead of a bang, there only came a hard cough. The side window of a sedan shattered and Lyons hastily worked the bolt once more and fired again. This time, the spare tire attached to the rear of the speeding SUV dimpled for a second, and then the vehicle disappeared behind a bus.

Nodding in satisfaction, Lyons replaced the weapon and started back into the nightclub, but Blancanales and Schwarz appeared in the doorway, soaked to the skin and without the professor.

"He's dead," Blancanales said without preamble. "Caught a piece of shrapnel in the eye. If his glasses hadn't broken, I never would known what killed him." The words hung heavy between the three men.

The clanging bell inside the wrecked club stopped, and now they could dimly hear the wail of an approaching fire engine.

"Let's go," Lyons said in a flat tone. "I hit their SUV with a tracer. We can still do something useful if they know who hired them to take out Gallen."

Nodding somberly, the Stony Man operatives got into their vehicle and took off, their expressions dark and foreboding. Their shot in the dark had paid off, then was snatched away by blind fate. So be it; bad luck was a part of every soldier's life. They accepted the defeat and moved on. There was still a mission to accomplish, and Able Team was grimly looking forward to tangling with those last two mysterious hit men. This gunfight was far from being over.

While Blancanales got their weapons ready, Lyons merged into traffic and Schwarz activated the tracer. The map on the dashboard shifted to another view of Memphis, a tiny blinking dot creeping long the DeSoto Bridge into Alabama.

Heading that way, Lyons could only hope that Phoenix Force was doing a lot better in Finland. There were still fifteen days to go before America was safe. Or burned out of existence.

CHAPTER SIX

Durres, Albania

A tiny bell jingled above the woman as she pushed aside the door and walked a young boy into the grocery store. The boy pulled along with her was scrawny, his clothes badly tattered, but they were clean, freshly washed every day in the small enamel sink of their little apartment.

Crooked in her free arm was a wicker basket filled with a neatly folded clean cloth. In spite of the heat of the day, she wore a shawl around her shoulders to help make her appear older and less desirable. The fact that she was married and with a child meant nothing if certain people decided she might amuse them for an afternoon. Dimly, she remembered that once police had patrolled the city streets. But that was so very long ago she was starting it think it was a fantasy.

The bright sunshine shone through the clean windows onto the mostly empty shelves. Few canned goods were in sight and even fewer vegetables. Only the liquor section was packed with shiny bottles of imported beverages, and she scowled at them in open hatred.

On the sunny streets outside, a skinny man was walking a donkey up the cobblestone street, the sounds of its unshod hooves echoing off the clean rows of tan buildings. In the distance was the large stone fortress of a forgotten king. The communists had made it into a prison, but when they left, the fortress had been abandoned, the ancient symbol of Albanian freedom now only painted on the outside to render it pretty for the few visiting tourists. The thought made the woman tighten her grip. Tourists! She hated them worse than the Fifteen.

"Momma, you're hurting me!" the boy whimpered.

"Life is pain." She sighed, but eased her grip and went about the little shop making choices.

Placing the goods on the counter, she pulled out a handkerchief and carefully counted out a small pile of coins. She knew the precise amount, but some foolish part of her always wanted to count them again to see if magically their numbers had increased. But there had been no miracle in the night, and she put aside the cans of condensed soup.

"Just these," she said to the man behind the counter. "Plus, a small bottle of milk and a loaf of the yesterday's bread."

Nodding, the grocer put the items into her wicker basket one at a time as if they were precious jewels that easily shattered. Then he paused, and also slid in a package made of folded newspaper.

"If you eat the fish today, it should be okay," he said, not looking at the customer. "I like your husband and hope he gets better soon. Lots of work on the docks these days, eh?"

"Lots of work," the woman replied, reaching out to touch the basket with a trembling hand. "For the young and strong."

He looked up, and the teenage girl thanked him with her eyes. The man turned away quickly, ashamed that there wasn't more he could do to help. But there were many poor in Albania, just so many poor and starving these days.

Keeping a good grip on her son, the young mother shuffled from the store and into the warm sunlight. Going to the corner, they waited for the brand-new traffic light to change. There was no traffic, and only a few rusted cars parked on the street, but there were severe penalties for breaking the law, any law. At a young age, she had learned to obey and avoid the backrooms of the police stations at any cost.

Nobody was moving at this early hour of the day. Those who had work were busy trying to earn a living, everybody else was simply attempting to stay alive, and dream of leaving Durres for someplace, any place, far away from the grimy seaport.

Suddenly a loud car horn blared and a convoy of military Hummers rolled around the corner.

"Dragons," the woman whispered in terror, then ducked her head respectfully and hoped she had been fast enough to avoid a beating. Men were hit with rifle butts and boots, the fate of a woman, young or old, was far different and much worse.

The first Hummer was filled with armed guards in livery, the second contained a young laughing man surrounded by girls, their long blond hair blowing in the salty breeze. Loud music played from a stereo and the Hummer veered slightly as if the driver was drunk. Following close behind was a military half-track, the men in the cab wearing machine pistols in shoulder holsters, the dozen guards riding in the back carrying AK-47 assault rifles. There were a few gray smears on

the side of the armored personnel carrier where soft-lead bullets had ricocheted off the thick armor.

Driving straight through the red light, the convoy roared up the hill, the old man rushing out of the way frantically. Refusing to move, the donkey brayed loudly, then was violently slammed aside by the lead Hummer with a meaty thump. The body fell to the sidewalk, a thick rivulet of blood flowing from the slack mouth of the dead animal.

Taking a corner, the convoy passed out of sight, the smell of the diesel exhaust lingering behind in the air like the reek of a badly infected wound.

"Momma, who was that?" the boy asked softly.

"Our king," she replied, starting forward once the light changed. Without meaning to, she glanced at the mansion cresting a nearby hill. The vast estate was surrounded by a tall stone fence topped with glistening coils of deadly concertina wire. Armed guards walked along the top of the buildings, and she could hear the faint barking of guard dogs. Massive searchlights were mounted on the rooftop gardens and rocket batteries were on open display. A colorful flag fluttered from the top of a pole, but instead of the two-headed eagle of Albania, it was a complex design of filigree encircling some stylized lettering.

"Our king," she repeated softly, protectively tightening her grip on the child. "Now, hurry along and stop asking questions. Questions are bad, remember that."

"Yes, Mama. But we don't have a king, Mama," he insisted in puzzlement.

Standing on the cracked sidewalk, the breeze ruffling through her ragged clothing, the young woman sighed deeply, feeling an icy shiver run along her spine. "Oh, yes, we do," she said. "In fact, we have fifteen kings…."

Kadriouski Estate

STANDING ON THE BALCONY of the east wing, Slobodan Kadriouski smiled down upon the rustic city surrounding his hilltop estate.

Colorful homes of tan bricks and bright red tiles extended down the gently sloping hills to the busy seaport where half of the population worked day and night at the dockyards. Painted bright yellow, hoisting cranes loomed above the warehouses and cargo ships, their chains and cables relaying utilitarian metal boxes off and on to the waiting vessels. A storage yard was piled high with the boxes, the mix of colors supposedly stating where the box had been shipped from and what it contained: heavy equipment, dangerous chemicals, metal ingots, advanced electronics. Along with drugs, weapons and everything but slaves. The Fifteen did not traffic in such goods anymore. It was his only unbreakable rule.

That, and always make a profit, the crime lord thought in cold amusement. Money was power, and that was all that mattered these days. Raw power.

The city that was outside the stone wall surrounding his estate was old and crude, to say the least, mostly bare stone homes with red-tiled roofs. Pitiful. But inside the wall there were manicured lawns and swimming pools of azure water, along with an inflated dome, supposedly to protect a greenhouse full of delicate orchids. In reality, that was a private heliport where he kept a small fleet of gunships. Fight or flight, Kadriouski knew that a wise man was always ready for any contingency. There was only one gate, double sets of steel doors, flanked by squat pillboxes containing old WWII 88 mm cannons, more than capable of stopping any armored vehicle in the Albania army, such as it was, or NATO, for that matter.

The pillboxes had been bricked on the outside to make them more appealing to the eye, and neatly trimmed hedges surrounded them. But to a trained eye, there was no doubt that those were Draconian redoubts of lethal intensity.

A tattered object hung from a pole on top of the pillbox. The human scalp was visible from the street outside, a somber reminder of what happened to the only news reporter who had managed to get inside the compound.

"Your afternoon repast, sir," a liveried butler announced, wheeling a small cart onto the balcony. A silver bowl full of crushed ice supported a smaller bowl of caviar. There were several plates of assorted miniature pastries and a full magnum of French champagne.

Without speaking, Kadriouski held out a hand, and the butler quickly scooped some caviar onto a tiny slice of toast and passed it to the old man. He took a sniff, a small bite and then spit it out.

"Bah, it's warm. Throw this garbage away, Isaak!" the crime lord snarled, smacking the silver dish with a hand and sending it to the polished marble floor. The antique dish hit with a ringing crash and bounced away, sending the prime Russian Beluga caviar everywhere.

Gushing apologies, Isaak rushed forward to scoop the caviar off the floor, and scurried away, bowing constantly. The fury of the old man was getting worse every day, and often servants were fired from their service for the most minuscule offenses. The poor bastard who got caught stealing some silverware was thrown off the roof to land on the cobblestone street, horribly mangled, but still alive. Kadriouski had posted guards to prevent anybody from helping the thief, including the local ambulance service, and it took the man four days to perish of exposure. It was a death that nobody ever wished to see again.

Glancing sideways, Kadriouski watched the butler depart, almost smiling at the groveling. The crime lord liked it when the lower classes understood their place in the hierarchy of the world. Albania might mean nothing to the United Nations, but it was the gateway for all of the heroin in Europe, and he was its absolute master. There were kings and presidents on foreign lands that did not have his level of authority. He was the head of the Fifteen Families, the undisputed rulers of Albania, along with several smaller cities in Kosovo, Macedonia and Serbia.

His family had been smugglers and bootleggers for generations, their secret empire created in the Middle Ages, and blossoming into full fruition under the Nazi regime. No matter who was in charge, they always need the illicit services and goods provided by his blood-kin. When the Communists departed, the nation had been in total chaos, without any kind of leadership. So he'd boldly stepped into the power vacuum, seizing total control with the aid of guns and a lead pipe. Those Kadriouski could not beat into submission, blackmail or bribe, he killed outright, until the government in the capital city of Tirane was only a sham used to impress visiting UN dignitaries, NATO peacekeepers and the hated Americans.

Taking out a gold cigarette case, the old man applied the flame of a silver lighter to the tip of slim panatela made with Cuban tobacco, and drew in the sweetly dark smoke. Oh, occasionally, some damn fool tried to bring about free elections. But the next day his brutalized remains would be in a crashed car full of cocaine and dead whores. Always on the lookout for a fresh market, some of the younger members of the Fifteen had taken to recording the torture session for the Internet. Snuff films, as the Americans called such things, were a hugely valuable commodity, and it only made sense

to reap as large a profit from the death of an enemy as possible. Waste not, want not.

A cool wind from the Kobar Mountains blew across the balcony. Shivering with a chill, Kadriouski tossed away the panatela and quickly went inside. The palatial room was huge, larger than almost any apartment in the coastal city. The floor was polished Italian marble, the furniture French Provincial, and the liquor cabinet mostly Scotch whiskey and the weapons cabinet a mix of German and American. The only thing made in Albania itself was the building and a few paintings on the walls. The vaulted ceiling was decorated with hand-painted mural of the Albanian struggle for freedom. Born in the communist regime, the old man truly appreciated the present democracy. It was the rule of law that allowed him the freedom to carve out an empire.

Going to a red-velvet settee, Kadriouski sat down heavily. His health had been decaying over the past fifteen years, and he knew death was close at hand. The skin hung loosely from his old bones as if he were an overcooked chicken. Only his teeth gleamed in perfect health, but then, his old rotting teeth had been removed and new ceramic ones bolted to his jaw by a Swiss dentist, supposedly the best in the world. The man performed the operation while watching a live monitor showing his wife and three children being held hostage by armed guards, the so-called Dragoons of the Fifteen Families. The term was supposed to be some obscure English phrase for soldiers, and the old man had assigned it to their bodyguards simply because he liked the sound of the word. Dragoons. To the people of Albania, the word soon became Dragons, as the guards killed without conscience and took whatever they wished without payment. In the legends, a great knight would always ride to the aid of the besieged villagers and save them

from the horrible dragon. But this was real life, and not even Interpol or NATO special forces had been able to deter the raw power of the hated Dragoons.

Looking at a framed photograph on the mantel above the huge fireplace, the old man sighed deeply. His bloodline was broken, and he was alone. Soon, a successor would have to be chosen, or else the Fifteen might have a civil war over the matter. That would be bad for profits. There was somebody he had been training to take his place, but that dream was gone.

A soft clearing of the throat announced the presence of Isaak again, and Kadriouski looked up with a scowl. "Yes?" he snapped impatiently.

"The first of the guests has arrived, sir," Isaak said, with a slight nod of the head.

Grunting in reply, the crime boss rose from the settee and hobbled down the hallway to the second-floor patio. Going through a set of doors composed mostly of bulletproof glass, he went to the granite railing and looked down at the front drive.

As the double gates swung open, a convoy of Hummers and an APC rolled through. Driving past the tiered fountain, the cavalcade stopped at the front of the mansion, and armed guards helped one of Kadriouski's cousins out of a vehicle, along with some scantily clad women.

"Hi, Uncle!" the young man called, waving a bottle of brandy in the air. "Come on down and have a drink!"

Exercising massive patience, Kadriouski merely shook his head, and the drunken youth stumbled away with his women. When the entourage was out of sight, the old man hung his head in shame. *May dear God protect me from my own family.*

The gates had barely closed with a dull boom when they began to cycle open once more. This time it was a black Cadillac limousine, closely followed by an armored Bentley, a Jaguar sports car surrounded by guards on motorcycles, another convoy of Hummers… On and on the parade of criminals flooded in through the armored gates, parking in their assigned spots and spreading out across the estate.

Standing in dark rumination, the old man watched the Fifteen Families gather below his vantage point. They had come from all over Albania; from the Elsani clan who resided in the mountains, to the Morteli who lived almost exclusively on their boats. Yachts, oil tankers, fishing trawlers, the Morteli had been pirates for six hundred years, and the ocean had to have gotten into their blood. They seemed to relax only with water under their boots. Kadriouski liked that. They understood their place. None of them would ever made a good leader, however.

As the adults began to form clusters to discuss business, the nannies herded the small children off to play in a far corner of the garden. Kadriouski was pleased to see them all so well behaved. It was important for children to learn the facts of life early, when to be quiet and when they should scream. This was good training for when the little boys and girls became men and women and assumed their natural position as the masters of Albania.

Along with whatever part of the world we can steal for them, he added. His successor was somewhere down there, a cousin, a niece… The crime lord shook his head. This was too important a decision to make without due regard. It would require a lot more thought.

Snapping his fingers, Kadriouski reached out and Isaak gave him a chilled glass of champagne. He took a sip, then

drained it in a gulp, hobbling forward to join the rest of the noisy people in the council room downstairs. Remaining on the patio, the butler started to clear away the trash.

In dribs and drabs, the relatives were casually meandering inside, chatting about their wives and lives, and children, cars, a new mistress or an old friend. Slobodan Kadriouski scowled at that last part. He did not approve of family members making friends with outsiders. Business acquaintances, of course. Those were necessary. But not a friend who could ask for a favor you did not want to grant, or worse, turn on you and endanger other family members. Somebody once said that it was lonely at the top, that a king ruled alone. It was true, and it was not true. Kadriouski ruled with a hundred blood-kin.

"...so I had to take the boy out back and beat him with a belt until he saw reason," a man in a tuxedo said.

"I can understand his reasons for wanting to date a cousin," a large man replied, twirling the ice in a highball glass. The crystal reflected the overhead light and cast rainbows over the two drug barons. "We live a very insular life. But has nobody explained to him the facts of life?"

"Well, I did that day," the first man replied, clenching a fist until the knuckles cracked. "Then I took him to the best brothel in Rome, and had them teach him the rest."

"Bella Luna?" the big man asked.

"Of course! It is where I lost my cherry, and now he is no longer a boy."

"But not yet a man, eh?" a plain woman asked, standing stiffly in her ball gown of silk and gold. Her wrists jingled with every movement from the multiple layers of silver bracelets and bands.

"Too true. But I will have him kill somebody soon. First things first, old friend. First things first."

The cousins roared with laughter, drawing displeased looks from a dozen other relatives who clearly disapproved of jocularity at such gatherings. The Fifteen were here for business, not to have a good time.

Moving through the mixed crowd, the crime boss shook hands with everybody, exchanging brief greetings. Tall, short, fat, thin, old, young, pale as milk, dark as mahogany, the Fifteen Families was a cross section of humanity. Kadriouski had made sure of that from the first day he took control. Too many families started marrying their cousins, and soon, there were only simpletons. Feeling a surge of anger, the old man tightened his hand into a gnarled fist. That would never happen to the Fifteen! They were feared and respected. Intelligent and strong. That was the key, to be both. There were a thousand enemies who wanted them to fail and perish.

And while that might happen some day, the old man declared privately to the universe, it would not happen while he drew breath! The face in the photograph on the fireplace mantel came unbidden to mind, and he forcibly dismissed the memory. Let the dead bury the dead. It was his job to concentrate on the future.

Going into the next room, Kadriouski began to slow down slightly and a butler handed him a walking stick of knobby African ironwood. Hobbling to his chair, the old gangster sat with a grateful sigh, then loudly rapped the stick on the table.

"All right, everybody sit down, sit down," he commanded, his voice picked up by a microphone built into the chair and booming across the room.

In ragged stages, the criminal lords of Europe took chairs, and maids refilled their glasses without being asked. Then the servants departed, closing the doors tightly behind them.

"So, Grandfather, why the emergency meeting?" asked

Fatima Morteli, using a rouge stick on her lips while looking into a compact mirror. The buxom sixty-year-old woman was wearing a Christian Dior gown cut down to the navel. A long time ago, Morteli had been an incredible beauty, and while her sultry looks had faded with time, she still considered herself gorgeous. In some circles of society that might have been found amusing, but not even family members teased her about the vanity. Fatima Morteli was the chief enforcer for the Fifteen Families, and had still enjoyed personally killing her enemies with a chain saw.

Leaning back in his chair, Kadriouski started to speak when the closed doors were slammed aside and in walked a handsome young man in a white linen suit.

"Sorry that I'm late," Sakir Elsani said, walking into the room. The doors closed behind him, cutting off the sight of his two personal bodyguards often referred to as Beauty and the Beast, but never to their faces.

Tall and slim, Elsani moved with the purpose of a machine, every motion seemingly calculated to the nth degree for sheer efficiency. His clothing was painfully clean, and hung loosely off his wiry frame. An expensive-looking watch was strapped to a wrist, and prison tattoos adorned both arms from a brief indiscretion as a teenager. Under his tailored jacket, a S&W .357 Magnum pistol rode in a tailored shoulder holster, a ruby glittered from his left earlobe and a small gold crucifix hung around his neck.

Moving through a weapons scanner, Elsani heard the warning beep, but did not stop. The defensives were there for the staff, not for the high-ranking members of the Fifteen. They were expected to be armed, and a bodyguard without a weapon was merely a shield. It had been many years since Uri Bodna had tried to seize control of everything in a blood-

bath that had almost destroyed the crime family, but everybody remembered those bloody days. Bodna had been stopped by Slobodan Kadriouski, and measures had been taken to make sure such a disaster would never happen again. Not a member remained of Bodna's bloodline, and even several prostitutes that he used regularly had been eliminated just in case there might have been a bastard child on the way. The Fifteen Families did not believe in forgiving, forgetting or mercy.

"Hello, cousin," a large beefy man hailed, puffing away on a cigar. "Are you the reason for this unscheduled meeting?"

"Oh, what is it now?" an elderly woman demanded in a nasal voice, her hands perched on the bejeweled head of a hardwood cane. "Some new encoding machine to protect our communications, or is it another computer to transfer our money about? Your mad love of science costs us millions every year!"

"Sakir also makes us ten times what he costs," Kadriouski announced sternly. "Check the books if you wish. So the boy gets whatever the hell he wants."

Taking his seat, Elsani almost smiled at that. Only at these meetings was he ever referred to as a boy. "Thank you, Grandfather," he said. "But this time I come to bring a gift to the family." He paused. "A gift of the world."

"Bah, we already have that!" a fat young man laughed, slopping some champagne from his glass onto the table. "We control all of the heroin in Europe, all of it! And with the new deal to exchange heroin for cocaine with the Colombians, we'll soon also control all of the drugs in Europe."

"I said the world," Elsani repeated, trying not to show his annoyance. The man loved to hear the sound of his own voice

and was always talking too much. That was a dangerous trait Elsani planned to have Beauty and the Beast correct at the end of a knife as soon as it was possible.

"What, do you mean, like Africa?" the drunk scoffed. "A bunch of starving people without a coin to spare. We sell guns to the governments, but the people have nothing. Who gives a shit about Africa?" He liberally poured more champagne, only some of it reaching the inside of his glass.

"And what about America?" Elsani said softly, keeping his tone soft so that the others would have to strain to hear. "North America, South America, Australia, United Kingdom, Russia, Japan, China. All of it. Everything."

"You lie," the drunk muttered into his glass.

Slowly, Elsani smiled. "No, I do not."

There was a long pause among the family members as this startling announcement was slowly digested.

"And you actually have a plan to make this possible?" Harridan Jarvo asked, rubbing the side of his broken nose. With anybody else, the ugly man would have considered this merely bravado, or a bad joke, but not Elsani. "Some way that we can force out the Russian Mafia, the Yakuza and all of our other competition?"

"War is expensive," a prissy man said, filing his nails. "And if NATO gets involved, there could be real trouble."

"There is no need for a plan," Elsani said, looking at the faces around the table. "And there will not be a war. At least, not one that involves us. NATO will take out the other organizations for us. We control NATO, the United Nations, everybody and everything."

"Care to explain that, boy?" Kadriouski commanded in a whipcrack tone.

"Absolutely, Grandfather."

"This better be good," Fatima Morteli said, resting her powdered cheek in the palm of a manicure hand.

"For many reasons, I must be circumspect in the details," Elsani said, touching his wristwatch.

In response to the electronic signal, a small plasma screen rose up from the table in front of each member of the gangsters. The flat screens pulsed to life displaying a full-color map of world. Not a rendering, or vector graphic, but a real-time broadcast of Earth from an orbiting satellite.

"Are we astronauts now?" One of Elsani's cousins laughed, his arm in a sling. The recent wound had come from the Russian mob trying to gain control of the man's shipping concerns, slipping drugs and weapons into legitimate orders and then retrieving the illicit goods before the customer took possession of the shipment. If the goods were discovered, the customer took the fall. It was a smart deal, and the Russians wanted it badly. They paid for the attempt in blood, with small, but important, pieces of the men mailed to their mothers in Moscow. The Russians were smart and tough, but always folded when their families were threatened. It was their greatest weakness and what kept the Fifteen Families in control of Europe. Only once had the same tactic been tried of them. A Greek drug lord had kidnapped the pregnant wife of a member of the Fifteen Families and offered to exchange her for a cargo ship of heroin. In response, Slobodan Kadriouski immediately sent out the Dragoons in Ashanti gunships, and bombed the remote mountain villa out of existence, with the pregnant woman still trapped inside. Nobody ever bothered a member of the family again.

"If you were an astronaut, cousin, the shuttle would never get off the ground," Elsani said, smiling without any warmth.

The overweight man snorted, but withheld any further comments.

"Now, back to the topic under discussion…" Elsani paused, waiting for another interruption. When none was forthcoming, he continued. "These are the superpowers of the world." He tapped each in turn with a finger. On the other screens a corresponding white dot appeared at exactly that spot. "America, the United Kingdom, France, Russia, India and Australia. These are called the superpowers because they alone have nuclear weapons."

Fatima Morteli started to speak, but he cut her off.

"Oh, Pakistan and a few other have nuclear bombs, but no way to deliver them," he said quickly. "And that fat fool in North Korea…to be honest, who knows what that lunatic wants or has? Now it is rumored that several of the larger terrorists groups have stolen nukes, but they're afraid, or unable to use them, and thus don't really count." Elsani again tapped the monitor. "For all intents and purposes, these are the rulers of the world. The Big Six." He glanced over a shoulder. "Only now it is the Big Seven. Albania is now a nuclear power."

"You stole a nuke?" Morteli scowled, wiggling her fingers to dismiss the trivial matter. "We have done such things before, and then sold them at tremendous profit to those lunatics in the Middle East. This is not news, it is not even new."

"Unless our cousin has a different meaning," Harridan Jarvo suggested cagily.

"Yes, I do. I have found a way to detonate a nuclear weapon from a great distance. Now, I do not mean that there is a theory and that, maybe, some day, perhaps we will be able to build such a device. It is here, now."

Excited murmurs came from the assembled gangsters.

Leaning back in his chair, Elsani spread his arms grandly. "In fact, I already used it to destroy several nuclear-weapon caches in America, Russia and China."

"You're joking!" a skinny man exclaimed. "If that were true, then we would have heard about it on the news!"

"Not necessarily," Kadriouski said unexpectedly. "Those governments would try to cover up the explosions as tests, or accidents, if at all possible." He looked directly at his grandson. The man smiled. "But you already considered that, didn't you, son?"

So now it was son, eh? The subtle shift to the new word did not go unnoticed by Elsani. "True," he answered. "I specifically choose targets well away from large cities. America and the other governments want these explosions kept secret just as much as we do to prevent a worldwide panic. Can you begin to imagine the riots that would happen if the word spread the nuclear bombs were detonating randomly? Or worse, that they were being remotely controlled by terrorists?"

Slow smiles began to form on the ring of faces.

"You're insane," the drunk whispered, slurring his words. "If America learns we're behind this…"

"They can and will do nothing," Elsani shot back. "That's just the point. They cannot do anything! If there is the slightest sign of troops coming our way, a million Americans die. With the touch of a button I can remotely trigger every nuclear warhead in the United States. The death toll would be in the millions! We have them by the throat!"

"By the balls," Morteli said, her eyes narrowing slightly in excitement.

"My God, America on her knees," a man whispered, licking his lips greedily. "We could demand anything from them! We…we could—"

"Nothing," Elsani corrected. "We ask for nothing."

"Are you mad? They would empty Fort Knox for us!"

"And this is why you are in charge of our casinos," Kadriouski retorted hotly, slamming his stick on the table. "Gambling and whores is all you know. A blackmailer will always fail if he asks for too much. If you get photographs of a married man having, say, a homosexual affair, then you trade them to him for a reasonable amount of money. And afterward you give him back the photos and the negatives."

"But…" the man began in confusion.

"Push too hard, ask for too much, and the victim will decide that if he has nothing to lose, then he'll risk everything and try to take you out himself. Suddenly a simple business deal of exchanging goods becomes a battle with members of the family dying, perhaps even yourself! Keep your word, give the man back the photos." Kadriouski grinned. "Although you naturally assign a close watch over the man for when he does it again. This time the price is doubled. That is only fair. But he will understand and be reasonable, blaming himself, not us."

"If we asked to be recognized as the sovereign rulers of Albania with full UN status, that would be too much and America would send out a hundred thousand soldiers and ten thousand spies to find us, and smash the device," Elsani added, choosing his words carefully. *Can't let it slip where the Icarus is located.* "But if instead, we simply tell the United Nations Security Council to do nothing, nothing at all, they will comply, and with them off our backs we can spread out across the world and increase our drug trade by billions of euros and dollars."

"What if they deactivate all of their nukes?" a young cousin asked. "How long would it take the United States?"

"In my estimation, six days," Elsani said honestly. "So in three days we hit them with an ultimatum to give us the access codes to the satellites that monitor their weapons systems."

"Or else?"

"Exactly. Or else."

A heavy silence filled the conference room as the family members considered the matter from every angle. If this went wrong, they would be killed. But that was a daily hazard in their business. The danger was minimal, while the possibility for profit, and revenge on their enemies was virtually unlimited. A genuine win-win situation.

"So, who do we contact first?" Kadriouski asked, lowering his head like a bull about to charge.

CHAPTER SEVEN

Stony Man Farm, Virginia

Refilling the coffeepot, Aaron Kurtzman stared at the bubbling machine impatiently, as if he could accelerate the process of heating water by sheer willpower. After a few moments, the man wheeled away from the coffee station.

Taking his half-filled mug back to his console, Kurtzman set it down on a clear area where the paint had been removed exactly the same size of the mug.

"Any word on Able Team?" he asked Huntington Wethers, sliding his chair into position. Taking a healthy sip of coffee, he started flipping switches with his free hand.

"Unfortunately, yes," Wethers said, scowling over his pipe. "Professor Gallen is dead, killed by gunfire at a nightclub. Carl and the others are going after the killers in an effort to burn the rope." As a former university professor, Wethers had never heard of the phrase before joining Stony Man. But it certainly was logical enough, rather like cracking a cipher in its own way. An agent would force the killers to tell who hired them, and then go after those people and force them to tell

who hired them, and so on until finding the people in charge. Burning the rope. Lighting the fuse would be a more appropriate colloquialism.

"If they need anything, let me know."

"Will do," Wethers replied.

Damn, Kurtzman thought. The professor was dead. What else could go wrong?

"More bad news," Carmen Delahunt announced, sliding off her VR gloves to flex cramping fingers before sliding off the helmet. She blinked at the overhead lights for a moment before continuing. "The French navy has begun dumping their nuclear warheads into the Mariana Trench."

Caught in the middle of a swallow, Kurtzman stopped drinking. That section of the Pacific Ocean was two miles deep! After the warheads were crushed flat, they'd merge with the molten lava at the bottom. The Puerto Rico Trench was a lot closer, but there was no molten stone at the bottom. Those weapons were gone forever. It seemed an extreme way to dispose of their nukes. It was the Maginot Line all over again. The French were brave and smart, excellent chefs, artists, scientists. Heck, the parachute had been invented by a French aviator, who with no other way to try it, had simply jumped out of a flying plane to see if it worked. Now that was real balls! However, when it came to the military….

"Bunch of damn fools," Kurtzman said, shaking his head.

"And the hits just keep on coming," Akira Tokaido said, removing his headphones to massage his temples. "I've just received a coded message from Hal. The White House has issued an executive order that all covert operations in Albania are to be halted and recalled home. Immediately. Even our Navy ships are leaving the Baltic Sea. There is no reason

given, but on the list of people and organizations receiving the message is a Colonel John Phoenix.

"What was that name again?" Kurtzman asked, frowning.

"Colonel John Phoenix."

"Well, I'll be a son of a bitch," the computer expert growled, a smile slowly forming. "That clever bastard." John Phoenix was an old code name for Mack Bolan, one that he didn't use anymore, and the President would know that. The only people the defunct code name would mean anything to were the members of Stony Man. The President had to be incommunicado, and this was actually a message for Brognola and the Farm. Did this mean the Albanians were behind the nuke attacks? Or was the nation merely the staging area for some other group? The country was centrally located, and basically ruled by organized crime. Sending in a team would be difficult under the best of circumstances. Now it would be all but impossible.

Stealing a fast sip of the cold coffee, Kurtzman ignored the smell of the fresh brew at the coffee station and started typing away on his keyboard. Soon the main wall monitor was scrolling with the names and descriptions of every terrorist group and criminal cartel in that area. The Black Eagles, COBRA, the Kosovo Protection Agency, formerly the Kosovo Liberation Army…

"My God, there are hundreds of terrorist groups," Delahunt muttered, brushing out her hair and using an elastic scrunchy to make a ponytail. Sliding the VR helmet back on, she shook her head a little to get comfortable, then slid on the gloves once more and delved back into the data stream.

"Think it might be the Fifteen?" Tokaido asked, reaching past a pack of chewing gum for a sandwich. He lifted the plate and took a sniff, deciding the egg salad was still good, and

started to eat quickly. The body needed food, as well as sugar and music. Sad, but true.

"If we've learned anything over the years, it's to expect the worst," Kurtzman declared. "You concentrate on thulium, while I get as much data as we can on the Fifteen Families."

"Aside from the fact that they make the Sicilian Mafia look like the Girl Scouts?"

"Hell, son, they're all cast-iron bastards." Kurtzman drained his mug. "Hunt, better inform the teams and switch Phoenix Force to Albania. Send them to… What's the capital city, Tetamon?"

"Tirane."

"Right, and cross-reference the Albanian files with the Finnish records. See if anybody has connections in both countries."

"Not a problem," Wethers said, removing his pipe. "But we don't know yet that the Albanians are even involved."

"Well, we'll soon find out," Kurtzman said, accessing Interpol files, all of the screens on his console scrolling with arrest records and mug shots.

The Isle of Sardinia

THE SOFT ECHO OF the dripping water went on and on endlessly. Never faster or slower, but as regular as a heartbeat.

Huddled under a pile of dirty straw, the half-naked woman was tightly curled into a fetal position, asleep and lost in the dream again. She was young and free, with her family at a party where all of the relatives were invited. Safe, and warm, and well fed. The dream, the glorious dream.

Trembling slightly, Anna reveled in its outrageous impos-

sibility when something disturbed the wonderful fantasy. Was…was that a machine gun?

Struggling to consciousness, Anna forced open her eyes to stare at the blackness of the cell. The echoing drip continued ever on, a metronome of creeping time. Sifting the straw, she sniffed and detected the homey stench of her waste hole in the chilly air. The straw underneath her threadbare shirt was soft from body heat. Reaching out a trembling hand, Anna found her dinner bowl exactly where she had left it, the cracked wood a visual memory to her probing fingers.

Everything in the little stone cell seemed to be the same. As it always had been, as it always would be until her death. Yes, please, God, kill me! Yet deep inside herself, Anna felt a vague unease that something in her unalterable stone box had subtly shifted.

Struggling to her bare feet, Anna brushed off the straw and flinched as a brand-new twinge painfully caused a cramp in her right calf. Gently massaging the knotted muscle, she angrily wondered if this was what had disturbed her precious sleep. But then, her joints were constantly getting stiffer, while her hair and nails had slowed in growth to have all but stopped from her lack of food.

Releasing her calf, Anna touched the back of her neck and felt the twin tendons rigidly extended outward from her spinal column. Anna didn't expect to last much longer, and looked forward to death immensely. The incredible fact that she still had all of her teeth was a miracle she attributed to the bugs. Cockroaches, centipedes, she had no idea, never having seen any of the things in the light. But Anna ate as many as she could capture, her hands fast and sure in the lightless expanse of her dank cell. However, the bugs seemed to be learning how to avoid her and even smearing some of her precious food

under the doorjamb was attracting less and less of her tiny companions these days. A dab of menstrual blood had worked just fine long ago, but her cycle had ceased completely... How long was it now? Years? Decades? The prisoner truly how no idea whatsoever how long had been confined down here by the hated Sardinian slavers.

My period stopped just about when they ceased coming to rape me, the woman mentally noted, the blurred images of the constant assaults all jumbled together in a fragmented nightmare. But thankfully she was too ugly to rape anymore now. The thought had been strangely reassuring at first, especially for such a beauty as herself. But now...she savagely shook her head. There was no past, no future. Only the eternal living hell of the present.

A dull boom echoed slightly, and the walls of the cell shook, causing a rain of dust from the dimly remembered wooden rafters.

There was a fight of some kind going on, she realized in shock. For a split second her heart leaped at the thought of being rescued. Then reality came crashing back and she prayed for the stone walls to collapse and crush her dead. That was her only hope of escape, a quick and painless death.

More machine gun-chatter became discernable, and another explosion, closely followed by two more.

Jerking herself awake, Anna realized she had passed out for an unknown time. Straining against the quiet, she could not hear any more sounds of battle. Was it over? Had there been a revolt of the slaves? Some sort of coup? She was unsure if that was the correct term. Could the slavers be...dead?

Her belly tingling with excitement, Anna shuffled toward the unseen door. Reaching out, she touched the granite block wall, the smooth, mortarless surface familiar, every niche and

irregularity an intimate acquaintance. While still allowed to wear clothing, she had heard horror stories of how some prisoners went mad from reoccurring nightmares of being buried alive. Perhaps it had been designed to do just that. Who knew? Even when she first arrived, her most powerful thumps on the walls and floors culled no response from other inmates. Likewise, neither did her screams out the tiny food slot in the iron-banded door. It was as if there were no other prisoners in the entire basement of the Sardinian cavern.

Only during her sleep did Anna allow herself to wallow in the pleasure of escape dreams. But she always awoke to the darkness, eternal darkness, the harsh reality. Although sometimes it was difficult for her to separate which was the dream and which the nightmare. Could she be delusional? Hopefully so. Anna eagerly welcomed the freedom inherent in total madness. Insanity would at least give her some small respite from the crushing isolation.

As she stepped away from the wall, soft sounds came again, and Anna trembled from the alien noises. Could this be another dream? No, impossible. The throbbing in her calf told her that. She was awake and something was happening here that didn't involve beating her. Hopefully.

Then she clearly heard boot steps. Heavy and regular. Men marching and the jingle of keys.

The slavers were coming back! At the thought, Anna choked on a laugh. Better to ravish a corpse fresh from the grave than the crone she was now. Yet there were always rumors of people with tastes in that direction. Not to mention the many enemies her family had made around the world. That's why she was kept alive and had been attacked daily for many months. As revenge for the business dealings of her brothers and cousins.

Backing into the corner, Anna crouched on the dirty straw,

piling it in front of her. As the noise increased, she violently shook her head to dispel the creeping madness. This couldn't be happening. Nobody was coming. There were no keys to her cell. She was alone and forgotten. Buried alive in a coffin of stone. Perhaps already a ghost! The urge to scream rose in to her throat, but all that came out was a hoarse whisper.

The multiple boots stopped outside her cell and a soft light flooded in through the slot of the door. Distorted shadows danced on the walls, and Anna frantically raked scraggly hair over her face as protection. The flickering glow was blinding, and her temples throbbed from the soft brilliance.

Frantically she dug her fingers into straw and found the shard of pottery from her first water bowl. Ceramic and breakable, she had gotten a wooden replacement. But the fools never noticed the sliver missing from the wreckage.

The end of the pottery shard had been lovingly honed on the walls until it was razor sharp, the curved handle wrapped with a cushion of her own hair for a better grip. It had been meant as an aid for when she decided to take her own life. But that was a mortal sin, the one avenue of freedom available to her forbidden by God. Then again, could the damned go to hell?

With the shard in hand, Anna waited, feeling only repressed fury, laced with a terrible fear. This was the only weapon she had. A million turns ago, in her prime, she could have killed a dozen men with her bare hands. She had been taught by the best combat-drill instructors in the world. Nobody could stand before her back then. Experimentally, Anna flexed her shoulders and felt no tightening of the skin from muscles. She had long ago stopped exercising. It only made her hungry and more alert to her surroundings.

There came a shuffle noise of boots on stone and then the jingling of keys again.

"You sure this is it?" a gruff voice demanded.

"The chart says so, yes, sir."

"God in heaven, what is that stink?" a woman snorted.

Anna became more alert. A woman? What was a woman doing with the slavers?

"Apparently, Lieutenant, the Sardinian bastards didn't wash down here very often, sir."

"Don't wash down here ever, you mean."

Anna was stunned. Bastards? Had…one of the people outside her cell door just insulted a Sardinian?

Suddenly the lock jangled and squealed a bit, but nothing more.

"Blasted thing is rusted shut," a man muttered. "Where's the oil?"

"Here, Sergeant."

Something poured out her side of the lock and dripped onto the floor. Through sheer willpower, Anna forced herself to stay still and not rush over to lap it up like a dog. This could be a trick. Some new torture of the slavers. With them, anything was possible.

The keys jingled again, there sounded a metallic fumbling and a very loud click.

Trembling, Anna inched deeper into the corner, shielding her eyes with one hand, the shard brandished in the other. From between her fingers, she chanced a brief glance toward the reflected light on the wall. It hurt to look at it, her vision was blurry with tears. But if she squinted hard, the pain was durable. All pain was durable. Prison had taught her that hard lesson. Then she jumped as something hit the door, but it did not open.

"Well?" a muffled voice demanded. "What's wrong now?"

"The door is unlocked, sir. Just been so long without moving that it is stuck."

"Use more oil."

"It's not the hinges, sir. The door itself." Another thump and some dust rained down to dance like mites in the rectangle of light. "The damp expanded the wood."

"Are we sure there's anybody in there?" the other woman asked in clear disbelief.

"The chart says yes."

"Should we use explosives, sir?"

The reply was muffled and could not be heard.

Explosives! The blast would kill her instantly! Moving closer to the door, Anna felt something move across her toes and she instantly grabbed whatever it was and stuffed it into her mouth. It wiggled and fought, but her molars cracked the long shell and she swallowed the bitter food without thought.

More clicks and clacks, more jingling keys.

"Corporal!"

"Sergeant?"

"Open this blasted thing."

There was a pause. Anna held her breath. Then a man shouted a martial-arts cry and the door slammed open a good two feet. Brilliant light flooded into her cell and Anna automatically rose into a combat stance, prepared to slash out with the shard.

Dark shapes filled the doorway as the door was forced open all the way to the wall, pieces of the wood falling off to be crushed under heavy combat boots. Black silhouettes stood behind the blazing electric lanterns, and Anna could dimly see uniforms and weapons of soldiers. Real soldiers. Briefly, she prayed to die in a fight and not tied to some table like a hog to be gutted for the amusement of others. The Sardinians had

threatened her with a turkey doctor for years until it almost sounded like a gift instead of a threat.

Slowly, time passed, and the armed soldiers did not enter the cell. "Hello, there," one of them said. Then suddenly they all backed away, holding their noses.

"Mercifully heaven!" a tall man cried, his voice muffled by a handkerchief. "It's even worse with the door open!"

"Why was this done to a child?" a slim soldier asked, his young voice thick with distaste.

"She's not a child anymore after fifteen years."

Feeling as if she had just been slapped, Anna almost dropped the pottery shard. How…how long had she been down here? Fifteen years?

The tall man turned. "Must be somebody they really didn't like, but there's no name on the chart," he said, lowering a clipboard. "Remember that, people. These slavers are beyond scum, and deserved to die. The next batch we encounter, just blow off their fucking heads on sight."

"With pleasure, Lieutenant."

Those slavers? Then…these were not Sardinians? Could her dream have been true? Had some group killed the slavers, and was this a…a… Her heart pounding painfully in her skinny chest, Anna lowered the shard and tried to get a better look at the strangers. Her vision was getting better with every passing moment. Dimly she could see their clean blue uniforms, the white symbol of NATO on the armbands and shirts. All of the men, and women, were heavily armed, but one was carrying a medical bag, the symbol of Hippocrates on his uniform blouse.

"What's that she's holding, a knife?"

"A shiv, sir."

"Oh, great, a homemade knife. Swell."

"Please, miss, drop the weapon. We're not here to hurt you."

Trying to control her breathing, Anna pushed her back tighter against the wall. Use their voices to guide your thrust, she reminded herself, but don't go for the voices, they would have hands raised to protect their faces. Go below, for the vulnerable stomachs, deep in, then jerk to the side for a lateral slice and fast kill. She could get one, maybe two if she was lucky. Then they would have to kill her. Release was only a yard away.

"Fine, have it your way." The big man sighed.

"Please, don't!"

"There's no other way. Now, stand back."

There was a scrape of metal and the flickering light from the electric lantern increased as the shutters were completely raised. To Anna it was as if the sun exploded. With a cry, she dropped the makeshift knife and covered her face with both hands, screwing her eyes tightly closed. Pain.

"Yeah, I thought that would do it. You and you, get her out of there," a stern voice commanded. "And be gentle! Lord alone knows what she has been through."

"Yes, sir!" voices chorused.

Don't hurt her. Did she hear that correct?

Footsteps came her way, and strong hands took both arms and bodily lifted her off the floor. Helpless in the grip, Anna was assisted out of the cell and into the blinding corridor.

As she crossed the threshold, cold sweat trickled down her back, and she felt giddy. More in control. Invigorated. But Anna was still blind, and she stumbled more than once in spite of the guiding hands. And nobody was hurting her.

"Too fast?" somebody asked.

Resolutely, Anna shook her head no, and made herself walk more erect. Then she reeled with the impression of space beyond ten-by-ten feet, and her stomach violently lurched.

Something must have shown on her haggard face, because the soldiers moved back fast.

"Watch out! She's going to be sick!"

With surprising gentleness, hands took her arms, and a cool cloth was wiped across her face and the back of her neck. The contact felt beyond any known pleasure. Suddenly childhood lessons came flooding back and she breathed in through her nose, out through her mouth. That was how you fought sea sickness. Concentrate on breathing, and not on what was happening around you.

"Feeling better?" a man asked.

There was a strong smell of tobacco in his breath. Wonderful. Weakly, Anna tried to nod.

"Here, take this," a voice said gently, and somebody draped a blanket around her bony shoulders.

Startled at first, Anna grabbed the cloth and hugged it tight, all the while wondering if this was actually happening.

"Can you walk?" a soldier asked, turning down the lantern to the soft glow once more.

For a moment Anna debated faking a limp, or fainting, but her stubborn streak choose that moment to rear up and forced her to nod. She was not a child anymore, or a whore, some toy for others to play with and cast aside. She was nobility!

"Yes," she whispered hoarsely, her throat raw from the Herculean effort.

"No, I don't think that you can." A man sighed. "You and you, carry her to the medics."

Medics? Excitement welled from within, and Anna tried to speak again, but her meager resources of strength had been drained and the world spun crazily until she drifted away on the softest cloud imaginable that smelled oddly of strong military detergent....

GROGGILY COMING TO, Anna felt like she was flying, floating through the air, and assumed it was a dream. A wonderful dream where soldiers had killed all of the slavers and rescued her in a magical blanket that smelled of clean soap.

Warily opening her eyes, the woman came fully awake. She was lying on a stretcher carried by large muscular men in military uniforms. There was an IV dripping a clear solution into her left arm, and her hands were covered with bandages. So it was true. The impossible had happened and NATO had come to her rescue. Incredible. The irony was almost painful.

Watching the view as the soldiers trundled along through the rough-hewn tunnels, ancient memories flashed of her ordeal in the cold disrobing room. Only now there were bloodstains all over the place, a blackened section of the floor told about the use of explosives, every wall was peppered with bulletholes and the floor was covered with hundreds of spent brass shell casings. There were no bodies in sight, and that made Anna feel sad. She would have so loved to spit on one of the dead Sardinians. Any one of them. Or all of them! In a wild fantasy, she imagined nuking the chain of islands out of existence. Then the woman went limp, exhausted from all of the excitement.

Confused for a moment, Anna realized that she had to have briefly passed out again because the next moment the group was moving through the tunnel and out into fresh air. Salty air!

The old, dried riverbed was full of people, hundreds of soldiers moving quickly around doing things. Several soldiers stood near a radio talking in hushed tones; a score of men and women stood guard holding assault rifles, and there was a long row of black plastic body bags off to the side. Anna tried to spit, but no saliva came. Her mouth was as dry as her soul.

Just then, a breeze blew over her and Anna desperately

filled her lungs with air she couldn't taste or smell. It was wonderful! Amazingly, she finally understood what the ancient poets of Earth had meant when they used the phrase "to drink the air like wine."

Past a large tent, a sort of field hospital had been created by setting out rows of folding cots, the green canvas beds full of young women wrapped in thick blankets adorned with the symbol for NATO. All of them showed signs of torture, and most were weeping uncontrollably, but several of them were simply gazing blankly into space, their arms slightly red from a recent injection.

As the soldiers set her stretcher on the rocky ground, Anna was confused by the other prisoners. They still looked plump and healthy, clearly only recent arrivals to hell. Yet they had gone mad? Pitiful. Then somebody laughed. Under the warm blankets, Anna flinched from the noise. It had been a long time since she had heard laughter.

Out on the ocean were four large warships floating near the shore, a score of small hovercraft moving back and forth transferring women of all ages and sizes. Separate hovercraft carried piles of body bags. Lovely, lovely, body bags. The stacks of corpses was the prettiest sight of her whole life.

A soldier moved nearby and she grabbed his muscular arm with scrawny fingers.

"Yes, miss?" he asked in bad Italian, the words slurred with an odd British accent.

"Who…" Anna asked in English, but broke into a ragged cough.

"Easy now," the man said. Kneeling alongside her stretcher, he took out a canteen and screwed off the cap. "Small sips only. Small sips, understand. Or else you'll just lose it again."

Eagerly nodding agreement, she did as directed. The water

was warm, slightly metallic and tasted better than the air smelled, if that was possible. It seemed as if life itself was flowing down her sore throat. Her stomach roiled from the invasion, and she had to have shown something in her face as the man instantly took the canteen away. But after a few moments, she nodded and he gave her more.

"Better?" he asked, laying the canteen on her blanket.

She ignored that. "Did…you…kill…" That was all Anna could say before her voice expired. Tired, she was so tired.

"Did NATO kill the slavers?" Running stiff fingers along his crew cut, the soldier furrowed his brow. "No, miss, we did not. Or at least, my company didn't. We were on patrol when orders arrived from the high command in Brussels to get here pronto. When we arrived, an Italian contingent was already here, ferrying out the prisoners…" As if suddenly aware of what he was saying, the soldier paused. "Don't you worry about that, miss. There's nobody here to harm you anymore."

Which means all of the Sardinians were dead. Excellent.

As the soldier moved off to aid a woman with a broken arm, Anna considered the mystery. If NATO forces hadn't attacked the slavers, then who had? Could it have been family members? But if so, then why didn't they rescue her themselves? It had to have been somebody other then her blood-kin. Perhaps the stupid Sardinians kidnapped the wrong girl, somebody's child or wife, somebody with the ability to find their missing love and mount a military rescue operation. A president, king, sheikh, prime minister…but then they left before releasing the slaves?

Because they didn't want to be seen, she comprehended in growing clarity. Somebody who needed to be secret. Some covert paramilitary group that was not a part of NATO. Not openly, anyway. The British SAS, perhaps, or the American

Delta Force. This sort of mission would be just their style, she thought.

A nurse stopped to check the IV drip in her arm, then crouched low to brush the stringy hair off Anna's face.

"Hi," the nursed said softly, adjusting the blankets. "Feeling strong enough to give us your name so that we can inform your family about the rescue?"

The NATO nurse looked like an angel in her spotless uniform, her clean hair pulled back in a tight ponytail. But the holstered pistol on her hip was truly beautiful.

I shall never again be without a weapon, Anna vowed, the decision filling her with a new resolve to live. To live and find the people who had freed her from the dark hell of the little room. To find them and thank them. Anna didn't care if it took the rest of her life. This was her goal, her reason to live. She would find the group, no matter who they were and no matter what it cost.

"Miss?" the nurse asked again in concern.

Summoning all of her strength, Anna whispered. "My name…is Anna Kadriouski… I am the granddaughter of Slobodan Kadriouski from Albania…."

CHAPTER EIGHT

Canberra, Australia

A strident Klaxon began to sound through the Parliament of Australia so loudly that everybody stopped whatever they were doing to stare at the nearest wall clock.

"All right, who's playing the fool?" a secretary demanded angrily, resting a fist on a shapely hip. "The question period for Parliament isn't until two, and it's five past ten in the bloody morning!"

"Maybe the clocks are broken," a young woman wearing glasses suggested shyly, hugging her armload of confidential reports.

The senior secretary turned on the newcomer. "All of them?" she retorted hotly.

"Perhaps some computer hacker—"

"Not even bloody Bill Gates could hack into our system. This is the Parliament, girl!"

The young woman blushed. "Yes, of course. Sorry."

Mentally, she chastised herself. This building was an invincible fortress of over 4,500 rooms, and so many levels she

had trouble keeping direction sometimes. Built into the side of a hill to not disturb the war memorial on top, the seat of the government resembled a boomerang set into a circle from the air, although flying directly over the complex was forbidden and strictly enforced by the air force. From the front, Parliament looked out upon Lake Burley Griffin, Old Parliament House and the WWII memorial. High above the partially underground building was a flagpole flying the colors of the sovereign nation, reaching almost three hundred feet in height, the pole was supported by four additional legs to brace it against the strong sea breezes. The complex was rich in history, and the pride of the nation. And now that she worked here, the secretary also vaguely knew how tight the security was these days: EM scanners, chemical sniffers and a host of technical things she could barely comprehend—including, the so-called "soft" X-ray scanners built into the jambs of the front doors. Anybody suspicious was examined right down to the skin. She had seen the pictures of people talking and walking along, their clothing only a ghostly mist around their naked bodies. Even tattoos could be seen. Yes, the chief was correct. There was no way to smuggle anything into Parliament. End of discussion, mate.

"Sweet Jesus," an aide muttered, making the sign of the cross. "Could there have been another terrorist attack in New York, or maybe Paris or…" The man stopped talking.

Or maybe it was us this time, the chief secretary realized, suddenly feeling cold. Perth maybe, or Melbourne! I have family there. Oh, please, dear lord, no.

From the hallway came the sound of people running. A moment later a horde of ministers and members raced past the open doorway of the office supply room and charged the corner to run across the Great Hall toward the House.

On every wall, the clocks were still beating out their two o'clock warning, which was when attendance in the House was mandatory for every member of Parliament. Having the alarm go off early was startling to the younger staff workers, and absolutely terrifying for the old guard. The prime minister didn't flip the switch for the emergency summons for anything short of a nuclear attack. But what had been nuked this time?

Smashing aside the double doors to the huge room, the ministers spread out to their assigned seats, trying to catch their breaths. The PM was standing at his usual place in the center of the room, his face a stern mask of impatience. Armed soldiers were standing in the public gallery on the second floor, and the press box was empty and dark, the television cameras covered with sheets.

"Okay…" the Minister of Health and Ageing gasped, holding a stitch in her side. "Who…died?"

"Is it…the queen?" another man wheezed, holding his side. "Is…the queen dead?"

Glancing at his wristwatch, the prime minister said nothing as a cadre of young members took their places on the back benches.

When the last member shuffled into the room, the prime minister turned off the alarms and blessed silence returned to the building.

"Sorry to interrupt your naps, gentleman and ladies," he began, the small joke receiving a smatter of smiles, "but I have the most grave of news." The smiles vanished. Good. Brace yourself, cobbers, here it comes. "At 9:45 a.m., Woomera was attacked and severely damaged by enemy forces of an unknown nature."

"Did you say it was destroyed?" the Minister of Defence

asked. "Was there a radiation leak of some kind from the new atomic engine at the ASRI launch facility?"

"Was it an earthquake?" asked the Minister of Foreign Relations. "Have we begun a rescue mission yet?"

There were a lot of hushed murmurs from the back benches. But the prime minister ignored that. There always were a lot of hushed whispers from the back benches.

"There is no rescue mission, and I said Woomera was severely damaged, not bloody inconvenienced. The base was decimated by multiple nuclear explosions."

"Somebody launched missiles at Woomera?" the Minister of the Environment and Water Resources asked in shock. "How could anything get that far inside our borders?"

"The bombs that exploded were our own," the prime minister said with a sigh. "They were from our own stockpile of tactical nukes at Maralinga, plus the tac nukes and those two big hydrogen bombs we had in storage for the United Kingdom. The tactical nukes triggered some kind of a chain reaction with the hydrogen bombs and…" He ran out of words. How do you describe a nuclear firestorm combined with a hurricane-force sandstorm that spread out for hundreds of miles without sounding insane? "We also lost the experimental nuclear engine being worked on at ASRI," he finished lamely.

Dead silence filled the room.

"But the Australian Space Research Institute is open to the public," the Minister of Defence said. "Woomera Village is less than a mile away from the launch facility. There are picnic grounds, a golf course, a playground for children…"

"Were there any civilian casualties?" the Minister for Schools and Universities demanded, crossing her arms.

"Yes, there are civilian deaths," the prime minister said honestly. "The tactical nuclear blast at the ASRI took out the

entire assembly building, the main launch facility…and the tourist resort. The death toll is believed to be well over ten thousand civilians."

"Bleeding hell!" the Minister of Defence cried out. "What about our military personnel at Maralinga?"

"The entire military base is eradicated above ground. Only the subterranean levels remaining intact, sealed off at the moment by meters of fused soil."

"What about the SpanTech shelters?" a minister demanded, banging a fist on the wooden railing. "Those are nukeproof. I saw to it myself, by thunder, when I was just a toffee-nosed junior in the ministry! How many of our people got inside the shelters in time?"

Oh, yes, the prime minister was well familiar with the famous adamantine shelters. The truncated pyramids cost millions of dollars each, so they damn well better be nukeproof. "Unfortunately, nobody reached the SpanTechs alive."

"None?" the minister roared. "But that's impossible! It only takes a few minutes to—"

"There was no warning, you damn fool!" the prime minister said furiously. "This was not a goddamn test that went awry. Every nuclear device, bomb, warhead, torpedo… everything in storage detonated at the exact same instant. The Maralinga Nuclear Test Range, Nurrungar satellite tracking station, Woomera space facility, Bunker 99, Woomera Village, the hotels, the tourists campgrounds…gone, they are all gone."

"There are no survivors at all?" the minister asked carefully.

"Possibly," the prime minister amended. "At the moment we are not in contact with anybody at what's left of Woomera."

"And why in bloody hell not?" somebody shouted from the back benches.

"Because the EMP blast knocks out the radios and tele-

phones," the Minister of Communications responded irritably. "Lord love a duck, man, do you ever read *any* of the memos we send out?"

The other man started to bristle, then shook off the matter and sat hard. Now was not the time to bicker like schoolchildren over marbles. Lives had been lost. That was what mattered right now. The man desperately wanted to know how the nuclear weapons had been detonated from a distance, and from the expressions of his fellow colleagues, so did they, but everybody knew better than to ask stupid questions. In security matters silence was golden. If the prime minister thought Parliament needed to know that data, then the members would be informed.

"Spies? Was it spies?" someone asked. "Or was it—" he snapped his fingers "—what's that word…saboteurs?"

Now, there was word the prime minister hadn't heard since before 9/11. "The exact cause of the detonation is unknown," he declared loudly, putting a wealth of meaning into the statement. "And while ASIS has nothing to report at the moment, the matter is being most vigorously investigated." He repeated that phrase. "Vigorously investigated."

Relief showed on many faces at the pronouncement, and the minister sat down in contentment. Good enough. If the Australian Secret Intelligence Service agency was on the job, then there was nothing further to do. They were the best. Every bit as good as MI-5 in the UK and the CIA in America.

"Hold on a moment, Woomera is twice the size of England!" a minister said unexpectedly. "That's well over 127,000 square kilometers! How could any amount of nukes…"

"Damn it, man, pay attention! I said that parts of Woomera were damaged," the prime minister explained tiredly. "We lost the weapons test site, the space center and tourist resort. Everything else is fine."

"What else is there, besides a million smegging miles of sand and rock?"

"The Stuart Highway is undamaged, as well as the airfields and railroads and the underground bunkers," the prime minister retorted. "Woomera has been badly damaged, but it's a long ways from being out of business entirely.

"Business… Oh, hell, without the launch facility, we'll lose that multibillion-dollar contract with Russia," the Minister of Education, Science and Training whispered, loosening his necktie. "Along with our new space contracts with Japan, Israel, South Africa… This is going to bankrupt the nation!"

"Aren't we insured against acts of God and terrorism?" a young back bencher asked stiffly over the murmur of grim voices.

Brushing back his thick crop of hair, the prime minister snorted in disdain. "Hell, no. Nobody could cover that policy. Commercial space travel but more dangerous than shoving your John Thomas into a fire-ant hill."

Laughter sounded at the joke, but it quickly faded away under the serious concerns being discussed.

Slowly, the Minister of Defence stood, his face dark and grave. "In consideration of the current status of the world, as well as our own brutal losses of men and equipment, I respectfully demand that the prime minister immediately activate the national-defence grid and place the entire armed forces on full war alert." He paused. "This should include revealing the new experimental F-35 Joint Strike Fighters."

"But I thought the F-35 was vaporware," a member asked, frowning. "Not even built yet. I mean, really now, stealth jet-fighters that can fly at Mach III and carry more weapons than a squadron of RAAF interceptors…"

Suddenly, the politician saw the faces of the other ministers and quickly went still. The jets existed? He felt a flash of anger at not being informed about such a development, but also an sense of pride knowing the superweapons were in existence and safely in the hands of the RAAF.

In the past, the main defense of Australia had always been its sheer distance from everything else in the world. The entire military was designed to repel invaders, break supply lines, and generally make it impossible for an enemy force to get a successful landing on Australian soil. The elite of the military were the Bushmasters, a special-forces unit named after the deadliest snake on the whole continent, and that was really saying something in Australia where even the toads are poisonous and a simple ant bite can kill you in less than a day. The Bushmasters moved in supercharged Land Rovers, lightweight, and with virtually no armor to speak of. But the elite force could swarm like bees to any spot in the entire nation in under twenty-four hours. Anybody landing a plane, or a ship, in Australia would soon find themselves surround by fifty thousand sharpshooters, men whose marksmanship rivaled that of the Mossad and the U.S. Secret Service.

"Order, order, please," the prime minister called out, swiveling to look at both sides of the House. He had been given authority to chair this assembly. Usually the House Speaker did.

Steadily, the low swell of voices became loud cries, demanding to know how this disaster could have happened, who did it and for the government to take immediate action. Patiently, the prime minister let the members rage for a few more minutes, then he snapped.

"Shut up!" he bellowed, abandoning parliamentary decorum. "That's enough nonsense, I say! We have to move fast, and with decisive action right now! First and foremost, we

need to inform the public that there is no danger from fallout. Woomera is too far away from any major cities, rivers or reservoirs for the fallout to pollute the drinking water or croplands."

"Is it?" somebody asked warily.

"Absolutely. There is no danger from fallout."

Heartfelt sighs were heard from both sides of the House.

That is, no danger of fallout on civilian towns, the prime minister amended mentally. But thankfully Woomera was as large as England, because a section the land size of Middlesex county was now a radioactive dead zone for the next ten thousand years.

"As for the matter of further explosions," he said, thumbing off the security seal of the file he held and folding back the cover, "will everybody please open the Nuclear Response report and go to page nineteen, Emergency Military Protocols…"

Adriatic Sea

WHITE CLOUDS FORMED a cottony layer across the sky, masking the ocean below. The air above the Cessna 404 Titan was crystalline-blue, beautiful and serene.

A blacksuit from the Farm was at the controls, flying with the natural ease of a born pilot. The fellow was tall and lanky, loose-boned as if assembled without enough parts. The name he gave was John Smith, but David McCarter thought that was probably a cover.

"So what's your real name?" he asked from the copilot's seat.

The man flashed a toothy grin. "Honest to God, it's John Smith, but you can call me Smitty." He chuckled. "There's a reason the name is used so often as a fake ID at so many

cheap motels, there really are a zillion of us." He chuckled. "Most of them from Wales."

That piqued his interest. "Anywhere near Mousehole?"

"Sorry, no idea," Smitty answered with a shrug. "I was born in Pontiac, Michigan, just west of Detroit."

Oh, well, it had been worth a try. Sipping a cold bottle of soda, McCarter slouched in the copilot's chair, trying to relax and enjoy the view.

When Phoenix Force reached the island of Sicily, the team had gone to a small private airport and gotten on board a waiting Cessna. It was one of McCarter's favorite aircraft, and was capable of carrying fourteen passengers, plus two pilots, making it large enough to hold the Stony Man operatives and all of their equipment. Also the twin engines was a safety feature the entire team preferred, having been in one-lung engines and having the single engine taken out by enemy fire. A spare engine gave them a measure of flexibility, rendering the Titan capable of taking significant damage, but still being able to fight or run.

A group of men lounged near the control tower, ignoring the Stony Man operatives intent on playing cards and drinking beer. But that was their job. The airport was a favorite of anybody wanting to enter or leave the island unobserved. Criminals, Interpol operatives, spies and smugglers. This was neutral ground. The guards were only there to prevent the ambush of another plane. Aside from that, the passengers could do whatever they wanted.

The Cessna had barely gotten airborne when the call came in from Kurtzman to change their course to Albania. That instantly made the SAS commando think about the Fifteen Families. Could they be behind all of this? It seemed way out of their league. The drug lords had been trying for decades to

break in the United Kingdom, and almost succeeded by selling the IRA rebels guns and explosives. But the SAS ran a sting operation that captured, or killed, a dozen of their people, all of whom supposedly worked for somebody named Uri. However, there had never been any confirmation that such a person existed, and the criminals were safely rotting away in Belmarsh Maximum Security Prison, which was about as unpleasant a little hellhole as Pelican Bay SuperMax in California, McCarter thought.

"Good news, NATO has the prisoners, and everything seems okay," Calvin James reported from the a rear seat, turning off the radio. "They found some poor soul locked in a special room. The Sardinians were starving her to death."

"We didn't kill those bastards enough," Rafe Encizo stated with a growl, shaking the cushioned envelope.

"Oh, they're dead enough," T. J. Hawkins said, thumbing fresh rounds into an empty clip for the MP-5 machine gun. "We simply didn't kill them soon enough."

"Next time, eh, brother?" Encizo said.

With a stern expression, Hawkins eased the loaded clip into the machine gun and worked the slide. "Next time," he agreed, sealing the deal with a voice as cold as the bottom of hell.

"We're approaching Albania," Smitty said, pushing the yoke forward, the Cessna dipping her nose to dive into the clouds. "Drop your socks and grab your armrests!" For a long moment, there was only white surrounding the craft, then they emerged and the coastline of Albania was visible below, the Adriatic Sea busy with ships.

Just then the radar started to beep and then something flashed past the Cessna in a blur, the airplane shaking from the brutal turbulence.

"Was that a missile?" Gary Manning asked, instinctively

drawing his Desert Eagle, although what that would do against a Sidewinder he had no idea.

"Tell you in a minute," McCarter muttered, staring hard at the radar screen. There were three blips, moving fast in a tight formation. If he didn't know any better, the man would have believed they were jetfighters. Except that Albania didn't have anything worth mentioning that could fly.

"We have just been ordered by NATO to leave the area," Smitty said, touching his radio headphones. There was a note of incredulity in his voice. "We have two minutes to turn and go back, or they will open fire."

"Come again?" Hawkins demanded.

"They will open fire on us. The nation is closed to all travel, land, sea and air." Smitty frowned. "Since when does NATO take orders from the Albanian government?"

"Then maybe it's not from the government," McCarter said, thoughtfully rubbing his jaw. Kurtzman had to have known this was coming and tried to get them in before the borders were closed. Unfortunately it seemed that they were a couple of minutes too slow.

Off in the distance, a 747 jumbo jet was banking at an angle, preparing to circle the small nation. Or perhaps go back home to its home port. There was no way of knowing. The radar screen showed other planes doing slow curves in the sky, all of them heading away from Albania.

"Okay, I just checked with Bear. The quarantine is confirmed. Albania is now off-limits to everybody by order of NATO. If we cross land, they will shoot us down," James said, lowering the headphones. "I have no idea what is going on here, but NATO Air Command is dead serious. We can't come in. Nobody can."

"Tell them we're out of gas," Encizo suggested. "If we don't land, we'll crash."

While Smitty tried that, the team got their parachutes ready.

"If we're that low on fuel, NATO has suggested crashing into the water," Smitty said in a wooden voice. "They'll try to send somebody next week to fish us out. Just don't try to swim toward shore. Or else."

Appearing from out of the sun, a pair of F-18 SuperHornet jet fighters streaked past the Cessna, the wash of the turbo engines churning the air and making the passenger plane shuddered even harder than before. The assorted packs and trunks stacked behind the double row of passenger seats rattled so hard that something made of glass broke.

Clenching his fists, Hawkins fumed. The Cessna was a good transport, tough and reliable as an old DC-3. But the Titan had less armor on it than a school bus, and even if the team had weapons that could challenge an F-18, those were friendlies.

"I can't believe the NATO pilots would shoot at a civilian plane," Manning said, but there wasn't a lot of starch in his words.

"Well, I'll let you know if it's true or not in ninety seconds," Smitty said calmly, sweat appearing on his forehead.

"What about our diplomatic passports?" Manning said, staring at the coastline. "Tell them we're on a humanitarian mission for the WHO."

"To be blunt, sir, I don't think they give a damn about the World Health Organization," Smitty replied, slowing the speed of the Cessna. "Look, I'm with you all the way. If you want me to try to land, I'll give it a shot."

In the far distance, an F-18 streaked across the sky, skimming just below the fleecy white clouds and then sharply

dipping down and firing a missile at the sea. A cargo ship heading straight for Durres was nearly hit.

"Turn back," McCarter ordered in frustration. "We'll find another way in."

"How?" Hawkins asked bluntly, his hands clenched so hard on the armrests that his knuckles were white. "Their radar is every bit as good as our own. How are we supposed to slip past a NATO patrol?"

"I'm working on it," McCarter said, staring out the window as the coastline angled away and began to recede into the distance.

Soon it was gone from sight.

CHAPTER NINE

Situation Room, White House

Taking a seat at the head of the conference table, the President looked over the assembly of military officers and intelligence agents. Everybody was there, FBI, CIA, Homeland, NSA and DOD. Everybody but Hal Brognola.

Cool and clean, the room was dimly illuminated to make it easier for the rows of technicians sitting at the wall consoles to read their screens and instruments. The different colored lights cast a sort of rainbow across their stern faces. A large screen on one wall was divided into six small windows, each showing a different news program.

"Report," the President said, accepting a folder from an aide. The seal was intact, and he broke it with a thumb and started perusing the files. The news was not good.

"Sir, word of the…incidents has spread over the Internet," the CIA representative reported crisply. "It's all those video phones. Pictures of the blasts have been posted on a thousand blogs."

"We crashed as many servers as possible," Homeland

Security added. "But for every one we take out, ten more pop up."

"And now the news media has gotten hold of the story," Navy Intelligence added, the woman's uniform looking as if it had just come from the dry cleaner's. The creases were sharp and the cuffs spotless. "CNN, the BBC…face it, the cat is out of the bag."

"Do they actually know anything specific?" the President asked, still reading the file. The environmental reports were not good. The radioactive clouds would sweep across farmlands and major cities. There weren't enough airborne isotopes to harm plants or people yet, but if there were many more nuclear explosions, or worse, even one thermonuclear explosion…

"Specifically? No, sir. The first reports were that America was in a nuclear war," an admiral said, scoffing at the concept. "As if any bombers or missiles could penetrate the SAC umbrella over America."

It was nice hearing the Navy speak so well of the Air Force for a change, but that was unimportant right now. "Be that as it may," the President said, finally placing the report aside, "how is the public handling the rumors? Any panic yet?"

The men and women around the table exchanged glances. If the technicians sitting along the wall consoles heard anything, they remained silent.

"Well?" the President demanded impatiently.

"Yes, sir," the NSA agent said crisply. "There have been some riots in New York, London, Paris and Tokyo."

"Damn." The President sighed. "Still, it could be worse."

Before the President could continue, the ceiling speaker cracked into life. "Paging Mr. Johnson," a soft voice said. "Paging a Mister Able Johnson."

The President went stiff. That was the cod phrase for a breach in the White House perimeter! Instantly the military officers in the room dived to the control consoles while the Secret Service agents surrounded the President with their bodies as a living shield, a dozen assorted handguns pulled into view.

With soft sighs, steel panels slid from the wall, closing off the three doorways, and oxygen masks dropped from strategic positions from the ceiling in case of a gas attack. A blank section of the wall slid back to reveal a small arsenal of weaponry, and every man and woman grabbed an M-16 assault rifle. Rocking the clips, the soldiers primed the ammunition, then slapped the clips into the breeches and worked the arming bolts. Several then cracked open the breech of the attached M-203 grenade launcher and thumbed in fat 40 mm brass shells. The color striping on the side marking them as antipersonnel rounds filled with razor-sharp steel fléchettes. A Navy lieutenant grabbed an Atchisson autoshotgun and clicked off the safety, while an Army colonel took an HK G-11. A brief glance told the officer that the batteries were fully charged. Good. The weapon used an electric spark to ignite the caseless 4.6 mm rounds, and the G-ll could fire off an entire strip-clip of 95 armor-piercing rounds in a single burst. Plus there were two additional foot-long clips for the SOTA weapon riding in Pickatinny rails nestled alongside the chambered clip on top of the rifle. More than enough to handle anybody wearing body armor.

With a crackle, the ceiling speaker spoke again. "Calling a Miss Jones. Calling a Miss Abigail Jones."

"All clear." The head of Homeland Security sighed and grabbed a nearby phone. "Okay, report!" he said in a good impersonation of the President. He listened for a minute, then hung up without saying goodbye. "It was just some antinuke

protestors, sir. They hopped the fence and made it to the rose-bushes before the Secret Service tackled them."

"How in hell did they get that far?" the President demanded.

"We don't have a toxicology report, sir," the man replied. "But it would seem they were high on PCP, Angel Dust."

Wonderful. A pair of teenagers drugged out of their minds on animal tranquilizers that made them immune to pain. "Was anybody hurt?" he asked. Translation: were any civilians shot in the head?

"Yes, sir, two agents got broken bones taking the protestors into custody. Our prisoners only suffered some cuts and bruises from the stun guns."

"Clearly, this situation is getting completely out of control," the head of the CIA said, rubbing his jaw. "Sir, if you would just allow us to go into Albania…"

"No, and that's a direct order," the President said, placing both hands on the table. "That matter is being handled, and that is all I can say for the moment."

The men and women present said nothing, but their faces clearly showed barely restrained impatience. Personally, the President understood how infuriating this had to be for them. These were people of action, combat veterans, and sitting around a table talking while somebody else took care of a major problem was just not their style. However, it was their job.

"All right, time to play hardball," the President said. "Recall every pilot we have and triple the protective umbrella of Eagles, Tomcats and Hornets around the nation."

"Sir, yes, sir!" an Air Force general said, his hand twitching to salute, but he stopped it just in time. This was his commander in chief, but saluting somebody while indoors was the worst insult a soldier could commit.

If the President saw the aborted gesture, he diplomatically

said nothing. "Also, I want the Pentagon to start arming B-17 stealth fighters with FAE bombs. And do the same for every nonnuclear ICBM that we have." He smiled grimly. "If—when we find the people responsible for all of this, I want to be able to do more than send them a harsh note."

The Fuel Air Explosive bomb was invented way back in the Vietnam war, used by Marines to burn out patches of jungle so rescue helicopters could make safe landings. The weapon was as simple as it was deadly. There had to be a hundred Hollywood movies where somebody blew out the pilot light on their gas furnace to fill the house with fumes, and then struck a match, the explosion obliterating the structure. A military FAE bomb did roughly the same thing, only in midair. The primary canister would burst, not explode, and spread out a huge volume of incredibly flammable gas fumes across the sky. A split second later, the core of the device would then explode, igniting the cloud and creating a fireball of staggering proportions. If the wind was calm, and the air dry, the explosion could extended for half a mile, which was larger than a tactical nuke. There was no fallout, no residual radiation, as this was purely a chemical explosion. Unfortunately, an FAE bomb couldn't work under water or in high winds, during a snow storm or when it was raining. It could level an entire city block, but not during the rain or in strong winds.

"Sir, nuclear warheads would be easier to exchange," the Navy Intelligence officer began, then stopped herself. "But if we go near those, they could be triggered. Understood, sir. We'll arm the conventional missiles ASAP."

Glancing at the map of the world, the President noted a high radiation count coming from Woomera, Australia. Another hit from the terrorists. God grant there were no fatalities. "Estimated time to completion?" he said.

"The bombers are already loaded and ready to go, sir," a general said bluntly. "As for the missiles, say, one hour per ICBM per silo. So it's just a matter of how many techs we put on the job."

"All of them," the President commanded. "Use all of them, every nuclear mechanic and weapons technician that we have in uniform. Haul them out of retirement if necessary. Now move with a purpose, people!"

As the people in the room got busy on the landline phones, the President looked at a clock on the wall just as it advanced a minute. Fourteen more days until all of the thermonuclear missiles were disarmed. They were running out of time and options. Soon, the Albanians, or whoever was actually behind the attacks would start making demands that the nation could not, or would not, fulfill. Then it would really hit the fan.

Bor, Albania

THE CITY OF BOR WAS quiet at that late hour of the night, the traffic nearly at a standstill and dockyards empty of activity. The wooden wharves were scrubbed and washed, the towering cranes quiescent and cold, the electric motors already lubricated for the next day's heavy work.

Shivering in the chilly night, Lucinda tried to make her last cigarette last as long as possible. She was dressed in fishnet stockings that wouldn't rip from the calloused hands of a drunk client, and a dark striped skirt able to hide a million assorted stains. Her blouse was white, suitable for reflecting the headlights of a passing car and highlighting her in the gloom. Her nails were painted blood-red, but worn along the edges from nervous chewing.

Unlike the prostitutes in American movies, there were no

pimps in Bor, and the streetwalkers were left alone to do their work, forgotten and ignored. Not even the Fifteen Families gave a damn about them. Why bother with pennies when there were millions to be made, was their credo. That only made sense.

Unfortunately, the bar across the street wasn't doing much business this night, and neither was she. If things didn't pick up soon, she was going to have to troll for work along the riverfront. The clientele was a lot different there from the dockyards. It was all rough trade that left her sore and bruised in the morning. But a girl had to eat, and that was life. Such as it was.

She heard the sound of tires crunching on the loose gravel, and a dull gray Hummer rolled into view around the corner of the oceanfront warehouse. The headlights were dark, and the machine moved through the swirling fog like a military ghost.

Instantly, Lucinda placed a shoe flat on the wall behind her to display some thigh and give a peek at the bare flesh under her skirt. Open for business! The old joke still made her chuckle.

Stopping a few meters away, the man behind the wheel got out and pressed the fob on the key ring, The headlights blinked once and the horn tooted as the alarm was activated.

"Hi, handsome," Lucinda called out in a friendly manner. This man smelled of real money, and she was not going to let him get away. The expensive car might be stolen, but his hands were clean and his shoes were polished. He wasn't wearing a fancy watch or anything foolish like that. But polished shoes were always a dead giveaway that a man had money in his pocket.

Facing the bar, the man paused in the street near a steaming

manhole cover, and slowly turned, his face registering shock instead of lust.

"Looking for a good time?" she asked, shaking her shoulders to make her pendulous breasts jiggle seductively. "I know a lot of ways to take the chill out of a man… Hey. Hey, I know you!" A smile broke out on her face, almost cracking the heavy layer of cosmetics. "Hey, Isaak! Well, well, long time no—"

The silenced gun in his hand coughed once, the soft lead bullet plowing into the woman's face. In a spray of blood, Lucinda was thrown backward and hit the brick wall with a sickening crunch. As she slowly slid to the dirty sidewalk, Isaak fired twice more into the woman, just to make sure that was she truly dead and not merely wounded.

Holstering the weapon, the butler glanced furtively around the dark street. But there was nobody else in sight, only a mangy dog eating a dead rat near an overflowing garbage bin.

Stupid bitch! Isaak raged, hurrying across the street. What were the odds of meeting a whore from Durres in Bor! Talk about dumb luck. He had specifically come this far to prevent such an occurrence, and he still encountered somebody who knew who he was! Just for a moment, the butler reconsidered his plans for the night, but the thought evaporated.

Reaching the door to the bar, he stopped for a moment. Now, what had been her name again? Lucia…Lisa…Lucinda! Yes, that was it. Lucinda. The plump whore hadn't been very good-looking, but she smiled a lot and would do absolutely anything for money. Anything at all. Exactly like him.

Ducking inside, Isaak saw the place exactly as he remembered it from his youth. Stifling a yawn, a grubby bartender was polishing glasses with a relatively clean rag behind the battered wooden counter. A couple of men drank beer at the

counter, a dozen more scattered about the tables doing the same. A skinny prostitute with buck teeth was sitting alone at a table, sipping from a large glass of vodka. Her left eye was badly bruised and her lip was cut. She drank carefully, trying not to get any of the fiery liquid into the open cut. A bald man in blue jeans with holes at the knees was strumming a guitar next to the broken jukebox, the front of the machine dotted with bullet holes, the stack of discs inside shattered into rainbow-colored trash. A couple of old men were playing chess at a corner table, half-filled mugs of beer by their elbows, the foam completely gone.

The floor was covered with peanut shells and sawdust, a good combination to absorb spilled beer. A thick haze of smoke covered the ceiling, the scents of tobacco mixing with stale beer, old sweat and cheap perfume. The skinny blonde was not the only prostitute who used the tavern as a base of operations.

As Isaak strode across the bar, the prostitute suddenly came to life, smiling broadly and dropping the front of her blouse to expose a surprisingly lovely breast adorned with a nipple ring. She started to speak, but then saw the dark scowl on his face. Quickly tucking her breast away, she returned to her drink, dismissing the newcomer as trouble and not a potential source of income. His shoes were polished, his clothes clean, but there was the look of a killer in his eyes.

At the wooden counter, Isaak rapped the surface with a knuckle, drawing the bartender's attention.

"Are they here yet?" Isaak demanded.

"Have I ever let you down before?" the man said blandly, as if completely unconcerned with the answer to his question.

"There is always a first time."

With a shrug, the bartender sighed. "They're in the back."

Grunting in reply, Isaak pulled a fat envelope from inside his jacket and tossed it onto the counter, the loose bills inside partially sliding out.

Pushing aside a badly scarred wooden door, Isaak found the storage room dim, almost dark. Instantly his suspicions were raised, but then there came the scratching sound and a match flared, revealing a cigarette in the mouth of man wearing a dark hat. Inhaling sharply, the tip of the cigarette glowed bright red and he exhaled through his nostrils. Then the match went out.

"Switch is to your left," he said in a voice like broken glass.

Fumbling along the wall, Isaak found the switch and pressed the top button. Strobbing into life, fluorescent tubes came on, filling the room with harsh illumination.

Two people sat on a stack of whiskey crates, probably recently stolen from a ship still moored at the commercial docks. The big fellow had a crew cut and fancy mustache waxed at the tips, just like in the old British movies. His clothing was of excellent quality, almost elegant, but his face appeared to be made from concrete there were so many scars. An AK-47 assault rifle rested across one leg, but his hand was nowhere near the trigger.

The woman was slim and rather pretty, with hair so dark it almost appeared to be blue. Her eyes were green and slightly slanted as if there was some Oriental blood in her ancestry. She was dressed in black Chino pants and a tight T-shirt that showed the outline of a sports bra. A 9 mm Steyr machine pistol lay on the whiskey crate nearby, the strap dangling loosely down the side of the wooden box.

"Summer days," Isaak said, and waited expectantly.

"Winter nights," the man answered correctly.

"Sorry, but I had to know that I was talking to the right people."

"Not a problem," the woman replied. "That's why we're here. To make sure that we are also talking to the right person."

What an odd thing to say. Curiously, Isaak looked at her directly and she smiled. But there was no warmth in it, and the butler had the feeling of being in the presence of a carnivorous animal.

"So, has the KPA considered my proposal?" Isaak asked, taking a seat on a barrel of sawdust. The back room smelled of stale beer and mold. "I can deliver the plans for the device in twenty-four hours."

"Considered it? Yes, and no," the man said in his horrible voice, and the woman laughed.

"You don't want the machine?" Isaak asked incredulously. "But think of what it would mean to Kosovo!"

"Fuck Kosovo." The woman chuckled.

Isaak was stunned by their attitude. And that was when it hit him. She was beautiful and he was ugly. Beautiful and ugly. A gorilla and an angel. Their names came unbidden to his mind: Daut Liniat and Vilora Kostunica, also known as the Beauty and the Beast. It took a split second for that to register, then Isaak turned to flee for his life.

He reached the door in a heartbeat, and when he threw it open there was Sakir Elsani holding a shotgun.

Forcing an expression of delight on his face, Isaak opened his mouth to speak, and Elsani fired. The noise was deafening, and pain exploded in the butler's stomach. Doubling over, Isaak began to retch vomit onto the floor, some distant part of his mind registering the fact that he had not been blown in two by a charge of lead buckshot, but merely hit by a soft-gel stun bag.

Rough hands grabbed him from behind and ripped off his jacket. In a surge of adrenaline, Isaak clawed for his gun, and it cleared leather before the woman stabbed him in the wrist with a stiff finger. Incredibly, his hand spasmed out of control and the weapon went flying to hit the floor and skitter away into the shadows.

Clamping both big hands on his arms, Liniat lifted the butler off the floor, and Kostunica searched through his clothes for any more weapons. She was efficient and shameless.

"He's clean," the woman said, then buried a thumb into his throat.

Agony filled his universe and Isaak struggled to breathe. Unable to fight back, his arms were forced upward until he thought they were going to leave their sockets. Then cold metal clicked around his wrists and he was painfully hauled off the floor to dangle a good yard above it.

"Please!" he begged, the words barely audible. "I meant no harm!"

"No harm?" Elsani said, resting the barrel of the shotgun on his shoulder. "But aren't you here to meet with representatives of the Kosovo Protection Agency to sell them information about Icarus?"

Isaak gasped at the use of the name out loud. "No, sir! I'm loyal to the Fifteen! I would never betray—"

With a guttural snarl, Liniat buried his fist in the man's stomach, and Isaak convulsed, unable to breath or even think clearly for an unknown length of time. There was only a red haze of pain.

"I said, you are a traitor," Elsani said, obviously repeating himself. "And completely stupid, besides. Did you truly think that we have never considered such an action by one of the

staff before? Every room is bugged, we read your mail and even know what you like to do with whores."

Crossing her arms, Kostunica laughed again, and the butler burned with shame.

"Let me kill the idiot," Liniat said, sounding bored as he exhaled more dark smoke.

"Oh, no, not yet," Elsani answered, walking around the hanging man. One of the butler's shoes had come off during his struggle, and the gangster kicked it away. "We have much to discuss this night. Such as, have you told anybody else about Icarus?"

In spite of his position, Isaak flinched at hearing the forbidden word out loud. "No!" he whimpered, hot tears running down his cheeks. "Never, sir. I would never betray a family confidence!" Then inspiration hit. "This…this was merely a test of how good your security is! I work for Slobodan—"

In blinding speed, Kostunica slashed out with the palm of her hand in a martial-arts blow, and the man screamed as white-hot pain exploded in his left side. It felt as if his kidney was on fire! Then Isaak heard the sound of dribbling water and was utterly mortified to discover that he was urinating and could not stop.

Stepping back a little, the woman looked at the writhing man without emotion and prepared to strike him again, but Elsani stopped her with a raised finger.

"Not yet," he said, passing her the shotgun. "Now, no more lies, all right? Or else we shall have to get more… enthusiastic in our questioning."

Unable to stop himself, the butler started to cry, great sobs racking his body.

"And you thought this was a threat to the project?" Kostunica said in clear disgust. "Oh, just kill him, and let's leave."

"And exactly what project is that?" a strange voice asked.

Spinning around, Liniat and Kostunica leveled their weapons at the five men walking out of the shadows. Elsani said nothing, tightening the muscles in his arm, preparing to draw the derringer hidden up his sleeve.

The newcomers stopped a few yards away. They were big men, heavily muscled and had the hard look of stevedores, dock workers. Yet they stood at ease in the filthy huge storeroom, neither apprehensive nor overly excited. Each man was holding a boxy MAC-10 machine pistol. The weapons were cheap and wildly inaccurate, but at that range the strangers couldn't have missed even if they were blind. The men had the look of muscle-for-hire, strongarm thugs. Yet they had gotten close to his best people unnoticed. Interesting. Casting a glance at the door, Elsani saw that it was still bolted on this side. There had to be another entrance.

"He owe you money?" one of the dock workers asked with a hard chuckle, jerking his chin upward to indicate Isaak.

In response, Kostunica worked the pump action on the shotgun, chambering a round for immediate use. Liniat did the same with the arming bolt on the Kaliashnikov.

"And you are…" Elsani asked, trying to decided which one was the leader.

"The Black Eagles," one man answered. "And there's no need to ask for your identity, Mr. Elsani."

The gangster bowed his head at the respectful answer. "I'll assume that you were also here to make a purchase?"

"No, sir," the man replied, a finger clicking the safety back on the MAC-10 and slinging the weapon over a shoulder. The other men eased their stance, but still kept the weapons in their fists. "We heard a rumor that the KPA was going to purchase some new weapons from the Fifteen, and we wanted in on the deal."

"I can see why," Elsani said, chuckling at the old-fashioned machine pistols. "Well, the deal has been canceled."

"Obviously," the man replied. "What happens now, sir?"

"You leave," Elsani replied in an icy tone.

With a shrug of agreement, the man walked to the door, threw the bolt and exited the storeroom.

"No! Please come back!" Isaak begged at the top of his voice. "Kill them and I'll make you rich! Millionaires!"

"Silence him!" Elsani barked.

Paying the others no attention, the leader of the Black Eagles closed the door with a muffled boom, cutting off the agonized screams of the man.

Leaving the bar, the five men walked out into the chilly night. They kept silent for several blocks until the leader of the group stopped them near a dirty alleyway full of broken marine equipment.

"Do you think they believed us?" one of the terrorists asked, casting back a glance in the direction of the bar.

"Of course," said another man smugly, sliding the MAC-10 machine pistol off his shoulder and tossing it into a pile of refuse. "People always see what they want to see. These cheap guns were all that fool saw, and thus he accepted our story about being the Black Eagles."

"As if we look like Albanians," a burly man said with a sneer, bending to open a rusty box. Inside was an oily cloth. Throwing back the top fold, the man exposed a layer of brand-new Heckler & Koch G-11 caseless rifles. Respectfully, the terrorist handed the first to the leader of the group, along with a spare 99-round stripper-clip. The stainless steel tips of the 4.6 mm armor-piercing rounds gleamed in the reflected glow of the distant streetlamp.

With expert ease, the Hamas commander loaded the weap-

on and checked the power status. The battery was fully charged and ready for combat. Good.

"Yes, this was almost too easy," Noah Yasmire said gruffly, sliding the deadly weapon into a cushioned holster under his heavy jacket. For a spit second, there was a glimpse of NATO body armor underneath the dirty clothing. "I was not sure that Isaak really had information about some superweapon in the hands of the Fifteen, but now it appears to be true. And coupled with the reports we have been hearing about nuclear explosions around the world…" He stopped talking for a moment, his eyes glazing over with the idea of a weapon that could trigger atomic detonations. The so-called superpowers would be brought to their knees, whimpering and begging for their lives like a whore in the street. With this sort of power, the Hamas could force the United Nations to officially recognize Palestine, and NATO would force the Jews to leave and give their land and cities back to the Arab people. Merciful Allah, the end of Israel was almost in my hands! he thought.

"What should we do now?" a tall man asked, peeling off a theatrical prosthetic from his face, the acne-marked sheet of plastic sticking to the clear skin underneath. "Should we go back and capture the criminal? There are only two guards." He tossed it away to land on a bloody boot, the rest of the body of the Black Eagle covered with a mound of fresh garbage.

"That we know about," a muscular giant muttered in an oddly high-pitched voice. "The Fifteen Families are rats scavenging in the garbage, but rats have sharp teeth, my friend."

"As do we." A short man chuckled evilly, a thin knife sliding from his sleeve into his palm. He flipped the blade in the air, then tucked it away once more. "I can make them talk."

"Little Aziz, you can make anybody talk," Yasmire snorted, slapping the torturer on the shoulder. "But that is not how we

gain control of this new weapon." Inserting a finger into his mouth, the terrorist removed the set of yellow-colored false teeth overlaying his own teeth and dropped to the ground. "Patience is called for this day. We now have confirmation that the device is real. Next, we must learn its location, and how it is guarded. Only then can we strike and claim this prize for ourselves."

"So we should follow this man when he is finished from killing the butler," Akhmed Rantisi stated, hiding away his own G-11 rifle. "Learn their movements, discover their secrets."

"And then?" Little Aziz asked, patting the knife hidden in his sleeve as if it were a living animal.

Smoothing back his hair, Yasmire said nothing in reply, but the man gave a cold smile as he lead the Hamas cell out of the dirty alley and across the cobblestone street to disappear into the dark night.

CHAPTER TEN

Red Fort Island, India

His harsh breathing sounded loud inside the steel hull of the ICBM, and the technician tried to ignore the noise as his gloved hands manipulated plastic pliers and micrometer on a bolt attached to the inner seal of the tactical nuclear warhead. Careful now…easy does it…

As the bolt disengaged, the hatch swung open, exposing a complex nest of colored wires, coaxial cables and sealed titanium pipe. There were security labels on everything, but thankfully he didn't need to get at that. Titanium was a triple bitch to cut through, even with one of the new carbon-dioxide lasers.

Plus, one wrong move and he would pierce the core. If there was so much as a pinhole in his rad suit, or the safety vest underneath, the man would spend his last days on Earth coughing out chunks of his lungs. The thought was not new, but still disturbing to him. He had long ago decided that if anything went wrong on the job, well, there was a good reason he always kept a loaded 9 mm Glock pistol near to hand. The nuclear technician told the base commander it was simply a

matter of ministry protocol. He had no idea if the man believed the lie, but the BC had never raised a fuss, and soon after that all of the other nuke techs started also going armed.

"Within a couple of years, it probably will be official protocol." He chuckled, his hands neatly clipping wires and cables. Almost there…main power was cut…as was the battery backup and the emergency Tesla coil. There, it was done. The warhead was dead, as inert as mud.

With a deep sigh, the technician relaxed. One ICBM down, fifty to go. As he started wiggling out of the missile, the meters inside his radiation suit started clicking, and the thermo-scan began registering a rapid increase in the internal temperature of the missile. But the warhead was dead! There was no power going to the circuit boards and microchips at all! Then he saw it, the thulium housing bolts on the armament flanges were crackling with static electricity. His mind went blank with any possible reason, but he knew what it meant.

"Thulium!" the technician shouted over the radio. "They're triggering the thulium! Tell New Delhi! It's the thulium!"

"Confirm, message sent," the base commander replied. "Can you get it out? Do you need any help?"

"There's a hundred bolts!" He grunted, clawing for the carbon-dioxide laser in the cushioned pouch on his tool vest. "There's no room in here for anybody else, so I'm going to try for a burn!"

"Confirmed!"

Thumbing the laser to full power, the man fidgeted as the device slowly built to operational level. By now, the sparks were everywhere inside the hull casings, jumping off every piece of bare metal. Only the rubber coating of the radiation suit saved him from electrocution. He bit a lip and aimed the laser at the shiny steel armor surrounding the core. If he could

just slice it apart, before the sparking set off the C-4 explosives around the uranium, then he'd die, but the base would be okay. As the wild strobing increased, his gloved hands itched to press the firing trigger on the laser. But if he did it too soon, it would only flash out and have to rebuild a charge from scratch. Damn the safety-mad paper pushers at The Fort in New Delhi….

Dropping the laser, the technician clawed at the flap over his holstered Glock. He didn't have to be neat now. He could just shoot the uranium sphere until it dented. That would alter the shock-wave implosion and everybody would be okay. He almost smiled. Even him. But as he tried to aim the pistol, the weapon slipped away from his gloved fingers and disappeared down the internal workings of the missile. The clanks and bangs seemed to last forever.

"Hammerfall!" the technician said overly loud into his throat mike, giving the code for a wild nuke. "We have Hammerfall!"

"Confirm!" the base commander said, his voice oddly flat. "Begin emergency launch procedure!"

The technician paused in shock at the words, then understood the hard logic. It would be a lot faster to launch the missile than to try to evacuate the entire island fortress. Ten thousand soldiers died or just him.

Suddenly there was a low rumble on controlled power, then a giant hand smashed him flat against the machinery, bits and pieces stabbing through the resilient material and going deep into his flesh. The pain was terrible, and he saw the blood splash on the hot metal, sizzling as it struck. But that didn't really matter now. The pressure increased rapidly as the ICBM soared through the atmosphere climbing ever higher. Incredibly, he was still conscious, and found himself floating inside the machinery. Just then, the laser clicked on. Grabbing

it with both hands, the technician wrapped a leg around a crackle stanchion and started burning his way into the nuclear core.

Lord of all gods, give me one fucking minute. That's all I ask. Sixty measly seconds! The scintillating energy beam bore in deep as the fat sparks began a lambent corona of blinding fury….

Huntsville, Alabama

REACHING THE BRIDGE, Carl Lyons kept well back from the SUV, trying to move with the flow of traffic and remain as inconspicuous as possible. Over in the passenger seat, Rosario Blancanales was wearing sunglasses and pretending to be asleep, his head resting against the closed window. In the rear of the van, Gadgets Schwarz was sitting cross-legged on the floor to stay out of sight, his fingers dancing across the miniature keyboard on his laptop.

It seemed to take forever for the van to cross the incredibly long box-tressel bridge, but there was nothing that could be done about that. Thankfully, there was a lot of traffic also going into Arkansas along this route. Down below them, the mighty Mississippi River flowed sluggishly around Mud Island, the final resting place for the *Memphis Belle,* the famous World War II fighter-bomber plane, the first to complete its tour of duty and be rotated home again. Beaten, battered and full of holes from German antiaircraft guns and bullet holes from warplanes, the *Belle* had done her tour with honor and was the pride of the city.

"Stay to the left," Schwarz said, stroking the mouse pad with a fingertip. On the screen was a B&W vector graphic of Alabama, gray lines showed the roads and a wide band of light

blue marked the Mississippi River quickly being left behind. Just ahead of them, a small red circle marked the car they were following. "They're bypassing the city of Crittendon. Take the next exit, and look for a two-lane blacktop."

"On it," Lyons said, maneuvering through the traffic. All around them, luxury cars mixed with trucks in a discordant array. The new South was a strange mixture of Internet millionaires and poor dirt farmers, which was working in Able Team's favor. It would have been easy for the mercenaries to spot a tail otherwise. Any vehicle that stayed with them from Memphis to the Arkansas countryside would be highly suspect. Keeping a careful watch on the other vehicles, Lyons tried to keep behind the larger trucks and oil tankers.

"Okay, take the second right," Schwarz said, adjusting the controls. Oddly, the memory of the bartender was fresh in his mind and disturbed him greatly. With a great effort, he forced the image of her smile away and concentrated on the task at hand. Didi was dead. Just another victim of the murdering bastards in the SUV. For a brief moment, a blazing rage flared in the man unlike anything he had ever felt before, and he took a strange comfort in relishing the raw emotion, savoring the fury.

Studying his friend in the rearview mirror, Blancanales recognized the expression on his face. Tactfully, he said nothing. It was funny, but he had barely noticed the woman behind the bar, yet it was obviously she had hit Schwarz pretty hard. But as always, the job came first. They could mourn the dead *if there was a tomorrow.*

Heading away from the heavy traffic on the interstate, Lyons slowed to put as much room between them and the SUV. The tracer had a range of five miles, and there was no need to keep a visual on the enemy. Slowly, the miles passed by, and the urban landscape became rolling countryside, the

farm houses miles apart. Herds of black-and-white cows dotted green fields and acres of lush golden corn rose high, their stalks bending in the breeze. Driving the van over a wooden bridge that seemed to have been constructed during the Civil War, the Stony Man operatives crested a low hillock and saw the SUV on top of the next hill less than a mile away.

"How did we get so close?" Lyons demanded, easing on the brakes.

"Beats me…" Schwarz said, running a diagnostic program for the tracer. There was a fast series of beeps, then a flat tone.

Topping another hill, Lyons started to ask if something was wrong when he saw the SUV parked on the side of the roadway, facing in their direction. Oh, hell.

"Guys, we've been made!" Schwarz said, shoving aside the laptop and slapping a ceiling panel. As the M-16/M-203 dropped down, he grabbed the weapon and worked the arming bolt to chamber a round.

"The bastards must have used the EM scanner to check their car and found the tracer!" Blancanales snarled, swinging up his assault rifle and shoving it out the window.

Stomping on the accelerator, Lyons raced off the two-lane and the other men braced for the impact. With a strident crash, the armored van smashed through the safety railing, sailing into the air for several yards over a rain gully before violently crashing on the grassy field. Everything loose inside the vehicle went flying, spare ammo, maps, soda cans, grenades and the laptop, ricocheting madly. The windshield cracked, a headlight shattered and the three men were thrown brutally against their seat belts. But the straps held, and Lyons sent the shuddering van careening across the flat landscape toward a nearby copse. The team needed cover ASAP before the mer-

cenaries opened fire. Out in the open like that, they were sitting ducks, ripe for the killing.

But streaking out of the bushes alongside the parked SUV, came the rapidly extending contrail of a LAW rocket heading straight for the speeding van.

"Take it out!" Lyons shouted, fighting the urge to veer away from the incoming projectile. But that wouldn't have helped matters. A U.S. Army LAW was a hell of a lot faster than a Ford Econoline van.

Leveling his assault rifle, Blancanales stroked the rifle combo's secondary trigger and the 40 mm grenade launcher belched fire and smoke, discharging a hellstorm of stainless steel fléchettes. Schwarz was only a split second behind him. The double cloud of military death dealers hit the rocket halfway and it detonated, the fireball swamping a tree stump.

Desperate to control the van, Lyons fought the vibrating steering wheel as his teammates reloaded just in time. Two more rockets flew from a distant stand of trees on top of a grassy knoll. Bracket fire! The Stony Man commandos triggered their weapons in unison, and the rockets detonated close to the trees. A whirlwind of leaves flew skyward from the twin explosions, several of the branches smashed apart. A bloody man staggered out of a copse, dark fluids pumping from the tattered remains of his left arm.

Drawing his Atchisson, Lyons stuck the autoshotgun out the rear window backward and watched the bushes behind them. Sure enough, another LAW rocket came streaking into view, and he instantly fired. The missile was torn apart by the stuttering barrage of double-aught steel buckshot and tumbled to the grass sizzling and smoking. The distance it traveled was not enough to arm the warhead.

"Incoming!" Blancanales shouted, sending out a burst of 5.56 mm rounds from his M-16.

Ahead of them, two more men stepped out of the shadowy trees, a black giant dropping to a knee as he levered a round into a Barrett sniper rifle. The other man had bright red hair and seemed to be having trouble working the arming bolt on a Barrett 25 mm rifle. Without a doubt, these were the men from the fight in the Grotto.

But where was the bald man? Lyons thought, cursing at the sight and abruptly veering to the left. The massive .50-caliber round would punch straight through the van, and the 25 mm would blow them apart like snowmen.

As his teammates sent hot lead at the mercenaries, Lyons started to flip switches, and a dense cloud of greenish smoke vomited from the rear of the van. Circling fast, he parked in the middle of the dense smoke ring, and the Stony Man commandos dived out the doors.

Separating quickly, they crawled along the ground, trying to see their targets through the military smoke. The Barrett rifle boomed, closely followed by the crash of a window, the noise echoing along the landscape, but there came no sound of a hit. Then the 25 mm Barrett thundered and a section of grass erupted into fiery chaos.

Triangulating on the two sounds, the Stony Man operatives fired back in long bursts. A man cried out, but he sounded in pain, but not dying. Good. They needed at least one of these men alive to question, or else they were back to square one on this mission.

Turning, Lyons sent a full drum of fléchettes toward the distant bushes, and a man staggered into view with a LAW rocket launcher dangling from a limp hand. A moment later, the weapon fired straight down into the dirt, not completely exiting the tube. Jerking wildly, the man was covered with the

fiery exhaust of the rocket, then his head and arms were ripped loose and horribly sailed away, tumbling through the air gushing crimson life fluids.

Aiming in the other direction, Blancanales raked the trees with his M-16, while Schwarz triggered the 40 mm launcher beneath his own assault rifle. A hail of bullets peppered him across the chest, ripping his shirt to shreds, but the NATO body armor stopped the rounds cold.

Hitting the ground, Schwarz rolled to a new position and started firing again, but now there was a growing red stain on his sleeve. Nobody in sight had an assault rifle, or a machine gun, so this new attack had to have come from the bald man. But where was he hiding?

Immediately, the Barrett .50 rifle spoke twice and then the 25 mm rifle discharged. The van was hit, the sound of crumpling metal drawing the attention of the Stony Man team. Then the vehicle detonated, the fiery red interior horribly visible through the green smoke.

Staying low, Blancanales rummaged in a pocket and thumbed a remote control. Promptly, the hidden thermite charges inside the Ford van cut loose, and triple explosions melded into a single titanic blast that sounded louder than doomsday.

On the knoll, the two surviving men broke into victorious laughter and stood to start forward at an easy gait, their hands expertly reloading their weapons.

Staying perfectly still, the Stony Man commandos waited and watched, carefully marking their targets. The foggy air smelled of burning metal and C-4 plastic explosives, the moist ground under their stomachs soaking into their clothing. As the two mercenaries strode past, the three men of Able Team rose and fired. Caught by surprise, the mercenaries cried out

as they were peppered with rubber bullets and stun bags. They fell screaming to the ground, their weapons discharging wildly into the sky.

Dropping his last drum, Lyons hand-loaded the Atchisson with spare shells from the ammo pouch on his belt. He had only steel fléchettes left. If the mercs gave them any more trouble, he would try to shoot at their legs to keep them alive for questioning, but that was a desperate gamble without the field-surgery kits left inside the burning van.

"This is the FBI!" Blancanales called out.

"Lower your weapons and surrender!" Schwarz added. The blood was trickling freely down his left arm by now, and he had to constantly wipe his palm dry on his pants to keep a grip on the assault rifle.

As if in reply to the challenge, the 25 mm Barrett rifle fired, the fat gout of muzzle-flash clearly visible inside the swirling military smoke screen. Blancanales triggered his last 40 mm stun bag and was rewarded with an audible crack of bones. But as the smoky figure fell, the 25mm rifle fired again, the high-explosive shell violently detonating against the crumpled chassis of the burning van.

In stark clarity, Lyons saw the second man briefly silhouetted by the blast. The long shape of the .50-caliber Barrett sniper rifle was gone. Instead the man was holding a cylindrical object and was yanking something free from the top.

A grenade! With no choice, Lyons emptied the Atchisson, the seven 12-gauge rounds coming so fast they sounded like a single extended discharge. Literally blown to pieces, the riddled corpse of the mercenary was slammed backward into the conflagration, and then a colossal fireball blossomed outward from the igniting charge of willie peter.

A wave of searing heat washed over Able Team and they

went flat, hugging the dirt and trying not to breathe in any of the chemical fumes.

As the heat wave eventually passed and the air cooled, the men crawled farther away from the blast zone and warily eased to their knees, the sights of their weapons sweeping the horizon for the last mercenary. But there was nobody in sight.

"You okay?" Blancanales asked, glancing at his friend.

"Just a flesh wound," Schwarz replied, wiping his moist hand across his Hawaiian shirt.

"There's somebody in the SUV," Lyons said, thumbing in more cartridges. "Could be our missing man."

Nodding in understanding, the other members of Able Team spread out, moving from cover to cover, staying behind rocks, tree stumps and bushes, approaching the civilian car from converging directions. Staying crouched behind the bushes, Blancanales leveled his M-16 and studied the man sitting motionless behind the wheel of the SUV. There was a blood-soaked cloth wrapped around his neck and his dark suit was rendered nearly black from all of the blood it had absorbed from the ghastly wound. His bald head was leaning against the wide window, a string of pinkish drool hanging from his slack mouth.

"Damn, he's dead," Blancanales announced, boldly standing and walking closer to the vehicle. An MP-5 machine pistol lay in his lap, the ejector port blocked by a spent shell. Even though dying of blood loss, the merc had still fired at the Stony Man operatives, trying to protect his partners. A lot of fools thought mercenaries were just muscle for hire, stupid goons who did whatever they were told, but in his experience they were some of the smartest and toughest sons of bitches alive.

"He must have caught one back in the bar," Lyons said, reaching out for the door handle, then paused and took his

hand back. "What do you want to bet this baby is rigged to blow if we try to get inside?"

"No bet," Schwarz said, sweeping an EM scanner across the chassis. The mercs were dead, but there was no satisfaction from their demise. "I'm getting a dozen readings. This thing is set to blow if we sneeze too hard."

"Try not to bleed on it, then."

"Is there a low-jack?" Blancanales asked over a shoulder.

"Not that I can find."

"On a new car like this?" Lyons asked, rubbing his jaw. "Interesting."

"Suspicious is more like it," Blancanales added brusquely. "Snap it along, will you, Hermann?"

Snorting in reply, Schwarz tucked away the scanner, pulled out his cell phone and started taking a fast series of pictures through the closed windows. There were some partially folded maps lying on the backseat, along with a lot of junk-food wrappers and empty plastic soda bottles on the floor mats. Clearly, the men were not a local crew, but had been sent to Memphis from someplace a long way from here. There was also a security light on the dashboard that was dark, but that meant nothing. The light could be easily set to only glow red when it was safe to enter, instead of when the alarm was active.

"Be sure to get the VIN plate on the dashboard," Blancanales suggested, watching the surrounding countryside for any suspicious movements.

Glancing up, Schwarz gave the man an exasperated look and went back to his job. The plates on the SUV were for Texas, but the retaining bolts were new. Clearly the vehicle came from outside the Lone Star state. The VIN should tell them where. The plate was bolted into place and could not be reached without removing the windshield. However, it was

partially covered with a map of Graceland. But that was an old trick of carjackers to prevent the police from doing a scan of the vehicle identification number and running a computer check. The map had to have shifted when the bald merc braked to a halt to set up the ambush.

Making sure the metal barrel of his weapon never made contact with the chassis of the SUV, Lyons studied the dashboard. A fancy CD player was installed there, but there were no jewel cases or loose disks in sight. Craning his neck, he checked the sun visor. People often had a CD stored in nylon slippers there for ease of reach. But again, there was nothing. The CD player was probably a fake, just a false front covering…what, a radio? Could be. The question was, could they reach the device and stay alive.

"Any chance of you defusing the traps?" Lyons asked, resting the Atchisson on a broad shoulder. "Get us inside?"

"If I had my laptop, sure, no problem, but now…" Schwarz shrugged, tucking away the camera phone.

"Fair enough," Lyons said. "Let's check the dead to see if anybody has a key to this rolling bomb."

Moving away from the SUV, the three men went back to the mercenaries and carefully searched through their clothing. All of the mercs had wallets full of cash, but no credit cards. Clearly, they were smart enough to not get trapped the same way they had found the professor. There was lots of identification: driver's license, insurance card, library card and such, including the fake FBI commission booklets, every piece of ID having a different name and home address. Nothing useful there.

Each man also had a cell phone, but the devices were so new they still had the sales sticker on the back. Using a pencil tip, Lyons tried hitting a memory call button and then redial,

but no phone numbers came up. Damn, these guys really knew their business.

"Well, I found this," Blancanales said, bouncing a steel ring in his palm. There was a fob attached to the ring carrying the emblem of the SUV manufacturer and a single key.

"Think we're far enough away?" Lyons asked, squinting up the road at the parked car.

"Only one way to find out," Blancanales said, aiming the electronic fob on the ring at the vehicle and pressing the button to unlock the doors. As expected, the SUV violently exploded, flipping into the air as burning pieces of the driver and the chassis sprayed outward in every direction.

"So much for burning the rope," Lyons said in annoyance as the blackened pieces dropped heavily to the ground like flaming meteorites. Strangely, the explosion looked like a TNT blast from the slight yellow tint to the flames. The mercs had access to military weapons but used TNT to rig their ride? That was odd, to say the least.

"What do we do, buy a Ouija board?" Schwarz snorted, laying down his assault rifle and pulling out a small first-aid pack from a pocket.

"No, we call Jack for a pickup," Lyons said, opening a cell phone. "With any luck, between their descriptions, VIN and fingerprints, Aaron can get a trace to their home base."

"Better than nothing, I suppose," Blancanales said, slipping the key ring into a pocket. Electronic locks sometimes also carried the VIN of a vehicle. It was a long shot, but that's what this whole assignment was rapidly becoming, a series of desperate gambles.

"Not by much," Schwarz added, awkwardly placing a sterile dressing on the wound and pressing down hard to make it stick. After a moment, the blood stopped flowing and the

man eased the muscles in his shoulder as the antibiotics and painkillers on the patch started working.

While placing the call, Lyons mentally reviewed the recent battles. His people were still alive, but the professor was dead, the mercs were dead, and both of the vehicles had been destroyed. Not exactly a stellar day for Able Team. Hopefully, Phoenix Force was doing a lot better in Albania.

CHAPTER ELEVEN

United Nations, Manhattan

The Security Council room was full of people, but dead silent. Nobody was talking with reporters, chatting on a cell phone, telling jokes or flirting with the secretaries.

Normally, the chamber was a bustle of activity, often the conversations were deafeningly loud, punctuated by cursing and brandished fists. The American ambassador felt like he was standing in a museum or a funeral home where the mourners were waiting to inform the family who was dead.

And it could be any of us, the American ambassador mentally corrected. A sobering possibility.

Standing off by himself, the French ambassador was deep in thought studying the painting by Norwegian artist Per Krohg, which spanned the wall of the council chamber.

"The phoenix arising from ashes," the man muttered, walking closer. The room was so still that his footsteps could clearly be heard. Although done in dreary colors, tans and grays, the Krohg picture was universally considered a symbol of hope for a brighter future.

If there was a future. With a sigh, the Frenchman returned to his assigned seat. The 164 chairs for the public were empty, the 118 press chairs were deserted. Even the temporary member seats were vacant: Argentina, Republic of the Congo, Denmark, Ghana, Greece, Japan, Peru, Quajara, Slovakia and Tanzania. Only the superpowers were here for this covert meeting. Although to be honest, the man amended privately, Israel and India had every right to attend, since they also had nuclear weapons. Pakistan and North Korean, too, but they were both total lunatics, in his opinion.

"This blockade is intolerable! We must send in troops!" China raged, looking at the other members of the council as if daring them to challenge the wisdom of the statement. "I say that we should invade Albania! Search every house, every garage, every school, eventually we will find these terrorists and hang them in the streets!"

"During which, old man, they will detonate every nuke in existence," the ambassador from the United Kingdom said slowly. "Before we do anything, we must know the facts of the matter!"

The Chinese ambassador waved that aside. "Facts? We have no time for facts! We must send in missiles!"

"I have heard that Faraday Cages—" the French ambassador started hesitantly.

"Are useless," America interrupted. "Our nuclear laboratory at White Sands was protected by a Faraday and it blew up nonetheless."

"Perhaps there was a flaw in their protective netting?" China said in smug satisfaction.

The American glared. "And perhaps you should stop trying to find an easy way out and knuckle down to the job, sir!"

"Are you calling me a coward?" the Chinese ambassador said quietly.

"No, just a fool."

"Enough!" the Russian ambassador roared, standing at the desk. "Good God, gentlemen, the terrorists would be delighted to see us bickering. We need clear thinking and fast action, or else these madmen will slaughter untold millions of people. Millions? Try billions! Followed by plagues from the unburied corpses, and food shortages from the radioactive cropland unable to grow any plants and…and…" He stared at the other ambassadors. "Nuclear weapons are the absolute last resort, not our first choice!"

"I have been told that Poland has an underground city that can hold almost a million people," France said slowly. "There are nuclear generators, hospitals, schools, factories, everything needed to wait out radiation storms."

"Except for the fact that it's full of Poles," America stated resolutely. "Along with enough heavy ordnance inside the tunnels to keep out any possible invaders. We might be able to kill all of them with enough nerve gas or tactical nukes, but seize the place intact? And in time to do any good?" The man vehemently shook his head. "No, that is impossible."

"I was merely making an observation," France demurred coolly as if scoring a point in a debate.

"I say nuke them, burn Albania to the ground!" China declared once more. "If we all send in missiles, they could not possibly stop every one!"

"But would the few that got through do the job?" America demanded logically. "Or would that only anger them into something unthinkable?"

"But Albania is killing our civilians!"

"No, terrorists are killing our people, not the legal government of Albania."

"Do you think this could be the Fifteen Families?" France

asked with a worried expression. "Seems rather big for a bunch of drug dealers." Albania, Serbia and Montenegro, Kosovo, the whole area was one gigantic headache for France since the Communists departed, leaving the entire region in total chaos.

"This could theoretically be the Fifteen Families," America said slowly. "The matter is being checked into."

"You've sent special forces into Albania?" Russia asked. "But that was strictly forbidden." The man began to smile. "Do you need any help? We have a squad of silent-kill experts ready to go at a moment's notice."

"And who would they kill?" the United Kingdom asked pragmatically. "The Fifteen Families could only be a ruse for the real terrorists, al Qaeda, Hamas... This could even be a plot by one of us to take over the rest of the world."

"Ridiculous." China snorted in contempt.

"True, but even more ridiculous things have been accomplished before in the past," Russia added. "Just imagine the tiny island of Japan attacking the colossal nation of China, the peaceful Dutch stopping the Nazi war machine in its tracks during World War II, or the primitive people of India forcing out the British." He began to count off events on his fingers. "Pearl Harbor, Roarke's Drift, the Battle for Britain, the Battle for Stalingrade, the fall of Troy...all of these things are quite ridiculous, yet they did occur."

Shifting some papers on the table, the Chinese ambassador muttered something under his breath too low to be audible.

"Be that as it may," the United Kingdom continued doggedly. "Something must be done before these madmen ask for the...I mean, demand the access codes to our spy satellites. After that..." The man raised both hands, palms up.

"So any ideas, gentlemen?" America asked, leaning forward on his arms.

"The terrorists must be using a satellite of some kind to aim their…whatever it is being called," France said. "This trigger device must be in orbit, there is no other way it reach so many nuclear arsenals and depots so quickly."

"It should be easy enough to shoot down a single satellite," Russia stated. "Once we know its location. But what are we supposed to do, simply sit here on our *zoopas* and wait for the next attack so that we can find the damned thing?"

"Do you know of any other way to locate the satellite?" China demanded.

The ancient enemies glowered at each other, then forcibly relented. This was neither the time nor the place.

"Okay, we take out all of them," suggested the ambassador from the United Kingdom.

"What was that?" America asked in shock.

"Destroy every satellite in space," the man repeated. "We may not have enough missiles, but there are other ways to kill a satellite. What about using the Dragon? That big laser the Chinese used once before."

"That was not us, but a radical splinter of Red Star," the ambassador declared formally. "And the Dragon is dead, smashed to pieces by American Special Forces. The Chinese government has no laser capable of striking a target in high orbit."

Not knowing if that was true, the American ambassador kept his peace. He had only heard rumors about the incident and did not know how much to believe. Delta Force was good, but he knew for a fact they'd been on a mission in Colombia when the Dragon was destroyed. And there had been other similar incidents around the globe; the slaughter of the Inter-

national Conference on Terrorism in Sri Lanka, the destruction of the European Space Agency headquarters in Brussels.
Did America have some sort of ultracovert antiterrorist organization? It was possible, but highly unlikely.

"So exactly how long would it take," he said, choosing the
words carefully, "for everybody to get everything they have
online and ready to strike at a target in space?"

Slowly, the worried and frightened faces around the conference table began to clear and all of the ambassadors reached
for the secure-line telephones that directly connected to the
leader of their nation.

Ptarmigan Base, North America

A DARK SILHOUETTE TRAVELED slowly across a pool of moon-
light reflected on the surface of the huge lake. The movements
of the man in the canoe were steady, stroking the paddle once
on each side to keep the little craft moving straight for the shore.

As the flattened bottom scraped on the muddy shallows,
Andrew Baldwin stepped into the icy-cold water and quickly
dragged the aluminum-hulled boat toward the shore. In spite
of his thick boots, the freezing temperature of the lake seeped
into his bones in only seconds and he rushed onto dry ground
with subdued splashing.

Setting the canoe on its side, Baldwin stomped his feet to
try to restore circulation. Goddamn, that lake was cold! he
thought. It made the Black Mountains of Albania feel practi-
cally warm in comparison, and that was really saying something. He remembered as a small boy hearing his father tell
stories about going into the mountains to break off some air
to carry back home and use to keep their apartment cool
during the summer. Baldwin always thought it was just a joke

until he visited the Black Mountains and damn near died of frostbite on the first day of summer. As the old saying went, the only good thing about Albania was leaving it quickly.

After feeling returned to his toes, Baldwin removed some packs from the canoe and laid them out on the frosty ground. Taking a fat nylon disk by the edge, he snapped it hard with a jerk of his wrist. A small tent sprang into shape, and he set it near a small depression in the ground lined with rocks that he regularly used for a campfire. There was no way to hide the canoe, so establishing a campsite was the best way to disguise his real purpose here.

Placing some fishing poles on a large boulder and tossing some wood into the firepit, Baldwin inspected the tableau and nodded in satisfaction. Good enough. Blowing into his cupped hands, he walked the perimeter of the crude campsite, checking for signs of others having visited the remote location. But none of the trip wires had been disturbed, and the digital camera hidden inside a dead tree showed only animals on the plasma screen readout. Satisfied, he deleted the JPEGs, and set the camera on automatic again. Any movement in front of the tree would be silently photographed. The man would have preferred a Colt .38 Auto-Sentry, but that sort of computerized machine-gun emplacement would have been a dead giveaway to any federal agent who stumbled across the sophisticated machine. It was better to stay low and keep out of sight, until America was subjugated properly and Albania ruled the world. Then the men could come out into the open and be hailed as the new kings of North America.

Such a lowly thought, Baldwin mentally chuckled, and the reality of the matter was only days away. Maybe even less if that old fool Slobodan didn't get in the way. The head of the Fifteen Families would be the first to go up against the wall

when Sakir Elsani finally took over. And he would not be the last.

There came a splash from behind and Baldwin spun around with a silenced Walther PPK .38 pistol in his hand, his finger on the trigger.

Standing in the shallows was a huge grizzly bear, a thrashing trout impaled on its sharp claws. Keeping his Walther aimed at the monster, Baldwin watched with a pounding heart as the beast slowly lumbered away, eating the fish while it was still alive. As it disappeared into the dark forest, Baldwin let out a sigh of relief and clicked the safety back on the snug .38 pistol. The Walther was perfect for killing people, but almost useless against a grizzly. There was some bear spray in his pocket as even military-grade pepper spray had no effect on the colossal animals. Different biochemistry from people, he sagely guessed, tucking away the gun. Unfortunately, the bear pepper spray had a very low success rate, about 50-50, and was to be used only in a dire emergency. In his backpack was a Neostad shotgun loaded with fléchettes that would have blown the bear in two, but then there would have been the problem of cleaning up the hairy corpse afterward. A twelve-foot-tall grizzly bear could easily weigh in excess of a thousand pounds. That was not something he could drag over a hill or roll into the lake by himself. The task would require a vehicle of some kind, and all motorized transport was strictly monitored in this preserve. Even the larger boats only had electric engines powered by packs of bulky batteries.

Environmentalists, bah! Baldwin sneered. What good was accomplished in not littering the woods when governments set off nuclear bombs on a regular basis? Americans were mad, that was all there was to it. But that would soon change after they took over. And if the worst happened, eventually the

radioactive death cloud would dissipate, then Elsani and his people would return from the island of Tasmania where huge stores of food, equipment and weapons were already stashed in the abandoned gold mines. There was still old minuscule amounts of gold in the surrounding ore, but not enough to make it worthwhile to extract. But there was enough to make the mines excellent sanctuaries from radiation. Gold and lead were only a single electron away from each other, and while lead was superior at stopping hard radiation, gold would do just fine if used in significant amounts. And the Tasmania mines were very, very deep.

Taking a large bag from the mound of supplies, Baldwin went into the bushes and removed his heavy parka and fleece-lined jumpsuit to don a surplus Russian scuba suit. Strapping a rebreather unit onto his back, the man slipped on a protective rubber hood, a full-face diving mask and a pair of Thinsulate gloves. Then he dropped the Walther into a plastic bag, closed it tight, and tucked the weapon safely away in a holster on his hip. It would be useless under water, but the man felt naked without a weapon at his command.

Tucking a set of swim fins under an arm, Baldwin checked the air flow on the mouthpiece of the rebreather and then walked directly into the frigid lake. There was a sharp drop-off after a couple of yards, and he stood on the edge of the precipice impatiently waiting for the thermal packs in his suit to activate. Soon a gentle warmth emanated from the strategically placed eight packs, and he stepped off the drop to sink into the cold blackness.

Clumsily, he put on the swim fins, then checked the glowing digital screen of the miniature GPS device on his wrist. Moving off at an easy pace, Baldwin swam through the inky water ignoring the shapes that moved in the shadowy depths.

There were a lot of fish in the lake, and even more plant life, but none of it was dangerous to a swimmer. After about a mile, he cracked a chemical glow stick and look around. Less than a hundred yards away was a sunken ruin of a nineteenth-century paddle wheeler. Using that as a visual guide, Baldwin followed a zigzag course through a field of boulders to finally reach an wide overhang of stone. Diving underneath the submerged escarpment, Baldwin realized there was less than a yard of space between the stone and the rocky floor of the lake. He felt a brief rush of claustrophobia before suddenly reaching open water again. Angling upward, he saw a dim light from above and pocketed the glow stick before heading for the surface. The thermal packs and the deep-sea diving suit held back most of the cold, but the very blackness of the lake seemed to radiate an unnatural coldness that seeped into his soul.

Reaching a set of aluminum stairs, Baldwin took off the swim fins and proceed up the steps until breaking into the air.

"Hold it right there," a man commanded, and there came the sound of an arming bolt being worked. "One wrong move and you're dead."

Staying motionless, Baldwin saw several Dragoons standing on a concrete apron, their gloved hands holding AK-47 assault rifles, the 30 mm grenade launcher looking like a cannon from this angle.

"Password," one of the Dragoons demanded, leveling the Kalashnikov.

Moving slowly, Baldwin moved the face mask and then the mouthpiece of the rebreather. "Shut the fuck up, fool, you can see that it's me," he snarled impatiently, grabbing on to the aluminum rails and pulling himself out of the water.

The guard wavered for a moment, then clicked the safety

back on and shouldered the weapon. "Sorry, sir, it's just that we…"

Grabbing the aluminum rails, Baldwin rose from the water and stepped onto the apron before pulling the Walther from a holster on his equipment belt and firing twice. The plastic bag around the pistol expanded like a balloon from the muzzle-blast, the thin plastic disintegrating from the twin lances of flame. The pair of .38 HEAT rounds streaked visibly through the air before slamming into the throat of the Dragoon. Stumbling backward, the man clutched the hideous wound with both hands, blood spraying out from the ruptured arteries. Ruthlessly, Baldwin fired twice more, hitting the guard in the groin, crimson spraying out from each impact. With a ragged sigh, the Dragoon slumped to the concrete and went still, the Kalashnikov rolling from his limp glove.

"Drop the gun!" another Dragoon snarled, shoving the fluted muzzle of the AK-47 into the kidney of Baldwin. The foggy words were visible in the cold air for a few moments.

Standing a few yards away where he could cover both men and the pool of water, the other guard watched and waited, saying nothing.

Doing as he was ordered, Baldwin released the weapon and it hit the concrete with a metallic clatter.

The guard kicked the pistol away. "Okay, now I want the password, or else I'm going to blow off your fucking—"

"Fat man," Baldwin said calmly.

The Dragoon paused for a moment. "Little Boy," he replied in Albanian.

"Einstein," Baldwin answered in English.

Across the cave, the other guard gave a sigh of relief and lowered his assault rifle.

"Sorry, sir," the first Dragoon apologized, removing the

barrel of the AK-47 assault rifle from the scuba suit. "But we were thrown for a moment when you killed Dimitros…"

"He was an idiot and deserved to die!" Baldwin snarled, "Nobody is allowed into the cavern without the proper password and countersign. Not even Carter or Elliot!"

That took the men a moment to translate. Sam Elliot was the name being used by Sakir Elsani, and Richard Carter was the one chosen by Ratho Curuvija. Keeping the same initials was supposed to make it easier for the scientists to remember their new identities. The man standing in front of them in the scuba suit was Agim Balat, now being called Andrew Baldwin. Yes, that was it.

"Now, help me get off this rebreather," Baldwin commanded, turning. "Then get rid of the body and send word for his whole family to be punished for this lapse. We do not tolerate mistakes!"

"Sir, I—I'm his brother," the second guard said hesitantly.

Releasing the chest harness, Baldwin waited, but there was no request for clemency, and the man's hands stayed off the trigger of the weapon. Excellent. Intelligence should always be rewarded.

"So, did you love your brother?" Baldwin asked, sliding off the heavy rebreather.

The guard seemed flustered by the odd question. "I…well, of course, sir."

"Good," Baldwin said, pushing back the rubber hood. "Then there will be no punishment for your family. But inform of them of what happened, and why they are being spared."

"Yes, sir!" the man replied gratefully. "Thank you, sir."

Baldwin regarded the young man carefully. "You are the junior of the guards?"

The man glanced at the other Dragoon placing the re-

breather in a charging rack set along the frost-covered stone wall. "Yes, sir, I am."

"When we find a replacement for this fool," Baldwin said, nudging the corpse with the damp toe of his shoe. "Then you—" he addressed the man at the wall "—shall be promoted to sergeant, and you shall became a corporal."

They both got a promotion? "Yes, sir!"

Shrugging in reply, Baldwin started down a rock tunnel, the frost on the walls thickening into a solid sheath of white ice. Carrots and sticks, he noted. Men were like donkeys, beat them, then pet them, and they'd do whatever you asked.

Following the tunnel through a maze of corridors and spiraling ramps, Baldwin reached a set of burnished steel doors and thumped it hard with a fist. As the metal pulled back, a delicious wave of warm air flooded out and the man breathed in deeply.

The room was covered with thermal paneling and a hundred thermometers, the needles on the mechanical gauges quivering deep inside a blue zone. Standing near a control console were two men dressed in jumpsuits, the top unzipped and folded down to their waists showing sweat-stained undershirts. Both of the men were holding 9 mm Steyr machine pistols. From underneath the stubby barrels extended a brilliant red laser beam that danced on the rubbery chest of Baldwin's scuba suit.

"Turn those damn things off!" he commanded irritably, making a gesture. "You two are worse shots than the family butler!"

"Which is why we use the lasers," Sam Elliot said in Albanian, taking his finger off the trigger. Instantly the laser beam vanished.

"We heard gunshots," Richard Carter said tersely, his eyes straying constantly to the closed doors. "Were you followed?"

"Don't be absurd," Baldwin said, taking off his gloves. He flexed his fingers in the warmth with obvious relish. "One of the guards made a mistake, so I removed him and assigned another in his place, that's all."

"That's all?" Elliot demanded, his voice rising slightly. "Good God, do you know how few guards we have at this establishment! If the Americans find out that we're here—"

"But they won't find us, if the proper safety precautions are followed. Understand?" Baldwin snapped, removing the thermal packs from the pockets set into the rubber suit. Unfortunately the packs could not be turned on and off at will. Once started, they continued to generate heat until their crystals were exhausted. With some regret, he dropped them into a metal waste can.

"Yes, sir, of course," Carter muttered, hurriedly tucking away the Steyr. "We meant no disrespect, sir."

Opening a wall cabinet, Baldwin nailed the man with a hard look, then smiled. Carrot and sticks, again. "Of course, my old friend. No harm done, eh?"

As the scientist murmured agreement, Baldwin opened some cardboard boxes in the cabinet and extracted replacement thermal packs to insert them into the suit. If anything did happen, he would have to leave quickly. Through the lake was the only way to reach the outside world, and without the packs he would freeze to death long before reaching the surface of the glacial lake.

"How are things progressing?" Baldwin asked, peeling off the suit and hanging it from a wooden peg jutting from the wall. The big man flexed his arms, relishing the freedom of movement, then he took the Walther from the rubber holster and slipped it into a snug nylon holster at the small of his back.

"All systems are go," Carter said, scowling at the multiple

computer screens lining the console. His memory was not quite eidetic, but close enough for him to multitask at the complex job of running the Icarus. "Temperature is high in the core, but still within operational tolerances."

"Not too high, is it?" Baldwin demanded, brushing back his damp hair. Already the curls were starting to rise back into place. He knew he was a handsome man, and often used that to open doors for business deals, especially when they involved a beautiful woman.

"Oh, no, sir, just a few degrees above zero," Elliot replied, pointing at a thermometer. "It must have rained recently on the surface. That always causes a minor flux, but we'll soon be back to normal."

"It better," Baldwin growled in warning, going to a kitchenette and pouring himself a cup of black coffee.

Here in the heavily insulated control room the scientists who operated the Icarus lived in relative comfort, unlike the poor guards walking patrols through the icy tunnels of the prehistoric glacier. Taking a sip, Baldwin recalled how he had once sat through a long boring talk by the two men explaining how a supercomputer was composed of superconductors, wires that offered no resistance to electrical impulses. This made the machine a thousand times more powerful than a conventional computer, and thus able to solve problems before other computers could even realize there was something wrong. The hitch was that for the superconductors to work, they needed to be kept icy cold, as cold as possible. Liquid nitrogen was normally used in laboratories and military installations. However, Homeland Security keep an uncomfortably close watch on any shipment of liquid nitrogen. Even the small ten-pound canisters sent to high schools for science teachers to use in classroom demonstrations. So liquid nitro-

gen had been replaced with Mother Nature and the Ptarmigan Glacier.

Strolling to the console, Baldwin took a seat and looked over the confusing array of buttons, switches, dials and keyboards. One was standard, but another was composed only of mathematical symbols. Did that operate the Icarus, or the supercomputers surrounding them?

"Prepare the Icarus," he said, holding the mug in his hands and letting the warmth seep into his fingers. "We're moving up the schedule to make the UN Security Council capitulate faster."

"To do what?" Elliot asked in confusion. "Sir, I don't know that English word."

"Surrender," Carter answered snidely in Albania. "It means to make them surrender faster."

Elliot sniffed at the rebuke, but said nothing.

"Something big this time," Baldwin said, studying a vector graphic map of the world. "Something that will really rattle their teeth. What's on the list?"

"Well, South Africa has a neutron bomb," Carter began hesitantly, looking at a monitor scrolling with numbers. "And it seems to be armed."

"Anything else?"

"Nothing really big, no, sir," Elliot demurred, typing a few commands onto a keyboard. "Nothing of the size you want. Just more tactical nukes. Most of them in out-of-the-way military bases or on ships far at sea."

"What about Oak Ridge laboratories?" Baldwin demanded. "That should have plenty of nukes, and it is very close to several major cities."

"We've tried again and again, sir," Carter said, frowning deeply. "They either have some new sort of shield protecting the nukes or…"

"Or else it's not exactly located where it is supposed to be," Elliott finished. "There is a small possibility that the U.S. government has lied about the location of the atomic lab, and it is located somewhere else in Tennessee."

"Really? That means they really don't want it damaged," Baldwin said with a chuckle. "Excellent. Make that your next target. Keep sweeping the entire state until you find the lab and blow it off the face of the Earth."

"Yes, sir," Elliot replied crisply, then added, "However, that may take some time. We have to realign most of the northern satellites—"

"I don't care what the technical problems are!" Baldwin snarled. "Just get it done, and soon!"

Humming in thought for a minute, Carter lowered a pocket calculator. "If successful, I estimate a death toll of ten to twenty million, sir."

Sipping his coffee, Baldwin said nothing for a long moment.

"Yes," he spoke at last. "That will do just fine."

CHAPTER TWELVE

USS: Harper's Ferry

Moving at only half speed, barely ten knots, the U.S. Navy transport ship cut through the choppy waters of the South Atlantic. Standing on the bow, the executive officer removed his cap and let the salty spray hit him in the face for a moment, then donned the cap again and started aft along the gunwale feeling greatly refreshed. Better than a hot shower and a cup of coffee, he thought.

Before being assigned to the transport, the XO had never heard of the West Virginia mining town before. But by the end of the first day, he knew everything about the place. Sailors love to talk. It was the primary recreation on any Navy ship.

The small mining town of Harper's Ferry was famous, or infamous, depending upon your viewpoint. Located at the headwaters of the Potomac River, during the Civil War the town had been of immense strategic value with its shipping docks, iron mines, coal oil and food from the surrounding farms. There had also been a Union Navy dock with several heavily armed riverboats in dock as protection from pirates,

and the Confederates, of course. In the early months of the war, President Jefferson Davis ordered his troops to seize the vital town and raise the Stars and Bars. They did so with amazing ease. Immediately, President Lincoln sent General Hooker to reclaim the town. But the Confederates took it back the next week, and then the Union troops reclaimed it the week after that.

Wartorn and battered, the little mining town soon held the questionable distinction of being the most invaded town in the world, and before the Civil War was finally over, Harper's Ferry had been seized almost fifty times by the North and South. The *New York Times* carried the story that the local bar owner would look out his bedroom window every morning to check the color of the flag flying above the town square, and then open his bar either wearing a butternut-gray cap or a navy blue, depending on who controlled the town.

A strange history for a town, and for the ship that bore its name, the XO mused dodging around a .50-caliber machine-gun platform. The state of West Virginia didn't exist until Lincoln created it by presidential decree when he needed an extra congressman to help swing a vote his way. The crafty old bastard, he thought.

The vessel had taken on a cargo of nine hundred boxes containing who knew what, the XO mused, hurrying past a depth charge launcher. The 350 men on board had a million ideas what the *Harper* might be carrying, from a dismantled bridge to a frozen army of busty Hollywood starlets, but nobody actually knew. The boxes had arrived welded closed and with orders to handle with extreme care. The fact that the containers were kind of shaped like coffins cheered nobody, and only helped fuel the wild speculations.

Normally, the *Harper* carried a dozen LAV-25 Piranha-class assault vehicles, along with two huge LCAC, landing craft air cushion, better known in the civilian world as hover-crafts. A transport full of transport, as the old joke went.

"Sir!" the XO said in greeting, giving a crisp salute.

Standing at the railing, the captain slowly turned his head and nodded in reply. "So, are we hard, son?"

The first time the sailor heard the phrase, he had been ter-ribly confused. Seafaring slang had a logic all of its own, and landlubbers never got it right.

"Hard as a prayer in hell, sir," the XO replied crisply. "All six of the MK 36 chaff mortars are loaded and ready to go, same as both of the Phalanx 20 mm Cheese…" He paused in embarrassment, then carried onward. "The same for the Phalanx Gatling guns. All six of the .50-caliber machine guns are manned and primed, and both of the 25 mm machine guns are ready for action."

Swaying to the motion of the ship, the captain gave a half smile. "You were going to call them Cheese Whiz guns, weren't you?" he accused gently.

"Well, yes, sir," the executive officer admitted honestly. "I know that the designation CISW should be pronounced as 'sea whiz,' but you know how it is with sailors, sir."

"I surely do, and Cheese Whiz is a lot funnier name for the weapons. Lord knows, I've heard sillier nicknames."

Diplomatically, the XO cleared his throat. "Sir, now that we're alone, may I respectfully ask about our cargo?"

Glancing over a shoulder, the captain briefly studied the canvas sheet covering the squat metal boxes filling the cargo bay. That should have been full of armored personnel carriers and hovercraft, or armed Marines ready for battle. Now the *Harper* was loaded with squat steel boxes lacking military

code numbers, bar codes, color stripes or anything else to even vaguely identify the contents.

"What's our distance?" the captain asked, looking back to the sea.

"Three hundred miles off the Florida Keys, sir."

"Far enough. Okay, son, we're carrying nukes." The captain sighed, pushing back his cap. "To be blunt, the big ones. Hydrogen and plutonium bombs."

The XO opened both eyes wide, but said nothing for a moment. Their hold was full of hydrogen bombs? He had personally overseen the loading of the cargo and knew there were exactly 914 of the big boxes. The *Harper* was stuffed to the maximum. They couldn't fit a spare bag of milk on board. "Skipper," he began softly, "this must be—"

"Most of the U.S. nuclear arsenal, yes."

The XO started to ask why, but instinctively knew better. Some things a good sailor didn't inquire about. He might get a truthful answer. "Are there any special orders, sir?"

"Yes and no." The captain grunted. "We are to sail around randomly, keeping strict radio silence, not even using radar or sonar, until Atlantic Command or the White House commands us to come home."

"Aye, aye, sir," the XO said, licking dry lips. "But if the scuttlebutt is true about somebody detonating nukes from a distance…"

"Son, if any one of these babies blow, then we will be afforded a direct view of the bottom of the ocean for about a millisecond."

"Aye, sir." The XO exhaled, feeling the responsibility settle on his shoulders like a lead-lined mantel. "Well, I guess it's better that a couple hundred sailors die than a million civilians."

Wiping the spray from his face, the captain glanced sideways. "Try a hundred million," he corrected gruffly, "and you'd be a lot closer to the real figures."

In the far distance, a dark shape appeared briefly on the horizon and then dipped below the sea and out of sight once more.

"Sir, what if another ship comes close, are we to evade, or use force to keep them away?" the XO asked, squinting for any sign of the other vessel. But it was gone.

"We are to evade," the captain muttered, tightening his grip on the railing. "And if that fails, and the crew of the other ship attempts to cripple us, or storm on board…then we self-detonate. Our cargo must not be taken intact."

There was an awkward moment between the two naval officers, with only the sounds of the waves slapping against the hull and the muted roar of the engines disturbing the thick silence.

"You mean, that we are ordered to detonate the scuttling charges, sir?" the XO asked hopefully.

The captain looked at the man hard. "No, son, we don't detonate those." He turned back to the languid sea, deep in his private thoughts.

CHAPTER THIRTEEN

Cartagena, Colombia

A warm breeze rustled the jungle trees, making the hanging vines move as if they were live snakes. Monkeys chattered in the tree-tops and somewhere off in the distance came the sound of a human scream, followed by the roar of a chain saw. The entire jungle went silent from the noise, and even the breeze seemed to pause for moment. The screaming came again, higher pitched this time, more wild and desperate, barely human. Then a large-caliber gun boomed and the shrieking mercifully stopped.

On the veranda of a palatial mansion, several old men in white suits and Panama hats sat at a black wrought iron table, the glass top covered with fresh bottles of beer and a half-empty box of cigars. The mansion was made of gleaming white stucco, with fancy iron railing at every open window. Grim men with assault rifles walked along the top of the high concrete wall surrounding the estate, with more guards situated on the rooftop, each of carrying a bolt-action sniper rifle or a U.S. Army Stinger missile launcher.

"So let me get this straight, amigo," the drug lord said

slowly around a cigar, the dark smoke trickling out of his nose. "The Fifteen Families are offering us total immunity from the DEA of the United States?"

"That is correct, sir," the liaison to Albania said. "The DEA, CIA, FBI, all of them. The Fifteen Families absolutely guarantee it."

"I dislike guarantees," the drug lord muttered, removing the cigar to inspect the glowing tip. Just like cocaine, these hand-rolled Cuban cigars were outlawed in the United States. Why were the Yankees so much against pleasure? Life was hard, often brutal and uncaring. If a little smoke, or some dust, made a man's day easier to bear, why should anybody else care? It was absurd.

"So how much do they want for this immunity?" a third man asked, both hands folded on the glass table as if at prayer. There were numerous religious tattoos on his arms, and a jeweled crucifix hung around his throat.

"Ten tons of product every month," the Albanian liaison said, lifting a bottle of beer and taking a long, slow drink. He set it down, the beer foamed up and over the sides of the brown glass.

The men around the table registered surprise at the amount, but said nothing out loud. The amount was huge, but not impossible to fill. The amount of cocaine demanded by the Albanians lent a note of credence to the offer. If this was some sort of trick by the Albanians merely to get a free shipment, it would mean open war between to the two cartels and that would mean hundreds of street soldiers dead and the sale of product drastically slowed for weeks, maybe months. That could translate into millions of dollars. Men could die, that was part of life, but the loss of business was intolerable.

"We shall need some sort of goodwill gesture on the part of the Fifteen," the chief drug lord said slowly.

Finishing off the beer, the liaison nodded in understanding. "Of course. They shall let you know in a few days when you can send across the first truckload. That one will be *gratis,* for free, but after that…" He rubbed his fingertips together.

A long minute passed, then another.

"Done," the chief drug lord said resolutely. "We'll start preparing the sample load for shipment tomorrow."

"And the DEA will really do nothing to stop us?" another old man asked, leaning forward eagerly.

Smiling, the liaison took another bottle of cold beer. "Stop you?" he repeated. "The U.S. Army will step aside and salute as you drive by."

Slowly, the members of the Colombian cartel started grinning at such a thought, and began making plans for a new distribution system throughout the continental United States and Canada.

Las Vegas, Nevada

THE DRIVE FROM THE Henderson Executive Airport was smooth and boring, Route 146 was devoid of billboards and gas stations as it fed the flow of traffic through the residential section of Sin City. Jack Grimaldi had picked up the team in a venerable Bell helicopter and flown them directly to a small unnamed airport in Alabama where they'd switched to a Cessna Sky-Master. There the team rested until hearing from Price that the next location to check was in Nevada. The team tried not to take that as a bad omen. They had once fought a nuclear terrorist on top of Hoover Dam, and almost died in an atomic blast. Nevada was not a state they recalled with fond memories.

Lyons picked up North 15. The traffic was light at that early hour of the morning, mostly limousines ferrying people to the

airport and a couple of buses hauling people back to Los Angeles from the plush gambling tables.

Checking the GPS map on the dashboard of the rented Cadillac, Lyons saw a soft glow infuse the horizon long before the neon splendor of the city came into view. The skyscraper array of casinos rose from the neon sprawl of Las Vegas like a Technicolor Stonehenge, and towering among the electric splendor was a shimmering pyramid.

Pyramids again, the man thought ruefully. How many of the things were there in North America anyway? The oldest known structures in the world were quickly becoming the most popular.

"And that must be the Luxor casino," Schwarz said, pointing at a blinking column of light that stabbed upward from the apex of the structure.

"How come the light isn't spreading out?" Blancanales asked curiously, folding away a map. "That's not a laser, is it?"

"Bet your ass it is." Schwarz grinned, leaning both arms on the top of the front seat. "The damn thing is visible for a hundred miles." His arm was still sore, and a little stiff, from the graze, but nowhere near painful enough to keep him from finishing the mission.

"A light that bright must be a terror to pilots," Lyons guessed, taking an exit for Interstate 93. The team wasn't heading for Las Vegas this trip, but northward to the White Pines Mountains, just past Yucca Flats and the Las Vegas Nuclear Testing Range. There hadn't been any reports of nuclear detonations there recently, but the man kept a close watch on the miniature Geiger counter attached to the dashboard with a strip of Velcro.

"The laser? Yep. Or rather, it was. The Luxor casino owners had to tone the beam down. It was mucking up the flight paths of commercial flights and flocks of birds." He grinned.

"That's not good for business to have a thousand geese flying over the city and, ah, relieving themselves."

"No shit?"

"Actually, lots if it. That's why they modulated the laser."

"Must have been a boom time for car washes."

"And hat sales, too," Lyons added with a soft chuckle, taking a curve and leaving Las Vegas behind. The town seemed to be a combination of casinos and amusement parks these days. Vegas had certainly changed a lot since the big corporations took over and replaced the Mob. Whether it was for better or worse, he really couldn't decide.

Heading northward, Lyons saw little traffic going in this direction, so he set the cruise control and reached over to a plastic chest and extracted a sandwich and bottle of iced coffee. It was going to be a long drive to the Jose Six mines.

The VIN of the SUV had proved useless, the sequence totally random and belonging to no car in existence. Plus, Aaron Kurtzman and his team also found no reference on the fingerprints of the dead mercenaries or the cell phones. But the spent shell casings had given up some information. Most of the 9 mm and .50-caliber rounds had been a bulk purchase by an ammunition distributor, and sold across half the nation. But the 25 mm shells had been a specialty purchase by the Jose Six Corporation, which apparently owned nothing but a post-office box in Las Vegas and an abandoned mine in the White Pine Mountain range. A thulium mine. That wasn't a positive ID, but more than good enough for Able Team to check out the place. Especially after Kurtzman ran an anagram check and discovered that a major river in Albania was the Vijose, and VI stood for the number six in Roman numerals. Obviously the name was somebody's idea of a joke that had just backfired on the terrorists.

Passing a brightly illuminated billboard, Lyons scowled as he read an announcement that prostitution was illegal in Clark County. Now, what was the point of that? he thought. Ten yards later there was another sign proclaiming the end of Clarke County, and just past that was a neon pink sign announcing that it was only a hundred yards to the Chicken Ranch. What the establishment offered was not mentioned, but to any interested parties it was painfully obvious.

"Las Vegas, the city that never sleeps," Lyons snorted in disdain. "Alone, that is."

Sitting in the passenger seat, Blancanales turned around fast. "Carl! You made a joke! Did you feel okay, need to lie down or something?"

Lyons's reply mainly consisted of two words.

Just then, a whitewashed building resembling an old-fashioned motel came into view. Sitting on lawn chairs alongside the swimming pool were a dozen women in bikinis and lingerie. They laughed and waved as the Cadillac drove by, several of them dropping their skimpy tops to display a wealth of feminine charms.

"Whew, now, that's that I call advertising," Schwarz said, rubbing his sore arm. "At the very least, you have to admire their gumption."

Rummaging in the cooler for a cola, Blancanales laughed. "Gumption, is that what the kids are calling it these days?"

"Yes, it is, Grandpa. Now, shut up and eat your gruel."

Crumpling up the sandwich wrap with one hand, Lyons stuffed it into a garbage bag and took the wheel in both hands again. Oddly, the busty prostitutes had made him think about the bartender in Memphis. Gadgets had liked her a lot, that much was clear, but the man hadn't said a word about her so far. That was just part of their job. Sometimes, innocent people

died in a gun battle, and there was not a damn thing they could do about it but keep the body count to an absolute minimum.

As a cop in Los Angeles, Carl Lyons had seen a lot of young police officers never get over that hard fact. They weren't gods, or supermen, just cops walking a beat and doing the best they could to maintain the peace. But sometimes mistakes happened and good people died, while the criminals escape unharmed. It was a bitch, but the cold, iron truth. Some police officers quit over such incidents, or transferred to clerical and never walked the street again. It took a special mentality to view everybody you saw as a potential enemy and a potential victim needing to be saved, at the exact same time.

Lyons knew that some of the older cops had jokingly referred to themselves as garbage men, because all they ever saw was the refuse of humanity: the pimps, wife beaters, muggers, car thieves, killers and rapists. A soldier grew hard in the field, but learned to relax on R and R, or at the barracks with their buddies. However, a cop was never off duty, even when he or she wasn't wearing the uniform. The job became your life.

In the distant past, Lyons had been at a party, a corporate picnic with some friends where everybody was getting drunk and telling old jokes as if they were brand-new. Then somebody mentioned that he was a cop and a circle of silence expanded around the man until he knew the party was over for him. The people there were not criminals under any definition of the word, maybe a few cheated on their taxes or had tossed a parking ticket, infractions hardly worth noting. But all they could see was the badge and the gun, not Carl Lyons. He'd left the party and started spending more and more time practicing on the firing range. Cops and soldiers, they were both vital to the community, and both totally misunderstood by the very people they protected.

There came a musical snippet from the rear seat and Schwarz unearthed his replacement laptop. "Turn here," he said, reading the screen. "We're about twenty miles away."

"Away from what?" Lyons snapped, going off the road. The hum of the tires become a steady crunch as the van started along a gravel road.

"Nothing," Schwarz replied, his face illuminated by the computer screen. "There's nothing near us but rocks, sand and some more rocks."

"Join the Army, see the world," Blancanales muttered, hauling up his M-16 combination assault rifle and dropping the clip to check the load.

This was supposed to be a soft probe, a silent in and out, without the Albanians even knowing they had been there. But just in case, the M-16 was loaded with HEAT rounds, high-explosive, armor-piercing, tracers. When fired they resembled something from a sci-fi movie, streaking through the air, hitting with hard bangs and splashing around the sizzling white phosphorous. They were dirty rounds, and the M-16 would need a major cleaning after even a few clips. But for general destruction, there was nothing more deadly.

Turning off the headlights, Lyons slipped on a pair of night-vision goggles and switched them to starlite mode. The darkness vanished and world became tinted a muted green.

Hopefully, this would let them get close to the mine without the terrorists knowing it. Unless they had radar or proximity sensors buried in the ground. Whoever was behind these attacks, the Albanians, KGB, the Fifteen Families, they had a lot of resources and state-of-the-art technology.

Slowly, the hours passed and the stars came out, filling the heavens with a twinkling blanket. Soon, the flat desert was replaced with low ground swells that rapidly increased in size

until the van was driving between jagged hills. Sharp outcroppings stabbed at the sky and windy arroyos stretched across the landscape like the claw marks of some mythical beast.

A rusty iron bridge spanned a dry river and Lyons slowed and drove across listening carefully for any sounds of the supports giving way. The old bridge creaked and groaned under the weight of the Cadillac, but the team reached the other side without incident.

"Clear," Blancanales said, checking the EM scanner in his hands. "No sensors on the bridge."

"Radar is clear," Schwarz added from the backseat, a luminous arm sweeping the screen of the computer. "But I guess that makes sense. This close to the Las Vegas Gunnery Range and Nellis Air Force Base, any radar source would be discovered with a few minutes and the troops would come pouring in like D-Day at Normandy."

"Nellis is part of the U.S. Space Command, right?" Lyons asked, easing the Caddy a little bit faster. A dark shape darted across the gravel road and he almost slammed on the brakes until realizing it was a coyote.

"Sure, it's full of stealth bombers."

"Any nukes?" he asked pointedly.

Blancanales looked out the window and into the dark night. "Lord, I hope not," he said softly.

A few more miles down the road Schwarz called a halt, and Lyons drove the Cadillac off the crude road and parked it near a tall group of cactus. "Okay, from here we walk," he said, killing the engine and putting the keys into the ashtray.

His partners donned night-vision goggles and, sliding on backpacks, the three men started to trot across the rocky ground, staying in a loose combat formation, their heads moving constantly back and forth scanning the night for anything suspicious.

After a while, they slowed at the sight of a dirt road coming off the gravel road, the entrance blocked by a splintery wooden barricade. There was a sign, but it was impossible to read, the paint was so old and faded. Staying clear of the dirt road, the team ran alongside, Blancanales using an EM scanner to check for sensors or land mines.

With the coming of the night, the heat of the day had quickly departed, and a chill had settled over the land. Reaching an escarpment, the Stony Man commandos paused to pull on camouflage-color windbreakers, then kept going.

Suddenly a shadow figure moved ahead of the team and they dropped low, holding their breaths as the thing moved off with a soft electric purr. Switching their goggles to infrared, the night turned black once more and they clearly saw a man riding a motorcycle. He was also wearing goggles, and had a rifle strapped across his back, the muzzle tipped with a bulbous sound suppressor.

Quickly sweeping the radio frequencies, Schwarz confirmed that nobody was on the air calling for help. The bike rider had to have missed the team when they'd stopped behind the escarpment to don their jackets.

Waiting until the man was out of sight, the team swept forward quickly, using the natural contours of the ground to mask their approach as much as possible.

Cresting a low rill, they paused and looked down upon the ruins of an old mine. Several wooden buildings stood near the large hole in the ground, the corroded remains of a hoist standing above the mouth of the mine, loose steel chains dangling down to clink softly in the chilly desert breeze.

Switching from starlite to infrared, and then to UV, Lyons could find nothing unusual about the place. It looked exactly like what it was supposed to be, an abandoned mining site.

Then he caught a wave of heat coming from a flat section of ground surrounded by the old, ramshackle buildings. It took a moment, then he understood the ground was actually the roof of a large building covered with sand and cactus to make it resemble flat land. The wooden buildings around the area were obviously serving as part of the disguise, hiding the square structure from anybody at ground level. Only from the rill could the difference in heights be discerned. A building within a circle of buildings. Sounded like their boys, all right.

Tapping the shoulders of the other men, Lyons pointed out the structure. Focusing his goggles in that direction, Blancanales nodded in appreciation at the expert camouflage and Schwarz snorted in annoyance. These terrorists were pretty damn bold establishing a hardsite only a couple of miles away from two major U.S. military reservations. Then he realized the genius of the matter. The Army would actually act as perimeter guards for the terrorists, routinely herding away civilians and keeping this area of the desert undisturbed.

Easing down the side of the rill, the three men reached the ground and checked again for sensors. This time they found some. Land mines dotted the dirt road and there were proximity sensors tucked inside every cactus in sight.

Kneeling on the cold ground, Lyons debated how to get closer, when the sound of the motorcycle came again, this time moving along the dirt road. Parking near the jingling hoist, the man climbed off the two-wheeler and refueled the bike using a ten-gallon container.

Instantly the team started forward.

As the man finished the task, he tightened the gas cap and turned just in time for Lyons to ram the stock of his Atchisson shotgun into the guard's stomach. With a hard woof, the man doubled over and Lyons hit him across the back of the

head with the steel barrel of the autoshotgun. The guard crumpled without a sound, twitched and went still. Pulling a bottle from the pocket of his windbreaker, the Able Team leader liberally poured the whiskey over the unconscious man and forced a couple of sips down his throat. Then he slipped a half dollar coin into his shirt pocket.

Already at the bike, Blancanales and Schwarz undid the gas cap and stuffed in a rag. Lighting the cloth with a match, they rolled the machine to the open mouth of the mine and shoved it over the edge. Tumbling freely, the motorcycle fell for quite a while before it hit something unseen, and the gas tank violently exploded, the noise sounding like cannonfire in the still desert night.

Instantly, lights came on, illuminating the road and the old machinery around the mine shaft. A few moments later men rushed out of the wooden buildings carrying AK-47 assault rifles.

"What the fuck happened?" a skinny man demanded, watching the sky. "Are we being bombed or something?"

"No, you idiot," another retorted snidely. "Something exploded inside the mine!"

Craning his neck, a man peeked over the edge. "Looks like Radovik's bike," he muttered.

"The moron was always parking it too close to the edge," another man snorted. "Any sign of him down there?"

"Not that I can see."

A sharp whistle pierced the night.

"Hey, he's over here!" a man shouted, kneeling alongside a still body. "I think... Lord, he reeks of whiskey!"

"Drinking on duty?" a large man snarled angrily. "Baldwin will cut off his balls for this!"

"Then we don't tell him," a short man said, slinging the

assault rifle over a shoulder. "Here, help me get him inside."

After a moment the big man grunted in agreement and the guards picked up their unconscious friend to begin hauling him toward the dilapidated mining office.

Masked by the shadows, nobody seemed to notice the trio of dark shapes easing over the rill and vanishing from sight.

Hauling the unconscious man inside the ramshackle building, the men moved straight toward a blank wall. At the last moment, it slid aside with a soft hiss. More men were standing guard inside behind a sandbag nest, a 20 mm rapidfire cannon mounted on a tripod nearby. The rest of the room was filled with bunk beds, racks of weapons, a full kitchen and a complex console. A monitor of the board showed a slowly rotating view of the mining camp outside.

"Is he dead?" a guard asked, checking over the body. There didn't seem to be any blood, but there were a lot of scorpions in the American desert. Not to mention rattlesnakes.

"No, just drunk," another man snorted in disgust. "Fell off his bike and it went into the mine."

"That was what exploded?"

"Yeah."

Lowering his AK-47, a guard muttered a long phrase in Albanian.

"Agreed, and afterward Baldwin will toss him naked into the ice lake."

"Well, he's sure not getting a deluxe suit at the Apgar."

"Nevada or Montana," another grunted. "We're either roasting or freezing our balls off."

"I'd rather be dodging scorpions than running away from grizzly bears."

"Too true, my friend. We should have stayed in Albania."

"Too late now."

"Damn, look at the knot on the back of his head!" a man cried out, gingerly parting the hair of the limp guard. "He must have hit a rock."

"Well, stuff him into a bunk and let him sleep it off. In the morning we'll bust his ass."

"Hey, is there any of his whiskey left?"

"Shut up, and start some coffee."

HOURS LATER, DAWN WAS starting to lighten the eastern horizon when Schwarz closed the lid of the laptop and placed it on the rear seat of the Cadillac. "Well, it took them long enough." He yawned, rubbing both eyes. "But I think that we finally have enough to make a good guess at the location of their main base."

"Agreed," Lyons said, starting the big engine and heading back the way they'd come. "Get Jack on the radio and have him fuel up for a flight to Montana."

"On it."

"An ice lake," Blancanales said thoughtfully, running an electric razor across the stubble on his jaw. "That's an odd location to hide a command center. Maybe it's just another hardsite."

Running stiff fingers through his hair, Gadgets mumbled something under his breath.

"What was that?" Blancanales asked quizzically, turning off the razor.

"I said," Schwarz repeated tiredly, "a command center near an ice lake makes me think of only one thing."

"A supercomputer," Lyons said, tightening both hands on the wheel. "That's what is probably controlling the Icarus. A supercomputer!" The clever bastards had found a way to avoid being tracked by the sale of liquid nitrogen. Just sink a super-

computer to the bottom of an ice-cold lake. Making the circuit boards and microchips waterproof would be easy, the Navy did it on every ship and submarine. And if the computer was located near the runoff stream of a glacier, the temperature should be plenty low enough. The man felt a surge of excitement. They may be finally getting close to the enemy.

"Unfortunately, there are a lot of glaciers in Montana, and even more grizzly bears," Blancanales sighed, putting the razor into the glove compartment. He sat back and rubbed a palm across his cheeks. "Any idea where we start?"

"The man said a deluxe suite at the Apgar," Schwarz said, unwrapping a stick of chewing gum and popping it into his mouth. "Well, there's an Apgar Lodge in Glacier National Park, Montana."

"Sounds like the place to start," Lyons agreed, glancing in the rearview mirror. The rill and escarpment were dropping away behind the car, and soon were lost from sight. He hated to leave the firebase intact, but killing the men would only alert their leader, somebody named Baldwin, that trouble was coming. That could make the man smash the computer and let the Icarus run wild, which would translate into a lot of civilian deaths. The lives of millions of people were riding on this guess, but it was the best chance they had to stop the terrorists.

And this time, Lyons added privately, we're going to play it low and slow. Not let the terrorists know a thing was wrong until they blew out their brains.

"Of course, we could be wrong," Blancanales said honestly.

"We have to risk it," Lyons stated grimly, steering back onto the gravel road. "So far, these people have always been one step ahead of us. This may be our only opportunity to catch up and bring them down hard."

"I just hope this works." Blancanales sighed deeply, gazing out of the window at the sunrise. "Because if we're wrong…"

The man didn't finish the sentence out loud. He didn't have to. Deep in somber contemplation, the team grew quiet as the big Cadillac cut through the dusty desert, climbing on top of the miles that separated them from a bloody confrontation with the would-be masters of the world.

CHAPTER FOURTEEN

Tokyo, Japan

The blunt steel prongs of the rake moved lightly through the loose sand, leaving behind an orderly pattern forced from chaos by the will of Man. The old artist paused to smile contentedly at the complex patterns he was making in the rock garden. Nearby was his young apprentice, intently watching every move of the master, right down to the placement of his sandals. The cherry blossoms were in bloom again and the entire garden smelled like a summer dream. Fleecy white clouds lined the clear blue sky.

Wearing a loose silk kimono, Rashamor Hoto stood on a wooden dock extending over the small artificial lake. He watched the old man use the rake as skillfully as a samurai warrior did a *katana* sword. One created peace, the other brought death. But those were merely different sides of the same coin called life.

More than six feet tall, Hoto stood a good foot higher than his father, with most of his body covered with tattoos: demons and dragons, fire and swords, mystic symbols, magic numbers and even a few of the signs of the zodiac, which always amused his Shinto friends.

Breathing deeply, Hoto drew in the sweetly scented air and felt the tension of the day flow from his body and back down into Mother Earth. The rock garden was his private sanctuary, and the only place in the busy world that he could go to obtain a few precious minutes of peace.

Bathing in a steaming wooden tub were several Japanese women, their slender bodies as pale as alabaster, their long ebony hair glistening in the sunlight like polished sin. Pleased with himself, Hoto mentally chuckled at that and repeated the turn of phrase. Polished sin. That was pretty good for a Yakuza boss! But then, poetry and war were the same thing, exactly like sex and business. If you were good at sex, then you were profitable in business. That was a law as natural and basic as yin and yang.

Laughter sounded from the bathhouse and several European women joined the others in the steaming water. The Caucasians were tall with long legs, their full breasts almost pendulous from the sheer weight of the flesh. The women had been hired as sex workers, for the private use of the Yakuza. Hoto dislike the odious notion of having sex with a slave. How good could the pillowing be if the other person was unwilling?

One of the women was a voluptuous redhead with pierced nipples, the golden rings supporting tiny silver bells. Sitting on the side of the tub, she caught the eye of Hoto and promptly raised a shapely leg to show where she was recently shaved. Hoto admitted it was a pleasing sight, but her pale skin and oversize breasts did not stir a fire in his blood. As his father had always said, the sweetest apples are the ones closest to your home. Japanese women knew how to treat a man like a real man. Cherry blossoms would always smell sweeter than hamburgers. Speaking of which…

Casually, Hoto nudged the wicker basket at his feet. It rocked slightly, causing a new swell of blood to stain the

fibrous material. Inside the basket was the recently removed head of the Albanian liaison, a member of the Fifteen Families. Hoto had tried to greet him courteously, and the dog had been insolent, making demands and issuing orders! Without waiting for permission, his personal guards had immediately taken off the head of the fool. Which was only right and proper. The Yakuza had been operating in Japan for three thousand years, and the rules of conduct were inviolate. Rudeness was intolerable and discourtesy brought swift death.

Now, if a man was a member of the Yakuza, the rules were much more lenient. Break a minor rule and a man lost a finger to the first joint. That was enough for nearly all to learn better. The men redoubled their efforts and wisely waited before acting rashly again. Hoto glanced at his left hand, the pinkie short and stubby. He used to wear a glove to hide his shame, but now he showed the missing joint as a badge of honor. The Yakuza boss had been foolish once, very long ago, now he was as wise as the ocean, as calm as the mountains.

Some of the new breed of Yakuza, what the Americans so amusingly called "young turks," never took any direct action themselves and always hired mercenaries to do their dirty work. They were forever trying to never fail and thus never to be marred. But how can a man succeed, it he does not try, if he does not risk all, to struggle and fight against the odds? Victory meant nothing it if was too easily gained.

Diamonds are only valuable because they are hard to obtain, Hoto mentally quoted the great zen master Zu. Those were true words, indeed. One of the reasons the peace of his little garden was so precious was that it took a tremendous amount of electronic surveillance and manpower to make sure he would not be disturbed.

Along the shoreline of the tiny lake were a dozen guards

carrying assault shotguns, the fat drums attached to the undersides of the deadly weapons heavy with the new fléchette rounds capable of tearing a man apart in less than a second. The men also carried swords and were very highly trained *judokas,* masters of the martial arts. A cautious man by nature, Hoto had always been adverse to accepting firearms into the Yakuza. Of course, the weapons were commonplace on the streets of America, Russia, Germany, most of the so-called civilized nations. But this was Japan. Street crime was virtually nonexistent. The main job of the police was to maintain the flow of traffic, give directions to lost tourists—and to closely watching the Yakuza to make sure it didn't go mad and start behaving like the Mafia or the dung-eating Jamaicans.

Which again brought him back to the Albanians. He plucked a rose from a bush and deeply breathed in the sweet perfume. If what the fool had said was true, if even half of what he'd said was true, things were very bad. The Yakuza could talk sense to most of the other crime lords in the world. But not the Fifteen Families. They were mad with greed and pretended to be royalty. Idiots. If they truly had control of this strange new weapon that could detonate nuclear weapons by remote control, then the world was teetering on the brink of a dark abyss.

Instinctively, Hoto knew that the Russians would try to cut some sort of a deal with the Fifteen, the French would surrender and the Chinese withdraw into the mountains and pretend nothing was happening, but the British and the Americans would take direct action. Probably by sending in special forces teams to kill the Fifteen and smash the machine.

In spite of the serenity of the garden, Hoto shivered. The mad-dog Albanians in charge of the world. The idea was beyond ghastly, it was the road to Armageddon. Most of his family had died in the Hiroshima blast and many more friends

afterward from cancer. It was true that the Yakuza dealt in arms, but never nuclear weapons. They had been deemed forbidden.

The decision finally made, Hoto reached into a flowing sleeve of his kimono and withdrew a tiny cell phone.

"*Ohio, Ashikaga-san,* please immediately call a council of the senior bosses," he directed, smelling the life of the rose again. "We must decide quickly how best we can assist the Americans and British to kill the Fifteen Families of Albania."

East Adriatic Sea

TWILIGHT COVERED THE WAVES as the Italian yacht *Bella Donna* raced across the choppy waters, heading straight for the coastline of Albania.

Far to the north a lighthouse swept the waves, and to the south was the busy ports of Vlone. But here, the beach was dark and deserted, the only discernable noise the crashing of the waves on the pebbled beach.

"Repeat, turn back, *Bella Donna!*" the loudspeaker slung under the belly of the NATO Black Hawk boomed again. "This is your last warning!"

Insanely the yacht continued on course. All of the running lights were extinguished and curtains covered every window. Wipers beat steadily across the windshield of the bridge and no lights showed from within. The ship had been crudely splashed with dark paint in a futile effort to make it less visible, the transponder and GPS had been disabled and the lowjack smashed. But the attempt had proved useless. NATO had caught the speeding vessel on radar fifty nautical miles out from Albania and immediately sent a SuperHornet jet do a flyover. But that had no effect. The craft refused to answer

a radio hail. So helicopter gunships had been dispatched from the tiny island of Corfu off the coast of Greece. Easily finding the yacht, the Black Hawks swept the craft with brilliant searchlights and thundered warnings from their PA systems, but the craft continued on at full speed.

Looking down from a throbbing Black Hawk, the pilot shook his head in disbelief. The crew had to be either drunk or out of their minds. The yacht was still five miles away and there was nowhere to hide. In fact, the vessel wasn't even trying evasive maneuvers! Just powering straight inward for the southern coastline as if the yoke was lashed in place. The thought gave him pause, but after a minute the pilot dismissed the crazy idea. Why tie down the yoke if there was anybody on board, and if nobody was on board, why send the yacht to Albania? He shook his head. Common sense said the crew was either drunk or a bunch of damn fools. He leaned more toward the lack of brain power.

"*Bella Donna,* this is your last warning!" His voice boomed over the sea. "Heave to and turn about, or you will be destroyed!" The challenge was repeated in Albanian, then Italian and finally Greek, just in case there was a translation problem. But there still was no response.

"Time's up. All guns…fire," the pilot said into his throat mike, and flipped the safety cover on his joystick and to press the red button underneath.

Instantly two Sidewinder missiles launched from the weapons pods on both sides of the first Black Hawk and a stuttering stream of 35 mm minirockets cut loose from the honeycomb pod of the second.

The distance was short, the target plainly visible, and the missiles hit the speeding yacht, punching deep into the hull before exploding. The two blasts tore the *Bella Donna* apart, the hull rising from the waters and separating just as the

35 mm minirockets hit, the series of fiery detonations stitching the craft from bow to stern. Every window blew out in a sparkling eruption, deck chairs went flying, the bridge broke free, the teakwood deck came apart like a jigsaw puzzle. Then the fuel tanks ignited and the annihilated vessel vanished in a fireball that lit up the sea for a mile.

As the burning wreckage tumbled down into the water, the Black Hawk did a low sweep of the surface, looking for any possible survivors. Maybe a few of the crew had jumped overboard at the last minute? But there were no lifejackets bobbing amid the sinking pieces of the yacht and the radio channels were clear of calls for help. Moving in a standard search pattern, the two gunships did a reconnaissance of the choppy water, but there was nothing in sight but the cold, dark sea. Feeling like murderers, the grim pilots relayed the information of the kill to their base commander, then turned and headed back to Corfu.

Deep under water, the men of Phoenix Force released the ropes that had been attached to the belly of the stolen yacht, and commenced swimming for the shore. It had been a wild ride, the men dragged along behind the yacht like fish on a stringer, while Aaron Kurtzman and his team directed the multimillion-dollar ship from their underground bunker in Virginia via a satellite link. But the desperate ploy seemed to have worked. NATO was gone, and there was nothing ahead of the five men but a long hard swim. The water was cold, but endurable.

Keeping low and skirting the irregular bottom of the ocean, the team members kicked steadily along, battling the tide and the currents until reaching the upward sloping shore. Briefly checking his wrist GPS device, McCarter changed direction slightly, bypassing the wreck of a speedboat nestled in a

gently waving nest of seaweed. Then the team cut through a school of fish and paused for a moment as a hammerhead shark appeared. But the killer of the sea was much more interested in the darting tuna than the five men. Consulting the GPS device once more, McCarter headed southward and suddenly the team felt a gentle pressure pushing them away from the shore. Redoubling their efforts, the men swam hard and fast, moving over a wide bed of oysters until entering the mouth of the lazy Vijose River.

Staying near the banks where the currents were the weakest, the team warily maneuvered past fishing nets and a silent graveyard of sunken ships and boats, a school of tiny anchovies flittering about attracted by the body heat of the scuba divers.

Reaching into his equipment belt, Hawkins pulled out a container and popped the top with a thumb, releasing an oily substance. As the bitter chemicals dissipated in the fresh water, the anchovies quickly went away, leaving the men in peace.

The sharks were less annoying, McCarter thought to himself, swimming past a jumble of broken concrete. Plainly, this had to be the remains of the old western Vlore city bridge that had been destroyed when the Communists took over Albania several decades ago. Or at least he hoped so.

There were numerous rusted chassis of civilian cars mixed among the broken masonry and what appeared to be an old Soviet T-54 tank. Albania may have been conquered, but it went down swinging. All of the team members noted the smashed tank and it was a sober reminder that the Albanian people were not the enemy, just the terrorists in charge of the Icarus.

McCarter started upward and for the northern bank, with

the rest of Phoenix Force close behind. Soon the men were slogging through murky silt, then thick mud. Rising from the waves, the members of Phoenix Force waded out of the river onto dry land. Instantly, the men leveled the MP-5 machine guns wrapped in airtight plastic bags. A road was nearby, squat concrete K-rails forming a crude safety fence along the mossy bank.

Waiting for a few minutes, McCarter could detect no sound of traffic. The night was still.

"Drop your rebreathers, and watch the perimeter," McCarter said, sliding on a pair of night-vision goggles.

Moving quickly, the team removed the bulky rebreather units on their backs and laid them out on the ground to drape a camouflage sheet over them before adding a protective layer of loose branches. Meanwhile, McCarter thumbed a switch on his goggles and the view went from infrared to starlight, amplifying the meager light from the stars overhead until the coastline was bright as day, although tinted a muted green in hue.

"Okay, the coast is clear," McCarter reported.

"Negative, we have incoming," James said, swinging a passive EM scanner upward. "One—no, two helicopters. Coming this way."

Darting into the bushes, the men stayed low. A minute later a pair of Black Hawk gunships appeared, moving along the river, their searchlights stabbing into the water and along both banks. McCarter bit back a curse. This was a tough spot for them if discovered. They didn't want to shoot at NATO personnel, but it was vital they reach Durres and recon the Fifteen Families. If a choice had to be made… Grimly, the man brought up his MP-5 machinegun and removed the standard ammo clip to replace it with one containing DU rounds. The

only thing that would stop a depleted uranium round was DU armor, and the only nation in the world that had any was the United States. The 9 mm DU bullets would punch through the hull of a Black Hawk as if it was cardboard.

Staying low, McCarter tracked the NATO gunships with the barrel of his machine gun. As the helicopters flew directly overhead, the team held their breath, hands tight on their heavy weapons. Then the Black Hawks continued onward and moved out to sea once more.

"That was close," Encizo said, easing his grip on a LAW rocket launcher.

"Almost too close," James added.

Nodding in agreement, Encizo tucked the unopened plastic tube back into his equipment bag. This would be a soft penetration, but if the Fifteen Families were behind the Icarus attacks, their orders were to burn down the mansion and kill anybody who got in the way. Unfortunately, the mansion was a home and there would be a lot of noncombatants there. Dark orders for a grim mission. Privately, the man much preferred missions like Sardinia where it was nice and clear who were the villains or the victims.

"Too close," Hawkins agreed, pulling out a sweater and blue jeans from his equipment bag and stripping off the wet scuba suit.

After everybody had changed clothing, McCarter used the GPS device to confirm their position, then checked a map. "All right, Durres is ten miles to the northwest," he said, slinging the equipment bag over a shoulder. The duffel had been deliberately stained and patched in several spots to make it appear cheap and not worth stealing. "But we better circle around and approach the city from inland to avoid NATO. We got past them twice, so let's not push our luck."

"Agreed," Hawkins said, slinging a haversack across his back.

Going into the hills, the team avoided all major roads and steered clear of every town and village. Several times along their journey, they took cover from NATO gunships and twice an aircraft in the sky was shot down by F-15 jetfighters to land with a thunderous crash in farmland. The ban on Albania was in full effect, but clearly other people were trying to gain entrance anyway.

"I wish them luck," James said, taking a drink from his canteen. "The more people that get into the country, the busier NATO will be."

"Amen to that, brother," Manning said, shifting the heavy Barrett sniper rifle slung across his back. The weapon was tucked inside a blanket to make it look like a bedroll, but it was still easily reachable in case of trouble. The DU rounds in the MP-5 machine guns could do a lot of damage to most military vehicles, but the 750-grain, steel-jacketed man-stoppers in the Barrett would got the job on anything short of a battlefield tank or an oceangoing destroyer. Neither of which likely to be encountered in Albania. The nation was clean and tidy, almost painfully so, but the poverty of the people was crushing. He was looked forward to meet the man in charge of the Fifteen Families and teaching him something new about justice.

Following an old goat trail through the winding hills, at one point the team moved past a military installation for the Albanian army. The fort was in ruins, several of the buildings burned to the ground, a few still smoldering. The front gate was padlocked, and a flock of birds was eating at random places. There were no bodies in sight, but in any major fire-fight, people lost hands and organs, which often got left be-

hind. Rescue helicopters were more interested in saving lives than gathering the wretched offal of warfare.

"According to Barbara, all of the soldiers are at Tirane, the capital," McCarter said, touching his earpiece. "NATO has a command post there, and the Albanians have dug in, literally. They're throwing up an earthwork bulwark around the city using bulldozers and dynamite."

"Down, but not out," James said, soundly oddly pleased. "Tough folks."

"Just like when the Communists invaded," Hawkins said dourly, his expression unreadable.

"Let's just hope that we can tilt the scales in their favor this time," Manning stated, adjusting the Barrett rifle slung across his back.

The team spent the night dodging military patrols and civilian police until finally reaching the outskirts of Durres. Here they had to leave cover and walk openly along the ancient cobblestone streets. Durres was built on a sloping hillside, but there were other hills visible around the city. Most were covered with homes or hotels, but one was topped by a huge mansion surrounded by a tall, stone-block wall. Another was crested with an old stone castle that looked like something from the Middle Ages. A third was truncated, flat on top, and there was only a bare, concrete apartment house in sight there, obviously left over from the days of the Soviet Union. That was their first destination.

Keeping their heads down and trying not to attract attention, the team saw several Hummers full of armed men driving along the cobblestone streets. The men wore dark blue jumpsuits with sidearms belted around their waists. But there was no military insignia. Several of the men had beards, and often scantily clad women were also in the Hummers with the troops.

Clearly these were not the Albania army, McCarter decided. Had to be private troops for the Fifteen Families. So they were moving in the open now. And why not? The country was under their control and the United Nations was about to surrender. What did they have to fear anymore? Nothing at all.

Aside from us, the big man added grimly, pulling his woolen cap tighter down on his head. So far, no blondes had been seen in the city, and his pale hair made the man far too noticeable.

"We should separate," Hawkins said, wiping his mouth on a sleeve to hide the words. "A big group like us stands out like a road flare in a latrine."

"Can't take a chance of getting interrogated by the city guards," Encizo added in agreement, scratching his face. On the flight over here, the team had learned a few basic words in Albanian—surrender, run, that sort of thing—but if any of them was detained and questioned, they'd have to fight their way clear, and that could blow the whole operation.

"Agreed. We meet at the hilltop in an hour," McCarter directed. "Keep in radio contact. If there's any trouble, call out the word *mercenary,* and the rest will come running." With that, he turned a corner to start casually walking away.

Each of the men took off in a new direction, melting into crowds and disappearing into alleyways.

Keeping to the back streets, McCarter found them too small for the big Hummers to traverse. The bricks lining the roads were old and cracked, potholes were everywhere and there was garbage strewed about. But there were a lot more people walking along the dirty back streets than there were out on the main roads. Keeping out of sight of the tourists, or avoiding the patrols? he wondered. Probably a little of both. It was wise to not be noticed in any dictatorship.

There were a lot of old people and children around, but

almost no men, and nobody was talking much. The hush of the Mediterranean city felt unnatural. Towns were boisterous and noisy, the bigger the crowd, the more clamor it made. He had always considered it a sign of prosperity. New York, Tokyo, Paris, the more affluent the city, the more noisy it became. Freedom was loud. But Durres was nearly silent, as if holding its breath. More than once, McCarter could hear his own footsteps. The calm before the storm.

Unexpectedly, somebody called out from behind McCarter and he recognized a few of the words: *you, hat, stop.* Coughing hard to pretend he hadn't heard, McCarter ducked into an alley and yanked off the dark wool cap to turned it inside out so that it was now brown, and jammed it back on. Small changes often were enough to escape notice. But just in case, the man drew his Browning Hi-Power and quickly screwed on an acoustical sound suppressor.

A gasp from the shadows made him turn in a crouch, the weapon ready to fire, and McCarter found himself looking into the terrified eyes of an old woman holding the hand of a small boy. Quickly lowering the Browning, he raised a finger to his lips, hoping they understood the gesture.

Radiating fear, the old woman nodded and pulled the boy protectively closer.

That was when McCarter noticed she wasn't old, but starving, and their clothing was rags. She couldn't be more than thirty, he decided. Until now, the man had felt only contempt at the Fifteen Families, but when faced with the victims of their greed for power, that changed to a cold fury. Checking the alleyway for any sign of pursuit, McCarter swore that whatever else happened on this mission, the Fifteen Families were going to face judgment day and go down hard. Whether they were behind the Icarus or not.

After a while when nobody came running after him, McCarter eased his stance and holstered the Browning back under his patchwork jacket and pulled out a small wad of money. Turning to thank the woman, the man was shocked to find her gone. She had to have slipped off the instant that he wasn't looking. Stoically, he tucked the money away and started for the apartment once more.

Less than an hour later, McCarter turned a corner and there was the Soviet concrete edifice. Walking around the ugly monstrosity, he saw an ancient Roman amphitheater set into the flattened hilltop. A black iron-pipe railing encircled the ruins, and there didn't seem to be a front gate or a kiosk for buying tickets. He guessed that people were not allowed inside and could only look at the two-thousand-year-old theater.

Glancing around to make sure he wasn't being watched, McCarter hopped the fence and started down the worn marble steps leading to the broad mosaic covering the bottom level. The ancient stone steps were worn from the passage of a million of feet, sandals, boots and sneakers over the centuries. Weeds grew in profusion, and some wild chickens were darting around. He smiled.

There were several broad bands between the layers of stone seats and dark tunnels led into the hillside. The blunted, cracked bases of marble were scattered around, proclaiming the might and majesty of the once-magnificent structure. However, the main floor was in decent shape. A couple of centuries ago, actors played roles on those very stones, men argued about the law or espoused philosophy and slaves were slaughtered for the amusement of their masters.

So, not a lot had really changed in Durres after all that time, McCarter noted dourly, pausing to glance at the Soviet apartment block rising above the amphitheater. The cheap concrete

was already starting to crack and crumble. A brand-new ruin was being born to join the faded glory of another lost empire.

Reaching the bottom of the stairs, McCarter circled the amphitheater and entered the northern tunnel. It took a moment for his vision to adjust to the dim lighting, but there was the rest of the team sitting on stone blocks.

"What'd you do, take the scenic route?" Hawkins joked, screwing the cap back onto his canteen.

"Ran into a patrol," McCarter answered, sliding his backpack to the ground. "But nothing major."

"Same here," James said, wincing slightly as he rubbed a leg.

McCarter frowned. "Are you hurt?"

"No, just met a street gang that really liked my boots," James replied. "It took a few moments to convince them otherwise, and one of the little bastards got in a lucky shot."

"They shot you?"

"No, but I've been kicked in the exact spot that a man least wants to encounter a steel-toed work boot."

Manning chuckled, unable to stop himself. "Leave any of them alive?"

James scowled, then broke into a grin. "Mostly," he replied. "Although several of them may not wake up until next week."

"Fair enough," McCarter said, then broke into a grin. "Got you right in the jumbles, eh?"

"If that means balls, yes."

Sharing a laugh, the team dutifully got out of their dirty civilian togs and pulled military fatigues and body armor from their duffel bags. Within a few minutes they were dressed and ready for full combat. The last thing each man donned was a blue-and-white armband decorated with the UN symbol for NATO. The armbands were more than a di-

version from their real identities. Anybody who ran away from them was probably a civilian, and anybody who pulled a gun at the sight of the armbands was a fair target to shoot. In warfare, it always helped to have some easy way to tell who was supposed to get shot and who wasn't.

Cracking some glow sticks, the men let them build to full brightness before proceeding down the weedy tunnel and into the dank hillside. After about fifty paces, a locked iron gate barred their way. Drawing his Beretta 93-R pistol, Hawkins fired once, and the padlock blew apart with a sharp crack. Swinging free, the gate squealed loudly as it crashed into the stone wall and a light rain of dust came down from the ceiling, along with a couple of cracked tiles from an unseen mosaic.

"Jesus, this place is a falling apart," Manning complained, grabbing the gate to make it stop trembling. "One grenade, and we'd be buried alive."

Closing the gate behind them, Encizo grunted in agreement, then shoved a rock against the metal to try to keep it closed. That should be enough for any casual observer, and if the team had to leave fast, there wouldn't be another lock to slow their exit.

Holding a glow stick low to see the uneven floor, McCarter took the lead and the team carefully walked along the dark tunnel. Tiny roots were sticking through every minuscule crack of both walls like the feelers of insects and the air was redolent with the smell of mold.

"You sure this goes to the castle?" Encizo asked, stepping over a pothole.

"Definitely. This used to be the private passageway for King Zogu to visit the ruins," McCarter replied. Down here the night-vision goggles were useless. There wasn't ambient light to use starlite mode, and infrared and ultraviolet would

also be useless. Unfortunately, the glow sticks didn't help that much, the illumination only reached a couple of yards beyond which was total blackness. It felt like he was walking down the barrel of a gun.

"King who?" Manning asked.

"Zogu," McCarter answered. "Ahmet Zogu, the national hero of Albania. He got elected back in the twenties and partially rebuilt the whole place by himself, roads, schools, hospitals, you name it."

"He got elected king?" Hawkins asked sounding amused.

"President," McCarter answered, stepping over a pile of loose bricks. "But the population back then was so badly educated, nobody knew what an elected official was, so they called him king, after a while it became his nickname." The man paused to ease past an obstruction, the stone cracked and rough. What had caused the partial collapse he had no idea. Artillery on the surface, perhaps. "He was a hell of a guy. Even though he was a Muslim, his first act was to ban veils on women and make cruelty to animals against the law."

"So why the secret tunnel to the ruins, then?" Manning asked from the darkness. "Assassins?"

"Yeah." McCarter sighed, bending low to get under another slab of rock. "The people loved him, but the Fifteen Families did not."

"What, these assholes have been operating since the twenties?"

"Since long before that. Over fifty times they tried to kill Zogu, he aced the last one himself with a knife to the throat."

"Sounds okay for a king," Hawkins said with a hard chuckle. "I can't imagine one of our modern-day politicians doing that."

"You got that right," Encizo agreed, then added, "Well, maybe in Australia."

"Zogu did a lot of good," McCarter said ruefully. "Until Mussolini invaded along with the Nazis. Zogu barely escaped with his life out this tunnel."

"So, that's how we knew about it."

"Exactly, he was planning on coming back one day with enough troops to free Albania, but… Aw, shit!"

All conversation stopped as the team encountered a wide pool of water that was not on their map. Dropping in a glow stick, McCarter saw that it was thankfully only a yard deep. Treading warily, the team slogged across the pool and climbed out the other side, leaving damp footprints in their wake.

"No more conversation," McCarter subvocalized into his throat mike. "We're too close now. Stay sharp, there could be traps."

Readying their weapons, the men of Phoenix Force continued onward, watching the floor and walls for any signs of improvements that could be hiding mines or sensors. Thankfully, there did not seem to be any, but after only a short distance they encountered another iron gate. This time, they picked the padlock and oiled the hinges before pushing it aside.

From here, the tunnel was in noticeably better shape, the floor smooth and even, and there was electric wiring along the walls running to light sockets with bulbs. Soon, they came to another door, solid wood this time, with a modern lock set in the middle.

Grunting in annoyance, Hawkins started to reach for some C-4, but McCarter stayed his hand and gave Encizo a nod. Pulling out a keywire gun, the man inserted the locksmith tool and pulled the rigger to shoot the lock full of stiff wire. Gently, he turned the gun and the lock softly clicked and disengaged.

Tucking away the explosive, Hawkins was impressed. The lock's brand was one of the best in the world. He didn't know it could be opened aside from using acid or high explosives.

Easing open the door, McCarter found himself in a large open room full of huge casks of wine, hogsheads that stood over ten feet tall. Curiously, Encizo tapped one and heard a soft echo. It was empty? That was when he noticed the bronze plaque on the wooden stand. The casks were a display. This was some sort of museum. It made sense actually. If King Zogu was such a hero, it was only fitting to make his home a national monument.

On the other side of the cellar, bright light edged the outline of a door. Crossing the wine cellar, the men crept up a flight of stone steps and again used the keywire gun to open a lock. Easing ajar the door, McCarter suddenly smelled beef stew, fresh bread and coffee. They had to be near the kitchen. He glanced back at the others to make sure they understood civilians could be present, and saw they had already pulled out cans of pepper spray to subdue the staff if necessary.

Exiting the cellar, they saw that the hallway was clean and brightly lit. There were paintings on the walls and the terrazzo floor had recently been washed. There were a couple of side doors along the hallway, but they proved to be utility closets, brooms and mops in one, a water heater in the next.

Using a tiny mirror on the end of a telescoping rod, McCarter peeked around the corner at the end of the hallway and studied the kitchen. Sure enough, soup was bubbling on the electric stove and a percolator was bubbling away. There was a huge wheel of cheese almost completely covering a wooden table, countless sausages hung in clusters from the ceiling and drying herbs festooned the far redbrick wall. In a corner was a modern refrigerator and over at a counter was a

short bald man humming to himself while chopping onions. He was wearing a cooking apron and didn't seem to be armed. From somewhere, there came the muted sound of a soccer match on the radio.

Stepping into view, McCarter approached the man, when he suddenly turned and gasped in astonishment. Then his face turned ugly with a snarl.

"NATO!" He spit, and flipped the knife at McCarter, then yanked an old Colt pistol from under his apron.

Dodging to the left, the Phoenix Force leader saw the knife flash by his head as he stroked the silenced Browning's trigger and sent a 9 mm round directly into the bald man's face. Caught in the act of puling the slide, the man jerked his head back and slid to the floor, blood gushing from the wound. Hawkins caught the body and deposited it gently to the floor. Muttering incoherently, the bald man shuddered all over, then went still.

Kneeling by the corpse, McCarter pushed up its sleeve to expose a tattoo of a Greek symbol laid over the number nine. McCarter grunted in satisfaction. Carmen Delahunt had believed that the castle of King Zogu had been taken over by the Dectra Nine terrorist group, but could not get a confirmation. It was nice to know that the woman was right on the money as usual. The Briton holstered his pistol and fisted his MP-50.

"Do we need anybody intact?" James subvocalized into his throat mike, snicking off the safety of his MP-5 machine gun with a thumb.

Starting forward, McCarter shook his head and stepped into the dining room. Two men sat there eating soup and listening to the radio. Dressed only in T-shirts, their tattoos were clearly visible. As they looked up, McCarter sprayed them

with a hail of 9 mm rounds from the MP-5, the fat acoustical silencer reducing the noise to only a fast series of hard chugs.

Spraying blood and teeth, the men fell out of their chairs, one of them actually getting hold of a revolver before collapsing on the floor. Preparing for a fight, the team waited for any reactions to the killing, but nothing happened. Soup and blood dripped wetly to the floor as the soccer game continued.

With their backs secure, the team now swept through the castle, going from room to room and ruthlessly exterminating anybody they found. Some men were asleep, one was on the toilet, five were playing cards in front of a roaring fireplace. But this was not the movies, and the covert operatives gave the terrorists no warning or chance to fight back. They were removed from this world as quickly and quietly as possible.

When the first floor was clear, the team started up the stairs and moved into a ballroom full of weapons and stacks of boxes marked with military symbols and numbers. They had the armory!

Clucking his tongue in disapproval, a man walked into view from around a stack of boxes full of Russian grenades. Ticking off items on a clipboard, the fellow jerked to a full stop at the sight of the five armed intruders. Dropping the clipboard, he threw up both hands in surrender, revealing his tattoo. Without a qualm, James jerked a wrist forward and a Randall knife slammed into the throat of the terrorist. Hacking for air, the man doubled over, stumbled against the boxes of grenades, blood pouring from his mouth. Stepping closer, James chopped at the man's exposed neck with the edge of his hand. The bones audibly broke and the man folded to the floor.

"Rafe, guard this place," McCarter ordered, glancing around the ballroom. "There're enough explosives here to blow our asses to the moon."

"Think they'd try to take us with them?" Hawkins whispered, easing out a nearly spent clip and gently inserting a full one. The empty he laid on a table covered with newspapers, the completed crossword puzzles done in ink.

"Let's not give them the option," James answered brusquely. On a nearby shelf was a stack of dynamite bombs alongside some children's knapsacks decorated with colorful cartoon characters, exactly the kind of thing they used to carry books to school. Vaguely, the man recalled Dectra Nine bombing some elementary schools in Kosovo and Montenegro. James barred his teeth in a silent growl. The bastards needed to die.

Just then, a siren began to howl and men started shouting upstairs.

"They know we're here," Encizo said, removing the sound suppressor from his machine gun. The device only reduced the foot-pounds of the bullets by a small amount, but every little bit helped.

"Then we don't have to be subtle anymore," Manning stated, getting out a grenade and pulling the pin.

Hawkins threw open the door, and Manning dashed out of the armory. Looking upward, he saw movement on the third floor.

"NATO!" he bellowed at the top of his lungs.

There came a series of virulent curses and four men looked over the railing while working the arming bolts of Kalashnikov assault rifles. Tossing up the grenade, Manning ducked back into the armory, and Hawkins slammed the door. A split second later there was a thunderous explosion, followed by piercing screams, then silence.

"Move!" McCarter ordered, and the four men rushed out of the room and up the stairs.

Closing the door, Encizo moved to a work table and kicked it over, scattering the inventory reports everywhere. Crouching behind the impromptu shield, the Stony Man operative aimed his MP-5 machine gun on the door and started softly humming Beethoven's Fifth Piano Concerto while waited for the first person to walk through without first giving the arranged knock.

Reaching the third floor, McCarter and the team stepped over the remains of the four terrorists and took off in different directions, their weapons chattering briefly at anybody with a tattoo or a gun.

Moving into a bedroom, Hawkins got a burst of 7.62 mm gunfire in the chest. The body armor defected the rounds but the man had the wind knocked out of him. Fighting to draw a breath, the Southerner dived to the side, firing his MP-5. The steel-jacketed 9 mm manstoppers hit the Dectra Nine killer smack in the belly and punched clean through his bulletproof vest, blowing out his life onto the wall behind. The terrorist gave a low moan as if about to be sick, then he slumped to the bloody floor and toppled sideways.

Turning a corner, Manning flinched as a shotgun blast exploded an oil painting on the wall, the splinters and ricochets nearly blinding him. Dropping flat to the stone floor, he saw a man working the slide on a Remington 12-gauge. The man was standing behind a massive mahogany beam that supported the ceiling rafters. The ancient wood was roughly a foot thick and looked more like an eighteenth-century battering ram than anything else. Stroking the trigger on the Barrett, Manning sent a .50-thunderbolt into the beam and blew a fist-size hole clean through the wood and the terrorist.

Manning worked the arming bolt on the titanic rifle and continued along the corridor, looking for more prey.

Approaching a closed door, James paused and, sure

enough, a line of holes stitched the wood paneling from top to bottom. Crying out in pain, James stomped a boot on the floor and waited. When he heard nothing moving inside the room, he emptied his MP-5 into the door and then crashed through, drawing his Beretta. For a single instant, he could not spot anybody in the room, then the door to a cabinet swung open exposing a crouching terrorist with an Uzi machine pistol in target acquisition. Both men fired at the exact same time. As the body crumpled to the floor, James reloaded his MP-5 and continued the bloody manhunt.

Removing his knife from the throat of a still shuddering terrorist, McCarter started up the stairs, then quickly jumped over the railing to fall the couple of yards to a couch. A heartbeat later, a sizzling stream of tracers screamed down the stairs, fired from a M-60 machine gun behind a sandbag nest.

Must be close to the command center for them to use this kind of ordnance, McCarter realized, pulling the pin on a grenade. He waited until the firing stopped, then released the arming level and flipped the grenade in a lofting arc.

The terrorists yelled as the grenade sailed past them to land inside the nest. One man dived for the grenade while the other tried to scramble over the sandbags. Neither succeeded in their endeavors. Ruptured sandbags and gory chunks of flesh formed a hellish geyser that filled the landing with pure chaos for a several moments. Already moving, McCarter ran through the smoky destruction, hopping over the remains of the nest and throwing his shoulder against the sagging ruins of an elaborately carved set of double doors.

A pair of men were inside the spacious office, struggling to erect a Colt AutoSentry, but they were having trouble feeding the ammunition belt into the computer-operated weapon. Shooting them both in the head, McCarter went past

the falling bodies and straight into the a side room. He expected trouble, but the place was empty, the radio and radar softly humming away. There was a leather suitcase on the floor, loose cash sticking out from the top, as well as a satchel charge of C-4 plastic explosive, loose wires dangling from the side and contacting to nothing.

"Bloody amateurs," McCarter growled in contempt, turning off the radio and radar. The men had probably planned to attach the detonator wires to one of the machines, most likely the radio, so that they could send a signal and blow up the place from a safe distance. What a pair of bleeding twits, he thought. Not even a U.S. Army satchel charge would do much damage to this granite block of a building. It was designed to resist cannonfire. A demolition charge might wreck the third floor, but not much else. The place was a fortress, as sturdy as Gibraltar.

Just then, McCarter turned at the sound of a footstep, then eased his grip on the machine gun when Hawkins came into view.

"The place is clean," the commando reported, fresh blood splattered across his fatigues. But none of it belonged to the covert operative. "Calvin and I had some trouble on the roof, but nothing we couldn't handle."

Suddenly a scream came from out of nowhere and a body flashed past an open window. A second later, there came a juicy crack from below and the noise stopped.

"I hope that didn't land in the street," McCarter said, resting the barrel of his machine gun on a shoulder. The heat felt good on his cheek, even if the barrel was painfully hot. But that was okay. Only the living experienced pain; the dead felt nothing.

Arching an eyebrow, Hawkins didn't even deign to reply.

"Fair enough." McCarter smiled. "Come on, let's check to make sure the view is everything we heard it was."

Going into the office, the men walked over the smoking debris to the east windows and carefully parted the curtains. Spreading out below the castle was the city of Durres, the red-tiled roofs stretching all the way to a hill topped by a large mansion surrounded by a high stone-block fence.

"Everything under control?" Manning asked, entering the room with James. Both men had bullet holes in their fatigues, but there was no sign of blood. Their weapons were held two-handed and ready for combat.

"Go get Rafe," McCarter replied, stepping away from the window. "I want that maser up and running five minutes ago."

Both men nodded, and left the room in a sprint. A few minutes later they returned with Encizo and the man immediately began setting up a sleek device on a tripod. It sort of resembled a paintball gun, but it was attached to a heavy set of lithium batteries. This was a CIA model bugging maser. The compact device emitted a thin laser that bounced off any reflective surface, such as a glass window, sending the beam right back to the unit, effectively turning the glass into a giant microphone. A whisper would come through as loud as thunder. Some older models required a small prismatic patch to be attached to the window first, but the newer models no longer had that limitation. As long as nobody in the mansion was operating a jamming device, such as a Humbug, the team could listen to any conversation taking place in any room facing the castle.

"Okay, that one's a bathroom," Encizo said, making a face. "Nobody in the next room…"

"Try working down from the top," McCarter suggested.

"I am. Now, please shut up," the man muttered, fine-tuning the maser to greater sensitivity. "All right, I have a group of women laughing about something… Another empty room…

Somebody snoring loudly…a couple having sex…a couple of men discussing… Bingo!"

Moving away from the viewfinder, Encizo flipped a small switch on his comm gear that would transmit the conversation to translation services at Stony Man Farm. A no-nonsense voice sent back a translation via a special frequency on the team's headsets.

"…it down, Sakir. I said, sit down boy!" an elderly man commanded. "We have a couple of hours before the celebration tonight, and I want to know more about this marvelous Icarus of yours."

The Stony Man team was galvanized motionless by the single word. This was a confirmation that the Fifteen Families actually did have control of the triggering device! Pulling out Navy monoculars, the team swept the mansion until focusing on the fourth floor, second window from the corner. An old man leaning on a bent wood cane was facing a young man lounging in a cushioned chair. He was handsome with dark hair and a diamond stud in one earlobe.

And that is the face of the enemy, McCarter thought grimly, tightening his grip on the monocular.

"WHAT DO YOU WISH to know, Grandfather?" Sakir Elsani asked, swirling a tumbler of brandy. He took a sip and nodded in approval. "Excellent year."

"Bah, stop wasting my time, boy. How good is your security? The superpowers will try at least once to kill all of us and destroy the weapon. Is it well hidden? Do you have enough troops?"

"The report is right there," Elsani said languidly, taking another swallow. "Can't you read?"

The old man seemed furious over the simple question, and started to raise the cane as if about to strike the man. Then he

relented and sighed deeply. "Actually, no," he replied through tight lips. "I can not read. All of my people report to me verbally. I used to trust Isaak enough to read reports to me, but…" He shrugged.

Setting aside the glass, Elsani laughed. "Yes, and look what happened to that trust," he said. "Isaak betrayed the family."

"Bastard! I hope he suffered."

"Trust me, Grandfather, he did," Elsani stated coldly. "Very well, sir, I'll tell you all of the important details."

The men of Phoenix Force had collectively held their breath. This was exactly why they'd taken the castle, and the gamble was paying off in the first couple of minutes. Once they knew where the machine was located, they could bomb the place from the air if necessary. Or if that wasn't possible, they'd infiltrate and destroy it from within. Either way, this was all going to be over in just a few seconds.

"But before I begin…" The young man reached into a pocket, retrieving a small egg-shaped device. Flicking a switch on the side, the speaker on the maser instantly began to howl.

"Goddamn it, he has a Humbug!" Encizo cursed, changing the settings on the machine. But it was no good. The howling interference continued on the entire floor of the mansion. A moment later the curtains were closed, making any chance at lip-reading impossible.

"At least one of them knows something about modern bugging techniques," Encizo muttered angrily.

"Confirmed," James said, reading off the screen of his laptop. "Sakir Elsani is a known member of the Fifteen Families. Linked to a hundred murders, Interpol believes he is the man in charge of the electronic security for the Families. Handles

the encryption on their bank transfers, radio scramblers, Internet scams, et cetera. Supposed to have a couple of bodyguards, no names listed, believed to be called Beauty and the Beast."

"Who's the old man?

"According to Bear, that is most likely Slobodan Kadriouski, the head of the Fifteen."

"Most likely…aren't there any photos?"

"None," James said, frowning. "The last news reporter that got into the estate never came out again. You can see his remains fluttering from the top of the flagpole near the front gate."

"The scalp?"

"Yep."

"Damn."

"Looks like our soft probe became hard," Hawkins stated, sweeping the estate with his monocular. "If we can't listen anymore, then we need that report the old man mentioned."

"Or we kidnap this Sakir alive," McCarter agreed. The wall around the place was so thick that guards were walking along the top. Zooming in, he found more guards walking on the roof of the stately mansion, and there seemed to be a pillbox set inside the imposing wall, right next to the front gate.

"Getting in is going to be a bitch," Encizo declared. "We'd need an air strike, and… No, the old man mentioned a party tonight! If all of the Fifteen Families come, then there will be countless small children, infants, newborn babies, along with butlers, maids, chauffeurs, mistresses, hundreds of innocent bystanders. Apparently everyone shows up."

"Then the mission just went covert again," Manning said, bringing up the Barrett and adjusting the Ziest telescope to study the estate. In his bag, there was a sound suppressor for

the mammoth rifle, but it only reduced the thunderous report to a loud boom. Hardly worth the effort.

Inhaling deeply, McCarter then exhaled twin streams of smoke through his nose. "Okay, they're having a party tonight," he said, dropping the cigarette to the floor and crushing it under his boot. "They're probably going to celebrate taking control of the world. Well, we can use the party as a diversion."

"How?" Manning asked, glancing over a shoulder.

Rubbing his unshaved chin to the sound of sandpaper, McCarter gave a hard smile and began to explain.

CHAPTER FIFTEEN

Glacier National Park, Montana

It had been a harried flight from Henderson Airport in Las Vegas to Glacier Airport in Montana, but Jack Grimaldi had gotten Able Team there in record time.

Renting a Jeep with four-wheel drive, the team took Route 2 through Columbia and drove straight to the park. Bypassing the Apgar Village Lodge, they rattled over a nineteenth century bridge made of railroad ties and headed straight for the park ranger headquarters.

Booting his laptop, Schwarz scanned the map of the parkland. A craggy ring of mountains edged the huge national park, and cresting the entire northern ridge were glaciers, massive slabs of ice hundreds of feet high and miles long. The icy runoff water created hundreds of creeks and rivers that in turn fed into five major lakes and a dozen smaller ones scattered all over the vast park. The temperature of the lakes was much too bitterly cold for swimming. But just perfect for operating a supercomputer, he noted. The bastards were using a glacier to cool their computer. The idea was so clever that

Schwarz almost felt admiration for the Albanians, even though he was eagerly looking forward to blowing off their heads.

"A military hardsite hidden inside a public park," Blancanales said, running stiff fingers through his salt-and-pepper hair. "Well, I suppose it was only a matter of time before somebody else decided it was a good idea."

"I suppose so," Lyons agreed, turning onto Going-into-the-Sun Road, and following the natural curve of Lake McDonald. "But with civilians all about the place, the Albanians are going to be hard to find."

As they traversed an old wooden bridge, the timbers rattled loudly, the lake water rushing over a small dam below them, crashing down a hundred feet to hit a rocky riverbed. The huge boulders were covered with moss to the top, but the water only reached about halfway. This had to be the dry season, the water levels at their lowest. That would help some, but not much. Glacier Park was a hundred times larger than Shenandoah National Park where the Farm was located, and the only aspect in their favor was that the computer had to be submerged in water near a glacier. The closer, the better.

A deep blue, Lake McDonald stretched out into the craggy mountains for twenty or so miles, the rocky mountains looming high above the thick forest. Dominating the horizon was a rugged mountain that marked the Continental Divide. A wooden sign on the side of the path said it was called "The Crown of the Continent."

"The sons of bitches could be looking at us this very moment," Schwarz said, stroking his mustache. "Checking out all of the new guests through a telescope."

"Or a sniper scope," Lyons added, forcing a smile on his face.

"How big is the place again, Hermann?" Blancanales asked, pulling on a red flannel hunting cap. The team had changed clothing on the way here from Nevada, and now were wearing hiking boots, heavy denim pants, red flannel shirts and insulated vests. The big lumpy vests were actually Thinsulated, and the rest of the bulk was composed of handguns, ammo knives, grenades and similar hardware.

"A million square acres. There are over seven hundred miles of hiking trails alone. The park has more than three hundred historic buildings, some of them old trapper cabins now refurbished for campers, log cabins, lakeside inns and five luxury hotels. There's even an abandoned railroad track that runs clear around the whole shebang."

"Not enough business?"

He shrugged. "Most railroads are in trouble these days."

"Sad, but true."

"Any chance of a thermal sweep from a NSA satellite?" Lyons asked hopefully.

"A NASA cartography sat would be better," Schwarz replied, scowling at the computer screen. "Bear already checked, and a thermal is useless. There's about five thousand tourists in the park, with campfires all over the place, along with a scattering of hot-water geysers."

"In a glacier park?" Blancanales said in surprise.

"Well, they're not located near the glaciers," Schwarz stated. "However, they really fuck up the thermals to no end."

"Okay," Lyons said, taking a turnoff, "if the satellites are useless, then we do this the hard way." Leaving Going-to-the-Sun Road, the Jeep bounced along a gravel path that had seen much better days. Slowing to avoid getting thrown out of the moving vehicle, Lyons engaged the four-wheel drive. The

sounds of the engine abruptly shifted, their speed slowed, and the bouncing was reduced significantly.

About a half mile ahead, the ranger station came into view. The redwood building was larger than expected, with a chimney at each end, probably to help stave off the cold when winter arrived. As they got closer, the team noted a line of Jeeps and one Hummer parked in a field of low grass bordered with railroad ties. All of the vehicles were painted a dazzling electric-orange. Blancanales grunted at the sight. No way the team could borrow one of those to recon the park without the Albanians spotting them a mile away.

A large sign in front of the redwood building listed office hours, along with various fees for fishing, camping, renting a log cabin and boating. Off to the side was a barn and corral with a couple of horses nibbling on a bale of green hay.

Easing to a stop at the end of the line, Lyons set the brakes, killed the engine and climbed out, pausing a moment to scratch and stretch as if tired from the long drive.

Chatting and laughing among themselves, Able Team sauntered over to the wooden porch of the ranger station, knocked politely on the door and stepped inside.

A blast of warm air hit them in the face from a heater attached to a ceiling beam and pointed downward. Quickly closing the door, they moved out of the stream of the rumbling heater and looked around. The station was a single huge room, with stonework pillars supporting the roof beams. A long wooden counter sectioned off the front, and behind it could be seen a dozen desks covered with papers, files and the usual effluvia of office work. Oddly, there were no people aside from a pretty redhead standing at the counter. She wore a badge and had a U.S. Army Colt .45 pistol strapped to her hip.

"Can I help you?" the ranger asked, laying aside a pencil and glancing up from some paperwork.

Instantly she was suspicious of the trio. The men were smiling, but there was a hard look about them, and not one was carrying a fishing pole or golf club. Hunting was strictly forbidden in the national park, it said so in the brochures, on the walls, everywhere the rangers could think of putting a notice. But every year fools always arrived with enough firepower to take Iwo Jima, and were absolutely startled that they couldn't run amuck in the woods blasting away at anything that moved. People! Animals at least killed just for food, not sport.

"Hi," Lyons said, smiling, extending a hand to display his Homeland Security identification. "We're here for a fishing license." Blancanales and Schwarz did the same.

"Come again?" the woman replied slowly, raising an eyebrow. She started to speak, but Lyons held up a warning hand.

"We're just here for a fishing license, ma'am," he repeated, tapping the ID, then pressing a finger to his lips.

She blinked. "Oh…okay."

Pulling out an EM scanner, Schwarz started to sweep the room then stopped and pointed to a desk, then another and finally one of the stone support columns.

"What…uh, what kind of fish are you boys here for?" the ranger asked, looking at the man and touching an ear. He nodded, and she went red in anger, a hand going to the Colt on her hip. Then with a force of will, the ranger eased her stance and rubbed the side of her face. "We've got trout to the north with more fight in them than Mike Tyson, and salmon to the south about the size of Buicks. But they're all catch and release, you know."

"No problem," Blancanales said, tilting his head toward the

door. "By the way, we found a wounded deer on the road. Want us to bring it in for you or…"

"Better show me where the animal is located," she said briskly, and lifted the wooden trap to walk out from behind the counter. "Just let me grab a coat."

"No problem, ma'am," Lyons said, tucking away his ID booklet.

Going to a closet, the ranger took out a heavy parka, then scowled as Schwarz scanned the garment before letting her slide it on. Zipping up the front, the ranger stepped into the blast stream of the ceiling heater and held open the door as the three men stepped outside. She joined them, and they walked away from the ranger station, the air feeling that much colder after the warm and toasty interior of the redwood station.

Surreptitiously, Blancanales took a picture of the woman with his cell phone and e-mailed it to Kurtzman at the Farm.

Stopping in the middle of the gravel parking lot, the ranger pushed back her fur-edged hood and scowled. "All right, what the fuck is going on in my park?" she demanded softly. "I'm the chief ranger here, and there hasn't been any word of an operation going down around here."

"And there's not going to be any official notice," Lyons said. "We're trying to keep a low profile, Chief…?"

"Taylor," she replied. "Ann Taylor."

Chewing the inside of a cheek for a moment, the ranger made a decision and started walking. "Well, if somebody has bugged the station… I'll assume that's what you were checking for. Listening devices?"

"And found," Gadgets stated, patting the EM scanner inside a pocket.

She snorted at that. "Okay, if we're bugged, then this must be major trouble. What is it, drug smugglers again?"

"Much worse than that I'm afraid," Lyons said, easily keeping pace with the woman. "Homeland doesn't bother with narcotics or gun running."

"Damn, it's terrorists," she said, coming to an abrupt halt. "Who do we have hidden in the hills, Osama bin Laden?"

"That's classified," Lyons said in a friendly tone. "Now, how come the chief ranger was working the desk?"

In spite of the situation, she almost smiled at that. He had to be an ex-cop or something. He understood the hierarchy of the station politics. "Had to," Taylor replied honestly. "Everybody else is out with food poisoning. There's just me and a couple of new guys to patrol a forest larger than Rhode Island."

Without comment, the Stony Man operatives exchanged meaningful looks. Right, all of the rangers at the national park where the terrorists had a base got sick from food poison on the same week of the attacks. Anybody who considered that a coincidence was operating with one brain cell short of insanity.

"How did they all get food poisoning?" Blancanales demanded suspiciously.

"Weekend barbecue. Guess the pork was bad."

"And why aren't you sick?" Lyons asked pointedly, a smile on his face, but inside the pocket of his vest the man eased off the safety of his .357 Colt Python. The tiny noise was lost in the gentle mountain wind.

"I'm a vegan, a vegetarian," Taylor answered proudly. "Only had the corn bread and potato salad." She shook her head. "I could hear my staff losing dinner in the bushes for hours…" Suddenly, the woman snapped up her head. "Holy

shit, we were poisoned by—" she made a vague gesture "—whoever the hell you Feds are after."

"Most likely," Lyons admitted, impressed that she figured it out so quickly. "Actually, we're all lucky to be alive. These are real hardcases we're dealing with, and they kill without warning."

Inhaling through her nose, the ranger let it out slowly. "So why the hell did they bug the station?"

"Probably to keep a watch out for people like us."

That took the chief ranger a moment to digest, and she clearly didn't like the flavor. "Those dirty sons of bitches," she muttered vehemently. "Okay, guys, how can I help?"

"With information," Schwarz stated bluntly. "Have there been any unusual deaths in the park?"

"Anybody gone missing, drowned but the body was never recovered, that sort of thing?" Blancanales added.

"In a park this size? Hell, yes," Taylor replied, hitching her gunbelt. "We have a couple of thousand tourists wandering about the place, plus a hundred scientists checking our glaciers, so some damn fool is always falling off a cliff or breaking a leg. We have a search and rescue helicopter, a Black Hawk, and it gets a lot of use. Know the type?"

"Vaguely," Lyons said, successfully hiding a smile.

"As for deaths," the woman said, thoughtfully biting a lip. "We have about ten thousand signs telling folks not to feed the grizzly bears their hands…" She paused as the men chuckled at the old joke. "But some nitwit will still try to bounce a rock off a griz, and then they act surprised when the bear retaliates and eats them."

"Are there a lot of grizzlies here?" Schwarz asked, looking over the serene vista of the mountainous parkland. The evergreens reached down to the shore of the blue lakes and snow-

capped mountains rose impossibly high. In the very far distance was a large white expanse that the man knew was one of the parks many glaciers.

"We have too many grizzlies in my opinion," Taylor replied, crossing her arms. "I've been wanting to thin down the population for years, but we're only armed with pistols and shotguns. Those didn't do jackshit against a twelve-foot-tall, 600-pound, fully grown griz. For years I've wanted to get a Barrett Light Fifty, or even an old-fashioned Holland & Holland .575 elephant gun. But the state procurement office insists those would only endanger the precious tourists." She shrugged. "Guess we're just too far down on the list to be considered important enough."

"Which would you prefer?" Lyons said, shifting his boots on the frosty ground. "A double H or a Barrett Light?"

What was this, a bribe? The chief got angry for a minute, then relented. She was planning to help the Feds, so why not also get the desperately needed weapons?

"Well, if you're going to offer me a reward for helping out," she said in explanation, "then I'll take the Barrett. Thanks. Plus two hundred rounds."

"Done," Lyons said. "You'll have it in a week. And you'll get the weapon whether or not you tell us what we want to know. I don't bribe the police."

"I'm not a cop."

"Close enough for me."

Chief Taylor broke into laughter, revealing previously unseen dimples. "Fair enough! By God, we need that rifle. Make it two, and I'll personally escort you around the place for a week. Two weeks! One for each Barrett."

"We don't have anywhere near that long," Lyons replied

honestly. "And you can't come with us. Just tell us where the greatest amount of unusual deaths occur."

"No, forget that," Blancanales interrupted, his eyes brightening with comprehension. "Where is the highest concentration of grizzlies?" The huge bears would make natural guards for the terrorists, and anybody the Albanians killed could simply be tossed to the animals as food. There wasn't much left after a grizzly mauled a body, aside from boots and gnawed bones.

"The largest population of grizzlies would be in the breeding grounds," the chief said slowly. "And that's also where we've had about a dozen people vanish over the past six months. It's why I wanted the rifle so much. Thought they had been eaten by the bears, but now…"

"Any chance there's a lake nearby?" Lyons added hopefully. "Or a glacier?" The terrorists in Nevada had mentioned the lodge, but that was near the ranger station, and there wasn't a glacier nearby for fifty miles. This had to be where they met, arranged for supplies and all. The base and the computer would be as far away from any settlements or hotels as possible.

Just then, Blancanales's cell phone vibrated, and he took the call. It was from Kurtzman and showed a government-issue ID photo of Chief Ranger Ann Taylor. It was the woman they were talking to.

"A lake and a glacier?" Taylor replied, turning to look to the north. "Sure thing. There's a big lake near the grizzly-bear breeding grounds that's fed by a glacier. One of our largest."

"What's it called?" Gadgets asked eagerly.

"Ptarmigan Lake," the woman said. "Coldest damn water in the whole park. No good for swimming. You'd die in minutes. Only bears and salmon like the place."

Along with supercomputers. Lyons glanced at the other two men. They nodded in agreement.

"We'll need directions," he asked. "Along with one other small favor…"

CHAPTER SIXTEEN

Stony Man Farm, Virginia

Entering the Computer Room, Barbara Price heard only the soft tapping of the keyboards, and knew the team had to be in a fight. Even under the worst of times, the hackers were joking and drinking coffee, unless they were facing some problem that could cost lives. Then they went dead silent and bent to the consoles as if weighed down with the importance of their work. Watching the team for a few minutes, Price turned and started to leave.

"Found it!" Carmen Delahunt cried out in triumph, her gloved hands touching the empty air as she accessed files. "I've found the Icarus… Shit!"

Throwing the VR helmet off her head, the woman cringed, turning away from the console and trembling.

"What happened?" Kurtzman demanded, looking up from his monitor. He tried to slave his controls to the woman's and found no signal.

"It blew up…" Delahunt said shakily, taking off the gloves and wiping the sweat off her pale face. "I found the satellite,

and hit a a wall of intruder countermeasures of tremendous strength, unlike anything I've ever encountered before, and then…it destroyed itself."

"With you still inside the virtual-reality matrix?" Akira Tokaido whispered. "Those bastards tried to scramble your brains!"

"Damn near worked," Delahunt said with a weak smile. "A long time ago I was in a car crash with a semitruck. This felt pretty much like the same thing, only inside my head."

"So the Icarus is destroyed?" Price asked, walking over to the trembling redhead. She patted her on the shoulder. "Well done, Carmen."

"Destroyed?" Delahunt repeated, as if she had never heard the word before. "Hell, no, when I was inside I found ten, twenty relay points. There must be a fleet of these things in orbit around the world."

"Interesting," Huntington Wethers muttered thoughtfully around his cold pipe. He removed it from his mouth and tapped the stem against his cheek. "We knew there had to be two or three of the satellites because of the timing on some of the strikes. But ten of them…" He shook his head.

"Or twenty," Tokaido reminded him, scowling fiercely. "Okay, if we found one, then we can find the rest and…"

"And get your entire console scrambled," Delahunt shot back. "Akira, this satellite didn't have an operational system, it was ground controlled."

"Great!"

"By something huge," she continued unabated. "And I mean, motherfucking huge."

That caught Price by surprise. She didn't think she had ever heard the women use profanity before.

"How huge?" Kurtzman demanded, pushing away from his

controls and turning the wheelchair so that he faced her directly. "Are we talking another Cray supercomputer? Do these Albanian assholes have a Cray?"

"Worse," Delahunt replied, a little color coming back into her cheeks. "Much worse than that. I think we're facing a Thunderbird."

The rest of the hackers went silent.

"A what?" Price asked scowling. "Is that some form of advanced antiintruder software or—"

"It's a computer," Kurtzman said, cracking his knuckles. "A supercomputer, brand-new on the market."

"Well, it can't be as powerful as a Cray Mark IV," she began with a forced chuckle. But the woman stopped when she saw their grim faces. "Are you telling me, this Thunderbird is equal—"

"Better," Kurtzman said, inhaling deeply. "The Dell Thunderbird is, oh, hell, I don't know, ten times more powerful?"

"At least," Wethers stated, crossing his arms. "Carmen, my dear, are you sure it didn't track you back to here?"

"Initiating emergency shutdown protocols," Tokaido said brusquely, his hands flying across the keyboard.

A shutdown? Price was stunned.

"Are we talking the same Dell company that makes the inexpensive home PC?" Price asked in surprise. "Is this thing is good enough to hack us? I didn't think anything could attack a Cray Mark IV!"

"Yes, the same Dell," Kurtzman said with a humorless laugh. "They also make great big, incredibly expensive computers for industry, the military, NASA, the Atomic Energy Commission and the NSA. The most powerful supercomputer in the world is an IBM Blue/Gene, but the second best, and the absolute fastest, is the Dell Thunderbird. Christ, it

must have a thousand servers and more terra-floppies... A Dell T-Bird could easily smash through our firewalls and ICE to take over our Cray and turn the automatic defenses of the Farm against us. Launch every SAM we have in the bunkers to have them turn around in midair and come right back."

"Are you serious?"

"As a heart attack."

"Shit!"

"Ready for shutdown," Tokaido said woodenly, a finger poised above a glowing button.

"Well, stay that way," Kurtzman growled, wheeling back to his console. "We're down, but not out of the fight yet." It looked like Able Team was right on the money when they thought the Albanians had some sort of supercomputer hidden in Montana. But a Thunderbird! Without the access codes, his team might as well throw rocks at an aircraft carrier as try to hack that monster. But there were other options.

"I've already started gaining access to the IBM Blue/Gene supercomputer at NORAD," Wethers said around his pipe. "If the Dell finds us, at least we'll have some backup." Moving at blurring speeds, binary commands scrolled by his monitor.

"Activating safeguards," Delahunt announced, pulling on her VR helmet once more. Instantly, automatic scramblers kicked into action, disks were spit from computers so the data on them could be accessed in any manner and several slave computers physically disengaged from the main console, also terminating any possible cybernetic raid. The mighty Cray was no longer attached to the physical ordnance of the Farm.

"Also, scramble some stealth bombers from Edwards Air Force Base," Price said, staring hatefully at the vector graphic map of world on the main wall monitor. "I want them on the

way to Glacier National Park and ready to destroy it if need be. But no nukes! Only conventional weaponry."

"The entire park? Are you sure…" Delahunt started slowly, her gloved hands slowing in their manipulation of the electron streams.

"Absolutely. Also, have a couple of Army battalions ready to invade the park," the mission controller added, "with full armor support! If Able Team calls for assistance, we better be ready for anything. We're only going to get one shot at this."

"On it," Kurtzman said, his large hands relaying the messages. "By the way, got any idea what we're going to do about that unknown number of Icarus satellites in orbit?"

"Yes, I do," she said, walking to the wall phone and making a secure call over a landline. "Hello, Hal? We've got trouble…"

Kadriouski Mansion, Albania

SAFELY SURROUNDED BY THE five-story-tall mansion on all sides, the enclosed plaza was full of working servants preparing for the evening celebration. Over in a huge gazebo, a full orchestra was tuning its instruments, and the catering staff hurried around to the soft musical sounds of clinking glassware. Steam tables were being aligned along a rose trellis and in the center of a massive buffet was an ice sculpture of a two-headed eagle, the symbol of Albania. The number fifteen had been delicately added to the translucent base.

Going to a stone obelisk, a new head butler slid aside a disguised panel and flipped a switch. For a moment nothing seemed to happen, then the bottom of the Olympic-size swimming pool began to rise, the crystal-clear water flowing through a series of small vents, until the mosaic was flush to the surface of the patio.

Snapping his fingers, the butler directed a squad of house-men to roll out an expensive cashmere rug across the tile in preparation for the evening's dance. The guests might go swimming later, especially if the new shipment of cocaine was tested for its purity, but first and foremost, came the formal dance. This was a night of nights! Not because of the thriving business of the Fifteen Families, but because after so many years, little Anna was finally coming home.

But a child no more, the man mentally corrected himself. When kidnapped she was sixteen, now she would be in her early thirties. He shook his head sadly. He could almost feel sorry for what the Fifteen Families would do to the bastard who had ordered her capture.

Armed guards walked the rectangular roof of the mansion in groups of three, one man carrying a radio, another binoculars, the third a bolt-action rifle with telescopic sights. All of them wore body armor and carried machine pistols and grenades. It was absurd to think that anybody would be insane enough to disturb the joyous celebration, but the guards were ready for anything, just in case.

WATCHING THE PREPARATIONS from the roof of a nearby apartment house, Phoenix Force stayed low in the dark shadows. Their black combat fatigues blended into the shadows, and the faces of the commandos were slashed with black camouflage paint.

"Looks like it's going to a hell of shindig," Hawkins subvocalized into his throat mike, both hands tight on his monocular. "How do you want to play this, David, straight up?"

"Roundabout," McCarter replied, threading a sound suppressor onto the barrel of his Browning Hi-Power Pistol. Back at the Farm, Cowboy Kissinger had acquired a small supply

of the infamous KGB Silent Bullets, but the rounds carried only half-charges. So while they were absolutely silent, only giving a subdued click when discharging, their penetrating power was pitiful. The former SAS commando much preferred the gentle cough of an acoustical suppressor, the 9 mm parabellum bullet hitting with full power. The hammer was about to fall in Albania, and this was no time for half measures.

Just then a long black limousine pulled up to the front gate and honked a horn. The street guards checked under the vehicle for bombs while the steel gate was slowly lowered into the ground, the top of the wide metal slab forming a smooth path through the thick stone wall.

"These boys don't miss a trick," Manning said, gently working the arming bolt on a MP-5 machine gun, the deadly Barrett hung across his back. "But then, Lord knows they have enough enemies."

Normally, the expert sniper watched the other team members from some high vantage point while they went into a danger zone. But this time, he was going along. Durres was too dangerous a city for anybody to be left alone. The team stayed tight on this probe.

"Yeah, including us," Encizo whispered, then quickly added, "Heads up! Four o'clock."

Turning to train their monoculars in that direction, the team members saw a strange pair of people walking through the set of French doors in the mansion. The man was wearing a tuxedo, but was so heavily muscled he seemed about ready to burst apart at the seams. His head was shaved clean and a terrible scar bisected his ugly features. There was a Heckler & Koch G-11 caseless rifle hanging off a shoulder and his jacket bulged on the left side from a holstered weapon. The

woman was gorgeous, wearing a blue satin dress that showed off a lot of very shapely legs and a deep bosom. Her hair was up in a complicated coiffure and jewelry sparkled around her throat and wrists. But she also was carrying a weapon, a Neostad shotgun and the handbag slung over the opposite shoulder bulged with oddly shaped items.

"Beauty and the Beast," James said, adjusting the focus of the monocular. "If they're still here, then so is Sakir Elsani. He doesn't take a piss without them nearby."

"Think they're actually as dangerous as they look?" Encizo asked, memorizing their faces.

"Are we?" Manning snorted in grim amusement.

"I sure am. Don't know about you, though."

"We try for the report before snatching Elsani," McCarter said, lowering the monocular to check his watch. "And ignore Slobodan. The son of a bitch is so old that he could have a heart attack on us and then we'd really be in Barney."

"That means in trouble, right?" Hawkins asked, trying not to smile at the Cockney slang. It showed up in McCarter at the oddest times.

"Very deep trouble," the man gruffly replied. "Besides, if we can get in and out again without them even knowing, that will give NATO a big edge when they attack." McCarter checked his watch again. Two more minutes. "Time to move, people."

Without a sound, the Stony Man team slipped off the roof-top and down the old wooden fire escape to disappear into the night. Left behind on the roof was a squat package plugged into an electrical outlet, the power source being the main reason they had chosen the former hotel as their surveillance point.

Ghosting from shadow to shadow, the men of Phoenix

Force kept low as they proceeded around the walled estate until reaching the southern side. There the granite wall was solid, without doors or windows. Pulling out an EM scanner, James said nothing as he found several proximity sensors buried in the concrete sidewalks. Calmly, the men waited as the seconds ticked away to zero hour.

Checking his watch one last time, McCarter pulled out a small radio control box, extended the antenna to its full length, checked the batteries, then pressed a button. Instantly the northern sky was rife with gunfire, the chattering of the heavy-caliber weaponry only a distant murmur.

Suddenly the guards on the wall began to shout and bright searchlights crashed into life on top of the Kadriouski mansion, the beams sweeping across the city to focus on the former castle of King Zogu. Explosions dotted the massive structure and the sound of machine guns seemed to be increasing.

"Fucking Dectra Nine assholes chose a bad night to decide who was in charge again," a man muttered, raising a pair of Russian field glasses for a better look. "The idiots! The old man will have their balls for breakfast, eh?"

But there was no response from his friend.

"Vorha?" he asked, lowering the glasses and glancing behind.

Crouching near the motionless body of the guard, McCarter pulled his Gerber combat knife from the throat of the dead man, just as Hawkins climbed into view holding a rope.

The stunned guard had only a split second to register the grappling hook attached to the knotted rope when Hawkins fired his Beretta, the flame only a subdued flicker at the end of the sound suppressor. The gun gave a soft cough, and the other guard staggered backward, almost going over the edge

to topple inside the estate when McCarter grabbed him by the belt and hauled the dying man back into the darkness. Struggling for air, the guard tried to shout out a warning, but Hawkins covered his mouth with a calloused hand and fired the Beretta 93-R at point-blank range. The man jerked at the impact of the bullet and sighed into death.

A few moments later the rest of the team was atop the wall. Lowering the dark-colored rope inside the estate, James slithered down and took a defensive position in the dense shrubbery until the others joined him on the grass. Shaking the grapple loose, Encizo rolled it into a coil and slung it over a shoulder, then the team proceeded swiftly along the base of the wall to the eastern side of the mansion, far away from the banquet tables and orchestra.

A couple of guards stood near a set of French doors, liberally pouring champagne into their coffee mugs to hide the indiscretion. Keeping low behind a rosebush, McCarter moved a finger, indicating the order, and Hawkins nodded. Rising together, the men fired in unison, the guns chugging softly. Just as he set their champagne bottle into a silver bucket full of ice, a guard doubled over and toppled to the rug, blood gushing from the hole in the back of his neck that had previous held his spinal column. The other guards gasped at the sight and went for their guns when more coughs sounded. Groaning into death, the men doubled over from the searing pain in their bellies and tumbled off the patio onto the grass.

Moving quickly, Manning and Encizo pulled the bodies under some laurel bushes and James poured out the champagne to wash away the small traces of blood. In seconds it was all over, and the only indication that anything had just happened in the library was a faint smell of gun propellant, which was mostly masked by the aroma of the French champagne.

"How long will the fireworks last?" Manning subvocalized, sweeping the MP-5 across the manicured lawn, looking for targets.

"The AutoSentries have enough ammo for about ten more minutes," James replied over the radio link. "Then the C-4 satchel charges cut loose in the armory and the whole town will be watching the castle blow itself apart."

Loosening the grapple, Encizo swung it back and forth a few times to loosen his muscles, then he spun the aluminum hook around in a blur and let it fly. The cushioned grapple soared over the fifth story and landed without a sound. Testing the rope, the little Cuban nodded to the others and started climbing up fast, going hand over hand.

Reaching the rooftop, he swung up his silenced Walther PPK .38 pistol and eased around the brick flue of a large chimney.

Standing on the other side of the roof were two more guards, staring at the pretend battle raging inside the castle. Dropping prone on the asphalt-covered walkway, Encizo gave a low groan. As the two men turned, he groaned and rolled onto his side. As the armed men rushed closer, Encizo waited until they were far enough away from the edge and then fired a fast four times, tracking both of the gasping men as they collapsed into death.

Going around the chimney, the Phoenix Force pro found the other men already on the roof, James pulling up the rope and placing it in a neat pile in the darkest shadows, just in case the team had to leave the same way it gained entry.

Going to their bellies, the team crawled across the roof until reaching a decorative brick kiosk. James checked for traps, while McCarter tricked the lock with a keywire gun and

Hawkins oiled the hinges. A second later the lock disengaged and the door swung open silently.

Taking the lead this time, Hawkins proceeded down the stairs, keeping his feet on the extreme edges of the steps where the old wood would be the strongest and least likely to creak. At the bottom of the stairs was a steel fire door with bright light coming from under the jamb. There was a handle, but no visible lock. Obviously it was barred on the inside. Slapping a small wad of C-4 on the hinges, Hawkins attached wires and waited with a finger on the detonator. The timing had to be exact on this or else.

"Ready…on my mark," McCarter whispered, checking the military watch on his wrist. "Three, two, one…now."

Covering his face with an arm, Hawkins tripped the C-4 and it cut loose just as the light under the door went out. A moment later the C-4 charges in the castle on the next hill detonated, sounding like distant thunder.

Easing the door out of the way, the team slipped into the dark hallway and positioned the door back into place. A close inspection would show that it had been blown, but they were hoping the house guards for the Fifteen Families were going to be too busy checking out the battle at the castle to bother with the rooftop. The EMP bomb on the roof of the old hotel should have blown the electric circuits for about half the city, hopefully making it appear the explosions at Castle Zogu had cut an underground power line. It should take the Fifteen Families hours to figure out the truth, and by then the Stony Man team would be long gone.

Spotting a video camera attached to the wall, Manning spray painted the lens black to make it seem out of order, even when it came back on line. McCarter did the same to another camera, and the team moved stealthily along the carpeted

hallway and down the stairs to the fourth floor. So far, so good. Everything that used transistors or chips seemed to be down. The team also carried advanced electronics, but all of their equipment, from the laptop to their radios, was shielded from an EMP blast. Hopefully, none of the guards also possessed shielded radios.

Voices could be heard coming from the lower levels of the estate, most seeming to be curses mixed with hysterical laughter. Obviously, some of the people at the party had to have arrived drunk. Risking a glance out a window, McCarter saw that candles had been distributed, the mob of well-dressed people eerily illuminated by the flickering flames. Flashlights bobbed about the crowd, and suddenly a row of luxury cars turned on their headlights. McCarter was shocked at the sight, then realized only the vintage cars, Rolls-Royces and Bentleys were operating. All of the flashy new cars like the Cadillac limousines, Lexus sedans, Ferraris and Lamborghinis were dead.

"Always did think cars were relying too much on electronic parts," Hawkins whispered, nodding at the sight of elderly adults herding children into the few working vehicles. Good, soon all of the noncombatants would be gone, greatly reducing the possibility of an innocent bystander getting hurt in a firefight.

Suddenly a flashlight swept across the window. Quickly, McCarter and Hawkins stepped back into the shadows, and the beam moved onward. After a moment the men relaxed when the beam did not return and continued down the hallway to rejoin the rest of the team.

Reaching a set of double doors, the team took cover as Hawkins knocked softly. They heard the sound of footsteps, and one door was swung aside by a beautiful woman carrying

a candle. She was dressed in only a flimsy negligee, the strap off one shoulder exposing her left breast.

"Slobodan?" she asked, squinting into the hallway.

Holstering his Beretta, Hawkins stepped aside and James fired a stun gun. The compressed gas hissed as it sent twin barbs flying, hair-thin wires trailing behind. The woman gasped as they penetrated her lacey clothing. James flicked the setting to medium and pressed the switch. The box hummed softly, and the woman went stiff as the 50,000 volts coursed through her thin frame. As she started to collapse, Hawkins caught her in his arms. The candle hit the carpeting, throwing hot wax before going out.

Moving swiftly through the doorway, the team made sure there was nobody else in the spacious office, while Hawkins carried the woman to a couch. Gently laying her down, he checked her pulse and breathing.

"She's okay," the big man reported, pulling a duvet off the back of the couch and covering the woman. Just a girl, really, she could not have been more than eighteen. "But we better make this short. If the head of the Fifteen is expected here soon, he's going to have company, and some of them may have guns."

"Only some of them?" Encizo said, arching an eyebrow as he came out of the bathroom. "Clear."

"Same here," Manning reported, closing a closet door.

"Rafe, James, watch the hall." Checking the GPS device in his hand, McCarter went to a window with the curtains closed, then turned and walked to a table set between a pair of chairs. There were dirty glasses reeking of alcohol on the table, and the ashtray was full of cigarette and cigar ash. There was also a business-size envelope laying in plain sight. Lifting it, McCarter pulled out the papers inside. Unfolding

them, he found four sheets of a heavy linen paper covered with orderly typing. Turning over the pages, he muttered a curse, then laid them on the table and started to flatten them as best he could.

"Shut the drapes!" he ordered. "I think we have the report but it's in what I will assume is Albanian."

"Any numbered sequences?" James asked hopefully. "That could be the access codes."

"Negative, only text."

As the drapes were pulled on the rest of the windows, Encizo joined his team leader, flicked on a small halogen flashlight and aimed the bright beam at the pages. Flicking open a cell phone, McCarter took a shot of the top page, then slide it aside to get the second, third and fourth. Rafe turned off the halogen and tucked it away as McCarter pressed a transmit button and the images were relayed halfway around the world to the Farm.

"Got them," Kurtzman said in their ear jacks. "Translating now… Good work, this is the report that we wanted. Finland invented the machine…the KGB killed the scientists and stole the blueprints…built a dozen of them… Damn, Barbara, there's a dozen of the damn things in orbit, not two or three!"

"On it," Price replied softly from the background.

"Any codes?" McCarter demanded impatiently. "We're in kind of a hurry here."

"So I guessed," Kurtzman retorted. "Supercomputer relays the commands off commercial telecommunications satellites to each Icarus, not through them, off the outer hull. The clever bastards are bounding radio signals around the world like a pool player shooting the cue across a table full of balls… Must try that myself sometime… Computer is located in America where the Yankees will never think of looking for it."

"Think again, asshole."

"You got that right… Damn, no mention of the precise location of the Thunderbird."

"They have a T-Bird?" James said sharply.

"Bet your ass, but Able Team is on the way… Shit, sorry, the rest is a plan for world domination. Turn Russia against the U.S.A., seize control of the Watchdog, Keyhole and Echelon satellites, disband the United Nations…but no access codes."

"Damn. Thanks anyway. Out," McCarter muttered automatically. He closed the lid on his cell phone, terminating the connection. "Okay, time for Plan B," he growled, stuffing the report into a pocket of his fatigues. "We have to find Sakir Elsani and get the access codes from him."

"No problem," Hawkins said, removing the sound suppressor from his Beretta. "Let's go to a party."

CHAPTER SEVENTEEN

Rocket Force High Command, St. Petersburg

There was a knock on the door and it swung open to reveal a colonel dripping sweat and panting for breath. "Sir, we have just received a dispatch that Vladivostok has been hit! As are all of our reserve MiG-99 and the F-35 fighters at Minsk!"

"I see," the general said slowly, placing aside a Most Secret report on the Albanians. "Is there any word from the Kremlin?"

"Yes, sir. The president has informed us that there has been a command issued by the terrorists—"

"What was that again?" the general interrupted with a roar, standing to push back the chair with his legs. "They have given Russia a *command*? Did I hear that correctly?"

"Yes, sir," the colonel replied smoothly, passing over a sealed envelope embossed with the seal of the Kremlin. "We have been com—strongly requested to launch all of our remaining ICBMs at these targets in Europe and North America."

Scowling darkly, the general looked at the list. These were all major NATO bases, along with Interpol headquarters, Edwards Air Force Base in California, Cheyenne Mountain

and northern Virginia. That would be FBI headquarters, the CIA, the Pentagon and who knew what else. Perhaps the Fifteen Families really was behind all of this, these were exactly the people they hated the most. The general started to speak, but stopped himself. If they were to attack America, were they going to launch at Russia in return? And what about Britain, France and the Chinese? Were the mad fools in Durres trying to start a global nuclear war? His next words could herald the end of the world. Was that why he was born, to betray Russia and smash civilization?

"How soon is this to be done?" the general asked.

"Immediately, sir!"

"I see." The general sat down and scowled fiercely. *Command*. The word left a bad taste in his mouth. No civilian had given him a direct order since the end of the Soviet Union, and he had shot the escaping KGB agent in the back.

"Now, listen to me very carefully, Colonel," he said slowly, choosing his next words most carefully. "I want you to order the special forces troop to take control of our silos and machine gun the missiles."

The officer blanched. "What was that again, sir?"

"You heard me, soldier," the general growled, crumpling the paper in his fist. "Have the troops destroy the missiles! Shoot holes in the fuel tanks so that they cannot launch!"

"But, sir—"

"If the terrorists want these targets destroyed, then somebody is breathing down their neck hard. This is a desperate gamble to force us into submission." A cold smile formed on his stern face. "But they made a bad mistake thinking Russians make good little slaves. I refuse."

"But this comes from the President!"

"Who never served a day in the military. I refuse to obey

the terrorists. Now, order the missiles destroyed." The man laid a hand on the pistol holstered at his hip. It was not a ceremonial piece there just for decoration, but a deadly functioning weapon, the grip worn from so much use during the last days of the Soviet Union. "Destroy those missiles!"

"I…" The colonel licked dry lips, then stood taller and grinned. What the hell, a man could only die once. At least he would do so standing on his feet and not cringing like a whipped dog. "Yes, sir. The troops will be dispatched within ten minutes!"

"Make it five," the general replied, glancing at the wall clock. The White House had already contacted him about a possible attack on the terrorists. He had said no before, but now knew it might be their only hope. So be it.

As the colonel hurried from the office, the general lifted a receiver from a recess in his desk and touched a blue button set among a row of other colors. There was a fast series of clicks.

"Oval Office," the President of the United States said. "Have you reconsidered, General?"

The big man took a deep breath and let it out slowly. "Yes, I have," he replied in halting English. "When do we strike?"

Glacier National Park, Montana

LOOKING LIKE LAWMEN OUT of the Old West, Able Team was galloping along a hiking trail through the thick forest. Constantly checking their GPS device against the landmarks listed on the ranger map, they stayed parallel to the Flat Belly River to keep out of sight.

There had been a Bell and Howell helicopter available for them to use, courtesy of Chief Taylor, but the team needed to stay low-key in their approach to the possible terrorist base. Boats were also much too visible, and the old Jeeps made

more noise than a cement mixer, so they opted for horses. The animals were bridle-wise and surefooted, well-muscled powerful geldings who accepted the heavy packs of equipment as if they did this sort of thing every day.

Staying off the foot trails and roadways reserved for the rangers and game wardens, the men of Able Team took most of the day circling around the campsites and hotels to finally approach Ptarmigan Lake from the far side. Several times they caught glimpses of grizzly bears moving among the thick foliage, and their hands tightened on the cans of bear spray the chief ranger had provided. Thankfully, the horses sensed the bears long before the humans could, and always increased their speed to leave the area as quickly as possible, so there had been no grizzly encounters.

Cresting a low hillock, the Stony Man operatives slowed their panting mounts to a gentle walk and studied the rugged landscape spreading out below. The blue water lake was empty of boats, the surface shimmering like a mirror. Snow-capped mountains rose to the north, along with gigantic white slabs that twinkled from the runoff water trickling down their sides. These were the last few glaciers remaining in America, and soon they would be gone.

A thick blanket of green pine trees covered the rolling landscape, and somewhere off in the distance, the men clearly heard the call of a bald eagle.

"Now, I thought those were almost extinct," Schwarz said softly, rubbing a palm along the muscular neck of his mare. The horse nickered softly in reply.

"Not for a couple of years," Lyons said, rocking his hips to the motion of the horse. He hadn't gone riding in a long time and was remembering why he didn't like it. "In fact, I recently heard that swarms of eagles were eating small pets

someplace in Alaska, becoming such a nuisance that the locals were asking for federal assistance to get rid of the birds."

"Kill bald eagles?" Blancanales said, taken aback. The man was riding with the reins loosely held in one hand, the other carrying his M-16 assault rifle.

"No, not kill. Just chase them away."

"Did the state government help?"

"Told the folks to go screw a rolling doughnut." Lyons smiled. "I paraphrase that, of course. The politicians said it much nicer, but that was the gist of the statement."

"Good."

Stopping at a small waterfall gushing directly from the cracked rock face of a hill, the men let the horses take a drink, while they climbed down to stretch their aching legs and ran some scans of Ptarmigan Lake below with passive instruments.

"Nothing on the EM, infrared or UV," Schwarz said, fine-tuning the focus.

"Looks ordinary," Lyons added with a scowl, lowering his binoculars. "Think we might have the wrong place?"

"I'd say no," Blancanales said, bending over to pick up something from the ground. He tossed the item from palm to palm, then flicked it to Lyons, "What do you think of that?"

The Able Team leader made the catch and scowled. It was a shell casing from a neckered down 7.62 mm round, exactly the type used in an AK-47 assault rifle. Turning it over, he saw there was no serial number on the bottom, unlike those used by the mercenaries back in Alabama. Only government agencies had the facilities make shell casings like this, unmarked ammunition that could not be traced back to them. Correction, Lyons amended mentally. Government intelligence agencies *and international criminal cartels.*

"Okay, get hard," he directed, pocketing the spent shell. "No unnecessary chatter, stay alert for video cameras, land mines and snipers. You know the routine."

"Hell, we invented it," Schwarz whispered with a half smile, unbuckling a strap and sliding a pack off his horse. Adjusting the straps, the man donned the pack himself and shrugged a few times to get the heavy weight comfortable. Then he draped a winter camouflage poncho over himself and eased into the snowy bushes.

Doing the same, Blancanales then smacked the horses on the rumps and got them galloping off to the south. That was the shortest distance out of the breeding grounds and would soon bring them to a safe area. Joining his friend, the two men started meandering through the trees and shrubbery toward the lake, trying to stay out of sight as much as possible. Lyons had already gone ahead of them on the point position.

Circling a copse of trees, the Able Team leader paused as an EM scanner flickered, and he artfully moved past a camera hidden inside a dead tree. He didn't know what kind of camera it was, but better safe than dead.

Dropping to his belly, the Lyons crawled along a pile of loose boulders and rose again in their penumbra only to go motionless as the sight of a hairy form lumbering through a wide passageway amid some laurel bushes. A bear tunnel, he realized, and from the golden tint of the fur it had to be a grizzly. Quickly pulling out the bear spray, Lyons thoroughly doused himself from boot to poncho, hoping the stink would repel the animal if it caught his smell.

Suddenly a bush shook and a large hairy face thrust into view sniffing hard. Startled, Lyons did the only thing he could think of and yanked out the can to spray it directly into the face of the monster bear. Snorting and coughing, the bear

shook its head, making angry noises. Backing away for some distance, Lyons brought up the Atchisson autoshotgun. The weapon would definitely kill the large bear, but it would also announce to everybody within ten miles that somebody was in the area with military weapons. He clicked off the safety. *Come on, spray, do your stuff....*

Shaking the yellowish droplets off its whiskers, the grizzly turned away from the man and started rubbing its face in a patch of snow, rumbling and whimpering unhappily.

Easing into the bushes, Lyons put as much distance between him and the bear as he could before turning and sprinting away. Whew, he thought, score one for modern science.

Heading toward the lake again, Lyons spotted his teammates crouching near some bushes on the icy shore. They were already out of their ponchos and parkas, exposing the black scuba suits underneath. As he joined them, Blancanales opened his backpack and removed a Navy SEAL rebreather unit. Unlike a pressurized air tank, the rebreather left no bubbles behind to rise to the surface and mark the presence of a diver.

"We heard the howl," Blancanales said softly, strapping on the device. Placing the mouthpiece between his teeth, he tried a few breaths, then nodded in acceptance. "Glad you're still with us."

"Me, too," Lyons answered, easing his backpack to the ground. "Cut it kind of close there for a minute."

"So the spray works?" Schwarz asked, slinging his M-16 assault rifle across his chest. The weapon was barely distinguishable inside the multiple layers of watertight plastic.

"Sort of," Lyons muttered, shrugging off his outerwear. "But it took a whole can to get rid of one bear. If there had been two of them..."

Blancanales pulled a strange-looking pistol from his side holster.

The U.S. Navy had successfully denied the very existence of the Heckler & Koch P-11 pistol for decades until it was finally unveiled under the *Public Information Act*. The weapon was a version of an underwater pistol invented in 1976 by the Soviet Union. When the Joint Chiefs finally were informed about the bizarre weapon, they gave Heckler & Koch the task of recreating the gun, but didn't provide any technical details. All that was known was the Soviet weapon did exist, and it was lethal. After a dozen false starts, H&K finally delivered the G-11. The oversize revolver held five rounds, 7.62 mm steel darts encased in blocks of solid propellant. A pull of the trigger electronically ignited the block, and the dart took off. This was totally different from the Soviet weapon, but each of the underwater guns worked perfectly, aside from a diver not being able to reload the weapon in the field. Both aquatic revolvers had to be shipped back to the factory to be reloaded. A soldier had only five shots, no more, so the Navy SEALs had quickly learned to make every shot count. Oddly, a decade later, H&K used the exact same technology to create the G-11 caseless rifle, which ironically had a bad problem of misfiring if the propellant blocks got moist.

"Too bad it wasn't a girl bear." Schwarz chuckled, sliding on his face mask.

"Why, looking for a date?" Lyons replied, wading into the lake and spitting into his mask before slipping it on. The extra moisture kept the glass from fogging and making a diver virtually blind under water.

Blancanales snorted a laugh, and if Schwarz had a reply it was lost as the men waddled into the gentle waves of the frigid lake and sank below the surface. A terrible cold seized

the limbs of the Stony Man operatives, piercing their wetsuits like needles. Then the heater packs came to life and a soothing warmth cocooned them, banishing the terrible chill.

Silence filled their world, the only dim sounds coming from their own breathing and the gentle slap of the waves overhead. Then that was gone and they descended into the thickening gloom of the glacier lake.

As total darkness encased them, the men switched on small UV lights attached to their facemasks. The ultraviolet light penetrated further than visible light and could not be seen unless the enemy was also wearing a UV-sensitive facemask. The lake bottom was all blues and purples to the Stony Man team, the curving landscape surrealistic and slightly unnerving. A school of fish swam by, visible in the wash of the three UV lamps for only a few seconds before they disappeared into the Stygian gloom again.

In the tinted shadows below, weeds waved like windswept grass and the wreckage of an occasional rowboat was seen scattered amid the boulders and endless fields of broken gravel left behind by the retreating ice sheets.

The cuff between his sleeve and glove opened for a moment, and Blancanales stiffened from the icy pain, then the gap closed, and he continued onward. Never mind the terrorists, the team was already in a world of death. Without their heated suits they would have died within minutes.

Swimming slow and steady, the Stony Man team constantly checked their GPS device until reaching the middle of the glacial lake. That was where the enemy supercomputer should have been located, but there was nothing in sight but a large flat area of crushed stones, the remnants of the glacier receding over hundreds of years.

Pulling out a small conelike pistol, Schwarz did a slow turn

in the dark water, listening intently. However, the sonophone was picking up nothing unusual in the mountain lake. More fish, the brushing of weeds against each other, a sliding rock, more fish... Then he paused and boosted the sensitivity to maximum. Dimly, he heard men talking and laughing. But under water? Was there a frigging submarine in the lake?

Staying out of the way of their teammate, Lyons and Blancanales floated anxiously nearby, keeping a close watch on their air gauges, until Schwarz looked at them in triumph, gave a thumbs-up and started to swim earnestly toward the south. They quickly flanked the man and made sure their weapons were ready for combat.

Twice more, Schwarz stopped to check the source of the voices, then started to swim again in a new direction. Long minutes passed before the jagged slope of the shore came into view, along with a large rocky overhang. Lyons tapped Schwarz on the shoulder and tilted his head as a question. The electronics wizard tucked away the sonophone and nodded. This was the source of the voices. Whether it was the base of the terrorists was another matter entirely.

Studying the area, Blancanales noted that there was a steady stream coming out from below the rocks, and the water temperature dropped drastically until it was just above freezing. This had to be where the runoff from the Ptarmigan glacier flowed into the lake. But that didn't mean... Then he scowled and swam over to a nest of weeds. There among the plants were several chemical glow sticks, some of them partially buried under silt, but others clean and fully exposed. Somebody had been visiting this site for quite a while. Weeks, maybe months. Waving for the others, Blancanales pointed at the weeds, and they shared knowing glances.

Spreading out, the Stony Man commandos swam into the

stream, the mounting chill noticeable even through their heat packs. The passage beneath the rocky slab and the bottom of the lake became uncomfortably narrow, but then the rough stone rose sharply. Turning off their UV lights, the team now saw a sparkling pattern of light reflected off the surface of the water from above.

Trying to stay in the shadows, the Stony Man commandos rose slowly, and were surprised to spot an ordinary aluminum ladder bolted to the side of the underground lagoon. Instantly, they drew their P-11 pistols and tried to see through the choppy water, but it was impossible. Knowing there was no other choice, the men of Able Team moved away from the ladder and hovered just below the surface to let their eyes adjust to the light. There was a concrete ledge edging the water, and two men were standing near the ladder, holding what vaguely looked like AK-47 assault rifles.

Trying not to make a splash, Lyons eased his head out of the chilly pool. Now he could see that the two men were wearing heavy parkas, and were indeed armed with Kalashnikovs. Both of them were smoking cigarettes, and each had a belt around his waist supporting an ammo pouch for spare clips, a sheathed Bowie knife and a couple of Russian army hand grenades.

Lyons smiled at the sight. Okay, whatever was going on here was most definitely illegal with that kind of ordnance on display. This was looking better and better. Behind the two guards, a tunnel led into the—no, not the rock face, the material wasn't dark, but a translucent bluish white. The glacier! There was a tunnel cut into the glacier, water trickling down the sides and flowing out into the lake along a pair of deep grooves set into the concrete floor.

Waving a gloved hand under water, Lyons gestured for the

others to join him. As silent as ghosts, his teammates rose into view, and they all started slowly toward the concrete apron. Just then, one of the armed guards turned to throw a cigarette butt into the water. It hit with a hiss near the Stony Man team. The guards blinked in surprise, then swung up their AK-47 assault rifles.

"Mother of God, the FBI has found us!" one of them cried out, working the arming bolt of his weapon. "Kill them all!"

In unison, the men of Able Team fired their HK P-11 pistols from under the water. The finned steel darts lanced into the air and slammed into the guards, spinning them, blood spraying on the icy walls.

The first guard crumpled in a heap, blood pouring from the multiple holes in his parka. Dropping his assault rifle, the second guard clawed for a grenade on his belt and Lyons raised the P-11 to fire three more times. The first dart missed the man completely, the second hit him in the leg and the third buried itself in his throat. Releasing the grenade, the man dropped limply to the concrete, holding his throat in both hands. The deadly sphere rolled along the apron and plunked into the lake water to sink out of sight.

Moving fast, the Stony Man operatives scrambled out of the water and rushed into the tunnel for cover, but a minute passed and there was no explosion.

Yanking out the mouthpiece, Blancanales exhaled in relief. "Guess he didn't have a chance to pull the ring," he whispered, turning off the rebreather. "Jesus, that was close!"

"No thanks to this," Lyons muttered in annoyance, angrily tucking the HK P-11 back into its holster. Three shots to kill a man only ten feet away? That was beyond pitiful. Out of the water, a P-11 was damn near useless. He might as well have thrown the gun instead of firing the darts.

Checking the bodies, the team found the guards were carrying Albanian passports and embossed cards in their wallets that said the men were couriers for the Albanian embassy and had full diplomatic immunity. Growling, Schwarz tossed the cards away. Some body armor would have served them better than legal niceties. This was the new breed of twenty-first-century terrorist, trying to hide behind the very laws they ignored.

Removing their swimfins, the men slipped on combat sneakers, then unwrapped the plastic bags around their weapons and carefully checked for any leaks. When satisfied, the team activated their transponders and tried to contact the Farm, but there was no response.

"We're too far underground for the signal to reach," Schwarz explained, shrugging off his rebreather and placing it on the apron. "And the glacier isn't helping any, either. Ice stops radio waves even better than water."

"Then we're on our own," Lyons said. "Come on, let's find the computer and shut these people down hard."

"Sounds like a plan to me," Blancanales said with a grim smile. But just then a siren howled deep inside the tunnel, closely followed by a lot of men shouting and the sound of running boots.

CHAPTER EIGHTEEN

NORAD, Cheyenne Mountain

"Wait for it…" the mission controller said in a patient voice. He watched the ticking clock on the wall. "Almost there…"

Digital clocks were silent, but the technicians had found that the metronome beat helped the staff through tense situations when major problems arose, as if at least one machine was still on their side. Silly, but true. In times of stress, the human mind found the strangest things to use as comfort—a pipe that you couldn't smoke anymore but kept in your mouth anyway; a favorite book placed prominently in view; a picture of a loved one. Cary Grant never made a movie without wearing his lucky red socks, and astronaut John Glenn refused to be launched into space until somebody first asked him, "Are you a turtle?" Soldiers, scientists, artists and statesmen, everybody had his or her little rituals for good luck. Maybe they worked, maybe they didn't. But if it put the person in the right mode for success, that was all that mattered.

The wall clock ticked once more.

"On my mark…launch," the mission controller said in a deceptively calm voice.

Hunched over their consoles, fifty technicians pressed glowing red buttons on their consoles until they locked into position. At the sight, a surge of excitement filled the lieutenant. All around the world, his counterparts did the exact same thing at exactly the same instant. The terrorists had made a critical mistake. Every nation that had nuclear weapons, invariably also had some sort of a space program.

Walking a step closer, the lieutenant watched the vector graphic of the world on the huge monitor as hundreds of blinking dots rose into the skies from every continent and ocean. Every antisatellite missile that could be primed had just been launched from land bases, war ships, or fired from jet fighters. The massive armada included all American F-22 Raptors from Edwards AFB, eight Russian MiG-99 stealth fighters and a previously unknown pair of British F-35 superfighters from Windmere base in the Midlands. Every nation that had the technology to join the fight had contributed whatever they could. Whatever they had. Only an hour ago, the terrorists had sent in their demand for the access code to the surveillance satellites of every nation. That was what everybody had hoped would never happen, but when the hammer fell, the UN Security Council had acted unilaterally. Before the world bent a knee to their new masters, the superpowers were going to do their best to take them down. Every satellite orbiting the Earth that could not be accounted for was being targeted for destruction.

Watching the numbers scrolling wildly along the side of the world map, the mission controller for NORAD privately admitted to himself that an awful lot of the stuff orbiting the planet was merely junk: dead satellites, abandoned projects, wreckage from the few known high-orbit battles, garbage

tossed out of Mir, a busted mirror from the Hubble upgrade…
there was a grand total of forty thousand satellites flying
above the Earth, and more than ninety percent of them had
been eliminated as possible targets. That still left about four
hundred targets to be hit by three hundred antisatellite missiles. The final calculations had come from somebody with
the code name Bear. Even with the combined military might
of the entire planet, the UN armada had just barely enough
firepower to get the job done. Far too many stockpiles of AS
missiles had been lost in the first few nuclear detonations. The
clever bastards knew exactly when and where to hit the major
nations, the mission controller thought. Yet in spite of everything, the odds were still slightly in favor of the superpowers,
and if nothing went wrong, in about two minutes the terrorists would find themselves disarmed.

And one fucking minute after that, the American officer
thought proudly, NATO would swarm into Albania, going
from street to street, house to house and room by room, if necessary, until every member of the Fifteen Families was found
and dragged off to The Hague to be tried for crimes against
humanity. The general consensus was that the immensely
powerful drug cartel had to be behind the terrorist strikes.
How could anything this big take place in Albania without
their knowledge and consent?

On the wall monitor a winking light vanished as a British
missile went off course and self-detonated. Come on guys, he
thought, keep it together! A Russian missile went wild and
veered off to nowhere, then an American turned rogue and
attacked a French missile blowing it to hell. That started a
chain reaction of scrambled signals that took six more lights
off the wall monitor. Then the missiles reached space, locked
on to their targets, hit and exploded. A strobing series of

flashes dotted the monitor from the north pole to the south pole. Dozens of bright lights became hundreds, the explosions overlapping one another on the monitor even though they were dozens of miles apart in space. Then it was over, and the map was clear once more of missile flights and unknown satellites.

"Every missile accounted for," a technician confirmed from her console while using a sleeve to mop the sweat off her face. "Three hundred and fifty-two missiles launched, three hundred and ten unknown targets destroyed."

"That's a confirm," the mission controller noted proudly. "Good job, people. With any luck, we just won the war."

"And if we didn't, sir?" a young tech asked, both hands poised over the controls of his console. "If we missed just one Icarus, then what?"

Forcing a brave smile, the mission controller started to speak when there was a white flash on the edge of the monitor near western China.

"Sir, a nuclear weapon depository in Outer Mongolia has just exploded," the woman reported crisply.

"The same in South Africa, sir!" another technician added. "Along with an Israeli air-force base along the Gaza strip."

A heavy silence filled the command and control room for NORAD, and the mission controller slowly turned to walk sluggishly to a wall phone and report to the President on their failure to eradicate all of the enemy sats. The UN armada had done its best, and failed. At least two of the enemy satellites were still alive and functioning, maybe all of them, and there wasn't a single primed antisatellite missile left to fire at them. Of course, more were being assembled, but they would never arrive in time to be of any use whatsoever. Now the matter was in the hands of the politicians. The world leaders either

turned over the access codes to the surveillance satellites and officially surrendered, or they pulled off a miracle. God help them all.

Kadriouski Mansion, Albania

GOING TO A WINDOW, McCarter carefully parted an embroidered curtain and looked outside. The line of departing cars was almost gone. Only a few remained, including a Russian T-80 APC that had a large ugly man and very pretty woman walking along the sides, carrying weapons.

"That must be Sakir Elsani!" McCarter said. In only seconds the man would be through the gate and out into the city. No time for half measures. He glanced around and saw a blockhouse located near the gate. There were no windows or air vents and just a single steel door. Okay, if the gate was hydraulic, then that had to be the pumping station.

"Rafe, blow the blockhouse!" McCarter ordered, throwing back the curtains. "Gary, disable the APC! Everybody else, cover fire."

As the other men rushed into position, Manning placed the 9 mm Heckler & Koch MP-5 machine gun on a table and swung around the Barrett .50-caliber rifle to work the arming bolt and chamber a round.

"We only have one of these," Encizo said, sliding a plastic tube from his backpack. The U.S. Army LAW had been liberated from the Dectra Nine armory in case the team need to blow down the mansion to cover their escape.

"Then don't miss, amigo," Hawkins snarled, flipping the latch to throw up the window, admitting the cool night air. Now they could hear the voices of the people below, and the sound of off-tune music. Looking around, puzzled, Hawkins

spotted the orchestra inside the large gazebo, the men and women still playing their instruments. Poor bastards had to be terrified, he thought.

"Three o'clock," Hawkins announced grimly.

"Got it. Heads up, people, friendlies in the gazebo," McCarter said, aiming the MP-5. "Mark your targets!" The former SAS commando had kept the sound suppressor on the machine gun. It retarded the velocity of the rounds, but added an extra twelve inches to the barrel and increased the accuracy over a long-distance shot.

Rushing past the fireplace and into a private bedroom, Encizo pushed aside the curtains and raised the window. Then he extended the plastic tube to its full length, sights popping up on top along with a large button that clicked into place. Aiming the LAW at the blockhouse, the Stony Man commando noted the direction and strength of the ocean breeze and shifted the sights just a little to the left. The solid steel door would be the weakest point in the structure. Besides, the light antitank weapon was designed to penetrate inches of metal, not yards of concrete.

Always go with your strengths, Encizo noted, laying a finger on the firing button. "Ready," he subvocalized.

"Ready," Manning added softly, almost too low to hear.

Impatiently, McCarter waited as, one by one, the antique civilian cars rolled out the gate until there was only the Russian APC. "Fire!"

Holding his breath, Encizo pressed the button. A lance of flame exploded from the aft of the tube and a fiery dagger blew out the front to shoot over the milling people on the ground. A heartbeat later, the 70 mm rocket slammed directly into the door, blowing it off the hinges, and a tremendous detonation erupted inside the block house. Roiling flame

gushed out the ruins of the doorway and one of the walls cracked. Smoke and noise poured out of the breach, and a steaming red fluid flowed onto the grass as if the concrete building was bleeding to death.

Even as the blast reverberated over the Fifteen Families, the wide steel gate began to slowly close, shoving the bulky Russian T-80 APC back into the estate.

Instantly, the men of Phoenix Force opened fire on anybody wearing the blue uniform of a guard. Men went tumbling, blood spraying everywhere. Then Manning unleashed the Barrett and a large dent appeared above the engine compartment of the APC. The ugly man and pretty woman near the military vehicle whirled with their weapons at the ready, trying to locate the source of the attack, then the rolling boom of the Barrett arrived. They snapped their heads toward the mansion.

Itching to train his weapon on them, Manning concentrated on the APC and hammered the relatively thin armor above the engine with another 750-grain round. This time the hidden hinges burst and the hood flipped up to fully expose the diesel engine. Instantly, the APC started rolling backward, away from the gate. But it was already too late. Coolly, Manning put another round into the APC, the block cracking, dark fuel pumping across the hot metal. The next round ignited the spilled fuel, wild flames rising from the smashed machinery.

Suddenly a hail of bullets peppered the side of the mansion, the windows noisily shattering. Hawkins jerked as an incoming round bounced off his body armor, and he replied with a long burst of steel-jacketed death dealers from the chattering MP-5 machine gun.

Squads of armed men raked the mansion, clearly uncertain from which window the gunfire was coming from. But others

clustered around specific members of the Fifteen Families to form a living shield and rushed them off to the parking lot of dead limousines. Maybe the vehicles couldn't move, but the armored chassis would gave the crime lords a lot more protection than empty air. Screaming obscenities, an old blind man wearing dark glasses pulled out a Desert Eagle pistol and waved it around in a threatening manner. A burly guard looked around to make sure nobody was watching, then slapped away the titanic handgun and grabbed the old man to drape him over a broad shoulder and start for the waiting limousines.

Just then, the thick fumes began to pour from the APC, rapidly expanding to swamp the front drive in swirling smoke.

"Looks like the smoke generator is still working," McCarter muttered, moving away from the window. Dropping a spent clip, he inserted a replacement and worked the arming bolt. "Okay, let's get Elsani.

"Alive," he added hastily as the team rushed toward the hallway doors. "We must have him alive!"

Charging along the hall, the Stony Man commandos took the stairs to the second floor, then paused to take a combat position on the balcony just as the front doors swung open wide and a dozen men in blue uniforms rushed into the building.

Using volley fire, Phoenix Force ruthlessly cut down the Albanians, and then the next wave of guards that charged inside close behind.

Going to a window, McCarter cast a furtive glance outside, then ducked fast. The glass exploded as a shotgun blast splintered the window, sending the curtains flailing upward as if the cloth were startled by the attack.

"Can't see Elsani anywhere," he muttered into the throat mike. "But I caught Beauty and the Beast—if that's who

those two gunners are—rushing into the rose arbor that leads into the back lawn."

"Then we cut him off," Hawkins said, pulling the ring on a canister and tossing the bomb into the lobby. The grenade hit and bounced once off the polished marble, then detonated into a writhing fireball, the white phosphorous blazing brighter than any searchlight. Outside, men shouted in Albanian, and fired a variety of weapons into the chemical fire.

Kicking out the wooden railing, Phoenix Force climbed down to the living room of the mansion, and took off along a wide corridor heavily decorated with flowers and oil paintings. As they passed the open door to a library, a shadowy figure lurched into view and they nearly fired until realizing it was only a liveried butler. Then the commandos saw the mini-Uzi machine pistol in his grip and blew the man away before he could trigger a round.

In the kitchen, a score of cooks and maids were huddled on the floor screaming and raising their hands in surrender. Rushing past them, McCarter and Hawkins checked for any impostors among the serving staff, and shot one man in a badly fitted white jacket, only one hand held high, the other tucked out of sight. The other servants scrambled away from the dead man, and he fell to the linoleum, a bulky 30 mm MM-1 grenade launcher clattering to the floor.

Pausing to snatch the weapon, Hawkins rejoined his team outside just as they engaged a squad of guards. Raising the MM-1, Hawkins pulled the trigger. It boomed in reply and the guards fell back, torn to pieces by the barrage of stainless steel fléchettes. More guards rushed into view, and the Southerner fired again. But the next 30 mm shell hit only the ground to start pouring forth thick volumes of smoke. As the rest of

Phoenix Force started firing at the guards, he angrily tossed away the MM-1. The weapon was packed with a scenario load, and since he didn't know the order of the rounds into the big revolving cylinder, the weapon was virtually useless.

Stepping into view from behind a splashing water fountain, a short guard fired an AK-47 at the Phoenix Force. The 7.62 mm rounds tore a path of destruction through the flowering bushes edging the patio, a single round ricocheting off the Barrett rifle held by Manning. The man jerked from the impact, then swung the deadly rifle around and stroked the trigger. A foot-long lance of flame extended from the muzzle, the discharge sounding louder than the stun grenades. The AK-47 broke apart as the .50-caliber bullet tore through it. His hands pulped, the guard went flying sideways, tumbling and turning until landing in a sprawl on the flagstone path. His uniform was soaked with blood and he didn't move.

Working the bolt to lever in a fresh round, Manning noted a group of men off to the side, struggling to don old-fashioned bulletproof vests. He ignored them. The vests would not stop the Teflon-coated 9 mm rounds in the MP-5 machine guns, and the weight would slow down the guards considerably. A win-win situation there. Then he spied a large man strapping on the harness of a XM-214 electric minigun, the enclosed Niagara-style ammo feed going over his shoulder. The big Canadian knew that was real trouble.

Centering the crosshairs in the battery that powered the electric motor of the weapon, Manning fired again. The casing shattered and fat blue sparks crawled madly over the twitching man. His mouth opened in a wordless scream, his hair burst into flames, both eyes burst and then the ammo in the gun detonated all at once. The weapon thundered apart like a bomb, the halo of shrapnel rattling the nearby trees and

bushes, shattering a score of tiny windows in a fancy greenhouse and cutting down a dozen more guards.

"Nice to have you on our side," McCarter whispered, taking out a group of armed guards to their left.

"Always glad to lend a hand," Manning told him, levering in a fresh round.

The grass all around Phoenix Force started puffing up and the muted sound of a machine gun was audible above them. Diving for cover, the Stony Man commandos turned to rake the rooftop with the 9 mm rounds of their MP-5 machine guns, and Manning added a single round from the Barrett. A stone gargoyle on the corner shattered and a guard holding a machine gun cried out on the roof, grabbing the bloody ruin of his face. Pieces of the gargoyle plummeted to the ground to land with heavy thumps in the manicured grass, then a Thompson .45 closely followed.

A helicopter rose above a stand of trees and began to move off, heading away from the hilltop estate.

As if right on cue, the distant castle violently exploded, the stack of C-4 satchel charges placed in the rear courtyard finally igniting. The staggering blast illuminated the nighttime sky and the departing helicopter.

"Elsani!" McCarter cursed, working a jam from the ejector port of his machine gun. "Head for those trees! If there's one helicopter…"

More gunfire erupted from the rooftop, but the Stony Man team ignored the incoming bullets and zigzagged through the flower beds, hopping over the sculpted rosebushes until reaching the trees. Pausing to take their bearings, with the leaves on the trees shaking from flying lead, Phoenix Force looked down upon a sandbag nest full of guards holding AK-47 as-

sault rifles. The ruby-red beams of aiming lasers were sweeping the surrounding foliage, searching for targets.

"Take them," McCarter said in a deceptively calm voice, pulling a grenade from his chest harness.

In unison, the team threw the deadly spheres. The AP grenades sailed high and exploded in the air, raining a hellstorm of shrapnel behind the sandbags. The guards briefly screamed, then went silent.

Sprinting around the barricade, the team found a small heliport holding three helicopters, one of them covered with a gaily striped pile of canvas. The Albanians had covered the airships with a circus tent. One of the helicopters was a totally useless Bell and Howell bubble chopper favored by TV news crews because of the wide visibility. However, the Bell held only two men and carried no armor. But alongside the tiny bubble chopper was a pair of huge NH-90 Agusta transports.

Topped by four titanium blades, the huge airship carried two pilots, ten paratroopers and could haul ten tons of cargo. There were three separate sets of control wiring just in case of damage from enemy missiles; the fuel tanks were self-sealing to anything short of a 40 mm AP round, and the fuselage bore a composite armor totally resistant to small-arms fire and shrapnel. There were two side hatches and a rear ramp for loading a small vehicles. It wasn't a helicopter so much as a flying bus, oddly similar to their own C-130 Hercules.

The Agusta was protected by smoke generators, smoke, chaff, flares, antiradar and a nitrogen spray to confuse heat-seekers. It was also armed with two Hellfire missiles, five-foot-long monsters that had an eight-pound HEAT warhead, an explosive that sprayed out white-hot molten iron.

As the team got closer, they saw a man in a flight suit,

blood pooling around his cracked head. Tightening his grip on the MP-5, McCarter glanced skyward. Elsani had just executed the other pilot so that he couldn't be followed. Bad move, asshole, the Briton thought.

"David," Hawkins said, eyeing the massive Agusta, "can you fly this warehouse?"

"Watch me," McCarter snarled, slinging his machine gun and climbing to the aircraft.

A few seconds later the rear ramp descended with the sound of controlled hydraulics, and the rest of Phoenix Force rushed inside to grab wall seats. Hawkins and Manning stayed at the open ramp in case of trouble, and sure enough a squad of guards charged out of the trees, firing assault rifles and shotguns. The incoming lead ricocheted harmlessly off the mighty Agusta. The same was not true for the Albanian thugs when Hawkins and Manning replied in kind.

As the Rolls-Royce engines of the airship began to build in power, the turboprops started spinning faster and faster, until the huge aircraft was surrounded by a small hurricane.

A short man burst out of the trees, a Carl Gustav projectile launcher held expertly in his hands.

Instantly, the two defenders fired from the hip.

The spray of 9 mm rounds from the MP-5 stitched the handman cross the chest, knocking him backward from the multiple impacts. But no blood showed, only some sort of dark metal beneath his tattered shirt. Body armor! Then his head exploded from the .50-caliber round of the Barrett, a ghastly spray of bone, brains and blood smacking into the trees and bushes. As the corpse fell, the Carl Gustav fired, the deadly projectile going straight up to loudly detonate in the empty air.

"Wreck that other Agusta!" McCarter commanded from the flight deck, flipping controls.

Turning in that direction, Manning put three fast rounds into the fuel tanks of the transport. However, the large holes soon stopped leaking fuel, but it had been enough. Rearing back, Hawkins threw a thermite grenade. The canister hit the asphalt and rolled along to thunderously detonate near the other airship. The blast rattled the craft and ignited the liquid pooled on the ground, the sizzling thermite and aviation fuel combining to create a roaring inferno that licked hungrily at the tanks directly above.

"Now would be a good time to take off!" Hawkins suggested, then jerked backward from an incoming round. He hit the deck and rolled clear, the rest of the team firing to take out a guard standing behind the sandbag wall.

In a rush of power, the Agusta lifted off the heliopad and started moving away from the estate. As the rear ramp cycled shut, a crackle of gunfire came from below, but the Stony Man operatives were not concerned. The handguns and assault rifles were no longer a threat.

"Radar is clear," Enciso said, taking the copilot seat. A rainbow of lights reflected on the man's somber face as he worked the compact control board. "I can't find Elsani. Switching to infrared… Ah, there is he! Almost out of range. But not quite yet."

"Stay sharp," McCarter directed, adjusting the trim of the rotors.

Durres spread out below them, twinkling lights marking streets and cafés. In the harbor, cargo ships sat dark and imposing, the only illumination coming from the neon work lights of the tall skeletal cranes hauling crates onto waiting trucks.

A lot of those were probably full of drugs and weapons, McCarter thought grimly. But there was nothing the team

could do about that now. Elsani was most likely running straight for a bolt hole. If they were lucky. Or worse, a hardsite with enough state-of-the-art munitions to hold off NATO. And us, too, he added grimly. We have to force him down somehow and get those codes.

"Heads up!" Encizo called out from the console, a glowing screen beeping softly. "We have incoming at seven o'clock."

Checking that direction, McCarter saw four small helicopters appear on the horizon. The man cursed as he caught the radar silhouette of the airships. These weren't new choppers, or police helicopters, but Italian air force Mongoose gunships. Tough and heavily armed, the little brutes carried tons of weapons and were harder to stop than an avalanche. If memory served, the Mongoose came with a tribarrel 20 mm electric cannon and two weapon pods packed with Mistral missiles. Designed to take out tanks and warships, a Mistral would punch completely through the Agusta before detonating. Nimble and fast, the deadly Mongoose was the only military gunship designed and built entirely in Europe.

"Is NATO after us again?" Hawkins growled, loosening his seat belt.

"There are no markings on those gunships," James said, looking through a window with his monocular. "Must be more guards from the Fifteen."

"Hold on, mates!" McCarter shouted, flipping gangbars on the control panel. It took him a few precious seconds to find everything he needed, but suddenly the Agusta seemed to explode as thick smoke poured from the 35 mm clusters. Chaff and sizzling flares shot out sideways, briefly leaving visible contrails.

Blips appeared on the radar as missiles leaped away from the Mongooses. Watching through the windows in the side

hatch, the rest of Stony Man team braced for a hit. But the chaff got two; the missiles veering off wildly to attack the metallic confetti. The flares fooled a third, the heat-seeker diving for the magnesium charge and detonating in empty air. The fourth also went for a flare, but seemed to be distracted by the chaff halfway, then it violently exploded. The Agusta rocked from the trip-hammer blast as a hail of molten steel peppered the outer hull. On the flight deck, half of the controls went dark, then flickered and came back strong as the auxiliary systems automatically engaged.

"Readying a Hellfire!" Encizo called, his hands moving across the dashboard.

"Don't! We may need those for Elsani, and there's only two!" McCarter snapped, swinging the Agusta back and forth to try to avoid any possible cannonfire. Sure enough, a split second later, there was a stuttering roar from somewhere behind and a double line of tracers shot past the Agusta. The Briton released chaff and flares, coolly noting that they were almost out of both.

A missile streaked past the Agusta, heading for nowhere, then there came the sound of metal on metal and a cold wind whipped through the interior. The Agusta turned abruptly, the turbo-blades lowering pitch. Fighting to maintain control, McCarter dimly heard a loud boom from the cargo hold. What in the bloody hell… Manning!

Off to the left, the trail rotor of an Albania Mongoose seemed to explode, the shattered blades flying out like shrapnel. Instantly, the gunship began to rotate out of control, white vapor pouring from a ruptured fuel line and thick smoke coming from inside.

Standing brazen in the open hatchway, Manning fired the Barrett again, while the rest of Phoenix Force unleashed their MP-5 machine guns.

The windshield on a second Mongoose cracked into a spiderweb from the .50-caliber round, then the hail of DU 9 mm rounds hammered the military aircraft and the Plexiglas gave away completely. The pilot and gunner threw arms in front of their faces, but were cut to ribbons by the bulletproof plastic.

The third Mongoose tilted and surged forward, trying to protect the damaged aircraft. The Barrett spoke again, the hull of the gunship dented, but penetration was not achieved. Using the last of the DU rounds, the rest of Stony Man team switched clips and poured volumes of steel-jacketed lead at the intact Mongoose. The hot slugs ricocheted wildly, throwing out a display of white sparks as brass cases flew through the Agusta to fall musically to the metal deck, and fall through the open hatch.

The first Mongoose was falling behind, spiraling toward the ground in a controlled descent. But the second Mongoose was out of control, the bleeding pilot and gunner acting as if they were blind. Turning on their axis, the nose cannon fired randomly, and two more Mistral rockets launched from the weapon pods to streak right past the Agusta and head toward the farmlands below.

Arching around the other gunships, the fourth Mongoose got in the clear and the triple-barrel 20 mm cannon vomited a stuttering flame of death that raced directly toward the lumbering troop ship. Holding on with both hands, McCarter pulled the joystick to his chest and banked sharply, almost spilling Manning out the open hatch, but James and Hawkins caught the man by his belt and hauled him to safety. More smoke and chaff were unleashed, and a missile detonated close behind. A single heartbeat later, a halo of shrapnel arrived, pounding the Agusta like hard rain. An aft window shattered, several holes appeared in the thick walls, and

Encizo cried out as he fell onto the radar screen, blood spreading across his fatigues.

Swinging the MP-5 behind his back, Hawkins grabbed a ceiling stanchion and staggered for the rear of the transport. There was a row of lockers there, and he was hoping for the best. Experience told him that no drug dealer in the world would have an escape vehicle that wasn't carrying weapons. He only hoped one of them might prove useful.

"Lighten the load!" McCarter commanded, clutching the stick in a death grip. "Throw out everything you can!"

Moving fast, the men started tossing out the few boxes in the cargo hold, uncaring of what they contained. One of them hit the edge of the hatch and burst apart, creating a white whirlwind of powdered heroin before being drawn outside by the cold wind. The medical supplies went next, followed by the extra jumpseats and spare oxygen canisters.

Pulling a knife, Hawkins jimmied the lock of the first locker and flung open the door. It was full of parachutes. Moving to the second, he found winter parkas in a variety of sizes. Mentally crossing his fingers, Hawkins opened the third and found a neat a row AK-47 assault rifles, along with spare clips and a bag full of grenades. All good stuff, but useless at the moment. Then he spotted gold. Yes!

"Open the other hatch!" Hawkins bellowed, heading for the open hatch. He'd need a lot of room to pull this off.

Swiftly, the rest of the team did as requested, then scrambled to put as much distance between them and the big Texan.

Leveling the HAFLA, Hawkins tried to track the fourth Mongoose and then stroked the trigger. Smoke gushed from the four-barrel weapon to fill the Agusta, and a volcano of flame roared across the empty deck and out the open hatch.

Lancing through the air, the 70 mm napalm rocket missed

the undamaged Mongoose by a yard. As the 20 mm cannon returned fire, Hawkins aimed again, trying to sway with the motions of the big transport, and sent off two more rockets at the dented Mongoose.

They both missed, but then the Barrett thundered and the windshield cracked. As the other Stony Man operatives started firing their 9 mm machine guns, the pilot wisely withdrew, dropping rapidly out of the clear blue sky.

"Three down, one to go," Encizo said sluggishly, reading the radar screen, a hand clamped on to his dangling left arm. Blood was slowly dripping onto the deck. "Number four is trying for a lock… No good! Our jamming is better than his S and D!"

"How's the nitrogen?" McCarter demanded, too busy flying the giant helicopter to read the overhead board.

"Almost drained." Encizo coughed, then turned his head to spit red on the deck. "His heat-seekers will be able to lock on us in only a few minutes."

"How many does he have left?" James demanded, firing the MP-5 in short bursts.

"Two! And the bastard only needs one," Manning growled, levering in his final round for the Barrett. Damn it, the team was equipped for a commando raid, not a dogfight! What good were hand grenades against a gunship?

"Then we're going double-H!" McCarter announced, and the bulky transport swung around in a tight curve to again face the deadly gunship.

Surprised by the unexpected tactic, the Mongoose started to move away fast when the HAFLA and Barrett spoke together. The windshield shattered into sparkling pieces a heartbeat before the last 70 mm rocket arrived. It slammed into the screaming pilot and out the back of his chair to detonate deep inside the gunship.

As the fireball blossomed in the sky, McCarter swung away from the blast, letting the undamaged belly armor of the Agusta take the shrapnel.

"Sky is…clear," Encizo announced weakly, the words slurred. "No sign of other gunships, or Elsani."

Grabbing his field medical kit, James went to the front of the aircraft to check on his friend.

Tossing away the spent HAFLA, Hawkins closed the hatch and moved to the arms locker. Taking an AK-47, he thumbed a fat 30 mm round into the grenade launcher. It wouldn't do much to a Mongoose, but it was better than nothing.

"Firebird One to Rock House, come in, please," McCarter said into his throat mike, adjusting the frequency. "Fire to Rock, do you read me? Over."

There came a garble of static.

"Respond," he said, speaking clearly.

"This is Java Joe, and I read you loud and clear," Kurtzman said. "Just checking for eavesdropping, but we have no un-authorized listeners. Been visually tracking your progress via a NASA satellite, and I know what you want. Your quarry is twenty miles away, due east."

"Thanks. Try to keep NATO off our ass for a while."

"Not a problem. Professor Smoky has informed them you're members of the Fifteen Families and they have granted you unlimited clearance."

That was fast. "Many thanks, Joe. Stay close in case Christmas comes early."

"Understood, Firebird. Over and out."

In a rev of power, the Agusta swiveled and angled away in a new direction at its best speed.

"How's the fuel?" Manning asked, laying aside the empty Barrett and bringing up his MP-5 to check the clip.

Checking the overhead gauges for the reserve tanks, McCarter did not reply. The aircraft had lost a lot of fuel from the multiple shrapnel hits. Maybe too much.

"It'll have to do," he announced, killing every electrical system that was not vital to the transport. That would extended the fuel supply a little bit. If it was enough, only time would tell. "Better bundle up, boys, it's going to get mighty cold in here!"

Laying aside the AK-47, Hawkins went back to the lockers and started tossing out the winter parkas. As a precaution, Manning dug out a couple of self-heat MRE packs and put them alongside his canteen. Those would only give a couple of minutes of heat, but that could be all the difference between life and death.

While the team got dressed, the fuel gauge steadily dropped as the colossal helicopter headed straight for the snowcapped Korab Mountain range.

CHAPTER NINETEEN

Ptarmigan Glacier

Moving steadily along, Blancanales and Schwarz positioned themselves on either side of the subterranean passageway, and Lyons took the slot up the middle. The alarm kept howling, and they braced for an attack. But then it stopped abruptly and a strange silence filled the ice tunnel.

"They're laying a trap," Lyons stated with conviction. The air was horribly cold, every breath sending daggers into his lungs. There were only a few more minutes of heat from the thermal packs in the scuba suits, and then the cold would arrive with a vengeance.

"The big question is why?" Blancanales added softly, his eyes darting everywhere.

"And there's the answer," Schwarz said, thumping the frozen wall of the passageway with the stock of his M-16/M-203 assault rifle.

Next to the man was a small niche carved into the ice, a sort of a basin. It was filled with the water trickling off the

ice walls, and sitting inside was an electronic device, with rainbow-colored wires running in several directions.

"That's a computer server?" Lyons said as a question.

"Bet your ass," Schwarz replied, reaching into the water and touching the machine. A panel opened and he studied the interior without touching anything else. Muttering a curse, Schwarz moved down the passage and found another niche with a similar basin and a second server under the cold water. Stepping into the middle of the tunnel, he saw endless rows of the niches along both walls going out of sight. There was an intersection a hundred yards away, and rainbow-colored wires went into both branches.

"Yep, we're in trouble," Schwarz muttered, tightening his grip on the assault rifle. "This isn't a Cray supercomputer as we supposed, but a freaking Dell Thunderbird."

"Dell?" Blancanales repeated in confusion. "As in the guys who make affordable home computers?"

"I mean, Dell as in this baby," Schwarz replied, patting the U.S. Army laptop slung at his side. "They make PCs, and also build some of the most advanced computers in the world. Supercomputers that make the Cray back at the Farm look like an abacus."

"Bullshit."

"God's truth. The Thunderbird is not the most powerful computer in the world, but it *is* the fastest. This is what Sandy uses!"

Watching the corridor for any movement, Lyons bit back a curse. He knew the slang word. Sandy, meant Sandi Nuclear Security Laboratories. The very people assigned to protect the nation's nuclear arsenal from enemy hackers.

"Big deal, so it's one of the best computers in the world," Blancanales said, shoving the M-16 at the nearest unit. The

fluted barrel smashed easily through the plastic housing and busted apart the internal seals and cracked a circuit board. There came a low whine, and the server went dark, faint sparks crackling in the water.

"They bust easy enough," Lyons said. "So what's the problem?"

A machine gun cut loose down the tunnel, and ricochets zinged musically off the walls. But the gunfire wasn't coming toward them.

"They're doing a faint," Blancanales said, checking a grenade in his belt pouch. "Trying to draw us into the trap."

"What's the problem?" Lyons insisted.

"The problem is that the whole glacier is the computer." Schwarz sighed, looking around as if able to see through the ice walls. "There must be six or eight thousand of these servers in here."

"And how many do we have to smash to make the system crash?"

"Nearly all of them." The electronics wizard grunted, a chill running down his spine that had nothing to do with the surrounding mountain of ice. "But if we take out about half, then Bear might be able to smash through the firewall."

"Are you sure?"

"No."

"Great."

"So we smash thousands of servers, or find the control room."

"That's about the size of it, Carl."

Suddenly the chatter of the machine gun came again, louder this time, and closer. Then another spoke from a different direction.

"Okay, let's get busy," Lyons stated, walking to the next

niche and pulling out his Colt Python. The .357 Magnum revolver boomed and the underwater server exploded, the pieces flying randomly.

"Thousands of servers," Blancanales said with a frown. "Gadgets, we don't have enough bullets to take out anywhere near that many, and we can't call for an air strike with the ice blocking the radio transmissions!"

"I know." Pulling a knife, Schwarz slashed at the rainbow of wires running along the translucent wall of the tunnel. "We do this in shifts, I cut and you guys cover my ass, then Carl cuts and next you."

"Let's move, people!" Lyons said, pulling out a knife with his left hand. Accepted, they couldn't do a big kill as planned, but then, nothing was going as expected on this mission. They were going to have to nickel-and-dime the damn machine to death. Suddenly, the mission had changed from a lightning-fast blitzkrieg into an occupation.

Constantly rotating positions, the three men moved swiftly along the tunnel, cutting wires. At the intersection, they paused. The machine gun was firing to their left, so they headed directly for it. If the Albanians were trying to herd the team to the right, then that was precisely the direction they did not want to travel.

"David better get that access code," Blancanales stated, intently watching the next intersection for movement. The glacier was a maze, a crazy honeycomb of crisscrossing tunnels and side passages. Probably designed to confuse invaders. Unfortunately, it was working.

"Amen to that… Incoming!" Lyons shouted, crouching low and triggering a long burst from the Atchisson.

A roar of the autoshotgun combined with the chattering of an AK-47 and a hail of 7.62 mm bullets smacked into the frozen walls around the team, throwing off a sparkling spray

of ice chips and powdery snow. The noise of the two weapons echoed into the distance, becoming steadily fainter.

Dive rolling to a new position, Blancanales discharged the grenade launcher. The 40 mm shell of antipersonnel fléchettes exploded down the corridor just in time to catch three men charging out of a side passage. They were torn apart by the deadly barrage, their weapons firing wildly into the bloody ceiling.

Slashing a wire, Schwarz knelt and brought up his assault rifle, sending a spray of tumblers into a opposite tunnel. A man screamed in pain and blood splashed onto the floor. But two more rushed into view wearing flak jackets and carrying Kalashnikovs.

As Blancanales cut the next section of wire, Lyons burped the Atchisson. The five cartridges fired so quickly it sounded like a single long discharge. The 12-gauge rounds blew off the heads of the terrorists, and their bodies toppled sideways, arms flailing. Steam began to rise from the ghastly neck stumps as the Stony Man operatives raced past the corpses, reloading their weapons and cutting wires.

Pausing for only a moment, Blancanales took a grenade from a still twitching hand. A Kenwood transponder was clipped to the tattered belt, the radio smashed into pieces, wires dangling loosely.

Pulling the pin of the grenade, Blancanales flipped off the safety lever and tossed the grenade down a side corridor lined with servers. The team was already past the next intersection when the grenade detonated, filling the icy tunnel with fiery shrapnel.

"Fifty down, a zillion to go," Schwarz commented.

They heard the sound of running boots, several assault rifles firing single shots and then more running boots.

Moving in a standard two-on-two formation, six men charged around a curve in the tunnel. Ski masks covered their faces, their breaths puffing white through the black-knit material. All of them were carrying AK-47 assault rifles with 30 mm grenade launchers mounted beneath the barrels.

Dropping flat again, the Stony Man operatives fired from the ground, stitching the terrorists from knees to throats. Shouting with surprise, the Albanians went tumbling like rag dolls, blood gushing everywhere, their weapons firing into each other as they fell into infinity.

Scrambling to their feet, Able Team snatched the grenades from the corpses and tossed them into four more side tunnels, the explosions seeming unnaturally loud trapped inside the glacier. Running down the main tunnel, the men kept rotating positions, slashing at the wiring with their knives, never completely stopping, but never moving on until they were sure the electrical connection had been completely broken.

Reaching a central core, Lyons swept the upper levels for snipers, but there was nobody in sight. "I don't like this," he muttered, thumbing a couple of extra shells into the hot Atchisson. "Stay sharp."

"As a razor," Blancanales replied, trying to count the levels above them. There was a spiraling ramp that reminded him of the Guggenheim Museum in New York, probably where they got the idea, so it was difficult to even make a good guess. Twenty more levels, or maybe a dozen more. They were going to need a lot more grenades.

"Gadgets, any chance you could hack into the wires," Lyons asked, tapping the cable with the steaming barrel of the Atchisson. "Scramble their access codes so that nobody can use the Icarus satellites anymore?"

Hacking apart the wire on the opposite wall, Schwarz

glanced over his shoulder with an expression of scorn. "Hack a 264 tera-flop Thunderbird with a 50 gig laptop?" he asked incredulously.

Translating that to mean the task was flat-out impossible, Lyons started for the icy ramp, thankfully noting the rubber mats covering the slick ice for traction. But he only got a few yards when something came hurtling down the shaft from above and loudly crashed on the frosty ground.

Instinctively the team dived for cover and a split second later a deafening explosion and a blinding light flash overwhelmed them. But as the flare and concussion echoed away, they noted there was no accompanying sound of shrapnel hitting the shaft and that the ice walls were totally undamaged.

"That was a stun grenade!" Lyons cursed, swinging around the shaft and blindly firing the Atchisson. Suddenly the Albanians were trying to capture them alive? Hell, no, the bastards were trying to hold them in place for some sort of big kill coming their way.

"Here it comes!" Blancanales growled, triggering a 40 mm grenade from his M-203.

The hellstorm of buckshot hit the side of the ice ramp, blowing out a jagged chunk, and some sort of squat machine tumbled over the edge to land on the ground in a crash. It was an angular box with steel treads like a miniature tank. But before the Stony Man operatives could do anything, the machine extended robotic arms and flipped itself upright, the video camera and dish microphone on top spinning to locate targets, the stubby barrel of a machine gun precisely tracking the moves.

Even as the team aimed its weapons, they realized they were facing a SWARD. Originally built by the Army Corps of Engineers to defuse booby traps and unearth land mines,

the computer-controlled robot had later been armed and armored by the U.S. Marines. Literally a killing machine, the SWARD was rapidly becoming very popular with troops doing house-to-house searches. Virtually unstoppable, the SWARD was remote-controlled, the operator miles away in a bunker, far from the actual combat. When the SWARDs first arrived, the Iraqi insurgents often screamed and ran from the machines. Later, they rallied and would attack, and the SWARD would cut them down like summer wheat.

Hosing streams of 5.56 mm rounds from their M-16 assault rifles, Blancanales and Schwarz saw the bullets rain harmlessly on the body armor of the robot, then Lyons emptied the rest of his ammo drum at the SWARD, the barrage smashing the dish mike but doing nothing to the ferruled cable feeding the video camera. Even the lens seemed to be bulletproof.

As the machine instantly turned in his direction, Lyons fired the Atchisson again as cover and rolled behind the smashed piece of the ice ramp. A split second later the chunk slammed into the man, propelled backward by the chattering stream of .22-caliber rounds flying from the SWARD's stubby machine gun. Then the bullets went high and swept along the frosty wall, ricocheting wildly. Staying low, Lyons grunted as several hit him in the back, his NATO body armor stopping the small-caliber rounds easily, but the sheer number of them was intimidating. Then Lyons felt a warmth trickle down his left arm and knew he had caught one. There was little pain, so it was probably just a flesh wound. Dismissing the minor injury, the Able Team leader used a tiny mirror attached to the end of a telescoping rod to peek around the cracked chunk of ice. The SWARD had taken a position in the center of the shaft where it could cover both ramps easily. The stubby barrel of the .22-caliber machine gun never stopped moving as the

video camera searched for targets. By now, Blancanales and Schwarz were nowhere in sight having retreated down the curving tunnel to find some cover.

Studying the robot, Lyons saw that there were grayish marks all over the chassis from a 5.56 mm round that had hit it, but the SWARD was undamaged. It had fallen thirty feet and landed in fighting shape. In the same breath, Lyons cursed and praised the U.S. Marines for their fine engineering. If the machine started moving, he was a dead man.

Casting aside the Atchisson, the big ex-cop eased out his Colt Python and worked the slide to chamber a round as quietly as possible. The SWARD should be deaf with the dish mike gone, but there could be a secondary mike hidden among the armor plating and metal arms. There were several tools tucked inside the boxy limbs, including a drill, a wrench and a pair of clippers suitable for cutting the wires on a bomb. *Or removing clunks of flesh from a throat.*

In a burst of speed, Lyons rose, fired twice and dropped down again. The SWARD responded a moment later by shooting bullets randomly, high and low, the armored treads turning the machine in a full circle. But it didn't charge the ice block. Risking the mirror again, the man grunted at the sight of the busted video camera hanging from the armored chassis by sparking wires.

"Okay, now it's blind and deaf," Lyons subvocalized into his throat mike, holstering the Colt. "That buys us some time, but soon enough more guards will arrive and we're fish in a barrel."

"Gadgets, any idea how many .22 rounds it carries?" the disembodied voice of Blancanales asked over the radio link.

"Sure, I helped design the thing for the Pentagon," Schwarz whispered in reply. "A SWARD carries twelve hundred

.22 rounds, along with a hidden 12-gauge shotgun they're holding in reserve for when we charge."

"But it's blind."

"Doesn't matter. There's a built-in mass proximity sensor that can tell if we try to sneak past the machine."

"Will a 40 mm shell kill it?"

"Nope."

"Then we don't even try," Lyons said, feeling the old rage build inside, but he forced it down for the time being. Only a cool head would beat the machine and its hidden controllers. "On my signal, hit it with your grenade launchers as a diversion."

"As a… And what will you be doing?" Blancanales asked intently.

Just then the wailing siren turned off and a ringing silence filled the tunnels and shaft of the Montana glacier.

The reserve troops were about to be deployed.

"On my mark…" Lyons muttered, pulling the pin on a thermite grenade. These had been brought along to destroy the enemy supercomputer if it was under water. Thermite burned so hot that it could melt tank armor and actually consumed the oxygen in water to flare even hotter than normal if submerged. "And…now!"

The 40 mm grenade launchers boomed and the SWARD was covered with antipersonnel fléchettes coming from two different tunnels. The machine rocked under the double assault, and Lyons dropped the arming lever on the canister of thermite and rolled it across the slick ground. The grenade came to rest about a foot from the SWARD. The .22-caliber machine gun swiveled down to aim at the canister and the grenade detonated in a hellish fireball.

Lurching forward, the SWARD lumbered out of the con-

flagration, but the sizzling thermite clung to its side. Metal dripped off the robot like silvery blood, an armored cable snapped, then the left set of treads sagged and broke in the middle. Something exploded loudly, throwing out pieces of machinery, then the .22-caliber rounds started cooking off, sounding like a hundred firefights happening at the same time. Suddenly, blue electrical sparks could be seen through the glaring light of the thermite.

"Go! Go! Go!" Lyons ordered, and the Stony Man operatives charged into the central shaft.

Darting past the flaming machine, the men raced for the undamaged ramp, their combat sneakers slipping on the ice several times before they were past the hellzone.

Crippled, but still fighting, the SWARD began to fire the shotgun randomly. Reaching the next level, the Stony Man team paused to pull out two more thermite grenades and toss them down. The central core of the shaft became alive with writhing flame, and the air began to reek with the metallic smell of cooking thermite. The entire glacier seemed to rock from the trip-hammer blows, then an odd splintery noise sounded and Lyons turned to see a zigzagging crack extend along the ice wall for several yards. Water began to ooze out like clean blood. It formed a puddle on the floor and started trickling down the ramp, making it impossible for anybody to follow them from that direction.

Or for Able Team to retreat. "Time to go," Lyons said, pulling his knife again and slashing at the nearest set of wires.

The others were right behind him, cutting wires and tossing grenades down side corridors. They finished the second level and just reached the third when they heard the sound of running boots once more.

"Surrender or die!" an amplified voice boomed down the

central shaft, the words reverberating off the shimmering walls.

In response, all three Stony Man operatives leaned over the translucent railing and sprayed their weapons upward, the muzzles vomiting fire and smoke. Somebody cried out in pain, and a moment later a body dropped past them to hit the burning SWARD with sickening results.

Now a hail of grenades dropped toward them, then sailed past the team to explode near the second level. Able Team paid them no attention, continuing to cut wires as fast as possible. But then an odd smell began to permeate the air; it wasn't unpleasant, just ripe and rather strong. Sort of like fresh horse radish… Mustard gas! Those hadn't been HE grenades, but gas bombs!

Exhaling as hard as they could, the men stumbled to the closest niche and plunged their faces into the icy cold water, rubbing vigorously to dilute any lingering traces of the horrific war gas. Mustard gas ate at a person's lungs, you drowned in your own blood. A horrible way to go. Fresh water diluted the compound and made it harmless, but inside the glacier the only water available were the tiny pools inside the wall niches containing the servers. The scuba suits would keep the gas off their skin, but one good whiff and the men would die in agony.

Splashing more water on their faces, the Stony Man commandos held their breath and took off at a full run past the rows of softly humming servers as a thin cloud of greenish smoke rose over the icy railing, gently wafted upward by the radiant heat of the burning machine below.

CHAPTER TWENTY

Korab Mountains, Eastern Albania

Craggy mountains dominated the horizon, low clouds moving slowly past the ragged tors and peaks. The range looked newly formed, rough and unfinished, as if freshly torn from the bowels of the Earth.

The huge Agusta helicopter moved steadily through the snowy mountain passes, the spinning turbo blades coming dangerously close to the rocky peaks. Sitting in the rear of the chopper, the ten guards were ignoring the view, concentrating on the job at hand and dutifully checking over their assault rifles. Wearing parkas from the lockers, they seemed nervous, but said nothing, getting ready for a pitched battle to protect their lord and master.

"Sir, the pilot of the last Mongoose just reported in," Vilora Kostunica said crisply, holding a headphone to her left ear. "He was damaged, but managed to land intact. All of the other gunships were destroyed by the invaders. Whoever the hell they are. Last seen, they were heading directly after us."

"How is that possible?" Daut Liniat demanded in a low

growl, peering out the aft window of the loading ramp. There was nothing in sight but clouds and mountains. "Do you think that we have a tracer on board?" Turning his head, the big man looked around suspiciously at the crates and boxes filling the rear of the cargo area. The Agusta was equipped for a long voyage, packed full of clothing, cocaine, gold bars and tons of munitions.

"The how of the matter doesn't matter," Sakir Elsani replied from the flight deck of the transport. With one hand on the joystick, the gangster was guiding the large helicopter through the deadly maze of rocky peaks with deceptive ease. He knew these hills like his own face. "But if the report is true, then we abandon the idea of trying to reach the fortress in Serbia and head for Kosovo. That's much closer. Once we're safe in the badlands, we can reestablish contact with Baldwin in Montana and this time, no more finesse. We nuke the superpowers into submission! This foolish attempt to capture me will cost them millions of lives."

Haughtily, Liniat and Kostunica laughed at the plan, while the guards hunched lower in their seats and said nothing. The Fifteen Families ruled Albania with an iron fist. Opinions were not greeted warmly. The men knew that they were little more than uniformed slaves. Armed slaves. But with the lives of their own families at risk, there was nothing to be done but obey the madman piloting the helicopter.

"There's the landing zone!" Kostunica announced, pointing downward.

Grunting in reply, Elsani guided the Agusta through a narrow mountain pass. The jagged rocks passed uncomfortably close to the huge transport. In the distance, a snow storm was blowing along the ridges, softening the rocky formations into gentle hills of glistening white.

The Korab terrain was wildly rocky, jagged slopes and razor-sharp canyons impossible to climb, or traverse. The trees grew in patches as if the mountain range had the mange, and most of the rock was serpentine, strangely flesh-colored with dark spots.

In his youth Elsani had traveled the world, from downtown Paris to the South Pole, but this was some of the worst landscape that existed. The mountain range almost seemed like an alien world not created for humans. This section of the Korab Mountains was a little slice of hell that even the Nazis and the Soviet Union hadn't tried to seize when they occupied the nation. Not enough people, not enough resources and it was difficult to reach. The locals had also learned the valuable lesson that it took weeks to build a bridge, and ten seconds to blow one up.

"Hold it, sir!" Kostunica snapped, raising a hand. "We have a thermal reading down below." She studied the screen closely. "I think there are some people waiting for us."

"Indeed?" Elsani muttered, easing the descent of the Agusta and checking the radar for any incoming missiles. But the screen was clear.

Some distance from the helicopter was a dark ledge that jutted from the sloping side of a mountain like the hand of a beggar. It was supposed to be flat and smooth, but now there was some sort of lump in the middle. A camouflaged tent? Perhaps.

"Sergeant, ready your men!" Elsani commanded. "You must hike to the tent and investigate."

Releasing their seat belts, the guards gathered near the side hatch. Easing it back, Liniat waved them through. Jumping from the helicopter, the guards hit the ground, a few of them slipping on the icy rocks, but quickly scrambling to their feet again. Separating fast so as not to offer a group tar-

get, the guards headed toward the mysterious formation. This could simply be some shepherds or a couple of lost mountain climbers, but in case it wasn't...

The howling wind was stiff, but manageable, and the guards soon found the entrance to the tent. A tarpaulin had been stretched across several boulders to offer protection from the inclement weather, a dusting of fresh snowfall masking it into an recognizable mound.

Using the barrel of his AK-47, the sergeant gently pushed open the flap to the tent and saw a dozen men snoring softly in sleeping bags clustered around a smokeless cooker. Waves of heat radiated from the little stove. Stacked neatly in the corners were mounds of weapons and crates of food. The roaring wind had masked the sound of the helicopter's approach.

Stepping back outside, the sergeant looked up at the nearby helicopter and shook his head. Nobody they knew.

Leaning closer to the windshield, Elsani ran a thumb along his throat. *Kill them.*

Returning to the tent, the sergeant wordlessly directed his men to assume firing positions, when one of the snoring men awoke and stared in horror at the armed guards.

"No, wait!" he cried out. "We're the—"

Uncaring, the guards cut loose with their assault rifles, mowing down the sleepers. A few cried out in shock, but most simply slept into their own deaths.

"Just like butchering hogs." A guard chuckled, dropping the spent clip and inserting a fresh one.

"Make sure they're dead," the sergeant ordered, watching the bloody corpses with grim intent. Failure was not accepted by the Fifteen.

Ruthlessly, one of the guards walked among the tattered corpses, and shot every dead man in the head with his

AK-47, even when it was clearly not necessary. Upon reaching the man who had awakened, the guard chuckled to see the fellow had tried to reach a Steyr machine pistol, but died in the attempt. Laughing softly, he shot the corpse twice in the back and then once more in the head for being so stupid.

Pulling out a radio, the sergeant set the code and frequency. "Clear, sir," he announced.

"It better be," crackled the grim reply.

A few moments later the huge Agusta landed outside, the wash of the blade throwing the loose snow off the tent and fluttering the canvas.

Stepping from the hatch, Elsani stood and lit a cigarette while Liniat and Kostunica hauled out bundles of skis and poles. The key to any escape was to make sure that you could not be followed. And where they were going, no helicopter could pursue.

While Liniat assembled the equipment, Elsani and Kostunica walked to the tent and glanced inside.

"Sir, do these people look familiar?" the woman asked, curling a lip in disdain.

"Yes," he said slowly, flaring his collar against the cold. "Back in Bor. Said they were the Black Eagles, but their shoes were much too good. I assumed they were al Qaeda or the Hamas. Any papers?"

"None," the sergeant said, rising from the bodies. He started to say more when a low mechanical beat filled the air.

"Helicopter!" Kostunica cursed, rushing outside.

Moving fast, Elsani was close behind the woman and stopped to stare in disbelief at the black speck in the sky coming their way. Impossible. This was flatly impossible!

"By the blood of Zogu, it's the other Agusta!" Kostunica scowled, clenching a gloved fist. "How the hell did NATO find us?"

Taking a step toward the helicopter only yards away, Elsani stopped himself. As much as he burned to shoot down the NATO bastards, the open ledge was not a good place to make a last stand. Because that was what this would be—his last stand.

"Get the poles!" Elsani snapped, zipping his parka closed. "We're leaving right now!"

As the sergeant and the rest of the guards rushed to clamp on the skis, one man held back and walked hesitantly over to the gangster.

"Sir?" he asked softly, the word visible in the cold air.

"What?" Elsani demanded, slipping the safety loops for a pair of poles over his bulky gloves.

The man swallowed. "I'm new and…sir, I don't know how to ski. Should I take the helicopter and—"

Bringing up a hand, Sakir grimaced and the glove exploded, the .44 dum-dum round from the derringer removing most of the man's face. Spraying out blood, the guard reeled backward, his assault rifle firing a long burst into the air before he crumpled onto the dirty snow. Tossing away the ruined glove in annoyance, Sakir bent over and yanked one off the man as a replacement.

"Sergeant, hide a Claymore mine under the body," Kostunica commanded. "Then follow us!"

"Yes, ma'am!" he replied with a salute.

Nodding at the gesture, the woman started toward the brim of the ledge, completely ignoring the oozing corpse of the dead guard. Anybody who could not ski was a weak link, and should have been removed swiftly. Mercy had no place in the real world. The slums of Durres had taught her that hard lesson as a small child.

Going to a angled section of the ledge, Elsani pushed off, closely followed by Liniat and Kostunica, and then the rest of the guards. The snowy ground was a gentle slope with

nothing to bar the way, and in a few seconds the group was streaking into a forest, the spreading branches completely hiding them from the air. Elsani and his people had practiced doing this before the first Icarus was launched. Only a fool forgot to build a house with no back door.

"Why haven't they attacked?" Liniat demanded in confusion as they maneuvered between the trees.

"We are moving too fast," Kostunica responded smugly. "There is no way they can track us!"

"Fools!" Elsani snarled, zigzagging around a depression and going airborne for a few seconds before landing and sweeping onward.

Although he tried not to let it show, the man was terrified. How had things gone wrong so fast? The men invading the mansion were clearly more than NATO soldiers. Some sort of special forces unit? American Delta Force? British SAS? It didn't really matter. This was a desperate attempt to obtain the access codes from him before their governments officially surrendered. The man stopped abruptly and removed one of his gloves. Reaching into a pocket, he pulled out a piece of paper and shoved it into his mouth, chewing frantically until able to swallow. There, done. The codes were gone. There was only one other source, and they would never get that while he still lived. If he fell, so did the world. The mushroom clouds and burning cities would be his funeral pyre.

"Look, there they are!" Kostunica shouted, pointing a pole at a set of black lines cutting through the fresh snow.

Turning sharply, Elsani donned his glove then led the way along the railroad tracks, and soon the terrorists reached a small log cabin built just below the snow line. It was a way station with an emergency radio and food supply in case an avalanche blocked the tracks. But his people had take it over months ago.

Twisting around, the people came to a halt in a spray of snow and quickly kicked off their skis and hiked the short distance to the cabin, their boots crunching into the snow. Pausing to glance through a frosty window, Elsani saw several bodies splayed on the floor of the cabin. Some hunters had tried to steal the food and gotten killed by the antipersonnel mines hidden in the cabin.

"Check the bikes," Elsani ordered to the guards. "Daut, Vilora, lay a welcome for our visitors."

But before the man and woman could move there was a deafening explosion from the other side of the log cabin, the windows shattering and the whole building shaking so hard the tiles came off the roof. A rain of white droplets sprayed over the landscape. Elsani recognized the falling material as molten iron. That had been a Hellfire missile!

Just then, the second Agusta swept into view, roaring up the hillside to hover above the smoking ruin of the log cabin.

"This is NATO!" a voice boomed in weirdly accented Albanian, as if the speaker were unfamiliar with the language. "You are under arrest! Surrender!"

"Sir?" Liniat asked, moving back toward the motorcycles. Several of the machines had toppled over, the frames bent and useless.

"NATO my ass, they're the KGB!" Elsani screamed, playing on the ancient fear of the Soviets. "Kill them! Blow them out of the sky!" That Hellfire missile had to have deliberately missed the log cabin in an effort to stun them into submission. The fools.

Swallowing hard, the guards rushed toward the helicopter and started firing their AK-47 assault rifles, wildly hosing streams of bullets at the hovering transport. The barrage of 7.62 mm hardball generated threw off a wealth of bright

sparks, then explosions began to pound the Agusta as 30 mm shells from the stubby grenade launchers were deployed.

Taking cover behind a wood pile, the sergeant was working the arming bolt to clear a jam from the ejector port when he heard revving engines. He turned to see three motorcycles streak away from the wrecked cabin, tossing something in their wake.

"Bastards!" the sergeant bellowed, swinging his weapon toward the departing trio when the rest of the parked bikes were torn apart in a fast series of powerful explosions. The noise was beyond deafening, then something hot slammed the sergeant in the chest. Feeling oddly numb, he was unable to pull in a breath and slowly sank to the ground still muttering curses until a soothing darkness engulfed him forever.

Landing the Agusta amid the smoking wreckage, the men of Phoenix Force scrambled out of the transport and started carefully firing single shots at the escaping motorcycles.

"Shoot to wound!" McCarter snarled over the radio. "We must have Elsani alive!"

But a moment later the rapidly accelerating bikes took a sharp curve in the road and went into a dark tunnel to disappear from sight.

Ptarmigan Glacier, Montana

LISTENING FOR SOUNDS from below, ten guards stood uneasily shoulder to shoulder at the ramp to the fifth level. AK-47 assault rifles were tight in their gloved hands, their breaths puffing out visibly in the frigid air. None of them knew a thing about what was going on, except that there had been a lot of gunfire and that most of the other Albanians inside the glacier had ceased to answer their radios.

Suddenly, a hail of incoming bullets hit the frosty roof

above them, showering the startled men with stinging ice chips. Ducking for cover, they blindly fired their weapons in return. But the barrage continued with only split-second breaks, as if two men were firing one at a time. But what would be that point of that? Unless…

"Run!" a guard shouted, standing upright. "This is a diversion!"

"Too late," Lyons growled, stepping into view and cutting loose with the Atchisson autoshotgun.

Even as the terrorists started to pivot, the deafening stream of 12-gauge cartridges tore the men apart, the barrage of fléchettes chewing through the ranks, arms and legs flying from the bodies until there was only bloody carnage strewed across the icy floor. Incredibly, a disembodied hand tightened on the trigger of a Kalashnikov to fire off a single round, but then there was only the ringing echo of the sustained discharge.

Moments later, Blancanales and Schwarz raced up the ramp from the fourth level, wet rags tied around their mouths as protection from the deadly mustard gas. Their eyes had stopped stinging by the third floor, and after that it was becoming noticeably easier to breathe. The honeycomb of tunnels running through the mountain of ice was simply too big for a single tank of mustard gas to fill, and every whiff that touched the cold water running through the wall niches dissolved and was rendered inert and totally harmless.

"Any trouble?" Lyons asked, dropping the spent drum from the Atchisson now that his teammates had joined him. With no more spare drums, or clips, he quickly started thumbing individual rounds into the hot belly of monstrous weapon.

"Only for them," Schwarz agreed, craning his head to check for snipers on the next level. "These boys have been on sentry duty for too long. They move slower than a clerk at the

DMV." Oddly, there didn't seem to be any movement on the next level, which was very strange. That should be the heart of the glacier, and the location of the control center for the Albanian supercomputer.

Gathering the few undamaged weapons from the dead terrorists, the team spent a minute launching 30 mm shells into the branching corridors, taking out as many additional servers as possible. But each man kept one live shell in the his own grenade launcher, in case of emergencies. This was probably going to be a long battle coming up, and the team was already dangerously low on ammunition.

"Stay sharp!" Lyons subvocalized into his throat mike, easing toward the last ramp. "The sons of bitches have nowhere to run, which means they'll dig in and really start fighting."

"Too bad for them," Schwarz muttered, his M-16 held in one hand, a AK-47 in the other.

"Hold it," Blancanales said, stopping abruptly.

The other two paused, their eyes sweeping the area for danger. But nothing was in sight.

"This is wrong," Blancanales said under his breath, studying a blank section of the wall. Exactly where another niche containing a submerged server should be located, there was only translucent ice, smooth and featureless, quite unlike the rest of the tunnel walls, which had irregular surfaces, pitted and rough.

Acting on combat instincts honed over a hundred battles, the former Black Beret brought up his assault rifle and unleashed the last grenade. The distance to the wall was short, but just enough for the Russian round to arm. It hit with a thunderous crash, snow and icy chunks splaying outward mixed with fire and smoke to reveal a badly dented steel door.

Aiming their own captured Kalashnikovs, Lyons and Schwarz added the destructive power of their 30 mm rounds and the door blew off its hinges to reveal a second door. Dropping the assault rifles, the men tossed grenades and moved away fast.

The double explosions rocked the central shaft of the glacier and the door was ripped from the surrounding walls to hurtle into the room beyond like a pile driver.

Moving low and fast, the team swept through the jagged doorway. Acrid smoke was billowing in the air, making it difficult to see. But as the wall vents started sucking away the fumes, the Stony Man commandos could see a dozen guards splayed on the dirty floor. A line of computer consoles and furniture machines had been piled up to form a crude barricade, but the thick door had crashed through the impromptu defense to smash the guards aside. The AK-47 assault rifles had been hammered into the men, the bent wood and cracked plastic almost cutting them in two. Pools of blood were everywhere.

"Check for survivors," Lyons ordered, then realized that he could not see his breath. The air in this room was warm and dry. That was when the swirling cloud of smoke cleared enough for him to spot the bank of controls edging the bottom of a large window. Down below was a twinkling maze of servers set deep inside a pool of water carved out of the glacier.

"This is it, the control room!" Schwarz cried, shouldering his rifle. Shucking his gloves, the man raced across the field of bodies to take a seat at a console. Several of the stations had also been torn apart by the explosions and airborne door, one whole section of controls dark and lifeless. Saying a quick prayer, the electronics wizard flexed his hands a few times and started to type on a keyboard.

Staying alert, Lyons and Blancanales watched for any suspicious movements in the room. But it seemed to be empty. There were no other visible doors, or means of exit.

"What's going on?" he muttered, moving closer to the window. Just for a moment, he thought there had been some movement among the submerged servers. "There's not an underground base in existence that doesn't have an escape hatch in case of trouble. It's here somewhere, trust me."

A trickle of sweat running down his face, Lyons started to speak when he noticed it, a large section of the concrete wall without any sort of power outlet, thermal gauges or anything else, unlike all of the other walls.

Indicating the area with a jerk of his chin, Lyons and Blancanales got between the blank section and Schwarz, then opened fire. The 7.62 mm rounds punched through the fake concrete and there came the screams of pain. Moving the assault rifles in a classic figure-eight pattern, the two men poured hot lead into the area until the disguised door broke free and swung open wide. Inside was a small room lined with gun racks. Four guards lay dead on the floor, along with three men wearing casual clothing and not carrying a weapon of any sort. That was the clincher, and there was no need to ask if those were the people in charge.

As the Stony Man operatives grimly advanced, one of the terrorist leaders stirred slightly. Raising a blood-streaked face, the man muttered something inaudible at the invaders and there came a soft click from his fist.

Instantly, a white-hot flame flared on the control panel and Schwarz cursed as he pushed away from the console, throwing up a protective arm. The flame raced along the bank of controls, melting the keyboards and monitors. Rivulets of molten plastic ran onto the terrazzo floor and a thick black plume of acrid smoke began to fill the control room.

Ruthlessly, Lyons fired again into the pile of bodies to stop any further activity, and Blancanales grabbed a fire extinguisher from the wall and sprayed the length of the control bank until the tank ran dry. But it had been a useless gesture, the man recognized the metallic reek of thermite and knew there was nothing in the world that could stop the rampaging self-destruct charge.

Coughing from the thick smoke, the men of Able Team moved out into the icy cold tunnel to catch their breath.

"D-did you…" Lyons started, but stopped to hack for a few seconds to try to clear his throat. "Did you get in?"

"Yes, and no," Schwarz huffed. "I was able to give control of the Thunderbird to the Farm before the fire hit."

"Great," Blancanales wheezed, sounding like an old man. "Well done."

But Schwarz vehemently shook his head. Pulling out a canteen, he took a drink, gargled and spit out dark fluids. Then he drank deeply before passing it to the others.

"What's wrong?" Lyons demanded, watching the smoke billow about inside the control room, the fumes creeping out of the smashed doorway to crawl along the ceiling like a wounded animal trying to escape. The ice on the nearby walls was starting to glisten with moisture from the waves of heat pouring from the thermite conflagration. The blaze was dying away, but there wouldn't be much left of anything in the room but charred wreckage and bodies.

"Bear said that all of the remaining Icarus satellites have been locked to focus on America," Schwarz said, reaching out to touch a damp wall and then rub his hand over his face. "In about fifteen minutes, every nuke in the country, no matter where it is hidden is going to detonate."

Blancanales muttered a curse. The death toll would be un-

imaginable! "Okay, we smash the computer," he declared, starting back into the cloudy room.

"We can't." Schwarz sighed. "Even if we had enough explosives to get through that plastic window, Bear needs the machine intact to turn the satellites off. That is—"

"If he had the access codes," Lyons finished grimly. "The Fifteen Families kept the key to their weapon in Albania while the lock was in America. Smart. No chance one of the guys in there might have it?"

"No way in hell," Blancanales replied. "If these folks had the access codes, then they'd be in charge and the first thing they would have asked NATO to do was bomb Albania off the map."

"Damn. Whoever was in charge of the project was smarter than any of us thought."

"I'm afraid so, Carl."

Just then, something crashed inside the control room and a fresh volume of black smoke poured from the interior.

"There's nothing we can do," Schwarz said solemnly, frustration heavy in his voice. "Now, everything depends on Phoenix Force."

CHAPTER TWENTY-ONE

Korab Mountain Pass

"After them!" McCarter shouted, charging forward, his MP-5 throwing out a halo of hot lead. But the three bikes vanished into the black tunnel.

Holding the only surviving Albanian guard roughly by the collar, Hawkins spoke into his cell phone for a moment.

"Where does that tunnel go?" Kurtzman demanded haltingly in Albanian. "Answer, or die!"

"What is death to me?" The guard sighed, slumping his shoulders. "If I talk, my wife and children will be sold into slavery. Do to me what you will, but I will not talk."

Angrily, Hawkins raised a fist, then threw the man to the ground. There was no threat he could possibly make that would be more terrifying to the guard than his family in chains.

"Well, there's no tunnel on the map," James announced, hunched over his laptop. There was a new dent in the titanium sheathing, but the machine was still working perfectly. "Must be something brand-new."

"Or something the Fifteen Families kept secret for just such an occasion," McCarter snarled, dropping a spent clip and reloading. "All right, we…" The man paused as Kurtzman gave a succinct report about the battle in Montana over the radio.

"Fifteen minutes?"

"Thirteen, now."

"Understood, over and out," McCarter snapped. "We got ten minutes to get Elsani or else the blood hits the fan. Rafe and Gary with me in the Agusta. We'll try to find them from the air. Calvin and T.J., go check the—"

But the two men were moving among the smashed motorcycles, checking to see if any of them might still work. A couple on the outskirts of the blast didn't seem too badly out of shape. James found one that only had a flat tire, and Hawkins located a bike that was in fine shape, aside from badly leaking gas from a split fuel line. Both would be useable if the men had only an hour of free time to do some basic repairs.

Suddenly a hurricane of wind whipped around the decimated log cabin, blowing the loose snow around with stinging force as the Agusta climbed into the sky and started after the escaping terrorists.

Finding a bike that looked okay, James straddled the seat and tried kicking the machine alive. The engine sputtered and coughed, then died away. He tried again and it backfired louder than a Magnum pistol, then sputtered into a smooth purr of controlled power. Hallelujah! Without waiting a second for his friend, James took off in a rush, the spinning rear wheel spraying out loose gravel. In only moments he was inside the tunnel and gone.

Slinging his machine pistol over a shoulder, Hawkins

levered the last motorcycle upright and climbed into the saddle. The dashboard was smashed, but the fuel tank was still intact. Braced for failure, he turned the handlebar controls and kicked hard. The big engine came to life with a roar.

"Here I come, Cal," Hawkins subvocalized into his throat mike, steering the BMW toward the tunnel and switching on the headlights.

"Don't wait for me," James replied, and Hawkins passed the man. "The fucking motor died and I have no idea what's wrong."

"Then follow on foot!" Hawkins snapped, pouring on the juice and crouching over the handlebars to lower his wind resistance. It might already be too late to catch the terrorists, but he had to try.

Taking a curve, Hawkins saw daylight ahead and shot into the open. From somewhere he could hear the throb of the Agusta, but it was not in sight. Then another turn took him into a second tunnel. Driving through the darkness at breakneck speed, just for a second Hawkins caught a whiff of exhaust fumes and knew that he was close behind Sakir Elsani and the others. Making a battlefield decision, the man began throwing away everything he could to lighten the load and move faster. His MP-5 went first, then the ammo belt with all of his spare clips. Next went the med kit and his canteen. The backpack was impossible to reach without letting go of the handlebars, so Hawkins simply cut the straps and shrugged. It tumbled away into the gloom, and the BMW responded with a surge of power.

An experienced rider, Hawkins knew that BMW made a motorcycle that had a transmission like a car, rather than a drive chain, and the machine was eerily quiet. Perfect for a recon or midnight escape. But this lumbering monster was

nothing but muscle, the Twin-V engine hammering between his legs as if trying to break free. The speedometer was smashed, so Hawkins had no idea how fast he was traveling, but the blur of the ground told the man it was at killing velocity. If he fell from the machine at this speed, without a helmet or protective leather jacket, he would be dead before the second bounce.

The road swept to the left again, longer this time, until it almost seemed like the tunnel was curving back onto itself. Then daylight appeared as a speck in the distance and the Stony Man commando dimly heard the roar of the other bikes. Hot damn, he was on their heels! The odds were still three to one, but that couldn't be helped.

"Lone Star to Leader, do you copy?" Hawkins shouted into the throat mike over the noise of the powerful engine. But there was no reply, only the soft hum of the open mike in his ear.

Just then the tunnel emptied onto a flat vista of bare land. To the left was a field of stones stretching off to the Kosovo Mountains, to the right was a featureless, treeless plain. Kosovo made the most sense, but then he spied a faint dust trail from the plain.

Hunching low against the chrome handlebars, Hawkins headed in that direction, trying to accelerate the hulking BMW through sheer willpower.

Dust began to sting his eyes, and Hawkins slid on his night-vision goggles and dialed for infrared. Sure enough, there were three blobs in the distance near some sort of a bridge. In shocking realization, the man understood what was happening, and ripped the heavy goggles off to throw them away.

Squinting against the wind, Hawkins dimly saw the three people standing on the bridge doing something, then they climbed on the motorcycles and started away again. Throwing

caution to the universe, the man raced across the cold plain toward the structure, the clusters of red dynamite sticks soon coming into view. Without hesitation, Hawkins shot onto the wooden bridge, the fuses burning down fast, and reached the other side a full heartbeat before a volcanic eruption detonated behind him.

The shock wave almost made the motorcycle topple over, and he fought to keep it on course. Then the flaming debris arrived, burning timbers and flaming chunks of wood spraying across the Albanian desert everywhere. Something hit Hawkins hard in the back, and he grunted from the impact, then something grazed his cheek, going through the empty space of the window. Hunkering lower, the Phoenix Force commando felt blood on his face and knew that he'd missed being decapitated by a scant inch. The thought sent adrenaline surging through his body, temporarily banishing the cold as a sort of berserker mania came over the soldier.

"Is that the best you assholes got?" Hawkins shouted defiantly.

Ahead of the man, the three people on motorcycles turned at the cry and openly gawked in shock at the lone rider plowing through the roiling cloud of the explosion.

Without a word, Elsani twisted the throttle on the handlebar and shot away fast. But Beauty and the Beast stayed behind, climbing off their machines and drawing weapons.

Lowering his speed a trifle, Hawkins drew the Beretta 93-R from his belt and emptied the clip at the two, hoping to land a head shot. The ugly bald man jerked back, blood and teeth spraying out from a head strike, but the pretty woman crouched low and opened fire with her AK-47 assault rifle. The rounds kicked up dust spouts where they chewed into the ground, and started coming his way fast as

she tracked on the motorcycle. Unable to reload at this speed, Hawkins twisted the throttle to full power again and charged directly at her. It was a desperate attempt to rattle the terrorist. A professional soldier would simply stand his or her ground and keep firing until Hawkins died, and then jump out of the way of the bike. But did she have the guts? Only one way to find out.

Her eyes flashing wide, Vilora Kostunica suddenly understood what the other man was doing. He was suicidal! Frantically diving to the side, she hit the ground rolling, and Hawkins streaked past the other BMW, tossing something small and round in his wake.

Moving away fast, Hawkins heard a curse, the Kalashnikov started up again, and then the willie-peter grenade detonated, throwing out a hellish corona of sizzling white phosphorous. Glancing in the rearview mirror, Hawkins saw the female terrorist covered with burning chemicals, her assault rifle still firing away at nothing. Then the grenades on her belt exploded in a staggering cacophony.

Straight ahead, Hawkins could see Elsani veering off toward a second wooden bridge. Then a deep throb filled the air and the Agusta came into view around a jagged rill. There came a flash of light from the belly of the transport and a white-hot missile shot through the air to strike the bridge. The middle span blew apart, the rest of the structure breaking into pieces and tumbling away into the river chasm below.

Rapidly braking his bike to a full stop, Elsani could only stare in wonder at the totally unexpected attack. This was not the sort of thing he expected from NATO. Who were these people? His mind spinning with escape plans, the terrorist chose the easiest and got off the BMW to flip open the top of the cargo rear compartment and haul out a parachute.

Let's see the UN lapdogs follow me into the chasm! Elsani thought smugly, running toward the edge of the abyss. There wasn't enough space for the machine, and if they tried, the helicopter would snap off its rotors and crash in fiery ruin. There was nothing these fools could do to stop him now! he thought in triumph.

The nameless river below would float him into Serbia, where there was a cave containing a large cache of money, food, weapons and several vehicles. Everything Elsani needed to reach Poland. He had established a fake identity there many years earlier, and now was clearly the time to use it. When the nuclear war began, he would be safe in the underground city with the Poles. All he had to do was to avoid being captured for just a few more minutes. The roar of an engine came from behind.

Struggling into the parachute, Elsani turned to see Hawkins dive off the speeding BMW motorcycle. The terrorist tried to dodge, but Hawkins spread his arms wide and the two men collided, bones audibly breaking from the brutal impact.

Rolling to his feet, the Phoenix Force commando found his right arm useless. Pulling a clip from his pocket, he stuck it into his mouth and dropped the spent clip from his Beretta, when Elsani slammed into him, driving a knife into his belly. The steel blade slid off the NATO bodyarmor, and Hawkins kneed the man hard in the crotch. But the Albanian only grunted and pulled out a derringer to fire point-blank. The .44 dum-dum round hit like a sledgehammer, knocking the air from Hawkins's lungs and he lost the clip.

Whirling, Hawkins rammed an elbow into the terrorist's face and felt the man's nose shatter. Blood gushing out in a torrent, Elsani fired the derringer, again hitting nothing, then unexpectedly turned and pelted for the edge of the cliff.

Pulling out his survival knife, Hawkins threw it and the man cried out, the handle of the combat knife jutting from his leg. But the terrorist did not fall and continued toward the river chasm and freedom. Only a few meters to go…

Tackling Elsani from behind, Hawkins brought the down the mass murderer, burying a thumb into an eye until the orb burst. Shrieking in pain, he slashed out wildly with his knife, catching Hawkins on his broken arm. The pain made his vision blur, so the Stony Man commando grabbed the man by the throat and started squeezing with all of his strength. Turning red in the face, the terrorist thrust again and again at his adversary, the blade sliding off the armor to cut deeply into his unprotected arms. Hawkins hung on, redoubling his efforts, grimly determined to never let go. However, the blood loss was having an effect and the big man felt his strength start to weaken. The knife cut a gash along his throat, blood seemed to be everywhere, and Hawkins let go of Elsani's throat to try for the other eye…

Wriggling and kicking, the terrorist threw off Hawkins and scrambled to his feet to lurch for the edge of the land when there came the deep boom of a shotgun and the man jerked away from the precipice as if hitting an invisible wall. Gasping for air, Elsani clawed inside his clothing for something, and the Remington shotgun again spoke, the 12 gauge stun bag slamming the terrorist in the chest. Convulsing, he pulled out a cell phone, the shotgun boomed once more and he spasmed with pain, going still.

Seconds later, the hurricane wind announced the arrival of the Agusta. It landed hard near the two men, and the rest of Phoenix Force clambered out of the transport. Leaving behind a trail of blood, Hawkins was pulling himself along with a single hand, still perusing the terrorist leader.

"Cal, see to T.J.!" McCarter commanded, slinging his MP-5 machine gun. "Gary, watch for incoming. Rafe, with me!"

As the others moved to their assignments, McCarter and Encizo went to Elsani. Kneeling alongside the unconscious terrorist, McCarter briefly checked for booby traps, then examined the cell phone.

"No way in hell is he going to wake up in time!" Encizo snarled in frustration, the deadly barrel of his MP-5 never wavering from the still form on the ground. "What do we do now, David?"

But McCarter did not answer. In the palm of his hand, he was holding the cell phone as if it were a ticking bomb. As the terrorist fell, he had tried to make a call. But to whom? Someone in the Fifteen Families? More of his troops? There was no way of telling until the man awoke, which was not going to happen for a quite a while. Too long to do any good.

Experimentally, McCarter pressed the first button. For most people that was their home number, or the office, whatever was the most important thing to them. What could possibly be more important to the terrorist than the Thunderbird in Montana? But nothing happened. There was no telephone number there or in any of the other memory slots.

"Try redial," Encizo suggested, looking tense.

Tapping the button, McCarter saw an impossibly long string of integers flow across the little screen, and then there came the familiar buzz and hiss of a modem connecting to a computer. Incredibly, the readout out the bottom of the screen gave the international code for America! The cell phone was connected to the Thunderbird in Montana!

"Firebird to Rock House!" McCarter said into his throat mike.

"Right here, Firebird," Kurtzman replied promptly. "Been waiting for your call. Do you have the access codes?"

"No, but I have a cell phone that's connected to the Thunderbird. Will that do?"

"Tell you in a minute," the man replied gruffly. "Tracing your location… Got the signal… Trying to piggyback on it into the computer…."

Suddenly the display screen of the cell phone began to flash with thousands of lines of binary code, and then the device turned off with a hard click.

EPILOGUE

Oval Office, White House

"So it worked," the President said, leaning back in the chair. "Thank God for that."

"Obviously, sir," Brognola noted from his chair. "Bear seized control of the Thunderbird and had all of the Icarus satellites realigning their orbits...fifty feet underground. The crash in Amsterdam was supposed to be quite spectacular."

"Anybody hurt?"

"Not a soul."

"Good." The President sighed in relief. "There have been too many lives lost on this already."

"Agreed, sir."

"Pity there is no way for us to ever learn how the Icarus worked," the President said, templing his fingers thoughtfully. "Is Aaron sure that he destroyed all of them?"

"Absolutely. And Sakir Elsani knew nothing about the machine, aside from the fact that it worked."

"Still a pity," the President repeated, as if trying to invoke a response.

But Brognola said nothing. Personally, he could understand how the politician would want the knowledge of how the Finnish weapon worked. It would be a devastating first strike in any war, exploding the enemy missiles as they left the atmosphere where the blast could do no harm. But it was better this way. A long time ago, Brognola had learned the hard lesson that some things were too dangerous to ever be used, even with good intentions.

Accepting the wall of silence, the President glanced at the report on his desk. "You'll be happy to know that the FBI and Homeland Security cleaned up the Albanian hardsite near the thulium mine. The terrorists really didn't give them much of a fight after getting the news that Sakir Elsani and Slobodan Kadriouski were both under arrest. With luck this may be the last we hear of the dreaded Fifteen Families, eh?"

Tactfully, Brognola didn't say a word. He knew better than to hope that a multibillion-dollar cartel would disperse merely because the top people had been killed or captured. Mack Bolan had taught him that hard lesson. The void would be filled. And some day Stony Man just might be called upon to burn down their house. Permanently.

Don Pendleton's Mack Bolan®

Appointment in Baghdad

A raid on a Toronto mosque reveals a
hard link to a mysterious figure known
only as Scimitar. He's a legend believed
to be at the center of an international
network of violent jihadists and
criminals, stretching across the
Middle East and southwest Asia.
Yet Scimitar remains a mystery within
an enigma, a brilliant, faceless opponent
whose true identity will force Bolan into
a personal confrontation for justice—
and righteous retribution.

Available May 2008
wherever you buy books.

TAKE 'EM FREE

2 action-packed novels plus a mystery bonus

NO RISK

NO OBLIGATION TO BUY

James Axler
Outlanders®

GHOSTWALK

Area 51 remains a mysterious enclave of eerie synergy and unleashed power—a nightmare poised to take the world to hell. A madman has marshaled an army of incorporeal, alien evil, a virus with intelligence now scything through human hosts like locusts. Cerberus warriors must stop the unstoppable, before humanity becomes discarded vessels of feeding energy for ravenous disembodied monsters.

Available May wherever you buy books.

JAMES AXLER
DEATH LANDS®

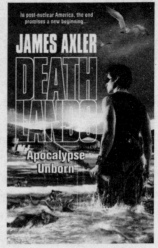

In post-nuclear America, the end promises a new beginning...

JAMES AXLER

DEATH LANDS

Apocalypse Unborn

Apocalypse Unborn

Reborn primeval in the fires of thermonuclear hell, America's aftermath is one of manifest evil, savage endurance and lingering hope. Traversing the lawless continent on a journey without destination, Ryan Cawdor seeks humanity in an inhuman world. In Deathlands, life is cheap, death is free and survival demands the highest price of all.

And there's no turning back. Or is there?

Available in June wherever you buy books.

ROOM 59

A nuclear bomb has gone missing. At the same
time Room 59 intercepts a communiqué from
U.S. Border Patrol agent Nathaniel Spencer.
But as Room 59 operatives delve deeper into
Mexico's criminal underworld, it soon becomes
clear that someone is planning a massive attack
against America…one that would render the
entire nation completely defenceless!

Look for

aim AND fire

by

cliff RYDER

*Available July 2008
wherever you buy books.*

GOLD
EAGLE ®

GRM593